Great th
This is n.

MW01277995

William Blake
The Washerwoman's Song"
from *Epigrams, Verses, and Fragments,*
1808-1811

Trees Are Lonely Company

Trees Are Lonely Company

Howard O'Hagan

Talonbooks   •   Vancouver   •   1993

published with the assistance of the Canada Council

Talonbooks
201 / 1019 East Cordova Street
Vancouver, British Columbia
Canada V6A 1M8

This book was typeset by Linda Gilbert and printed and bound in Canada by Hignell Printing Ltd.

First printing: March 1993

Acknowledgements: "The Tepee" first appeared in *New Mexico Quarterly Review* and in *Wilderness Men*; "Trees Are Lonely Company" first appeared in *The Tamarack Review*; "The Warning" first appeared in *Weekend*; "The Stranger" first appeared in *Queen's Quarterly*; "The White Horse" first appeared in *Macleans*; "Ito Fujika, the Trapper" first appeared in *Prairie Schooner*; "A Mountain Journey" first appeared in *Queen's Quarterly*; "The Woman Who Got on at Jasper Station" first appeared in *Esquire*.

Canadian Cataloguing in Publication Data

O'Hagan Howard, 1902-1982.
    Trees are lonely company

    ISBN 0-88922-327-0

    1. Men—Canada, Western—Fiction. 1. Title.
PS8529.H35T7 1993   C813'.54   C93-091341-8
PR9199.3.O42T7 1993

Foreword

The nine men whose lives are traced in the following pages are of the West. The three Indians — Almighty Voice, Gun-an-noot, and Tzouhalem — being born there, knew no other world than their limited tribal range, except for Gun-an-noot, who had a brief and deadly glimpse of the "outside."

The six others, white men, where westward-seekers, who sought out the West and came to know it. The three Indians, by circumstance, lived upon the fringes of the society which bore them, Almighty Voice and Tzouhalem leaving bloody trails in their wake. Similarly, the six white men, though more as a matter of choice, scouted the western rim of civilization in whose cities they found no peace. One of them was to hang his name upon a tree. Another to have his partner's lungs slapped across his face. Still another heard death come to him from overhead as he trudged up a river in the far northern tundra.

These nine men, Indian and white alike, have a further bond of union: they met life alone in the sombre forests of the Pacific slope, in the uptilted land of the Rockies, on the northern prairies, or in the wastes of the Arctic. Even Tzouhalem, with his gang of cutthroats, was a man apart, and Grey Owl, though often married, kept to himself the imposture which enabled him to confront mankind.

The writer knew two of these men as persons. I was the "doctor's son" who went with "Old" MacNamara up the ghostly Grantbrook in Chapter 1. Jan Van Empel, the Dutch-born artist of Chapter 9, I knew in Jasper, Alberta, and later met him while I was taking a pack outfit by Berg Lake behind Mount Robson, British Columbia. The device of the third person was used to preserve the same point of view throughout the book.

Howard O'Hagan
February 14, 1958
Victoria, B.C.

Contents

The
Black Ghost

For the North American Indian tomorrow was but the promise of another yesterday. His was a collective, or tribal, conscience and he lived by age-old ritual, accepting without question the beliefs it imposed and the restraints it exacted. Life outside the group had little meaning for the tribesman deprived of its social nourishment.

As a result records reveal few "loners," as distinct from "outcasts," among the tribes of the West — solitary men, voluntarily shunning the company of their fellows. "Loners" — or "wilderness men" — are the product of a civilization whose society they have, in large part, rejected. They are a true phenomenon of a rugged frontier land, wandering its deserts and mountain valleys under a back pack, or with a pack animal, prospecting for minerals or making a precarious living from a trap-line.

"Old" MacNamara — if he had a proper first name he took it with him to the grave — was one of these, a man whose very eccentricities made him typical of the breed. Grizzled, time-worn, he seemed never to have known youth, yet at seventy-five he was lean and wiry, beak-nosed, with eyes as cold and pale as twin chips of glacier ice, and he could still hump a sixty-pound pack twenty miles in a day over a mountain trail. In 1920 he lived in an earth-floored log cabin on the north shore of Yellowhead Lake. Named after a yellow-haired half-breed trapper, Tête Jaune, who in the early days had his cache, or fur depot, not far away, this five-mile-long body of water, laid like a narrow slab of amethyst below the peaks of the Seven Sisters, is today on the main line of the Canadian National Railways just west of the Alberta boundary and drains into the Fraser, which reaches the Pacific near Vancouver, B.C., five hundred miles to the southwest. MacNamara arrived at the lake and built his cabin about 1907, before a locomotive whistle had troubled the stillness of the valley.

Like most loners, he kept his early years in shadow, but the name is a well-known one around the Bay of Fundy and it is possible that he sprang from there. He trapped and laboured along the fringe of the sub-Artic forest in Saskatchewan and Alberta. As settlement advanced, he retreated, snowshoes, rifle and traps, and the clothes upon his back his sole possessions, until he found himself on Yellowhead Lake in the mountains two hundred miles north of the Canadian Pacific Railway at Banff, Alberta. It is man's fate to be overtaken by that from which he flees. MacNamara's was no exception.

By 1915 two rail lines, the Grand Trunk Pacific and the Canadian Northern — now part of the Canadian National, one on each side of the valley, held his lake in a cincture of steel. The little paradise where streams trailed like lengths of lace from mountain bosoms, where moose wallowed in the muskeg, the beaver slapped his tail on the water, and the golden-crowned sparrow loosed his plaintive note was his no more. It had been invaded by brawling construction crews, by the blast of dynamite and the roar of the steam-shovel. These left in their wake, facing MacNamara from across the narrows of the lake, a divisional point on the Canadian Northern: Lucerne, a town of three hundred, with a depot painted red, a coal tipple, a marshalling yard for freight cars, and a smoke-belching roundhouse from which came the ring of hammer on metal and the groan of machinery as though within its walls giants were met in haphazard and clangourous contention.

Mountains are loneliness and mystery. To them, throughout the ages, man has gone, humbly and afoot, to dream his dreams and seek his God. MacNamara's dreams were an old man's dreams, of youth which was his no longer, of life, a winding trail stretching behind him whose final summit he was about to mount. He found his God in the eerie winter silence or as he bowed his head to the wailing ghost of the blizzard. He found Him, too, in the lapping of summer waters and in the white clouds asleep against the peak.

But now MacNamara shared the valley with another sort of man — with railroaders, a locomotive foreman, two store-keepers, a pool-hall operator, a schoolteacher, and a doctor. It seemed that all his life he had been pursued by locomotives and that at last they had caught up with him. However, he had come so far that he could go little farther. Abandoning his trap-lines around Yellowhead Lake, he climbed over the shoulder of the Seven Sisters and put up another cabin on the head of the Grantbrook, a creek flowing into the Fraser below the lake. His winters he spent up there, his summers at the lake. MacNamara was to outlast the town and in the mountains behind it was to meet two opponents as relentless in their pursuit as steel.

A bridge had been built across the narrows of the lake and over this he would occasionally go, morose, growling, not speaking if he could avoid it, to buy groceries with money from the furs he had sold. In the town, which was no more than a street of log cabins laid out in the wilderness, he was thought to be eccentric and a miser. At night boys would sneak across the bridge and look in the old man's window. More than once they saw him, coal-oil lamp glimmering on the table, sitting like a man besieged on an apple-box before the tin stove and facing the door with his .32 Winchester across his knees. The sight gave grounds for grave suspicion.

September was the time of MacNamara's release. A flock of sixty or seventy mountain goats inhabited the upper reaches of the Seven Sisters, and, by studying them, he could usually foretell the weather, for they carried in their systems a built-in barometer. With certainty they signaled the approach of the equinoctial storm and the season's first snow. Forty-eight hours before the storm began, the goats would commence to cross over the mountain from their late summer range on its farther northern slope. In late summer and fall, after shedding his coat, the goat is a glistening white, so white that, in the awaited September day as MacNamara watched and the whole flock came over the Seven Sisters, they were like streamers of snow, whose harbingers they were, drifting down the dark gullies between the peaks. The storm might last three days, carpeting the valley and mountain slopes with wet, heavy snow. In a few days it would have melted in the valley and on the lower slopes, having heralded the coming of Indian summer. It was then that MacNamara, after oiling and testing his rifle and filling his packsack with groceries, would set out for his cabin on the Grantbrook to get his winter's meat. Above the cabin in an alpine meadow, were moss-fringed pools, like circled images of blue dropped from the autumn sky they mirrored. Here in the early morning and late evenings, hooves clicking, antlers tossing, the caribou came down from the higher slopes to drink. Some of the meat MacNamara "canned" in jars and stored it against freezing in a root house. Some of it he smoked in long strips Indian-fashion over a slow-burning fire of willows. These dried strips he chewed on the winter trail.

During the summer of 1920, short of funds, MacNamara had sawed and split the winter's wood for the town doctor and so became acquainted with the doctor's son, a seventeen-year-old youth locally called "Slim" who was home from his studies at McGill University in Montreal. After a proper interval of two or three weeks, when the boy had taken to visiting him at his cabin, MacNamara opened up and told him of the "caribou pools" on the head of the Grantbrook. He showed himself, unexpectedly, to be an artist in words and brought the scene alive. Late that September, when the goats had made their annual migration over the Seven Sisters, he invited Slim to go with him and watch the caribou come down to drink.

Despite his parents' objections — for MacNamara was "no fit company for man or beast" — the boy went. Rather than climb over the shoulder of the Seven Sisters, they walked down the railroad eight miles to the mouth of the Grant-brook on the Fraser. The doctor had arranged with the locomotive foreman to provide a "speeder" for this part of the journey. MacNamara would have none of it. He wanted no truck with "any goddamned railroader."

By nine o'clock in the morning MacNamara and Slim had

left the railroad and were heading up the Grantbrook. A few years before, fire, attributed by MacNamara to an "ignorant" railroader, had swept the valley. Skeleton-like grey snags pointed to the sky and "deadfalls" encumbered the ground. Clambering over the down-timber, sweating under his pack, brandishing his rifle, MacNamara raised his voice in protest, though most of his words were lost in the roar of the white-toothed river. He was not unaware of the opinions of the townspeople about him. Money! They thought he hoarded it. The truth was, he was lucky to make enough from his traps to buy flour, bacon and tea and the snuff he chewed, tucked under his lower lip, its brown juice oozing from his mouth. Before the railroad came, things had been different. Around Yellowhead Lake he had prospered and had sold his fur to a trader who came by in the spring with a dog team. The day-long progress up the Grantbrook was less a journey than a drawn-out series of vituperations aimed in general at the human race and in particular at the railroaders of Lucerne. Long pent up in silence, MacNamara seemed eager for the release of speech.

The fire had extended only halfway up the valley, and by the afternoon Slim and his host were walking on the soft moss of the primeval spruce and balsam forest. By sundown they reached the cabin. As it was too small to hold both of them, they laid their blankets under a balsam tree. Around midnight Slim awoke to find that he was alone. Then he heard MacNamara's voice a short distance off in the timber and remembered what he had been told in town, that the old trapper "talks to the trees." Slim wisely kept his own counsel and feigned sleep when the other returned to bed.

The next evening, over a feast of caribou steak, bannock, and tea, MacNamara spoke of "the Thing." He had met "the Thing," he said, on Huna Creek. The Huna — pronounced "Hoona" — rises below Mount Robson, 12,972 feet, highest peak in the Canadian Rockies, a two-day journey from the head of the Grantbrook. MacNamara had gone in there to look over the trapping possibilities. He was alone. He was emphatic that no other man was within miles. He knew. He had thoroughly cruised the valley.

He was talking now of the early days just after the advent of the railroad. It was late October, he said, when the willows and alders had long ago shed their leaves. He walked upstream, the Huna on his left, deep, quiet moving, between ranks of tapering spruce and lodgepole pine. Crossing an open slide, where the willows grew, he saw where a grizzly had been digging for a ground squirrel. The hole was "big enough to hold a kitchen range." That night MacNamara made camp under a spruce by a rock bluff above the river. To his right, babbling and chattering over pebbles, a creek fell down into the river and from it he took water to make his bannock and boil his tea. He cut boughs of balsam, laid them, and spread his blankets.

At midnight he awoke. He knew the hour because the Dipper was due east of the Star. He woke up "wide-awake." One coal glowed in the ashes at his feet, like a red eye watchful of his sleep. But what had awakened him was not that, nor the night's chill, nor the river's low hum, nor the forest's creaking. He had been roused by a sigh, a sob, and then a crashing in the bush. Lifting himself on an elbow, he heard the splashing of a heavy body in the waters of the creek, downhill and fifty feet from him. Surrounding him, clinging to him was a beastlike smell which bunched the skin upon the nape of his neck and burned his nostrils as if, surely, it rose from within himself.

He got up, pulled on his trousers, sat down and pulled on his hobnailed boots. He kicked the fire and it sparked up from slumber. The valley wind fanned into flame the brand he took from it. Rifle in his hand, the river to his left, he walked down to the creek whence he had heard the splashing.

There in the pebbles, in the light of his torch, MacNamara saw the tracks. They resembled the tracks a barefoot man might make, a man heavier than himself for they sank deeper into the pebbles than his own. At first he thought they were bear tracks, remembering the grizzly digging he had seen the previous afternoon. A bear's plantigrade hind foot leaves a track similar to a man's, although a bit broader. But a bear has four feet and whatever had made these tracks used only two. They were not as clean-cut as if they had been in clay or mud. Still, they showed up clearly among the smooth, round pebbles, water slowly seeping into them. Close together and not in line, as though the man had staggered, they led across the creek.

From its edge, holding his torch high, MacNamara looked over at the opposing wall of darkness. The trees grew there as thick as prime marten fur. The creek was shallow and he might have forded it. Instead he went back to his campfire, wading in the shadow cast by his torch. A man in the dark, even with a rifle in his hand, is a helpless creature.

MacNamara put more wood on his fire. For once in his life he was lonely, and his back against the forest was chilled. The tracks had him puzzled. What would a man be doing, where no earlier sign of man had been, wandering about the night unshod and with no light to guide him? Why did he ford the stream? Whence had he come and where was he going? He recalled myths he had heard from the Indians to the West, of a strange race roaming the high mountains, the "Susquhavey," neither man nor beast, but something clawed, fanged, and furred and in between the two. It was then that he began to think of it as "the Thing."

For a while he dozed, rifle against his lap. When he awoke the fire had burned down again to coals and ashes and the cold of early morning with the scent of coming snow was around him. As before, it was not the cold that had awakened him. It was "a presence" which had returned. Mac-Namara heard a stir in the bush, not this time by the creek, but in front of him and on a higher level, across the fire upon the open bluff above the river. He slipped away from his fire a short distance to where, unseen, he could better see.

He heard a grunt or a cough. A dry twig broke under an alien foot. He saw nothing, even at the end, nothing he could point to, aim his rifle at, and exclaim, "There it is!" What he saw was the darkness between him and the bluff above the river. He saw it approach, take on form, yield itself to deadly purpose, until within the dark there was the growth of deeper dark. It endured. It loomed and cut from his vision a twinkling star. It breathed and its breath showed pale against the greying sky. From its breath came the "beastlike smell" which scorched his nostrils. MacNamara called out, "What are you?" No answer came.

He rested the barrel of his rifle on a stump and emptied its magazine into "the Thing That Walked like a Man." He jumped quickly aside as it thrashed about in the bush, its groaning like a tremor under his feet. Then it loomed upright again, black, threatening, though dimly seen, standing for a moment above the river, unassailable as a mountainside. It swayed and toppled back. It fell from the bluff, and its roar as it hit the waters sixty feet below floated on the river's roar.

Fright, in its sudden coming, can rob man of reason. It can hold him helpless in its vice or send him in headlong flight to his doom, and MacNamara in the stillness following the thrashing in the bush, the groans, the imminence of a horror for which he had no name, was frightened. Fright shook him like a gust of wind and bathed him in the moisture of its sweat. He had killed. What had he killed? The further thought touched him, faint as the echo of the mad loon's cry, *whom* had he killed?

MacNamara did not wait to see. He did not wait to see what in full dawn the green waters of the river below the bluff might reveal, washed upon the bank or tangled in the branches of a fallen, outthrust tree. Gathering up his blankets, his pot and pan, his axe, and cramming them into his packsack, clutching his empty rifle, he fled the scene of his confusion and his dismay. In half darkness he fled downriver, whence he had come, stumbling against trees, tripping over down-timber, floundering knee-deep through beaver meadows. By morning light he was crossing a slide, pushing through the autumn's barren willows. Their branched stems, like arms with unfleshed hands, waist-high, neck-high, wrapped around him as if to detain his flight. He did not pause to accept the handshake that was mortal. All day long he half ran down the valley, and for each step that he took, another was at his side — the measured tread of that from which he fled, the black ghost, the sobbing phantom of the bluff above the camp above the river. . . .

MacNamara paused in his recital to look across the campfire at the doctor's son. "No," he said, "I never went back up that ghost-haunted valley. Not to this day I haven't."

There in the forest night, with the wind sighing and the river murmuring, his tale had not seemed incredible and the old man with long white hair, staring into the campfire as he spoke, was only a sorcerer reading the story in the coals. MacNamara was making his own contribution to the lore of the "man-beast" that walks the mountains, in North

America as in Asia. In Asia rumours persist of "the Abominable Snowman." In British Columbia an expedition was formed in the spring of 1957 to hunt the "Susquhavey" in the mountains of the lower Fraser River. Atavistic man is forever seeking in the shadows that which he most fears to find.

Many a solitary traveller in the forests below austere summits has looked over his shoulder at the touch of "a presence" and has turned and hurried on his way, fleeing from he knew not what.

> Like one that on a lonesome road
> Doth walk in fear and dread,
> And having once turned round, walks on,
> And turns no more his head;
> Because he knows, a fearful fiend
> Doth close behind him tread.
>
> Coleridge, *The Ancient Mariner*

It has been said that the "strong, silent man" of the outdoors is thought to be strong because he is silent and is silent because he has nothing to say. MacNamara, though no conversationalist, was not one of these. His interests did not extend to "the outside" but were limited to the mountains and the land in their shadow. His world was part real, part fantasy, and before a receptive audience he would talk of it in lengthy monologue. Often he stopped in the middle of a sentence and would not speak again for hours, nor answer when he was spoken to.

During the next few days he and young Slim tramped the valley and crossed over its head onto the Arctic-flowing waters of the Miette and Snaring rivers. From a pass they saw in the distance the gleaming spire of Mount Robson, described by two Englishmen, Milton and Cheadle, who passed below it in 1863, as "a giant among giants, immeasurably supreme."

MacNamara by now had built deep in the timber on the Miette, a second trapping cabin, an easy day's journey from his first. The fact that the Miette, falling into the Athabaska, was in a Dominion game preserve, Jasper Park, where trapping was prohibited, troubled him not at all. To trap there was a gesture of defiance. Besides, rangers did not travel that part of the park in the winter because, aside from MacNamara's, no cabins had been built. In the summer, when they rode though with a pack outfit, they kept to the trail and had not discovered the cabin, which was well off the beaten path.

While they hiked, and again around the campfire, Mac-Namara unburdened himself to the doctor's son of what he called "the strangest hunt" of his life. It took place on the heads of the Miette and Grantbrook and lasted without a break for almost three weeks, from the previous mid-November into early December. Before its end, in despera-tion, he was "fit to gnaw the bark off a spruce tree." The hunt began with the "Day of the Track."

MacNamara's staple catch as a trapper was marten, a member of the weasel family and the size of a half-grown cat. Shoulder-high in the trunk of a spruce or balsam, he would chop a niche about the width of his hand, push his rancid bait well back into it, and then drive two long nails through the top of the niche so that their points were less than an inch apart. The marten, a tree climber, pushed his head in under the inward-sloping nails to reach the bait and the sharp points of the nails against his skull would keep him from withdrawing. In a day — or two or three, depending on the weather — he would freeze to death, his body curling up against the tree trunk. As trapping goes, it was a gentle process: it broke no bones, it left the pelt unscarred, the fur unblemished. MacNamara would come by and pick his fur from the tree much as a farmer plucks apples in his orchard in the fall. For fisher, fox, and lynx he used the conventional steel-jawed traps.

The November day that he saw "the Track" was sunny and bitterly cold. He was breaking trail from his Grantbrook cabin to the one on the Miette. He came upon a porcupine waddling through the snow and beat its brains out with a club. Trappers have no love for the quilled waddlers. They chew up axe-handles, saddle gear, anything impressed by man's sweaty hand with the taste of salt. They find a chink between the logs of a cabin, or a crack under the door, and they gnaw it wider and move in, chewing through the legs of bunks, leaving their barbed quills in the blankets. They gnaw through the supports of loaded shelves, spilling their contents on the floor, and they will destroy any leather that may be about. However, the porcupine MacNamara killed that morning in the timber above the Grantbrook was the last he was to lift his hand to in anger.

He went on, climbing out of the timber onto the alplands. There the snow was beaten hard by the wind and on his snowshoes he walked upon its crust. He came to a rocky outcrop where the wind had eddied and the snow had drifted — soft as flour and, in the shadow, blue as ink. There he saw the track. One track.

It was large as a monstrous wolf's track and almost round, but, unlike a wolf track, it showed a "thumb." Nor was it a lynx track because it had claws. It was the track of a wolverine.

Of course, it was not the first such track that MacNamara had seen, but until then his country had been singularly free of this nemesis of the trapper. The wolverine, snake-headed beast, weighing up to thirty pounds, with side bands of rust-coloured fur meeting at the base of a stumpy tail, is the largest of the weasels. It is sly, ingenious, and stubborn, following in the trapper's steps, springing his traps, gobbling the bait, or devouring the fur caught in their jaws. What it fails to eat it may carry away and "cache" or forever spoil by spraying it with the fetid scent from its anal glands. French Canadians know it as the "carcajou" or "the glutton."

MacNamara's track was fresh, made the night before. Weak-eyed, the wolverine usually shuns the light of day and hunts in the darkness. The old man studied the track thoughtfully. The one lone track made him vaguely uneasy. It seemed to have been set down there like a challenge, or as a portent in the snow, and he felt that, even as he studied it, he was being watched by a pair of red-rimmed myopic eyes.

He tramped on across the alplands and down into the thick timber of the Miette Valley, and there in the powder snow, between the blazes of his trap-line, he picked up the tracks of the wolverine. They were not put down now in individual pad marks. With nothing to distract him — for MacNamara had not yet set his traps — the wolverine had loped along in great bounds, clearing with each one twice the distance of a snowshoe stride.

He had, inevitably, visited the Miette cabin, toward which

MacNamara was proceeding, but he had not harmed it. Nor had he bothered the adjoining cache of flour, bacon, rice, and other supplies that MacNamara had packed in from the railroad and stored there wrapped in canvas. The cache was a platform supported by four spruces, their trunks limbed and ringed with stovepipe. Other trees nearby had been cleared away, so that the cache was a small elevated island in the forest. The crude ladder which MacNamara used to climb the fifteen feet up to the platform leaned against a lone-growing jack-pine fifty feet away.

The pad marks showed that, though the wolverine had not molested the cache, he had at least carefully inspected it. He had also sprayed one of the trees.

MacNamara was sure that he would return. He knew, too, that the wolverine would not easily be taken. Wolverines have chased trappers from their trap-lines and sent them back into town, hollow-cheeked and stuttering, fleeing a menace whose only shape and identity were in the depredation left behind.

In the morning MacNamara rigged a surprise for his un-welcome neighbour. He bloodied his hands with a snowshoe rabbit he had snared overnight, and he rubbed blood on the barrel of his favourite .32 Winchester Special. Over the mouth of the rifle he lightly tied a strip of fat bacon rind.

He cut a forked willow stick and set the mouth of the rifle barrel in it, about a foot above the surface of the snow, the rest of the barrel hidden in the willow bush and only the bacon rind protruding. From the bacon rind he ran a length of fish line around the butt of the rifle, around the willow to which it was fastened — he had smoothed away the bark with his axe — and then to the trigger, where he knotted it. He loosened the safety catch of the rifle. Finally he swept out his snowshoe tracks with a branch of spruce and replaced them with tracks made with the severed hind foot of the rabbit.

The tracks went in and out of the willow bush, a rabbit's natural winter food and shelter, and they made nice reading in the snow. They would lure the wolverine to the bacon rind, and when he yanked at it the fish line would pull the trigger and feed him a meal too heavy for even *his* hardy digestion.

Content with his morning's work, MacNamara tramped back to his cabin on the Grantbrook.

Though he saw no new sign on the way, the wolverine had apparently circled the trail to reach the cabin ahead of him, and he had got into the place by ripping shakes from a corner of the roof. The floor was covered with a mixture of snow, sugar, rice, flour, and syrup. The mattress had been gutted, and the blankets lay shredded on the floor beside the bunk. The stove had been overturned. In the soot and the flour — which had been hanging in a sack from the ridgepole — were the tracks of the wolverine, and the cabin was drenched with his nauseous odour.

MacNamara camped outside in a clump of balsam that night to avoid the stench. It took him two days to set the cabin to rights, and even then he could still smell the wolverine. He threw the fouled and tattered blankets into the bush and slept cold beside his fire, wrapped in a canvas pack cover.

The third morning, he snowshoed back to the Miette cabin, where he had set the rifle. He found the rifle, fired, lying muzzle down in the snow. The bacon rind had disappeared, but there was no wolverine, its brains blown out, lying beside the willow bush.

The well-trodden snow told the story. The wolverine had approached the bait and backed away from it several times. Then he had gone, cautiously, around behind the rifle and, by accident or design, tripped the trigger. At the report, he had leaped twenty feet or more into a patch of juniper, from which he took off into the timber. He had returned after a while, though, and licked up every remnant of bacon rind scattered over the snow by the blast of the rifle.

MacNamara was stumped. Despite the fact that he had rubbed rabbit blood over his hands and gun, the wolverine had still scented man in the setup. He had figured out the function of the fish line and the meaning of the rifle — unless the whole thing were blind chance, which MacNamara didn't much think it was. Why was the wolverine, presumably still unscathed by man, leery of man's scent? Very young animals do not fear men. They are taught to fear by their elders, or learn through experience to fear them.

There was more for MacNamara to learn that day. He went over to his cache and found that the wolverine had been there too. Where a few days before he had merely sniffed around below the platform, now he had made several tries at getting up to it.

It was all there in the snow, as clear to MacNamara as if it had been written. After sliding back a few times the wolverine had shinnied up one of the tree trunks. MacNamara had been careless in the way he sheathed the trunk with stovepipe. They should have overlapped, each upper end coming down a bit over the one below. The wolverine had been able to dig his claws into the interstices between the strips and so made his way to the top.

The whole winter's grubstake had been hurled into the snow, and every sack of flour, sugar, beans, and rice ripped open and despoiled by the wolverine's scent. Each item represented not only its price at the store in town, but also the labour and sweat of back-packing it the difficult miles from the railroad. MacNamara would have to make a round trip to town to replenish his supplies. Here, on the head of the Miette, was a four-footed, evil-smelling marauder trying to take his trapping grounds away from him.

The wolverine, satisfied with the damage he had done to the cache, had left the cabin alone. MacNamara's cabins were never anything to brag about — a man could barely stand upright in either of them, and if two men shared one there was just room for one man to lie on the floor between the bunk and the stove — but the old man was thankful for shelter that chill November night. He made a supper of bannock and tea and rice and raisins from the small store of food on the cabin's shelves.

The next morning he performed an exacting ceremony. He built a fire outside in the cabin clearing and let it die down. He piled green balsam boughs upon the coals, placing them in layers until they formed a mattress. He stretched himself, fully clothed, upon them, and soon, though the temperature around him was well below zero, the sweat was streaming from him. After half an hour he got up. He had practiced a lesson he had learned from a Cree hunter in the early days, that steaming balsam is supposed to remove from clothing and moccasins all taint of human smell.

For several days he ran his trap-line to indicate to the wolverine that he was carrying on as ususal. Below one of his marten sets he set a jagged-jawed Number 5 trap and dusted it over with snow. When he came by the following day, the trap had been turned over and sprung. Part of a marten's scalp remained, caught by the spikes in the tree trunk. The wolverine's tracks were in the snow below.

Taking frequent balsam baths, MacNamara continued to cover his trap-line, back and forth between the two cabins. He dropped oily and scented bait in the middle of the trail and set traps on each side of it, thinking that the wolverine, passing around the bait before he took it, would step in one or the other of the traps.

Where a creek flowed free from ice, MacNamara put the bait, fully exposed, on a boulder in the stream. He set his trap in the shallow water midway between boulder and shore, and on the pan of the trap he set gently a flat stone on which the wolverine would step while reaching for the mess of fat and meat.

Often MacNamara circled the trail to a spot in it where deadfalls or an outcrop of rock permitted him to lay two poles across it. Crawling out on the poles, he dropped his trap, the snow around it untouched with the fresh tread of snowshoes.

He took from his pocket his Ingersoll watch, wrapped it in canvas, and buried it in the snow. Its ticking, slight though its sound would be, would cause the wolverine to stop and investigate — for, being intelligent, he was highly curious. Above the watch, upside down and completely covered with snow, MacNamara spread the jaws of his trap, knowing that the habit of his wary antagonist was to put his paw beneath a trap to overturn and spring it.

He dropped a big fishhook, baited with fresh rabbit meat, on the trail and chained it to a heavy piece of down-timber which was loose and would act as a toggle.

More than once he set up his rifle with its gift of bacon rind. He came back to find the fish line leading to the rifle's trigger severed by the wolverine's sharp teeth. The fishhook had been sniffed at and ignored. The traps had been sprung and the bait taken. The watch, so carefully buried in the snow, had been dug up and carried away, the trap above it tossed to the side of the trail. In one trap, however, was a porcupine, evidently caught only minutes before and held by his tail. More in sorrow than in anger, MacNamara knocked out its feeble brains. He was after other, bigger game.

It went against MacNamara's grain to use strychnine. He believed that poison spoiled fur and, by habit, avoided it. Instead he inserted sharpened, bent twigs of willow into balls of fat and froze them outside his cabin door. When the wolverine swallowed one of these, it would melt in his stomach and the willow would unbend and pierce his intestines. This was a strategy the Eskimos used to kill wolves.

He let the balls of fat fall casually here and there along the trail and through the forest. The wolverine ignored them.

After more than two weeks the old trapper was hollow-eyed and exhausted. He was no longer stalking the wolverine. The wolverine was now stalking him, his pad marks imposed upon the snowshoe tracks. MacNamara discovered himself glancing more and more over his shoulder or starting up from his blankets under a spruce, for nightfall often came upon him when he was far from his cabin, to peer into the darkness at a ghostly form of his fancy flitting between the trees. He was engaged in a contest, fighting for his winter on the trap-line, for his livelihood, for his stake in the wilderness and the only way of life he knew. He was pitted against an adversary with a mind as nimble as his and a body more agile than his own. The trap-line could no longer be shared. It must belong either to him or to the wolverine.

Then one sun-up, so cold that the trees were cracking, he had a glimpse of the wolverine about a mile above the cabin on the Miette. In all his years of trapping it was the first time he had seen one alive.

The animal was in a meadow from which the mist was rising, in a patch of buckbrush not more than fifty yards away. He lifted himself to his haunches, standing about two feet high, and held a paw above his eyes to shield them from the unaccustomed glare of the sun. Before MacNamara could raise his rifle, he had dropped to all fours and vanished into the brush. But the trapper had his trail to follow and lit out upon it.

The tracks led over the pass to the Grantbrook and from one bunch of scrub to another as the wolverine hunted and dug for the mice which lived beneath the snow. MacNamara lost the trail on a rock slide swept clean by the wind.

Two days later he cut the wolverine's trail again by a creek flowing into the Grantbrook. A warm spring bubbled nearby, melting ice and snow, and the tracks were so recent that water was still seeping into them. This time they did not go from bush to bush, but traced a circuitous mile through low-growing balsam and stunted poplar. Several times the wolverine had paused to rub his head in the snow, and once he had coughed up blood.

MacNamara was puzzled. He followed on across a steep, open slope, and then around and under a ledge of rock. Beyond the rock ledge the tracks led down to a tangle of spruce and balsam, a little higher than a man, their tips down-bent by years of wind, their branches extended like hands reaching out upon the snow.

As he came closer, the breath puffing grey from his nostrils, his beard iced about his lips, MacNamara unlatched the safety catch of his rifle, muffling the click with his moose-hide mitt. He sensed that his quarry waited in the cluster of alpine growth just ahead.

Approaching its edge, he stopped, listening for the crack of a twig, the rustle of a bough, or a laboured and solitary breathing. There was no wind blowing, and he heard only the silence against his ears — that and the throb of his heart. He took another step forward, hesitantly, aware that no animal in the bush, even a bear with cubs, was more to be feared at close quarters than the fanged, hump-shouldered wolverine.

As his foot lifted for another step, MacNamara recoiled and almost tripped as he attempted to go backwards on his snowshoes. The wolverine was there, in the shadowed recesses of the timber-line forest, standing up against the roots of a fallen tree. He was dying, but he snarled, showed his teeth, implacable in death as he was in life. Breath wheezed and rattled in his throat. His muzzle and face were so barbed with porcupine quills that there, in the tree-shrouded dusk, he resembled the bristled horror of a childhood dream. He brushed a cheek with a forepaw and coughed as he tried to dislodge the quills lodged in mouth and gullet. The next moment, too fast for thought, he was in the air, teeth slashing for the throat of the upright intruder into his final agony.

MacNamara saw the yellow fangs. He saw foam and blood fly from them. He saw the purpled tongue, studded with the gleam of quills.

His rifle butt met the wolverine's head in mid-air and brought the beast to the ground. A bullet behind the ear completed the act.

The wolverine was grizzled. Like MacNamara, he was an old-timer. But, unlike MacNamara, he had met a stupid and inferior adversary and he had lost.

Were it not for the porcupine, the wolverine would be the ruler of the bush. A bear tips a porcupine over with his paw, exposing the vulernable belly, and leaves the skin turned inside out, like a discarded mitt. The fisher, the marten's large and water-hating cousin, has juices strong enough to digest the porcupine's quills. The wolverine lacks the bear's skill and the fisher's digestion. Shrewd and crafty as he is in all other respects, he attacks the porcupine open-jawed, like a dog, and feasts upon barbed and needle-pointed death.

MacNamara reflectively skinned the wolverine — the fur, which will not frost, is used to line parkas — and when he had finished he began to backtrack upon the animal's trail. He found the place where the wolverine, unable to hunt because of the quills in his mouth, had spent the night beneath a windfall. Four or five miles farther on, after many devious turnings and well down into the forest, MacNamara approached a porcupine in a small natural clearing. Its back was bloody and gashed and almost bare of quills, but the animal still breathed and it twitched its tail weakly as MacNamara approached. He did not club it to death. In compassion, in gratitude —or for what other reason he could not say — he blew off its head.

Since then, a year before, though he had seen his share of porcupines, MacNamara said he had not harmed one of them. Before they turned homewards down the Grantbrook, Slim had evidence of his companion's conversion.

Returning to the cabin late in the afternoon, after a day-long hike over the alplands, they found that, during their absence, a porcupine had gnawed through the leather hinge on the lower part of the door and, pushing his head between door and threshold, had forced himself inside. He had not been there long enough to do more than shred one of a pair of moccasins.

MacNamara tried to grab the animal by its tail and pull it from below the bunk, where it had gone for refuge. A man may sometimes do this if he is quick and succeeds in slipping his hand under the tail. The underside has no quills. Those on the top slope backward and can be held down with the thumb.

MacNamara for his pains received a slap from the tail and a handful of quills, yet he would not kill, nor let Slim kill, the porcupine. As his hand was useless, he told the boy to go outside and get a short pole from the woodpile. For nearly an hour, while the other nursed his hand, cursed, and gave orders, Slim worked with the pole to lift or prod the porcupine over the high threshold of the doorway. Finally, when his trouser legs and pole were studded with quills, he won out.

By now it was moonlight. The porcupine waddled across the clearing, its back totally bereft of covering and pale as a woman's shoulders in evening dress under a chandelier. It climbed a bull-pine tree. "Get up there, where you belong, you prickly bastard!" MacNamara yelled, shaking his left fist. "Stay up there and grow quills and come down and get me another wolverine." The last word — "w-o-l-v-e-r-i-n-e" — echoed weirdly up against the mountains. By midnight, using coal oil, which seeps down into the quill to soften the barb, and a pair of pliers, Slim had extracted most of the quills from the palm of MacNamara's hand.

The next morning, hoisting their packs, they set out down valley for the railroad. Two miles in from it they were met by a search party of four, headed by Tom Young, the town's locomotive foreman. Young explained that, as they were overdue by three or four days, Slim's parents had become worried that "something had gone wrong."

At first MacNamara was speechless. His face flushed. The veins of his throat swelled as if they would burst. Then he threw his worn black hat on the ground and jumped upon it and, waving his rifle, shouted, "By the bleeding hind-quarters of the Lamb of God! By Christ and by Jesus! I know every goddamned branch of every goddamned tree in this valley! And you, you greasy railroader . . ." He sputtered into incoherent rage, pushed past the searchers, and strode on.

At the railroad the speeder was waiting. MacNamara would not accept a ride, nor would he permit Slim to walk with him to his cabin. The two never spoke again. MacNamara could not forgive the disgrace of having a party of railroaders looking for him in the mountains.

He died alone of pneumonia in his cabin late in November, 1924, bitter to the end and refusing medical help. During that summer Lucerne, as a railroad divisional point, had been moved to Jasper, Alberta, over the divide and twenty-two miles eastward. Ironically, when he died, MacNamara had outlasted the town by several months and again had the valley to himself.

Today Lucerne is only another deserted town in the mountains, windows broken, doors swinging open in the wind. There are those who say that the black ghost, delivered by MacNamara years ago on the Huna, on November nights crosses the bridge at the lake narrows and comes to haunt the town's one rocky street.

The Singer
in the Willows

His people, the Wood Crees, called him "Gitchee-Manitou-Wayo," or "Voice of the Great Spirit." The name in English became "Almighty Voice," and the young warrior was to prove himself worthy of it. He was not a "loner," but he made a lonely stand.

For twenty long months the name troubled a wild northern land, rolling west across the prairie grasses to the ramparts of the Rocky Mountains. Trapper, trader, and Cree Indian took it with them as they paddled down the rivers flowing northeast to Hudson Bay and north to the Arctic ocean. There, beyond the stunted tree line, it faded and was lost upon the tundra. It survived the blizzards of two winters until, in the hosts of swirling snowflakes, it seemed to toss like a banner above beleaguered tepees scattered upon the plain.

Inside those tepees, pitched within the awful shadow of a collective doom, the name was whispered as a hope by old men and women who knew they had no hope. Young braves, less tutored in a race's sorrow, shouted it as they danced and beat drums around their campfires. Blackfoot, Blood, Sarcee, and Piegan, still roaming as hunters through the foothills, heard its message as a challenge. Even lonelier than the natives of the country, who moved or squatted in uneasy groups, the white settler, turning the virgin sod, came home at night to his family and in the stillness sensed the name like a threat outside the walls of his log cabin.

In the end, after two winters, two springs, one fall, and one summer, the young man returned his name, Almighty Voice, to those who had given it to him and, while his aged mother keened his death song, died, and in the manner of his death made a legend for his people. The place he chose for his atonement was a ridge, topped with newly leafed poplar and willow in the Minnichinas Hills — the "solitary hills" — west of the town of Prince Albert on the southern edge of the sub-Arctic forest in the present-day province of Saskatchewan.

There the sun of his last day on earth rose early, and from a pit, dug with bare hands behind a clump of willow, Almighty Voice, with his companion, Going-Up-to-the-Sky, could hear the voices and feel the stir of the hundreds who had come to watch him die — settlers, half-breed trappers, and Cree Indians, ranged in a half circle on the slopes of the hills nearby, above them their two-wheeled carts and horses on the sky line. Below him, half a mile away, was the thin crimson line of the Northwest Mounted Police. The drama was well staged, the blue sky for its canopy and the green, wavelike prairie for its backdrop. Unseen, in the thicket before the pit, the bodies of three dead men lay.

Almighty Voice boomed out his death chant. His mother, Spotted Calf, fifty yards distant on a hillock, joined with him in a quavering treble. The ranks of the Mounted Police parted and a piece of artillery, a snub-nosed nine-pounder, was rolled forward. A final demand for surrender, translated into Cree by an interpreter, cut through the air. For a full minute Almighty Voice was silent. Then he lifted his voice again in defiance. A puff of smoke erupted from the gun's muzzle. At intervals, throughout the hot forenoon, the bombardment continued — a nation, an empire, waging war against two men on a hilltop. Poplars and willows were shredded by shrapnel, and leaves, ripped from their stems, rose up in clusters to fall back in slow, verdant showers. As the leaves fell and the echoes of each shot subsided, Almighty Voice was heard taunting the gunners.

At last, when the sun was at its zenith, the voice from the

willows was still. A fragment of metal had pierced the singer's forehead, leaving there on the brown skin a sudden red blossom. Beside him in the pit, Going-Up-to-the-Sky, fulfilling the prophecy of his name, shuddered in his last agonies. A shroud of dust hung over the thicket on the hilltop, like the tattered ghosts of two young braves ascending to the home of their fathers, where, for all eternity, warriors danced and sleek horses grazed belly-deep in meadows starred with flowers.

The dust marked the finish of the last pitched battle between the white man and the Indian on the North American plains. It was also the end of the most ambitious and crucial man-hunt in the history of the Northwest Mounted Police, today the Royal Canadian Mounted Police. In length of time, in distance covered, of men and issues involved, and in the theatrical setting of its climax, none other in their eventful record equals it.

In formal terms, the primary offense committed by Almighty Voice was the shooting of a white man's steer. Actually, his more grievous fault was that he had been born an Indian in a tepee of buffalo hides, and in turning the nine-pounder upon him the Mounted Police were duly performing the function for which they had been formed.

The year of the deed was 1897, late in the month of May. This was the decade of the "Gay Nineties." It is a decade remembered for "Diamond Jim" Brady, chorus girls, and champagne parties where couples waltzed and two-stepped to the tune of "Sweet Little Buttercup" and other sprightly songs of the day. However, in many respects, the nineties were anything but "gay." In 1893 there was a financial panic in New York City and on May Day, 1884, Coxey marched the ragged remnants of his army of unemployed into Washington.

In the spring of 1897 the world was converging upon London to celebrate the Diamond Jubilee in the reign of a dour and dumpy little woman, Queen Victoria, the "Widow of Windsor," who had imposed her will upon a quarter of the earth's surface and given her name to an age. In Europe, Greeks and Turks were fighting. On June 16, in Washington, President McKinley was to sign the treaty annexing the "Sandwich Islands" — Hawaii — to the United States. On the

West Coast hordes of gold-seekers were embarking for the Yukon to seek their fortunes in the grim and snow-topped mountains of the north.

In the spring of 1897 on the Canadian prairie a race of man was dying — and with it a way of life which had endured through the centuries. Another race, another era, impatient of all waiting, stood by to take over. The locomotive's whistle, laying waste the prairie silence, trumpeting beyond through the mountains, was to the Indian at once the requiem of all things past and the herald of a hoarse-voiced and unpitying future.

That future, with the Mounted Police as its law-enforcing arm, broke upon the Crees and the other tribes of Canada's western territories with the abruptness of catastrophe. The penetration of the western United States was a series of bloody Indian battles, but it was gradual and continued for more than half a century. Canada took over her West, on the other hand, in ten years — 1874 to 1884 — without a major campaign against an Indian tribe and, indeed, with only an occasional revolver drawn. The battle in the Minnichinas Hills was not against a tribe, but against an individual, Almighty Voice, and his comrade.

Chartered in London in 1670 for trading into Hudson Bay, the Hudson's Bay Company held most of the Canadian West as a virtual feudal preserve as late as 1869. Interested only in pelts, mainly those of the beaver, the Company discouraged white settlement in its territory and interfered little with the nomadic life of the aborigines with whom it traded.

Foremost among these were the forest-dwelling Crees, neighbours of the Ojibways, in today's northern Ontario and Manitoba. Supplied with steel traps and rifles by the Company's factors, they slowly pushed west and south until, late in the eighteenth century, they emerged upon the plains. There they infringed upon the hunting grounds of the Blackfoot, who became their mortal enemies.

The white man walked west in North America on a carpet of beaver skins, and no people did more to lay the carpet at his feet as he crossed Canada than the Crees. They trapped and hunted for him and guided him through the intricate waterways which were to lead him over the divides from Hudson Bay to the Mississippi and the Arctic, and from the

Great Lakes to the Pacific. And because, among the northern tribes, their women were the comeliest, they freely mixed their blood with that of Scottish factors and French Canadian voyageurs. The offspring of these marriages became a distinct breed of men, the French Canadian Métis, Catholic in religion, traditional in thinking, who were twice, in 1869 and 1885, to rise up and oppose the Canadian Government in its settlement of the West.

In 1869 that government purchased from the Hudson's Bay Company the immense Northwest Territories, stretching from what in 1870 became the Manitoba boundary seven hundred miles west to the Rockies and almost two thousand miles north from the international line to the Arctic. Vast tracts of the land were, in turn, to be handed over to the Canadian Pacific Railway. Students of Canadian history have dubbed the double deal "the Great Divide." To create an authority for the one that had been removed, the government organized the Northwest Mounted Police early in 1873. The mission of the Force, with an initial muster of less than three hundred men, was to patrol more than a million and a half square miles of prairie, foothills, forest, and tundra, an area comparable to that of Eastern Europe. White men had traversed this wilderness. In 1789, Alexander Mackenzie of the Northwesters, a rival fur-trading company later absorbed by the Hudson's Bay, reached tidewater on the Arctic by the river to which he gave his name. In the spring of 1793 he portaged over the Rocky Mountains by way of the Peace in the Mackenzie Basin, travelled down the upper Fraser, and walked overland to the Pacific at Bella Coola, the first white man to have crossed North America. Cree blood was in the veins of the men of both expeditions.

By 1873 other fur traders and explorers had made well-known routes of the North and South Saskatchewan, flowing into Hudson Bay, and of the Athabaska, which, like the Peace, drains through the Slave River into Great Slave Lake and the Mackenzie to the Arctic. Most of what remained between these established trails was *terra incognita* to the white man's eye and the few posts which the Mounted Police set up along its fringes were like ports looking out upon a sea whose shoals and currents had still to be charted. Across this undulating expanse, under the flag of their centuries-old freedom, wandered tribes of Indians, their numbers placed as high as fifty thousand. To keep in touch with them and induce them eventually to settle on reservations, the members of the Force used saddle horse and wagon in the summer, snowshoe and dog team in the winter. Cree half-breeds were their guides and dog-team drivers.

The Mounted Police, contrary to popular belief, were not composed of "gentlemen rankers," "Ne'er-do-wells," nor castoffs of wealthy English families, though some of these were to be found among them. Nor were they of exceptional physique. A survey in 1889 established that most of them were from farms, men who knew animals, who were accustomed to hardship and resourceful in acting on their own. Their average age was twenty-nine; height, five-feet eight inches; chest measurement, thirty-eight inches; and weight, one hundred and sixty pounds.

Their official motto was, and is, *Maintiens le droit* — To uphold the right. Unofficially they subscribed to the dictum "Without trouble" because, so few among so many, they could not afford it. In their dealing with an Indian group they took pains to explain that the law was alike for white man and for red. That they put their words into effect was manifest as early as 1877, four years after the Force came into being. Early in that summer the Blackfoot Confederacy, which, numbering more than fifteen thousand with the parent tribe, embraced the Blood, Piegan, and Sarcee, signed a treaty under their chief, Crowfoot, and became wards of the government, though they were permitted to continue hunting far afield from their foothill reserve. The Blackfoot were the most war-like people of the plains, foraying as far south as the Yellowstone into the United States. Other treaties had been signed previously with bands of Crees to the north and east, but the Blackfoot treaty, because of the number of people involved, and their reputation as warriors, was a turning point in the relation between white and red.

At the signing Crowfoot called the redcoats his "friends," and added, "they have protected us as the feathers of the bird protect it from the weather." He meant that the Mounted Police had kept their promise to protect his tribe from aggression by the Crees and his lands and young men from exploitation by white settlers and unscrupulous whiskey traders from south of the border. A measure of the morals of the whiskey trade exists in a formula for liquor sold to the Blackfoot and other Indians near Fort Whoop-Up about this time. Fort Whoop-Up, on the edge of the foothills, was just north of the international boundary. The recipe was: one keg of alcohol, Perry's Painkiller, Hosetter's Bitters, red ink, castile soap, blackstrap chewing tobacco and water, the whole well mixed and boiled before serving. The traders offered one tin cup of this concoction for a buffalo robe. It is small wonder that Crowfoot, palate and dignity outraged, was thankful to his benefactors, the Mounted Police.

In that same early summer of 1877 the Force — a handful of police with the mobility of a military unit — met their second challenge as they strove to keep order among tens of thousands of "hostiles." The Sioux chief, Sitting Bull, with four thousand of his followers, appeared in the Cypress Hills, north and east of the point where today Montana, Saskatchewan and Alberta meet. Fleeing from his massacre of Custer's 7th Cavalry on the Little Bighorn the year before, he claimed Canadian sanctuary. The presence of the redoubtable warrior and his hungry people posed problems not easily met. One was a further threat to the diminishing buffalo herds and the action the indigenous tribes might take against it. The other was that Sitting Bull, fresh from his victory over the "long knives," was a living symbol of what the Indian, armed and resolute, might achieve in resisting the authority of the white man.

Sitting Bull was granted sanctuary but he and his people, being properly wards of the U.S. Government, were denied rations, though they were free to hunt buffalo and other game. After five uneasy years, the hunt failing as the buffalo decreased, he surrendered in March, 1881 to the Americans at Fort Buford, Dakota Territory, a few miles from what is now Plentywood, Montana. In this year, Almighty Voice, twenty-three years old at his death among the willows of the Minnichinas Hills in 1897, was a boy of seven on the One Arrow Reserve, near Duck Lake, Saskatchewan, three hundred miles northeast of the Cypress Hills. There is no doubt that around the campfire he heard the saga of the doughty chief of the Sioux who, after defeating the white man in battle, was finally reduced by hunger to impotence and his proud following to a few dozen emaciated and ragged wretches. He may even have heard quoted Sitting Bull's words as he left on his journey of sorrow: "Once I was strong and brave. My people had hearts of iron. Now I will fight no more, forever. My people are cold and hungry. My women are sick and my children are freezing. My arrows are broken and I have thrown my war paint to the winds."

As he grew older the boy had further reason for pride in his race. He was the son of Sounding Sky and the grandson of Chief One Arrow. These two became leaders in the Northwest Rebellion when, in the spring of 1885, the year through-trains of the Canadian Pacific Railway began to cross the prairie, Louis Riel, a Métis, tried to carve a French Canadian, Catholic-dominated enclave out of the northern wilderness. Although the Crees were prominent in the uprising, it was not a conflict between Indians and whites, but rather a sanguinary dispute between the Canadian Government and a minority of its own people who had settled upon the plains, a dispute in which the Crees took part.

The Métis, many of them with Cree blood, were hunters and trappers. Like the Indians, they regretted to see the old days of freedom pass with the buffalo. Descendants of the early-day fur traders and voyageurs, many of whom had married Cree women, they had settled along the rivers on pieces of land with a ten-chain water frontage which stretched as much as two miles back into the prairie. This was the custom in French-speaking Québec, where most of them had their paternal origins. Its advantage was that it assured the settler not only water, but fuel and wood for building from the forest growth along the rivers. Furthermore, he was within calling distance of his neighbour.

The Canadian Government sent out survey parties from Ottawa to divide this land into mile-square "sections," in conformity with accepted practice outside of Québec. The operations were carried out summarily with no attempt at explanation. The Métis, understandably, regarded the surveyors as trespassers interfering with their rights as owners. The fact that they would still own roughly the same area of land in different form did not appease their indignation.

Louis Riel, who, from a previous foray against the authorities in a similar cause in 1869-70 at Fort Garry — now

Winnipeg, Manitoba — had taken refuge in Montana, came north again to build upon this new discontent. By profession a schoolteacher and in his middle years, he was thought by some men to be mad. Undoubtedly he had "visions" and a fanatic zeal and a gifted tongue to strive towards them. He saw himself as no less than the titular ruler of a kingdom in the Northwest. In following him the Métis, having no voice in the laws being foisted upon them from afar, had little to lose and a country of their own to gain. Or so their leader told them, and he promised the Crees and other tribes who might join in the effort that they would benefit equally.

The Crees, under Chief One Arrow, Sounding Sky, and another chief, Poundmaker, fought stoutly beside him. After months of fighting, with combined losses on both sides of more than a hundred lives, the Mounted Police defeated Louis Riel and his allies — but only after being heavily reinforced by militia from Ottawa.

Riel had many supporters in the East, notably in Québec. He was hanged for treason in Regina, new capital of the Northwest Territories, in a clamour of opposing opinions which shook the government of the day in Ottawa. Prison sentences were meted out to his Indian leaders, among them Chief One Arrow, grandfather of Almighty Voice, who served three years in Stony Mountain Penitentiary, Manitoba. It became a distinction which the old man bore proudly.

Chief One Arrow's band at Duck Lake, along with other Crees, numbering about twenty thousand, had treated with the government and gone on a reservation in 1876. The transition had been sudden. Up to that time, and since their coming to the plains, they had depended upon the buffalo for life itself. Its meat, sometimes dried, pounded, and mixed with saskatoon berries to make "pemmican," had been their main sustenance. Buffalo hides gave them blankets for warmth and covering for their tepees, and buffalo dung was often fuel for their fires. Above all, the hunting of buffalo taxed the full energies of their men and the preparation of the meat and skins kept their women busy.

Within ten years all this was gone. The railroad cut across the migratory tracks of the once teeming herds. As early as 1880 the buffalo had vanished from the Canadian prairie, because of overhunting and a cordon of virtually all the

Indians of the northwest states which prevented the northern migration of the one great remaining herd and penned it within the Missouri Valley between the Little Rockies to the west and the Judith Basin to the east. White settlers planted crops and turned cattle loose where once the buffalo had grazed. Instead of the rich red meat of the chase the Indian's subsistence was now handouts from the government — flour, tea, and occasionally beef delivered on the hoof. And even this did not always come through on time. More than once, over the protests of the Mounted Police, the government, in distant Ottawa, failed in its obligation. Hunger struck indiscriminately at Crees, Assiniboins, and at their hereditary enemies, the Blackfoot on the far side of the prairies up against the mountains. The Indians ate roots, hunted gophers and mice, haunted the police and trading posts, saw their old people and children perish, and offered up their young girls for sale.

Regina, now the capital of Saskatchewan, in the early days was known as "Pile of Bones." There the Plains Indians had piled the bones of slaughtered buffalo, pathetically believing that those still upon the prairie would not forsake the remains of their dead. One pile alone was said to contain the remains of 360,000 animals. With the coming of the railroad, the Indians polished the horns and sold them to souvenir hunters. The beggar's wage they received did not save them from hunger.

As they delved among the bones they may have reflected that, after all, the American way of dealing with their people was no less harsh in its final result than the Canadian. The Americans killed the Indians in thousands. Indeed, the international boundary from 1870 to 1890 was like a dike through which Indian blood seeped northward in scattered and torn human remnants seeking sanctuary.

Canadians, on the other hand, took away the Indian's source of living and slowly starved him to death. Canadians and Americans together had done more than that. They had destroyed the Indian's pride of race, their priests and administrators mocking his ceremonials and scorning his gods. He might have withstood the disappearance of the buffalo and retained his will to participate in the future if his right to human dignity had been respected. With the collapse of his

tribal structure — it could not exist without gods, ceremonies, or economic base — the Indian was spiritually, as
well as physically, deprived of all sustenance. By definition,
"to civilize," the word having its roots in the Latin *civis*, a
citizen, means "to make a citizen of." "Civilization" brought
no such privilege to the Indian. He was made a social outcast
in his own country.

Rumours passed through the reservations and hunting
camps of conspiracies hatched and confederations formed
to sweep the white man back whence he came. The red man
was strong in numbers. Sitting Bull and Louis Riel showed
before their final failures what they could do acting with
their brothers in a common cause. The old men shook their
heads, but the young men still donned war paint, danced,
and beat their drums. For a little while yet they would
believe in a future shaped from the glories of the past.

Then in 1890 a new hope swept over the Canadian plains,
affecting particularly the Crees. In far-off Nevada a Paiute
named Wovoda taught that an Indian Messiah would come
to the earth and return the continent to his people. The
Messiah, attended by the great chiefs and warriors of the
past, would appear on a mountaintop and word would go
forth to all the tribes to assemble below him.

Wovoda's was a peaceful, Christlike religion, and the ghost
dances which attended upon his teachings were no more than
its ritual. Yet they were brutally suppressed south of the line
and made a pretext for the slaying of Sitting Bull at the
hands of his own people in the Grand River Valley in the
high Missouri. This preceded the slaughter of Wounded
Knee, where American troops killed three hundred Indian
women and children and ninety men.

On April 13 of that same year, 1890, Chief Crowfoot died.
Steadfast in friendship to the white man, his hand held the
Blackfoot Confederacy in check for thirteen years and restrained his followers from joining in the Rebellion of 1885.
He died, attended by his chiefs and his three wives, in his
tepee, to the beat of war drums in the greening Bow River
Valley in the foothills. A Catholic priest, Father Doucet, was
present. He recorded and translated the dying man's last
words. Among them were: "In a little while I will be gone
from you, my people, and whither I cannot tell. From no-

where we came, into nowhere we go. What is life? It is the flash of a firefly in the night. It is the breath of a buffalo in the wintertime. It is as the little shadow that runs across the grass and loses itself in the sunset."

The western Plains Indian accepted the world as he found it. Except for the introduction of the horse, Chief Crowfoot's people, until the white man came, lived in much the same environment and fashion as their ancestors in Neolithic times. In contrast to the Indian, the white man is forever shaping a new world out of the old. In the early days of the West an angry shadow burned at his restless heels, urging him constantly towards the setting sun. His passage was to sear the buffalo grass from the prairies and lay waste the forests in his wake. Chief Crowfoot longed for the old days, but, knowing that they were now gone forever, he strove with tact and energy that the transition of his people from one age into another might be brought about without the shedding of blood.

Largely, he succeeded, and with his death the Mounted Police lost their most powerful ally among the native tribes. However, their authority was not to be seriously challenged until 1895. In that year Almighty Voice shot the white man's steer. Ironically it was a Corporal Dickson of the Force who, with a few careless words, formed him for his destiny and pointed him towards his fatal battle in the Minnichinas Hills twenty months later.

He was well fitted to become a storied figure, one whose name, after more than fifty years, still echoes over the rolling bush land and prairie where he had his birth and being. The son and grandson of the warriors Sounding Sky and Chief One Arrow, he stood more than six feet tall in his moose-hide moccasins — moose, though their numbers never compared with those of the buffalo, were hunted by the Wood Crees who lived on the margin of the northern forest. Almighty Voice's Roman nose, his black, piercing eyes, and the resonant, deep-sounding voice from which he took his name — these were the attributes of a leader. More than that, at the age of twenty-one, when a policeman's hand for the first time touched his shoulder, he was the best runner, the best hunter, and the deadliest shot on the One Arrow Reserve near Duck Lake. It was while hunting off the limits of the reserve one morning that he shot the steer.

The offense was not an unusual one for those days. Indians, as a rule, did not like beef. It tasted "sweet" compared to the tangier meat of the buffalo. However, inasmuch as all animals grazing on the land had once been theirs, they frequently failed to distinguish between wild and domestic stock. This was especially true if they were hungry, and hunger was endemic among the Crees in the years before the turn of the century.

One version of the story is that the steer was being held for the government, which later would deliver it as part of their rations to the band of Crees on the One Arrow Reserve. In killing it Almighty Voice was only taking in advance an animal already marked for the use of his people — for its flesh would be shared, according to tribal custom, among his neighbours.

The other version is that it was not a steer that he shot, but a white cow belonging to a settler named McPherson. McPherson objected when Almighty Voice vaulted his rail fence and trespassed on his property. They had angry words. To conclude the argument Almighty Voice shot over the white man's shoulder and killed the white cow. McPherson at once saddled up and rode to the Duck Lake detachment of the Mounted Police, fifteen miles to the east, and reported what had occurred to Sergeant C.C. Colebrook, who was in charge, with Corporal Dickson and a constable under him. The white cow, McPherson alleged, was a good milk producer and his particular pet.

The sergeant, a veteran of more than ten years with the Force, lost no time in setting out to bring the culprit in to justice, trailing an extra horse for the purpose. It was in keepin with Mounted Police tradition that one man should make an arrest in a camp of several hundred potentially hostile Indians.

The day was brisk. The breaths of the horses and the rider rose and mingled as they passed through gaunt poplar and willow whose leaves were shed. The country had the "hungry look" which comes upon it just before the snow.

The One Arrow Cree encampment conformed in this respect to its surroundings. Few people or dogs were about. Smoke puffed from the tepee tops. Some of the tepees were of patched canvas and blankets. Others were of buffalo hide worn so thin by long use that the skeletons of their poles showed through, suggestive of the half-starved humanity sheltering within from the raw northeast wind.

Colebrook picked up an interpreter on the edge of the reservation and with him rode to the tepee of Sounding Sky, where he expected to find Almighty Voice. The old man, since his part in the Riel rebellion of 1885, ten years before, had been under the eye of the Mounted Police. As befitted the eminence of its owner, the tepee was set on high ground, a bit apart from the others. Leaving his horses — they were taught to "stand" — Colebrook threw back the flap of the tepee and, with his interpreter, entered.

Stopping, coughing, as he peered through the pall of smoke from the slow-burning fire in the tepee's centre, the sergeant, through his interpreter, explained his mission to the shadowy figure in the rear whom he took to be Sounding Sky. He pointed out, in the well-tried formula, that the Force's duty was to be impartial. They protected the Indian and his stock. They had also to protect the white man and his animals against unlawful behaviour by the Indians. Almighty Voice was accused of shooting a white man's beef and would now have to come to Duck Lake, where he would be fairly tried the next day. Sounding Sky, Spotted Calf, his mother, and any others were welcome to attend the trial to see that he was treated fairly.

No word was uttered in reply. For a long minute of silence the white man's authority was at issue. Already, outside the tepee, a crowd had gathered about the two horses. Colebrook, with his red jacket, was solitary among alien people. He had his two men at Duck Lake to back him up. Beyond that the nearest support was at Prince Albert, another thirty-five miles to the east.

A tall form took shape across the fire and turned to rummage in a pile of blankets. He might be reaching for a rifle or merely for a harmless item to take with him on his journey. Colebrook moved aside as Almighty Voice, a blanket over his arm, stepped around the fire and out of the tepee. Doubtless he had been waiting for the policeman's visit. His crime at most was a small one. If he had to he would spend a few weeks in jail. There at least he would have warmth and food. Besides, his grandfather, Chief One Arrow, had served a much stiffer sentence after the uprising of 1885, and One Arrow, as everyone knew, was for that all the more respected by his people.

Almighty Voice shoved his way through the throng outside the tepee. With Colebrook at his side he threw his blanket over the extra horse and leaped lightly on to its back. Bare to the waist, wearing only a breechclout, waist-high moose-skin leggings and moccasins, he sat the horse with natural grace and arrogance. Two long braided plaits of black hair hung down his chest. His lip curled as he glanced at the sergeant. On the ride to the Duck Lake barracks he spoke not at all, nor did he show discomfort when, in the late twilight, snow commenced to fall and melt upon his naked chest and shoulders.

Almighty Voice rode first along the narrow trail. Colebrook, as he gazed upon the tawny back before him, had no means of knowing that within a few days he would be dead from his prisoner's bullet.

The log barracks, coated and chinked with white clay, lacked a proper cell, and Almighty Voice was confined to the guardroom with a heavy iron ball locked to his leg by a five-foot-long chain. Disdaining the straw pallet, he rolled up in his blanket and lay down on the floor for the night. However, he had little chance to sleep.

Corporal Dickson, who was on duty, was talkative and knew just enough Cree to make himself understood by signs. Further, he had been heard to boast that "once an Indian, always an Indian."

Now, tilting back in his chair behind the table that served as a desk, he looked down on the prisoner on the floor and told him that he would probably hang for the crime of shooting the white man's cow. According to what Almighty Voice later related to his people, the Corporal embellished his story, describing the scaffold that would have to be built and the crows that would perch on the hanged man's shoulders and peck at his eyes as his body dangled in the autumn winds, a reminder to other would-be transgressors against the law.

These were among the most expensive words spoken in the history of the Force. They were to result in the deaths of three policemen, one volunteer, and of three Cree Indians, and in the wounding of two policemen and one Métis, in patrols covering thousands of miles for the next twenty months and in bringing the countryside to a state of unease it had not known since the days of the Riel rebellion. The words were also to cost Dickson his rank and put him to digging a grave in frozen ground.

Strangely enough, Almighty Voice believed what he was told. Chief Buffalo Child Long Lance, a Blackfoot who became the adopted son of Spotted Calf, mother of Almighty Voice, and later a publicity man for the Canadian Pacific Railway in New York City, points out in his autobiography that Almighty Voice was then very young, only twenty-one, and "knew little of the white men except to fear them for their ways. He was not afraid to die. That we know. But to die for a cow that we needed for food . . . that was something he could not understand. He decided to escape."

Another point is that the young Cree, for the first time in his life, was held within walls and tethered to an iron ball. The experience was at once humiliating and terrifying to a hunter raised in the freedom of the forest and the plain — for, though placed on reservations, the Crees were allowed to hunt beyond them. To such a prisoner the threat of death was congruous.

Almighty Voice's chance to escape came at midnight when Corporal Dickson was relieved by a constable. The constable, weary from a day in the saddle, fell asleep, his head on the table by the low-burning coal-oil lamp. Almighty Voice, watching from under the cover of his blanket, slowly got to his feet and, carrying the iron ball in his hand, approached the table. The key to his leg iron was there, on a ring with several others, by the base of the lamp. For a minute he stood, weighing the iron ball in his hand with which he could have crushed the head of the sleeper.

Instead he set the ball quietly on the floor, fitted the key to the leg iron, and freed his leg. With another key, he unlocked the guardroom door and, returning the keys to the table, shutting the door quietly behind him, slipped into the shadows of the night.

Fifteen miles of prairie and bush land and the half-mile-wide South Saskatchewan River lay between him and the One Arrow Reserve. The distance and the river meant little. Not even a man on horseback would likely overtake Almighty Voice, given an hour's start, before he reached his mother's tepee.

Riding in to Duck Lake, Sergeant Colebrook and his prisoner had crossed the South Saskatchewan on a barge. Now Almighty Voice avoided the trail to the barge, where he might meet a chance traveller. Coming to the river several hundred yards below it, he laced together a raft of willow, on which he put his leggings and moccasins. Pushing this ahead, resting his hands on it for support, he kicked himself across to the north bank and before dawn reached the One Arrow Reserve.

It was only a few hours later that Colebrook came again for him, this time accompanied by the constable. Almighty Voice was still in his mother's tepee when the sergeant left, taking with him as hostage Sounding Sky. Inexplicably Colebrook accepted at face value the statements of father and mother that they had not seen their son since the previous day and failed to make a thorough search of the tepee. Had he done so he would have found Almighty Voice under a pile of sacks and skins near the door where Spotted Calf had hidden him.

That night he departed for the North on horseback. He took with him a double-barrelled muzzle-loader, ammunition, and blankets. Nor was he alone. His companion, also mounted, was a fourteen-year-old girl of his tribe, Marie, known to be the sweetheart of one Dumont, a Métis guide and interpreter who lived nearby. It is likely that she was a pleasing lass. Alexander Mackenzie commented that the Cree women had the finest features and the most enticing forms of any of the native women he had seen in his journeys across the continent.

The girl would not hinder the fugitive in his flight and, indeed, was a valuable adjunct to it. Almighty Voice, reverting to the life of his ancestors, would live off the country. As they did before they came out of the forest and onto the plains, he would shelter himself and the girl in crude tepees of spruce boughs and birch bark. His was more than a journey. It was an errand into the past, into the shadowland of his ancestors, where trees had spirits and rivers murmured of visions in the night.

To the north across the North Saskatchewan towards the

Barren Lands he would find moose and caribou. She would set up camp, dress and cook the game he killed, mend his moccasins and leggings, make him new ones from the skins she stretched and scraped — and when the day was done, offer him the warm solace of her young body.

The outraged Dumont was quick to appear at Duck Lake before Sergeant Colebrook with this latest news and to tender his services as guide in the pursuit which inevitably must follow. As the police in the city depend upon the informer and the stool pigeon, so have the Mounted Police thoughout their history looked to those among the Métis or half-breed population who, for a consideration, would betray those to whom they were allied by blood. With a knowledge of the country such as no policeman tied to his post could gain, the Métis made a further and invaluable contribution. Even today, in their wilderness patrols, the Mounted Police rely upon native guides.

The next day, with two saddle horses and a pack-horse, Colebrook and Dumont took up the trail of Almighty Voice. The search was not as haphazard as it might seem. Dumont did not need to cast about for tracks. Putting himself in the other man's place, he had only to decide where a man with horses would most likely go to find good feed, and the country which, with unshod horses, he would avoid.

After ten days Dumont was able to point to unshod hoof-marks in a patch of muskeg and beyond them to fresh horse dung. This was early morning. The two men rode on through bleak autumn meadows and through ghostlike clumps of white birch. Suddenly they were startled by a rifle shot in the distance. Almighty Voice had shot a grouse and they came upon him unexpectedly in a clearing as the girl was plucking it. The young Cree had not yet brought in his horses from their night's pasturage and made no attempt to escape. Instead he grabbed his rifle and levelled it at Colebrook's red tunic. "Another step nearer," he shouted in Cree, "and you are a dead brave."

Dumont relayed this message to Colebrook and added, "He means what he says." They were still sixty yards from Almighty Voice and the Métis advised the sergeant to pull up for a "parlay."

Colebrook, not permitting his horse to break its stride,

ordered Dumont to tell Almighty Voice that he was under arrest. The Métis obeyed, but reined his horse and refused to advance farther. Colebrook went on by himself to write his name and that of Almighty Voice into the annals of the Canadian West.

The girl, Marie, in a fringed suit of white buckskin, moved back into the birch thicket, the half-plucked grouse hanging by its feet from her hand. Almighty Voice and Colebrook faced one another alone. The Cree believed that if he surrendered he would be hanged. More than that, to surrender now would be to deny the proud tradition of Sounding Sky and Chief One Arrow and to mark himself a coward before the girl he had taken under his protection.

Colebrook, on the other hand, could not retreat. If he did so he might get a bullet in the back. But more impelling than any fear were the habits learned in more than ten years of patrolling the prairies. The outnumbered Mounted Police had maintained their authority by fair dealing and by bluff. When these were not enough, they fell back on raw courage. His one concession was to put his hand upon his revolver butt.

Almighty Voice called out a further warning. He did not realize, as he braced his shoulder against a tree and steadied his sights upon the approaching sergeant, that he was aiming not at one man, but at the first redcoat in an unending file of redcoats. If Colebrook fell, another would rise in his place. It might take weeks, months, or years, but, inevitable as the next day's dawn, a successor would appear to confront his killer. A man in uniform may be alone, but he is never solitary.

The heavy ball from the muzzle-loader caught Sergeant Colebrook in the neck, severing his spinal column and toppling him backwards from the saddle.

With a cry Dumont, forsaking all thought of regaining the girl, Marie, wheeled his horse and, trailing the pack-horse, fled. It was to be twenty months before another policeman set eyes on Almighty Voice.

A Corporal Tennant, summoned by Dumont from fire duty, came by with some others a few days later and recovered Colebrook's body. His saddle horse grazed nearby still saddled. Only his revolver and cartridge belt were missing.

At the Duck Lake detachment Corporal Dickson, whose

folly in the guardroom had brought about Colebrook's death, already reduced as punishment to the rank of constable, was given the grim duty of digging his grave in the hard November earth.

Now began a time of tribulation for the Mounted Police and of discontent and unrest over the whole Northwest. In 1879, near Fort Walsh in the Cypress Hills, far to the south of Almighty Voice's deed, a Blood Indian had murdered Marmaduke Graburn, a recently enlisted constable. It was two years before one, Star Child, was brought to trial and charged with the crime. The evidence was only circumstantial and he was acquitted.

The search for Star Child, though it was diligently conducted, produced among the Indians none of the alternating fury and exaltation which was to attend that for Almighty Voice. Star Child, who went free, was a small, ugly man known to be mean and revengeful. Murder would be in keeping with his character and only another frontier incident.

The case of Almighty Voice was different. Physically he was without peer among his people, the Wood Crees. He was a man noted for his courage and hunting ability and, until he shot McPherson's cow, had been law-abiding. In the eyes of the Crees his killing of the Mounted Police sergeant assumed the qualities of the man himself. It was not a crime, but a deed, and its perpetrator, far from being a murderer, was a victim and in time a "martyr" of the manhunt organized against him. Almighty Voice, in his flight from the law, became the living and gallant symbol of what his own people, and other tribes, had endured since the white man's coming and his lean figure, appearing only to vanish again, the elusive vessel of their hopes.

The man himself did not overtly encourage the myths growing up about him. Rumours were persistent that, from time to time, he spoke to gatherings of Indians, Blood and Blackfoot as well as Cree, inciting them to throw off the white man's rule. However, no direct evidence supports the rumours and the official account of the Mounted Police states that during the twenty months he evaded his pursuers he did not once show himself near his people.

Nevertheless, though he did not actively harangue them, the fact seems to be that he remained in touch with them and from them received food, ammunition, and word of the whereabouts of the uniformed men on his trail. Certainly he brought in the girl, Marie, and left her, with her baby boy born in the northern bush, with his mother, Spotted Calf, in the fall of 1896, a year after his encounter with Sergeant Colebrook.

A few days later his horse went lame and was found near Batoche on the South Saskatchewan, scene of the decisive defeat of Riel's forces in the Northwest Rebellion of 1885. The horse's back was still warm. Almighty Voice had taken off the saddle and blankets and thrown them on another horse, stolen from a nearby rancher. Though closely followed, he escaped behind the curtain of an early blizzard.

All during this winter and the succeeding spring the Mounted Police set out on leads furnished by informers and Indians thought to be friendly. Following information, often false, their patrols ranged south to the border, west to the Rockies, and north as far as the tundra. In those days, before the radio, telegraph lines existed only along the line of the Canadian Pacific Railway, near the international boundary and along the banks of the North Saskatchewan to Edmonton. A few additional lines reached Mounted Police posts such as Fort Walsh. The police, away from the telegraph, moved among people who were sympathetic to the man they sought and whose system of communication was better than their own. In 1885, during the Rebellion, it was an old woman of the Blackfoot who told the police at Fort Macleod in southern Alberta of the massacre at Duck Lake, seven hundred miles northeast, less than twenty-four hours after its occurrence. As telegraph lines had been cut during the uprising, it was several days before the news was officially confirmed. Flashing heliographs and smoke signals quickly carried news from one Indian encampment to another and relayed it on to the next.

While the police, their whole force numbering under a thousand, were tracing clues true and false across the immense prairies after Almighty Voice, their other duties continued. Thefts, whiskey smuggling, an occasional murder all made calls upon their time. Horse stealing was the most prevalent offense. Typical of the complainants against this activity and of the problems it posed for the police was a

Montana rancher who was camped near Fort Walsh. During the night, he said, Cree Indians had taken one of his horses. Describing the horse to the inspector of the local detachment, he said, "Wal, ye see, Cap, the doggoned hoss hain't no particular colour. I calls him 'Blueskin.' He hain't blue, but then I tell ya he hain't black, and ye cain't call him grey. He's a cantankerous critter, but I bets ye, ye cain't beat him with any ye got in your stables. Will ye take me on? I'll run him agin anything hereabouts." The inspector mildly suggested that the horse would have to be found before being raced. A patrol of four men set out, found the horse in a camp of three hundred Crees and, after a ride of fifty miles in seven hours of subzero weather, returned it to its owner.

Such routine efficiency did not shield the members of the Force from the ridicule attending their efforts to apprehend Almighty Voice. Young braves openly scoffed. "So many redcoats," they said, "and they cannot find one man." Others, referring to the circumstances and the cost of the widespread manhunt, it was a paltry one — jeered, "It costs only a hundred dollars to shoot a policeman. That's all a redcoat is worth." The lack of logic did not detract from the force of the statement.

Chief Buffalo Child Long Lance, the Blackfoot foster brother of Almighty Voice, writes that during this second winter and spring of the search, when rations were late and game was scarce, secret powwows were held by painted braves who urged that the present was ripe for the warpath. Blackfoot, Piegan, Blood, Assiniboin, and others were consulted. The Mounted Police, it was claimed, were scattered and baffled. The Indians were hungry, and now, for the first time since the days of Sitting Bull and Louis Riel, they had a leading figure around whom they could unite.

Though the old people held aloof, and the principal around whose name the hostile forces were tending to congregate did not show himself, shadowy figures danced around fires built within circles of tepees and shouts and songs echoed into the prairie night. With them, in its undertone of threat, was the beat of the war drum, the primordial heart-throb of the wilderness.

As though in answer to the resounding summons, Almighty Voice, a few days before the end of May, 1897, walked boldly into his mother's tepee. As well as Spotted Calf, his father, Sounding Sky, was there to greet him. The old warrior had been released from custody on the reverse premise of his arrest. It was now thought that, rather than assisting Almighty Voice in his escape, he would try to bring him in, having been promised that his son, who had been so grossly deceived by Corporal Dickson, would be granted every possible leniency.

Apparently Almighty Voice had come to his own decision. He announced to his mother and father that he was weary of hiding from constant pursuit. He would face his foe. Let them come and take him, if they could. The girl, Marie, staring up at him from across the tepee fire, his baby sucking at her breast, urged him to throw himself on the white man's mercy. Almighty Voice was adamant. He no longer trusted the white man. He had lived as a brave, and he would die as he had lived — and not strangle like a dog at the end of a rope. Almighty Voice had become a man dedicated to death, a death that would epitomize the courage and the fate of his people.

News of his reappearance had spread through the reserve and, even as he talked with his parents and common law wife, Napoleon Venne, a half-breed scout and informer, was galloping a foam-flaked horse to the Mounted Police detachment at Duck Lake. He returned with two constables to make the arrest.

On the outskirts of the reserve they pulled up their horses to reconnoitre, one of the policemen dismounting and pretending that he had to adjust his saddle cinch. The horse was uneasy, wheeling to face a clump of willow fifty yards distant. Venne, still in the saddle, reached for the horse's cheek-strap to hold him steady. A shot rang out from the willows and Venne, slumped in his saddle, was brought back to Duck Lake with a ball in his chest. The wound was not mortal. Almighty Voice, apprised of Venne's mission, had been waiting for the patrol and had selected the half-breed, a renegade to his people, as the victim of his open declaration of war upon the authorities. He now had two "coups" to his credit as a brave — a police sergeant killed and a Métis wounded.

Word of this further outrage was soon received at Prince

Albert, thirty-five miles to the east. In charge of the post was Inspector J. B. Allan, with more than twenty years of duty behind him on the plains. He mustered eleven men and by a forced march reached the Minnichinas Hills just to the east of One Arrow Reserve early the next morning. As he passed through Duck Lake, the local postmaster, Ernest Grundy, was added as a volunteer to the patrol.

Riding through the hills, Inspector Allan abruptly held up his hand as a signal to the small column to halt. Off to his left what appeared to be three antelope were moving up a bluff towards a thicket of poplar and willow. What he saw were the figures of Almighty Voice now joined by two companions, Topean and Going-Up-to-the-Sky, teenage boys who had vowed to stand with him and share his glory in his fight against the law. The glory would be measured by the number of "coups" they exacted before their own three lives became forfeit. For their ordeal they had stripped to breechclouts and moccasins and anointed their bodies and long black hair with bear grease. The three bodies, glistening under the sun, bent over as they climbed the steep slope so that they seemed to walk on all fours, from the distance could be easily mistaken for glossy antelope.

Almighty Voice stood for a moment to look back, and the Inspector, perceiving the reality before him, spurred forward with a command to surrender. When no reply came, and the three Indians continued their climb, he dismounted and with a Sergeant Raven proceeded up the slope. Near the top, where the willows were thick and his quarry had disappeared, he could see only a foot or two in advance. Hat pulled low, left arm over his eyes to protect them, revolver drawn, he pushed on, knowing that every step might be his last one. The noise of his passage gave notice of his whereabouts and the man above, already death's courtier, was one who would shoot on sight.

As he stood to shout another order to surrender, a ball from a muzzle-loader hit him in the shoulder, bowling him over. Just behind him Sergeant Raven fell, blood spurting from his groin. The battle of the Minnichinas Hills had begun, Almighty Voice and his comrades imprisoned on their crest. Should they attempt to come down from their leaf-enshrouded citadel, men on horseback would quickly overtake them. The score now stood: one redcoat killed, two redcoats and a Métis informer wounded.

Inspector Allan pulled himself deeper into the thicket, under a fallen poplar tree a few yards away. As he rested, panting, trying to ease into a position to relieve the pain of the wound in his shoulder, a dusky face showed over the poplar log and a pair of black eyes pierced his own. Then the eyes disappeared and the Inspector found himself looking up into eternity — the eternity inside the muzzle of the gun pointed at his forehead.

After his many years in the country he understood the words hissed at him. "Don't move," said Almighty Voice. "Give me your revolver and your cartridge belt and I will not harm you."

Inspector Allan shook his head in refusal, but he knew that he would be unable to resist if the other crept forward to take the weapon and ammunition from him. He rolled over to put himself in a shooting position. He had learned, at any rate, that Almighty Voice needed a better firearm than the one he carried. The revolver he had taken from Sergeant Colebrook's body was never found.

The Cree warrior spoke again, his gun barrel came forward an inch. "Now," he said, "I will take what you will not give me."

In the instant a bullet whined over the Inspector's head and buried itself in the log in front of Almighty Voice, raising a small dust of splinters. With the wounding of Allan and Raven the command of the police patrol had fallen upon a Corporal Hockins. He and another corporal, Hume, had snaked forward across the open sidehill and into the willows to aid the two wounded men. Already they had dragged Raven to comparative safety and had re-entered the thicket to rescue their inspector.

It was Hume who, hearing the demand for the surrender of Allan's revolver and cartridges, had crawled on his belly towards the sound and shot when he saw the warrior's head above the log. Now, with the retreat of Almighty Voice, he assisted the Inspector out of his deathtrap. In a further flurry of gunfire during the withdrawal, as the police later learned, Almighty Voice suffered a shattered shinbone while his young ally, Topean, was killed on the edge of a poplar grove by a bullet between the eyes. Almighty Voice and Going-Up-to-the-Sky were left alone in their blood-spattered thicket.

There, on the summit where no man could look down on them, with bare hands they dug a pit in the ground and camouflaged it so well with the branches of newly-leafed poplar and willow that those who held them under siege could pass within a few feet of it, unaware that two pairs of eyes watched, two gun barrels pointed. And men, after twilight that evening, came close to it — came so close that three of them did not return to camp to see the crimson of the sunrise as it spread over the Minnichinas Hills, lifting like great rollers out of the green ocean of the surrounding prairies.

After Allan and Raven were pulled from the thicket, in whose trembling leaves was the whisper of death, the police tried to set fire to it. Leaves and branches were too green to burn.

Hume and Hockins now called for volunteers to climb up the open sidehill and re-enter the patch of brush from which two wounded men had been lucky to escape with their lives. The patch of brush where Almighty Voice and Going-Up-to-the-Sky had elected to make their last stand was of no great extent. Outlined against the western sky, three or four hundred feet above the valley floor, it measured half a mile from north to south and was only three hundred yards across.

A darkness approached, leaving two men with the wounded inspector and sergeant, Hockins led eight volunteers — every man including Postmaster Grundy had stepped forward — up the sidehill and into the thicket. The men behind him were spread out, but to the watchers on the ridgetop, eyes trained in night vigilance, the movements of the willow tips under the sky's dim radiance, as well as the cracking of twigs and the laboured breathing of the climbers, betrayed where each man was. Corporal Hockins fell first, shot through the heart. Postmaster Grundy and a Constable Kerr were killed within ten feet of the pit where Almighty Voice and Going-Up-to-the-Sky crouched. The others drew back, leaving their dead. Almighty Voice's grim pilgrimage had now accounted for three Mounted Policemen and one volunteer dead, and two Mounted Policemen and one Métis wounded. Truly the Force had sustained a bloody nose. During the months of the Northwest Rebellion in 1885 its total losses had been only eight uniformed men killed in action.

In the morning Corporal Hume dispatched a rider to Duck Lake to summon help by wire from Regina, administrative centre of the Northwest Territories and headquarters of the Northwest Mounted Police. The message was delayed. It reached its destination late that evening when the frontier settlement of log houses, frame buildings and false fronts, and a palisaded police barracks was gay with flags and bunting and lively with the sound of a brass band.

The occasion was the scheduled departure for London, England, on the morrow of a picked detachment of the Mounted Police to attend the Diamond Jubilee of Queen Victoria's reign. There, vying with contingents from other parts of the world-wide British Empire, they would add the colour of their trappings and their feats of horsemanship to the splendid pageant.

To speed them on their way a ball was being held in the police barracks. It was attended by the officialdom and dignity of the Territories, many of whom, with their women, had been arriving in "the Capital" for days, by train, buckboard, or astride.

On the floor, under Union Jacks hanging from the beams, the blood-red jackets and gold braid of the men mingled and flowed with the billowing dresses of the partners in their arms. It is a matter of record that the tune they danced to, played by the police band on a raised platform at the end of the hall, was "Sweet Little Buttercup . . . safe in your sylvan dell . . ."

In the middle of a bar the music ceased. The dancers, caught in their stride, faltered and stood still, staring at one another, cheeks flushed from their exertions, at a loss to account for the interruption. Before they could draw breath, the band struck up again. Men sprang to attention, women hushed their voices as the doleful refrain of "God Save the Queen" signalled that the ball, begun barely an hour before, was at an end.

As the anthem finished, a thickset man with quick eyes and a long grey mustache, wearing the uniform of the Mounted Police, climbed the steps to the band platform and, telegram in upheld hand, asked for attention. This was

Assistant Commissioner J. H. McIllree, a true veteran of the plains. In 1874, as a sergeant, he was a member of the first patrol made by the Force. It left Dufferin, Manitoba, near the international border, on July 9 with the temperature 100 degrees in the shade. By wagon and horseback it travelled west to the Belly River, in sight of the Rockies, and on its return, bypassing Dufferin, reached Winnipeg on November 4 in 30-below-zero weather. The Force thus achieved one of the great forced military marches of frontier history, a total of 1,959 miles at an average of almost seventeen miles a day. Although they were a police force, this mission was a military one: the establishment of Fort Macleod.

Now on the platform above the dancers in the Regina barracks the Assistant Commissioner announced, "The Jubilee contingent will not leave for England in the morning. We have just received grave news from the North. Every available man is to proceed there at once." He said no more.

It was after he had left the platform, when couples were breaking up, the men hurrying for the door, that a name was whispered through the crowd, at first gently, and then, as its implications mounted, beating upon their ears and seeming finally to rise like a fearful shout to fill the hall. The name of Almighty Voice was one to give pause to men on their way to their duty and to women going back to their rooms for the night. For all they knew, in his reappearance near Prince Albert he might be the herald of the native uprising of which there had been so many rumours during the last few months of his pursuit.

To be ready for that eventuality McIllree took with him on the special two-car train leaving for Prince Albert at midnight the nine-pounder. Under his command were Inspector Archibald McDonnell, later Commissioner of Boy Scouts of Western Canada, and twenty-five picked men. The official responsibility for apprehending Almighty Voice had rested heavily upon McIllree. It was to his desk that the telegrams and letters from Ottawa arrived, pointing out its urgency. The issue between one hunted man and the authority of the white man's government now promised to be settled promptly.

While McIllree and his men made their overnight run from Regina to Prince Albert, nearly three hundred miles to the north, Almighty Voice and Going-Up-to-the-Sky waited in their thicket, deadly as two rattlesnakes, armed as they now were with the carbines and cartridges of Postmaster Grundy and Constable Kerr, who had met their deaths on the very ramparts of the pit. However, they had no food and no water. From time to time, as evidence was later to show, they crawled from their refuge to gnaw the bark of poplar trees. The bitter fare only increased their craving.

During the night Crees from the nearby One Arrow Reserve stationed themselves on the surrounding hills. They were joined by settlers, ranchers, and half-breed trappers from miles around who had come to see the final act in this stark drama of the plains.

The clear, star-studded silence was broken by the distant yapping of coyotes, the occasional hoot of an owl — which might have been Indians signaling to their brothers in the pit — and by a woman's voice. In the darkness Spotted Calf had worked her way up the bluff until she stood within fifty yards of her son. From her lonely place of watching she loosed into the night the plaintive and eerie notes of a Cree death song.

"Be brave, my son, die fighting," she chanted. "Remember your father, Sounding Sky, and your grandfather, One Arrow. Remember their deeds and die fighting." She knew and accepted the fact that Almighty Voice would die. Her fatalistic spirit forbade her to try to save him.

Out of the thicket came the reply, waking echoes in the hills. "Have no fear, my mother. We will die as braves should die. My leg is broken. We have no food, no water. We have eaten the bark of willow and poplar. To the length of my arm, so that my fingers bleed, I have dug into the ground of the pit in which we stand — and there is no water."

Then, coming even closer, Spotted Calf spoke to him in accents mothers over the world could understand: "I would hold you in my arms, my son. With my old body, I would shield you" — and then, proudly, raising her voice — "but I know that, as a warrior you would not desire it to be."

All night long she kept her vigil. The police, on guard below the periphery of the thicket, entreated her to desist and leave. They feared to have a woman's blood upon their hands. She would not be budged.

Towards morning Almighty Voice climbed out of his pit and addressed the Mounted Police. "Brothers," he called out, "here we are without food, without water. It has been a good fight. Send us food and send us water and, when the sun comes up, we will continue the battle." The plea, in the ancient tradition of warfare, marking the brotherhood of those who waged it, had its reply, shouted through the mouth of a Métis interpreter: "Surrender and you will have food and water, all the food that you can eat and all the water that you can drink." The temptation for Almighty Voice and his young companion was a sore one. They did not yield to it, and learned that the will of the men opposed to them was hard as granite and would not be dented. Mercy, pity, had no place that night in the Minnichinas Hills.

By the next afternoon, having made exceptional time, the contingent under Assistant Commissioner McIllree arrived from Prince Albert, trailing their piece of artillery. Reinforced with men picked up along the way, it included every redcoat who could be spared from routine duty in the adjoining districts. At that it numbered less than a hundred. The police strength, however, was increased by dozens of ranchers and Métis who had volunteered their services on the side of the law. History does not relate that among the assembled force was one, Private Dickson, of Duck Lake, whose callow words had brought them there.

Looking down from his self-chosen and impregnable eyrie, Almighty Voice may well have been impressed by what he saw, for it was a scene whose thousand actors, almost two hundred of them armed against him, attended at his bidding. Below him steel flashed, red tunics glowed, men went hither and thither, horses neighed and pawed the ground. Never before had the might of the western Canadian plains been arrayed in its splendour solely against one man and his disciple. It was a tribute to bring joy to the heart of a warrior who had determined to make his death a sacrifice and a memory of glory to his people.

On the bottom land, taking over command from Corporal Hume, Assistant Commissioner McIllree forbade further forays into the deadly thicket. Instead siege tactics were to be pursued, and logs were hauled into camp by horses so that, if the nine-pounder failed to do its work, men could advance behind, pushing them up the slope.

In the late afternoon McIllree walked out into the open and, through an interpreter, ordered Almighty Voice and his companion to surrender, assuring both that they would have a fair trial. "If you do not come out with your hands up," he said, "you will be blasted out. Much as we hate to see it, we have artillery here and at six o'clock, within the hour, we will begin firing."

A single rifle shot spoke from the thicket. It was directed not at McIllree, but at a crow flying above the embattled clump of willow and poplar. The crow fell, victim to the accuracy of Almighty Voice's aim, and he and Going-Up-to-the-Sky had their first morsel of food in thirty-six hours. The feat of marksmanship brought gasps from the assembly, most of whom were skilled in the use of the rifle.

The bombardment commenced on schedule. Dust, clods of earth, and broken branches erupted around the spot where the two warriors were entrenched and where the wood mouse and the robin had their nests. This and the succeeding day marked the only occasions on the North American continent that artillery had been trained against a mere fugitive from justice. Had the Mounted Police waited and laid siege to the ridgetop, hunger and thirst might have brought Almighty Voice out to them with his hands in the air. Probably the police feared that in the night his people might get sustenance and water to him, or that they might contrive his escape. After all, he had led the law on a fruitless chase for twenty months.

That he could pass through their lines in the darkness was to be proved within a few short hours. After a dozen rounds the gun ceased firing. Stillness fell upon the little valley, yet no one dared to enter the brooding patch of cover upon the sky line. As the late twilight faded a mocking laugh came out of the thicket. Almighty Voice had survived the cannon's rattle and he now, in clear, ringing tones, propounded a question for which his hearers had no reply: "I have lived as a man should live. Three redcoats, and one who came with them, have fallen to my bullets and my boy baby sucks at his mother's breast. I am a young man still, but my life is behind me. Why, then, should I be afraid to die?"

During the night, the second of the battle of Minnichinas

Hills, Almighty Voice left his pit and snaked his way through the cordon of police and volunteers on guard below the ridge. A bloody moccasin and crude crutch of poplar, which he had used to aid his crippled leg, were discovered the next morning within the lines. It is likely that he was driven by thirst to a desperate search for water. The moccasin and crutch served to explain a lone rifle shot which, during the night, had taken the hat off one of the police pickets. The mystery of the shot had been that it had come from behind him, from the camp of the besiegers.

Before dawn Almighty Voice had returned to the pit, for he was now death's diligent disciple. Once more Spotted Calf took up her place close by and, as the sun rose, joined with him in his death song.

Nor did she move when, at full daylight and after a further call for surrender, the bombardment recommenced. Progress and civilization were eager to resume their march. Settlement of the West must not be delayed. Overseas the pageantry of Queen Victoria's Jubilee was beckoning. One man and his teenage follower at this late date stood in the way. Other persuasion had failed. The language of the nine-pounder would brook no failure. Uttered from an iron-hard mouth, couched in words of shredded steel, backed by the acrid breath of powder, it would blow them from the face of the earth. Then the Empire, over the pit which had cradled their defiance and against which it had marshalled its utmost power, would continue its western march — but it is related that the redcoats who manned the gun, more than once after the lanyard had been pulled, turned aside to vomit.

Twice during the morning's bombardment Almighty Voice shouted his scorn at his destroyers. At noon, after a full hour of silence, James Mackay, who was to become a member of the Supreme Court of Saskatchewan, led a party of volunteers into the thicket. Cautiously moving forward, they were unopposed. Corporal Hockins' body had been rescued the preceding day, but on the edge of the pit, roofed with frail poplar and willow, they came upon the remains of Postmaster Grundy and Constable Kerr. Both had been relieved of their weapons and cartridge belts. The bark of nearby poplar trees was stripped where Almighty Voice and Going-Up-to-the-Sky had gnawed upon it. The latter was in the pit, gasping in his death agony. Beside him lay Almighty Voice, his forehead punctured by a piece of shrapnel. Six other wounds showed upon him. His body and that of Going-Up-to-the-Sky — he of the tender and hopeful name — were reverently carried down to the One Arrow Reserve.

In the bottom of the rifle pit was the hole which Almighty Voice had sunk to the length of his arm, digging for water. A few feet from the edge of the pit Cree letters were carved into a tree trunk. Father Lacombe, known during the 1860's at Fort Edmonton on the North Saskatchewan for his Masses against the cattle-killing grizzly bears, had, between them, devised a syllabic alphabet for the Cree language. Translated, Almighty Voice's words carved on the tree trunk read: "Here died three braves." Perhaps he referred to Postmaster Grundy Corporal Hockins, and Constable Kerr, who had fallen there to his rifle. Perhaps, anticipating his fate, the crudely carved letters were a memorial to himself, to Going-Up-to-the-Sky, and Topean, his other comrade in death whose body was recovered a few yards down the slope. It, too, was taken to the One Arrow Reserve to be mourned by its people.

The Crees returned to their tepees, the settlers and ranchers and Métis to their cabins. The Mounted Police limbered up their gun and went back to their various barracks — and the Jubilee contingent left only two days late for their appointment in London to celebrate the sixty-year rule of an old woman to which they had contributed the most recent of its bloody chapters. The South African war, in which many of them would serve, was more than two years in the future.

Over the Minnichinas Hills, where two braves for two nights and three days had challenged the power of that empire, more enduring than all the reigns of history, silence resumed its sway. It was broken only by the rustle of willow and poplar leaves, the lilting call of the meadowlark, or the clucking of the prairie grouse to her young.

Sometimes at night old men of the Cree Nation or men with Cree blood in their veins, passing that way and remembering their youth, will pause to listen. They may hear only the coyote laughing at the moon, or the great horned-owl speaking from a haunted hour. Sometimes, though, it seems they hear another sound. It comes from high up, from along the ridgetop, where the wind blows through the willows.

It is like an echo from far off and long ago, an echo of a death song from among those same willows. It is also the last echo from a fabled and valiant past. The singer in the willows pleads for water that the fight tomorrow may be a fair fight. He taunts the redcoats below him and tells them that he is not afraid to die.

The old men shake their heads and return to their cabins on the reserve between the two branches of the great Saskatchewan River. There, in their cabins, they may gather the children about them and tell them again of the last Cree warrior, Almighty Voice, who, with one companion beside him on the hilltop, held at bay for two nights and three days the best men that the queen from across the sea could send against him. Almighty Voice, they will say, was a man who died that his voice might live.

The Man Who Chose to Die

On a morning when the "Hungry Thirties" were only beginning, that of July 19, 1931 — a date recorded and underscored in the annals of the Royal Canadian Mounted Police — a man pushed a raft into the Peel River in the far Northwest Territories and, with his packsack and Savage rifle beside him, floated eastward down its sluggish stream. The Peel, rising on the east slope of the most northerly spur of the Rockies, drains into the delta of the Mackenzie at Fort McPherson, about two thousand miles north of Edmonton, Alberta.

Fort McPherson in 1931 was the headquarters of six or seven white trappers. Nearby were about two hundred Loo-ch-ux Indians and dozens of half-starved sleigh dogs turned loose in the summer to rustle for themselves. For white and Indian, when they were not out on the trapline, life centred about the square, frame-built, whitewashed Hudson's Bay Company's fur-trading post.

The man on the raft reached the little settlement late in the afternoon of the same day he had set out from up the river. He beached his raft — a crudely made affair with a platform of brush, its half dozen spruce logs bound together with rope and pliant willow. Dropping his pole, he hoisted his pack, picked up his rifle, came ashore and walked up to the HBC trading post. There — a man in his middle years, deep-chested, with remarkably large hands, a stubble of beard on cheek and chin, eyes sunk after long days of travel — he asked for his mail in a Scandinavian accent, giving the name of "Albert Johnson."

Two years before, airmail service had been inaugurated between the Mackenzie River delta and the "outside." Before that letters came by sternwheel steamer in the summer and by dog team in the winter. But mail for Albert Johnson? The storekeeper, rifling through the few letters on hand, shook his head. There was no mail for Albert Johnson at Fort McPherson on that July afternoon. There would never, never be mail for Albert Johnson at Fort McPherson, nor at any other postal counter in all that wide northern land.

Indeed, no one knew "Albert Johnson" — for probably this was not the name of the man who bore it. Today, more than four decades later, no one has spoken out to say who he was, nor where he came from. Named, he is nameless. And, as if to atone for that anonymity, back there in the early thirties, they gave him a title. They were to dub him the "Mad Trapper."

For almost two months that name was to blaze across Canada in newspaper headlines. In the North it was with men when they rolled into their blankets at night and waiting for them when they rolled out in the morning. It crackled in radio across the tundra. Because of it a ballad was born, still sung in western frontier camps, a ballad of the man, whatever his name, whom no one knew — a hunted man who led the Royal Canadian Mounted Police on the longest "hot pursuit" in their history. That of Almighty Voice endured longer, but, until the end, was a "cold" pursuit. With intermissions, for six weeks in sub-zero weather, Johnson was within virtual rifle shot of the best men who could be mustered against him and for six weeks, singlehanded, he held them off or eluded them. The drone of a plane in the Arctic sky, a master bush pilot at the controls, helped to bring him to his knees. It marked the first use in civilian aviation of a plane to hunt a man-killer.

Albert Johnson, as he styled himself — for a man to exist in the world of men must have a name — enduring more than most men could, an outcast of the Arctic with death at his heels, kindled a new figure of loneliness in the human imagination and so became the stuff of legend. These were the days when the world's markets had tumbled and stockbrokers threw themselves from office windows onto the pavement of Wall Street. On Fifth Avenue the unemployed sold apples. In Canada, as in the United States, men walked in gloom, not understanding the disaster that had come upon them. Loggers, miners, farm help looked for work and could not find it. The struggle of Albert Johnson against the forces which hunted him across the Arctic wastes became symbolic of their own. Like themselves, he, a trapper and, therefore, a workingman, was a victim of fate. As to the name he is best remembered by, Inspector A. N. Eames, during 1931-32 Officer in Command of the Western Arctic Sub-District, RCMP, at Aklavik, north of Fort McPherson, made a brief report. In his official account of the incident he wrote, "I note in press reports that Johnson is referred to as 'the mad trapper.' On the contrary, he showed himself to be an extremely shrewd and resolute man, capable of quick thought and action. A tough and desperate character."

This was the man then, as yet not fully revealed, who stood at the counter of the trading post at Fort McPherson, asking the storekeeper for his mail on an afternoon in July, 1931. In his situation he could have expected no letters. The request was a gesture, a futile reaching out for the touch of his fellow man — for already, to judge from his imminent activity, Albert Johnson realized that he was travelling on the border of that shadowed kingdom beyond which words do not carry. "A ... desperate character," wrote Inspector Eames. The root of the adjective is the same as that of the Spanish "desesperado" — transliterated into English as "desperado" — and means, literally, "without hope."

But if he was without hope — the spiritual sustenance of earthly endeavour — Albert Johnson was well supplied with another of man's essential needs. He had money, almost three thousand dollars of it, a trapper's small fortune — and, after turning away from the counter where he had asked for mail, he spent it lavishly for a trapper's supplies, buying clothes, grub, traps, and ammunition. Aside from the brief interchange required by these purchases he spoke little, except to inquire about the Rat River. The Rat River, like the Peel, down which he had come, is one of many which, like the spokes of half a wagon wheel, fan out to the south and west from the estuary of the Mackenzie below Fort McPherson. Because the river was one of the routes to the Yukon, the storekeeper thought that that territory was Johnson's probable destination.

Others thought so, too. Johnson had attracted the attention of the small populace of Fort McPherson for several reasons. One was his arrival there on a shakily constructed raft, rather than in the more conventional canoe or boat with outboard motor. Another was that, for a man who gave the appearance of having travelled far, he had a limited outfit — axe, rifle, pot and pan, and blanket, the bare necessities of living. Despite this he was "well heeled" and made no secret of it, although in other respects he was taciturn, even hostile, and did not squat down on his haunches to trade gossip with others of the country through which he had lately passed, as is the habit of men after journeys.

Johnson's aspect was that of one who lived beyond, and independent of, the community of his fellows. He gave nothing and asked little — except for his interest in the Rat River farther north down the Mackenzie. But a man always leaves something of himself behind, so that before Johnson, after a few days, drifted back into the wilderness whence he came, he had been tagged by his manner, by his speech, by a word dropped here and there, as an American Swede who hailed from the Dakotas.

After his departure downriver towards the mouth of the Rat, no more was heard, and but little thought, about Albert Johnson at Fort McPherson — until five months later. Until then — Christmas Day, 1931 — it was as if he had ceased to exist. Nor was that at all unusual. The North is a land of journeys and a man's arrival but the promise that soon he will be gone again.

However, in the meanwhile, Johnson had not been idle. Far from going to the Yukon, he had stopped sixteen miles up the Rat River and there built himself what amounted to a small fortress. It was on a point of land, a triangle, along two sides of which and around the apex the river ran. Back from the cabin land was cleared towards the base of the triangle, which consisted of a flat scrub spruce and willow.

The walls of his cabin — or fortress — were logs, roughly a foot in thickness, and its interior measured twelve feet by eight. The ceiling height was five feet in front and four in the rear. Although the doorway with a high threshold measured four and a half feet, only three feet of this was above the outside level of the ground. Heavy poles, under two feet of sod, formed the roof. There was one window by the door, twelve inches square. But this was not all. Johnson was not so easily satisfied. For his purpose he needed more than mere walls, so he fortified the outside of his cabin with extra logs and earth to a height of almost two feet. Inside, the earthen floor was sunk a foot and a half below ground level. Finally, between the logs Johnson cut rifle loopholes covering all approaches.

By Christmas time, when Fort McPherson was reminded that he was still among the living, his building labours had been long completed. The sod against the reinforced walls of his cabin and on its roof was now frozen hard as iron. Three feet of snow lay upon the cabin clearing and over the ice of the Rat River.

One other feature of Johnson's cabin bears remark. Trappers, as a rule, with little eye for a view, build their cabins in the protected timber, away from wind and storm. Johnson built his on a promontory overlooking the more than man-high banks of the river. His reason for putting it there was indicated by what happened later: he wished to have notice of anyone who came near. Johnson knew, when he set about constructing his cabin, that one day the world would come to his door, and he put himself in a state of siege to resist it. The riddle remains of why one man should set himself up on a lonely and God-forsaken hump of land and wait for what he dreaded most — a call from out of the night, the knock of an alien knuckle upon his door. Only this much has come to light, a light that is at most a glimmer: police records show that a man of Johnson's description and general demeanour, but with a different name, came from British Columbia into the Yukon in 1925 and spent the winters there trapping until 1931. While in the Yukon he bought a Savage rifle. Another report is of a man near the town of Nation in Alaska, close to the Yukon border, who made for himself during the same years a reputation of "violence and moroseness" by burning down cabins and "disabling" traplines. Why such acts went unpunished, is not said, nor has it been established that the trapper in the Yukon and the arsonist and trap robber in Alaska were the same man, nor yet that either of them was Albert Johnson.

However, the word that came out from Rat River to Fort McPherson on Christmas Day, 1931, tends, even if remotely, to link Johnson with the cabin-burner and trapline trespasser of Nation, Alaska. The word was brought by Indians. They complained that Johnson was interfering with their traplines.

Johnson was not hard up. As events were to show, he was carrying exactly $2,410 in the pockets of his mackinaw trousers — this after his extensive purchases at Fort Mc-Pherson. Yet he robbed the traplines of others. It was almost as if he had grown impatient. He had set up his citadel above the river. Now he wanted it to be tested — for he could have no doubt that his offense would bring quick response from the RCMP, whatever the leniency for similar depredations over the line in Alaska.

Certainly Johnson's conduct was not that of a man wholly in his senses — unless, as has been argued, he was the aggrieved party and the charges were trumped up against him by those who, for reasons that are not explained, wished to get him away from where he was. This version, though, does not account for his earlier doings: the locating of his cabin high above the river, the cutting of loopholes in its walls, and the throwing up of sod breastworks around it — this last being work which had to be done in summer and fall before the ground was frozen.

Johnson acted like a man who felt himself to be pursued and who had come as far as he could to evade those who were on his trail. Conscience, troubled by a secret guilt, may have driven him literally to one of the ends of the earth. If so, no unsolved murder or crime of consequence has been linked to his name. Sane in other respects, he may have been insane in the strength of his delusion. At any rate, he was tired of running and now paced his wind- and snow-beleaguered cabin, waiting for the inevitable tap upon the door. He had not long to wait.

Three days after Christmas, in the late morning of December 28, Constable A. W. King and Special Constable Joseph Bernard of the RCMP, carrying only side arms, climbed up to the cabin from the Rat River. Constable King knocked upon the door, stating who he was and why he had come. He received no answer. The door stayed closed. Johnson looked out at him through the small window. Then he drew a cover across the window. The two constables went back for further instructions to Aklavik, an eighty-mile journey by dog team down river ice.

There they told their story to Inspector Eames, a man in his middle years, of average build, with a soft voice, a quick and dancing eye, who had been seven years in the Arctic. In view of Johnson's suspicious behaviour, the Inspector issued a search warrant against him. With Constable R. G. McDowell and Special Constable Lazarus Sittichiulis as reinforcements, King and Bernard returned to Johnson's cabin before noon on New Year's Eve. The party carried rifles.

Again Constable King climbed up the riverbank and walked across the twenty yards of clearing to the cabin door. "Are you there, Mr. Johnson?" he inquired — a very mild inquiry, indeed, by one who had had his Christmas and now his New Year's Eve interrupted by a surly character up a little-travelled river and hardly one to elicit the reply it brought. That reply was a bullet through the door. It hit King just below the heart. Constable McDowell opened fire against the cabin from the riverbank, where he had been standing. Johnson fired at him twice through a loophole, but missed. During this exchange the severely wounded King crawled away from the cabin and by a roundabout route through the bushes made his way to the riverbank and down it to the safety of the tobaggan. Twenty hours later, writing an epic of Arctic travel, McDowell delivered him to the Anglican Mission Hospital at Aklavik. There he was to recover under the care of Dr. J. A. Urquhart — the same Dr. Urquhart who not long before had been host to the Lindberghs in their much-advertised flight across the top of the continent to the Orient.

Inspector Eames at once laid plans to arrest the trapper of Rat River and organized a party headed by himself and including McDowell, another constable, E. Millen, and five special constables. The eight men had with them forty-two dogs and reached Johnson's cabin on January 9, now in 1932 and again near midday, advancing towards it along a trapper's trail through the woods.

Johnson, as usual, was at home to greet them — nor during the ten days intervening since the wounding of Constable King had he altered his conception of hospitality. He must have known that he had shot, and possibly killed, a policeman. This was more than assault or murder. It was an outrage against the uniform, a bloody soiling of the cloth of authority, for which retribution is at once ruthless and relentless. The Mounted Police do not always "get their man," but they spare no effort in trying to do so. Yet, like one with the death wish upon him, Johnson had made no attempt to escape. If he had plotted it out step by step he could have contrived no grimmer destiny than that now awaiting him beyond his walls. For all that, he was to prove himself as fierce and cunning as the wolverine in his will to live and in his struggle to avoid the dark doom of man's vengeance.

He could hear the whisperings of that doom now close to him — but still farther away than he could have believed. He could hear it in the creak of snowshoes as Inspector Eames's party, debouching from the timber, dropped down under the riverbank below the cabin. Had Johnson gone to his window he could have seen the steam of men's breaths, and that of their dogs, rising in the brief daylight in a temperature that was 45 degrees below zero. He had invited the world to his doorstep. Acceptance came in a hail from below the bank when Inspector Eames, in his turn, invited Johnson to come out and surrender.

The men with the Inspector had been selected for their courage, their endurance, and their bushcraft, and when Johnson did not come out nor make a sign, though they heard him stirring about inside, they made a resolute charge against the cabin and succeeded in breaking down the door, but were driven back by "an exceedingly rapid fire."

The party retired under the riverbank. Johnson propped up the door and took up his station once more at his loopholes.

Inspector Eames made camp against the bitter cold and at night resumed the siege. The creak of snowshoes on brittle snow made it impossible for any of the police party, even in darkness, to approach close to the cabin without detection. At three o'clock the next morning, January 10, four pounds of dynamite were thrown against Johnson's door. Eames and Special Constable Karl Gardlund, a trapper, rushed forward to exploit their advantage, hoping to catch Johnson in the beams of a flashlight and dispatch him with their revolvers. He was ready for them and shot the flashlight out of Gardlund's hand.

In the moments before the flashlight was extinguished, Eames saw that the dynamite had not blown down the door. Only a few splinters of wood had been ripped away and the door was apparently still securely in its place.

Standing in the clearing, their positions starkly outlined by the slight reflection from the snow, Eames and Gardlund were exposed to deadly fire as Johnson crouched behind his loophole. They quickly separated and retreated under the riverbank.

The temperature was now close to 60 below. The rifles had to be left outside the canvas shelters on the toboggans. Brought inside, they would have "sweated" and then frosted up when they were taken back out into the open. Even with that precaution great care had to be used in their handling, lest a finger or hand be "burned" and leave its flesh on the frigid metal. The men wore moose-hide mits, like their moccasins, packed with duffel from Hudson's Bay Company blankets. The mitts were hung by a cord passed around the back of the neck so that when a hand was removed to fire a rifle the mitt would not drop to the snow and be lost.

In his flimsy shelter below the riverbank Inspector Eames reviewed the situation. He saw that in a siege as protracted as this one might prove to be the very size of the besieging party told against it. Men and dogs needed food and they were eighty miles away from their base of supplies at Aklavik. They had not come prepared for a long stay — although it would seem that they had had warning. In addition the cold was intense and winter winds buffeted them in their canvas shelters below the riverbank. In contrast, Johnson was well housed and warm in a cabin stocked with grub.

Eames and his men returned to Aklavik, leaving Johnson on his impregnable point of land. It was about this time that the sobriquet the "Mad Trapper of Rat River" was born. Only a man who was mad would continue a lone-handed battle against the Royal Canadian Mounted Police. He might run from them — but to stand and shoot it out, that was patent folly. However, if Johnson was mad in making his challenge he was eminently sane in the manner in which, from now on, he dealt with its consequences — for, as if to deny the name of "Mad Trapper," already sent out from the North by radio and splashed in printer's ink across the countryside, he abandoned his stoutly built cabin and fled into the bush. And this, failing outright surrender, was surely the path of reason.

When, on January 19, Inspector Eames came back to the Rat River with a stronger patrol, numbering, among others, Sergeants R. F. Riddell and H. F. Hersey of the Royal Canadian Signals at Aklavik, no smoke plumed from the cabin chimney. More significantly, the door was barred on the outside. Still, the police were cautious, for this might be a trap: Johnson, if not inside, might be hiding nearby in the timber, his rifle at the ready. Two members of the party crept closer to the cabin. They heard no movement, no sound of life within. The next morning they entered and searched but found nothing that would identify its owner. Johnson, in his flight, had cleaned its shelves of food.

Contact with him was not made again until January 30. Nor in the interval had he travelled far.

Before the snow flew, Johnson had made a pair of snow-shoes more than four feet long, steaming and bending supple birchwood and webbing the frames it formed with "babiche," or caribou gut. Today the snowshoes — along with his tea billy, and axe — are on display at the RCMP museum in Regina, Saskatchewan.

The snow in the Rat River country, and generally on the east slope of the northerly Rockies, is crusted and wind-blown. Avoiding the soft snow of the timber and creek bottoms, Johnson could travel on his snowshoes for miles without breaking the crust. Any slight track that he might make would be quickly covered by the wind, the almost ceaseless wind blowing westward across two thousand miles of barrens, forever sweeping clean the floor of a frozen kingdom.

On January 30 — Inspector Eames having had to return once more to Aklavik with the main party due to lack of dog food — four men he had left behind to track down Johnson came upon the fugitive camped in thick timber. Constable Millen, of earlier patrols, was in charge of the group of four. The others were Sergeant Riddell of the Royal Canadian Signals; Noel Verville, a trapper; and Karl Gundlund.

Johnson was camped where Bear Creek falls into the Rat, hardly a day's travel above the cabin he had left less than two weeks before. The advance party saw the smoke of his fire and, coming cautiously closer, heard him coughing as he squatted by it. Earlier they had discovered snowshoe tracks in the softer snow inside the timber. Following them up, they had no doubt that they were Johnson's, because every other man — trapper, hunter or trader — for miles around had been accounted for.

Riddell and Gardlund, shielding themselves in the willows, took up their post across the creek from Johnson's camp. Still, they could not see him, though they could almost pinpoint the spot in the timber where he was on the other bank of the creek at a lower level. They were to cover Millen and Verville, who were trying to creep up on his camp.

Millen, in command of the operation, was a tall, well-set-up young man of thirty from Edmonton, Alberta. A few years before, he had been stationed in the Alberta mountain-resort town of Jasper. There, in his crimson jacket, he had posed for tourist cameras on the platform of the railroad depot and in the summer evenings been a resplendent figure on the dance floor at the lodge across the Athabaska River. Perhaps on this day in late January, 1932, along Bear Creek in the Northwest Territories, on a sterner assignment, he remembered those gay days and the laughing faces and silken dresses — for this was to be his last patrol.

Under his snowshoe a frosty twig snapped. Johnson, suddenly aware of his danger, fired through an opening in the timber, but missed his target. From above, Riddell and Gardlund fired blindly into the campsite to protect Millen and Verville. When, after a time, Johnson had not replied,

Riddell and Gardlund dropped down to join their companions. Thinking that the trapper of Rat River had been killed or disabled by the rifle fire, Millen and Riddell, the two men of the four in their country's uniform, decided to penetrate the clump of twisted spruce and investigate — a foray as desperate as that of trailing a wounded grizzly bear into a thicket.

They had scarcely entered the shadows when a bullet, shot at very close range, whistled between them. Riddell went over the creek bank for shelter. Millen's rifle spoke twice and three more shots came from Johnson. Then there was silence — a sombre, listening silence. When Riddle crawled back up the bank he found Millen crumpled and dead in the snow. He had been shot through the heart. His body was put on a toboggan and taken back to Aklavik.

Now the cry was up for Johnson in earnest. So far he had picked his battlegrounds. The police had come to him in his cabin that was built for siege. Twice he had driven them off. Then they had come to him where he crouched, like an animal at bay, in a tangle of timber and brush. Again he had repulsed them — but whereas before he had merely wounded, this day he had killed. The brand of Cain was on his brow.

Constable Millen had been a popular member of the Force, and hunters and trappers from a hundred miles away snowshoed into Aklavik to offer their help in flushing his murderer out into the open. Some of them had heard of the murder by radio, others by word of mouth, for news is carried quickly in a sparsely-peopled land. Inspector Eames organized another patrol, this time of a dozen men, and once more set forth into the western barrens. On February 5 the patrol surrounded the camp from which Millen had been killed. Any hope they might have had that Johnson would be waiting for them was soon dispelled. The campsite was deserted and Johnson had a six-day start.

Had the police, earlier in the hunt, been able to establish a base camp on the Rat River and supply it by dog team from Aklavik they might have been able to maintain less interrupted touch with their man. Conditions were against them. Only a large party would corner Johnson, and supporting a large party indefinitely in those wastes of wind and cold was a formidable task for Inspector Eames with the resources he had at hand.

Johnson, of course, was not without his own problem of supply. The grub he had packed on his back from his cabin would not long sustain him — and, in any case, in his predicament, he had to travel light. He was equal to it and lived off the country, shooting and snaring ptarmigan and Artic hare. Under the best of circumstances this would have been no small achievement. A measure of Johnson as hunter and traveller and all-round outdoorsman is gained by realizing that he accomplished it in weather that was seldom above 30 below, that he had no shelter except a windbreak of stunted spruce, thrown up each day or night in a different spot, and that, finally, while hunting for food to keep alive, he himself was being closely trailed by the most redoubtable man hunters on the continent, namely the RCMP. Whatever his other qualities, Johnson was a man forged in the classic tradition of the North. Hardship was his daily bread and middle name.

On February 6 the police party discovered his tracks in the snow of a creek bottom. The country here was composed of rolling barrens, of willows which overtopped a man's head, and of ridges swept bare by the wind. Always blizzards wailed and mourned, lifting the snow at times a thousand feet into the air. A true blizzard, New York City editors to the contrary, is not snow falling. It is snow flung upward and being blown horizontally in stinging particles. A blizzard is like a mighty broom. It sweeps and propels all before it.

For three days Eames and his men followed Johnson up and down a maze of creeks. By day he camped cold, without a fire, hidden in the willows. By night he travelled, dropping over the divide from one watershed to another. On the divides, where he would emerge into the open, his tracks would disappear, obliterated by the drifting snow. To further confound his pursuers, it was found that he frequently reversed his snowshoes, so that when they thought they were closing in upon him they were in fact drawing farther and farther away. Often in darkness he would make a full circle, doubling back until he was walking in the tracks of his trackers, a will-o'-the-wisp, a veritable ghost of the tundra.

His judgement came from overhead. Stooped in a thicket, midday of February 7, he heard its whine through the fog of snow and swirl of wind. The late Captain W. R. — "Wop" — May had flown in from Edmonton. With him was Constable W. S Carter of the RCMP, also from the Alberta capital. Eames and Carter were now the only members of the Force on the patrol. Constable King had been wounded and Constable Millen killed. The others with Eames on the day of Wop May's arrival were volunteers. They were Sergeant Riddell of the Royal Canadian Signals, Special Constable L. Sittichiulis, E. Maring, C. Ethier (formerly of the RCMP), Peter Strandberg, K. H. Lang, F. Carmichael, A. N. Blake, August Tardiff, and John Greenland — each of them chosen for his stamina and ability in the northern bush and Barren Lands.

Wop May, who landed his single-motored plane near Eames' camp, had qualifications of a different order. A couple of years before he had flown the first airmail into Akalvik from Edmonton, two thousand miles to the south. As a reward for this and other distinguished services as a northern "bush pilot" — including that of flying through a terrific storm to bring vaccine into Fort Vermilion during a diphtheria epidemic in 1929 — he was awarded the McKee Trophy in 1930 for his contribution to Canadian aviation.

Before that he had served in the first world war, winning the DFC. It was Wop May, his machine guns jammed, his engine smoking, that Baron von Richtofen was chasing through the French skies late in the war when that German ace was downed by Roy Brown, another Canadian.

Probably the name of May was unknown to Albert Johnson, but Johnson could not be unaware of what a plane's presence on the scene portended for his future. May's function, weather permitting, would be a double one: when he was not scouting ahead for the hunted trapper he would be bringing in supplies to the base camp from Aklavik. Eames was now provided with an eagle's eyes and the equivalent of strings of dog teams between his camp and headquarters. His mobility was at once greatly increased, and he had assurance that it would no longer be wasted in fruitless and baffling search.

Still, Johnson was far from beaten. By February 13, six days after May's arrival, he was hardly more than twenty miles in a straight line from his camp on Bear Creek, where, on January 30, he had murdered Constable Millen — though he had walked three or four times that distance in backtracking and detours — and seemed now to be heading for the divide into the Yukon by way of the Bell River. To reach there he had another hundred miles of travel. Once he was in the Yukon, crossing it where it narrows towards the Arctic, another hundred would take him to Alaska. Possibly he had a dim notion of seeking refuge in American territory.

His gamble was that of a man who had no other choice or he would doubtless have made it earlier. It was not the distance alone that was against him — although a two-hundred-mile journey across the northern wastes in midwinter with his meagre equipment would give most men pause. A more telling obstacle than mere distance lay ahead. It was that over there, on the west slope of the Rockies, shielded from the prevailing winds of the barrens, snow conditions were different. The police knew — and so would Johnson — that once across the twenty-five-hundred-foot divide, he would be in powder snow. Even on snowshoes he would sink to his knees and be breaking trail with every step.

Johnson made the gamble. He crossed the high divide alone — a feat in itself for a team of seasoned men. On February 14, Wop May from his plane saw his tracks going down the Bell River. Johnson had passed only a mile from La Pierre House, first settlement over the Yukon line.

Turning off the Bell River, he went up the Eagle, his trail, like a narrow ribbon of lace, unwinding behind him. The man's endurance was outstanding. Those behind him had dog teams and a broken trail to follow. Johnson broke his own trail. Even so he was now covering thirty and forty miles a day, much of it in darkness, and living off the land — nor did he lose a chance to confuse his pursuers. Slogging grimly up the Eagle on February 16, he came into the path of a migrating caribou herd. He took off his snowshoes and walked where the caribou had walked. For ten miles he left no sign behind him. To those in pursuit it was as if he had vanished into the air or gone underground. However, before the day's end, Eames and his party came upon his tracks again and camped fifteen miles up the Eagle.

The next day, February 17, was to be the day of decision. Eames sensed, from the freshness of Johnson's tracks, that he was closing in on the outlaw and broke camp long before daylight. Sergeant Hersey of the Royal Canadian Signals and the trapper, Noel Verville, had by this time rejoined the main body with fresh dog teams and led the patrol up the valley. The fever of the hunt was upon them. Johnson, they knew, must be tiring and a bend in the river might reveal him to them. It did — but not in the fashion they had imagined.

Just before noon Hersey — formerly a schoolteacher in New Brunswick — drove his dogs around a low promontory and met Albert Johnson, pack on his back, rifle in hand, coming towards him — and only two hundred and fifty yards away. On December 28, on the first visit to his cabin on Rat River, Constable King, now lying wounded in Aklavik, had caught a brief glimpse of him through the window. Except for that, this was the first time that Johnson had been seen during the six weeks of the manhunt.

Apparently unaware that he was so closely followed, he was backtracking in another effort to throw his pursuers off the trail. Seeing Hersey, and Verville, who was close behind, he turned and made for the riverbank. There he would find cover in the timber and brush.

Hersey grabbed his rifle from the toboggan and with Verville ran to the opposite bank and opened fire, hoping to keep Johnson out in the open until the rest of the party caught up. Johnson, in a flash, wheeled about and fired back. His first two shots took effect, wounding Hersey in the chest and foot. This was the deadly shooting of the born hunter, the man whose rifle has become part of himself and who, in the perception of the moment, aims and fires by reflex.

Seeing Hersey downed and coughing blood, Verville went to his side to give what help he could. Johnson retreated up the river in the snowshoe tracks he had made earlier in the morning. Eames and the rest of the party came upon Hersey and Verville and then, after the Inspector had detailed Verville to remain with the wounded man, proceeded up the river in extended order.

Johnson, in full sight, fled before them and, though occasionally he whirled about to shoot at those behind him, was actually gaining upon them. For the second time — the first being weeks before at the cabin on Rat River — Eames called upon him to surrender. Johnson's answer was another blast from his rifle. Eames ordered his men to reply in kind.

Wop May, having taken off from La Pierre House, was now overhead, the entire panorama, with its diligent and contending morsels of life, unrolling below. The plane, flying in slow circles above him, seemed to affect Johnson with panic. A man distracted, he ran first for one bank of the river and then turned and ran for the other. Now at last he was truly "out in the open." The willows, the narrow creek bottoms, the gnarled and twisted stands of timber had yielded him up. Nowhere on the uneasy earth was there any longer cover for Albert Johnson. He was as exposed and naked as a black ant upon a white dinner plate.

Finally, he dug down in the deep snow in mid-river and came to bay behind the meagre protection of his packsack.

Soon his self-created enemy, mankind, was around him like hornets — and they would sting him until he died. They confronted him on the river ice and already looked down upon him through rifle sights from the thick willow bush above the riverbanks. Bullets whined about his head and splattered close to him in the snow. He squirmed when they hit him — but uttered no cry, gave forth no plea. He played his cards as he had called them, grim and silent to the end. At ten minutes after noon his rifle spoke no more. Albert Johnson, the trapper of Rat River, was dead.

The men who had pursued him came together over his body. Pulling them from police barracks, from trapline and cabin, he had been their demanding bond of union through weeks of Arctic cold and blizzard. Soon now, their bond sundered, their mission completed, they would disperse and go their separate ways.

One of them, Sergeant Hersey of the Royal Canadian Signals, gravely wounded, with Noel Verville, the trapper who tended him, was not on hand. Hersey was lying in the snow, not far away. Wop May saved his life by landing his plane on the river ice and taking him in little more than a hour to Dr. Urquhart at Aklavik at the mouth of the Mackenzie.

May, that day and the next, made a series of flights, taking out Inspector Eames, other members of the patrol, and Johnson's half-starved, bullet-ridden body. The clothes of the dead man had been searched. They found not a single

scrap of paper to identify him. In his pockets were the
$2,410.00.

An inquest at Aklavik on Feburary 18 brought forth the
following verdict from the jury: ". . . that the man known as
Albert Johnson came to his death from concentrated rifle
fire from a party composed of members of the Royal Canadian Mounted Police and others, Johnson having been called
upon to surrender. . . . We are . . . satisfied from the evidence
that the party had no other means of effecting Johnson's
capture except by the method employed."

Officially and physically Albert Johnson was as dead as
man could be — but, in dying, he had written a name in
blood upon the snow. Spring thaws had not erased it. It is
there still, scrawled across the Northland, the legend of one
man's fierceness, cunning, and endurance against the very
forces he himself had summoned to destroy him. It lives
because it is a story as old as the ages. Like a figure in Greek
tragedy, Albert Johnson was doomed and, like that classic
figure, sundered by his fate from those about him, he was at
last alone upon the stage, the shadows closing in upon him —
a man against the world, and against himself, one who chose
to die and yet, until his last breath, fought to live.

The Man Who Walked Naked across Montana

The case of Albert Johnson, the so-called "Mad Trapper," is that of a man bent upon his own self-destruction and demonstrates the extremes to which one man will go to accomplish his end. An example of the opposite, of a wilderness man who, on the very brink of extinction, refused to die, occurred more than a hundred years earlier far to the south when the Royal Canadian Mounted Police had not been born and the Arctic barrens were a scarcely-known land.

The man's name was John Colter. Stark-naked, weaponless, without food, pursued by hostiles, he walked through freezing nights two hundred miles across the then uncharted mountains of what is today the state of Montana.

His ordeal began soon after dawn in early October in the year 1808 when he heard the roll of hooves on the riverbank above him as he paddled upstream in his birch-bark canoe. Within minutes of his first alarm his partner, John Potts, travelling beside him in another canoe, was to be dead, his body "made a riddle of" with arrows. Within half an hour Colter himself, stripped naked, his face bloodied from being slapped with Potts' lungs and heart, was to be running for his life across the open prairie.

Pursued by picked runners from a band of three hundred Blackfoot warriors, he won his race — and went on from it to emerge as the protagonist of a saga of human courage, endurance and resource with few parallels in frontier history. Today, almost a hundred and fifty years later, the tracks that John Colter made across that western prairie live on as footnotes and scattered paragraphs in journals of his time as an example of what a man will undergo merely to survive.

He was born near Staunton, Virginia, in 1775, the son of Joseph and Ellen (Shields) Colter. He died in St. Louis, November 18, 1813, at the age of thirty-eight. Thomas James, a contemporary of his later years and a well-known trapper and trader, describes him as being "about five feet, ten inches in height and wearing an open, ingenuous countenance of the Daniel Boone stamp. . . . Nature had formed him . . . for fatigue, privation and perils. . . . his veracity was never questioned among us. . . . his character was that of the true American backwoodsman."

On October 15, 1803, Colter enlisted at St. Louis with the history-making Lewis and Clark "Corps of Discovery" for their overland journey to the Pacific coast. He served with distinction and is frequently mentioned in the Journals. Lewis and Clark were often separated, and Colter was the man usually selected to keep the two parties in touch, as he was the one favoured for a difficult and dangerous reconnaissance. On one of these forays he lost his horse and blanket over a canyon wall but saved himself and his rifle.

When the expedition on its return had reached the Mandan village on the Missouri, about fifty-five miles above the modern city of Bismarck, North Dakota, Colter asked for his discharge on August 15, 1806. Two trappers there, Dixon and Handcock from Illinois, had offered to outfit him if he would go with them for a winter's trapping on the Yellowstone. It was an attractive offer, especially as Colter felt that he "would be lonely in St. Louis."

His leaders granted his request as a tribute to his qualities, exacting from the rest of their company the promise that no other man would ask for his freedom until they had all returned to St. Louis. They wrote in their journal, "We were disposed to be of service to any one of our party who had performed their duty as well as Colter had done." The discharged man was given his pay voucher and a warrant for a grant of land, according to the terms of his enlistment.

Colter spent the winter on the Yellowstone. In the spring, deciding that he had had enough of the mountains for a while — he had been out in them now for almost four years — he travelled downstream towards St. Louis. At the mouth of the Platte he met Manuel Lisa, founder of the Missouri Fur-Trading Company, who was on his way upstream to trade with the Crows and Blackfoot. Lisa saw that Colter's experience would be invaluable in his venture and induced the mountain man to join his party.

Lisa built a fort at the mouth of the Bighorn on the Yellowstone and in the late fall of that year, 1807, sent Colter out alone into the mountains south and west to treat with the Crows and bring them in to trade. Here was a journey which would exact the most in "fatigue, privation and perils." It involved five hundred miles on snowshoes in below-zero temperatures into country never seen by a white man before and inhabited by Indians who, friendly today, might be hostile tomorrow.

Colter set out "with a thirty-pound pack and his rifle." Living off what game he could kill, he travelled up the Bighorn to the Shoshone (Stinking Water), then south to Jackson Hole. He turned west into Idaho through Teton Pass on to the head of the Snake River. Along the way he met with a party of Crows and fought with them when they were attacked by the Blackfoot. He was wounded in the leg. He would have added cause to regret the wound less than a year later.

When he returned to Lisa's fort in the spring he did so as the first white man to explore the valley of the Bighorn, the Tetons, Jackson Hole, the Wind River mountains, and the source of the Snake River. In his travels he twice crossed what is today Yellowstone Park and brought back the first description of its thermal wonders. The spring at the mouth of the Stinking Water became known as "Colter's Hell."

Colter was also a man of vision. Wagons, he said, could be put across the west side of the mountains through the wide, low passes he had discovered. This was the first prophecy by a man on the spot of the great western migration to begin four decades later.

Late in the summer of 1808, Lisa dispatched Colter to negotiate with the Blackfoot over the mountains two hundred miles to the west on the upper reaches of the Missouri. This was a hazardous mission. The Blackfoot were ill disposed. One of their men had been killed on the Marias River in 1806 while trying to steal horses from Lewis and Clark. Also they felt that the white man in trading favoured their enemies, the Crows.

On this expedition Colter was accompanied by John Potts. Like Colter, Potts was a veteran of the Lewis and Clark "Corps of Discovery" and had been discharged when the company returned to St. Louis late in 1806. There he had joined Lisa.

Potts is remembered today only from his association with Colter — except, apparently, among the Nez Percés, through whose territory, west of the mountains, the Lewis and Clark party had passed. Among these people his name, easy to recall, had been handed down so that in the 1930's one of their old men is reported to have said, "Potts, he boss other mans how to do funny dance and sing songs and all laugh." Potts appears here as a convivial caller of square dances and a leader of songs.

A more sombre destiny awaited him on the upper reaches of the Missouri. There, after paddling up the river from the mouth of the Yellowstone, when he and Colter did not at once encounter the Blackfoot, they put their time to use by trapping beaver, setting their traps in the late twilight, gathering them in in the early morning, and lying low through the day to avoid the chance of hostile eyes. When they met the Blackfoot they meant to do so in an open and formal manner, as emissaries of the Missouri Company, and not to be caught unaware.

On the October morning that Colter heard the sound of hooves above them, they were paddling up a stream six miles above Jefferson Forks on the Missouri, just to the west of present-day Bozeman, Montana. The sun was barely over the horizon and they pushed their canoes slowly upstream in the shadow of cottonwood and alder which lined the riverbank.

Colter, who had walked alone hundreds of miles through the mountains and treated with the Crows and fought against the Blackfoot, lifted his paddle and called softly across to his partner. "Did you hear what I heard?" he asked.

"Hell! It's only buffalo," Potts responded, thrusting his

blade into the water. "You're not scared, are you?"

The sanguine leader of square dances and bellower of songs was not to be deterred by the caution of his companion, who wished to pull up under the trees and from their shelter await and ascertain the nature of the commotion above them. He pushed on up the stream. Colter reluctantly followed. He knew enough about taking risks to avoid them when he could.

A hundred yards ahead, through a break in the tall-growing cottonwoods, the sun shone with a golden sheen on the smooth-flowing waters of the narrow stream. The two men, now paddling abreast, were almost past the gap when a gutteral voice caused Colter to turn his head.

There to his right and twenty feet above him and so close that he had to stretch his neck to see them, twenty or thirty Blackfoot warriors sat their horses, eagle-feathered bonnets and upraised lance points outlined against the sun. There was no mistaking the gestures and shouts of their tall leader, who, dismounting, ordered him and Potts to put in to shore. Colter saw that many of the other warriors had dismounted, too, and spread up and down the stream. Their bows were strung. The occasional rifle was at the ready. From the twenty or thirty men he had seen a minute ago, their numbers had increased, as if sprung from the ground, to a hundred or more. With their weapons they completely commanded the water. He motioned to Potts and they turned their prows towards the shore, where the Blackfoot were slipping down the soft earthen bank to meet them.

As Potts' canoe touched, a Blackfoot snatched the rifle stacked in its bow. Seconds later Colter stepped ashore, wrested the rifle from the warrior, and handed it back to its owner.

Potts, still in his canoe, dug his paddle in deep and backed into the stream. "This is no place for a white man," he called to Colter. "I'm going back."

"Don't be a fool. Come in and surrender."

Further conversation was interrupted by a gasp from Potts. An arrow had lodged above his hip.

"Are you hurt?" Colter asked.

"Hurt? Too bad to get away. Make a run for it. I'll get one of them anyway."

With that, kneeling in the canoe, Potts grabbed his rifle and shot square in the forehead the Blackfoot who two minutes before had seized it from him. Within moments, as Colter described it later, arrows had made "a riddle" of him.

Blackfoot waded into the stream and dragged the canoe ashore. They took Potts' body from it, dismembered it and, while two men held him, slapped the heart and lungs across Colter's face. Then they pushed and pulled their prisoner to the top of the riverbank.

There he saw that the party had again increased. At least three hundred warriors were assembled. Their faces were streaked with paint. Their blankets billowed in the wind. Their horses neighed and pawed the ground. For Colter it was not a question of escape. Rather it was one of how long his agony of dying would be prolonged.

From the Blackfoot a captured enemy expected no mercy. War and retribution were their mission in life and for years they were to remain implacable in their enmity towards the white man.

Centuries ago, according to Boas and other authorities, the native stock in North America migrated here from Asia across the land bridge which at that time closed the Bering Strait. Some drifted eastward to populate the forest and lakeland there. Others, following the east slope of the Rockies, reached the Great Plains, teeming with buffalo. Among these latter, the Blackfoot, including the Blood, Piegan and Sarcee, were late-comers and found themselves forced into the foothills between the plains and the mountains. Their name is said to have its source in the fact that other tribes, as they fought their way south, burned the land before them to impede their progress. Walking through it, their moccasins were blackened.

In the early 1800's the Blackfoot ranged from the Saskatchewan south to the Missouri. To the west, should they try to cross the Rockies, they were met by the Kootenays, the Salish, and the Nez Percés. From the north the Crees pressed upon them. To the east and south they fought to retain their holdings against the Assiniboins, the Shoshones, the Crows and other tribes. At the time of Colter's encounter with them this precarious balance was more than ever in doubt because the Crows, and others among their enemies, came between them and the fur traders with the latter's offerings of rifles, ammunition and other goods.

When Colter, who understood a little of their language and who, like most men of his time and place, was versed in sign language, protested that he had come among them to open trade relations with the Blackfoot people, they would not listen. The Lewis and Clark party had killed one of their young men on the Marias River when he was on a legitimate horse-stealing expedition. Manuel Lisa and other traders were friends of, and did big business with, the Crows, their inveterate enemies. Finally, and most damning of all, Colter was recognized by some among them as the white man who had fought with the Crows against them and been wounded in the leg the previous winter. To prove their point they ripped off his trousers and underwear, disclosing the hole in his thigh. Within seconds he was stripped naked.

Standing alone in a circle of warriors, Colter knew that the various discussions among them concerned the manner of his death. The relatives of the man Potts had killed waved tomahawks and were for dispatching him instantly. Older men shook their heads.

Colter noticed that a score or more of younger men were shedding their blankets and leggings until they stood reduced to breechclouts and moccasins. Each of them held a spear and several of them were sharpening the iron points with flat stones.

Colter still wore his moccasins. He was told to remove them. Then an old man led him across an open flat a quarter mile from the others and left him. Colter began to walk away, expecting every moment to feel an arrow or a spear point between his shoulder blades.

The old man returned, touched Colter on the arm. It seemed that he wanted to know if the white man was a good runner.

Colter, getting a hint of the trial in store for him and thinking of the many minutes that his mental torture had been prolonged, indicated that he was a very poor runner, indeed. The fact was that, while he could leave most men behind on a long overland journey, he esteemed himself no better than the average in a sprint. Shading the truth a little might get him a few extra yards start in the race that he now knew was impending.

He heard a whoop behind him and saw the young braves, those who had stripped to their breechclouts and moccasins, dancing on their toes and waving their spears. He looked ahead down the prairie, hills to the left, cottonwoods in their yellow autumn tints to the right. Six miles across the prairie were the Jefferson Forks of the Missouri. Beyond them, on the other side of the river, rose Gallatin Mountain, blue and hazy. Over the ten-thousand-foot mountain and down the Yellowstone to the mouth of the Bighorn was Manuel Lisa's fort, a bit more than two hundred miles from where he stood.

Another whoop and another quick glance over his shoulder told him that thirty or forty young Blackfoot, each one of them armed with a spear, had given him a lead of slightly over four hundred yards and had now set out to run him down. True, he might have been more quickly overtaken on horseback, but this, conceived by their elders, would provide a test of stamina for the young men, give them sport, and perhaps tame their restless spirits for a while.

Colter lit out in long strides across the prairie. At first he was tempted to slow up when a rock bruised the bare sole of his foot or the thorn of a prickly pear stabbed it. In the first few hundred yards the moccasin-shod Blackfoot had closed half the distance behind him.

If Colter, the man of "open, ingenuous countenance" and the prototype of "the true American backwoodsman" had thought of reaching Manuel Lisa's fort so far away at the mouth of the Bighorn, or even of getting to Jefferson Forks on the Missouri, still almost six miles distant over the rough prairie, he now dismissed them. This was a race in which Death held the stop watch. One misstep, one stumble and he had run his course. It was sufficient to live a minute at a time.

After a mile he had "found his feet," in the sense that he could ignore the pain they gave him and had got his second wind. More than that, he had gained a little ground on his pursuers. Their shouts were farther back. The Blackfoot, like other Indians, were inured to hardship, but would often yield under the sustained physical effort of which a well-conditioned white man was capable.

Colter, after months of wilderness travel, was in superb condition, and the hope came to him that, with luck, if heart and legs held out, he might yet gain life and freedom. His heart seemed to swell until it choked his throat. Foam flew from his lips. He fastened his eyes upon a stunted willow bush a hundred yards away and, losing consciousness of all else, made it his goal. Passing the bush, he seized upon a bunch of grass waving in the wind — so that his race across the plain became a series of sprints between these points singled out in advance.

But the Blackfoot, after what he later estimated to be about two miles, were drawing closer. Though, to save their wind, they no longer shouted, he could, in his imagination, feel their hot breath upon his neck. At any moment he might find himself biting the grass, a flung spear through his chest and pinning him to the ground.

Colter ran on. No longer did he see bushes or tufts of grass. His world was a red haze and life only a struggle for breath in the agony of his breast. Behind him all was strangely silent, as if he had been left, a last, lonely remnant of humanity travelling a deserted land.

A whoop, closer at hand than all the others, warned him that grim reality was still upon his heels. Colter put out his last strength. Suddenly blood, welling up from his overextended lungs, spurted from his mouth and flowed down his beard and chest.

On an impulse, knowing he had gone as far as he could go, he stopped and wheeled about, spreading his arms at right angles to his body, like a man already crucified. He saw, not more than ninety feet away, a tall, young Blackfoot running towards him, his arm lifted to throw his spear. The two of them had outdistanced the rest of the pack, who were half a mile behind.

Confronted with Colter — an apparition naked, bearded, and bloody standing beneath the mountains — the brave, in his attempt to halt, stumbled and fell — but before he fell he flung his spear. It buried its head in the ground by Colter's feet, shattering its shaft.

Colter wrenched the pointed part from the soil and before its owner could regain his feet, and over his gasped plea for mercy, plunged it through his heart.

Colter turned, ran on, now less than three miles from Jefferson Forks on the Missouri.

The other Blackfoot, coming up, gathered around the body of their fallen comrade. When they again took up the pursuit, Colter was a mile away.

Before they caught up to him, he had dived into the river, and as they flung spears at him he dropped beneath the surface and drifted downstream with the current. He knew the river well and remembered that a few hundred yards below was an island with a log jam on its upper part.

He came up under the log jam, head and shoulders above water, the rest of his body below it. The snow-fed water gripped him with an icy hand.

The log jam made a bridge to the left bank of the river, and soon Colter saw the moccasined feet of the Blackfoot above him and heard their shouted directions to one another as they searched for him beneath the logs, shoving their spears through likely openings. Shortly they were reinforced by the main body of warriors.

All day long, teeth chattering, their quarry lay within a few feet of their reach, his fear now being that they would set fire to his refuge and flush him out.

At twilight they departed without having set the fire. When darkness came, Colter clambered out of his hiding place and swam to the right bank of the river. He had escaped one peril only to meet another. His feet were cut and bleeding. The autumn night was cold and he was naked. He was hungry and he had no food, nor snare nor weapon to obtain it. He was alone and without shelter — and the nearest white man was at Manuel Lisa's fort two hundred miles across the mountains.

But Colter was a man who did not die easily. Believing that the Blackfoot would be guarding the pass below Gallatin Mountain, he set out at once to climb the mountain itself. He spent the night high up on the rocks, a night without food, clothes, shelter, or fire on a Rocky Mountain peak in October — a test few men have undergone. For Colter it was only an incident in a journey.

When dawn found him on the mountaintop, he would have been glad to go down to the more sheltered valley. On the mountain the cold wind keened about the rocks. But

Colter dared not move. The Blackfoot from below held the mountain under constant observation, not only because he had so far escaped them, but because they were hunters and instinctively on the lookout for the movement of game.

That night Colter gingerly picked his way down the far side of the mountain away from the Missouri. Difficult as it had been the night before to climb, descending in darkness was even more demanding. Climbing, he could feel his way with his fingers and what was above was outlined against the sky's dim radiance. Going down, he looked into a pit of blackness, knowing that with a misstep he might fall or roll hundreds of feet. Nor could he afford to dislodge a stone, whose clatter would give warning to any Blackfoot who might be watching below.

By morning Colter had safely crossed over the mountain from the Missouri watershed onto that of the Yellowstone, or the Roche Jaune as it was called in the early French Canadian style. He was now in the country of the Crows but feared to travel farther in daylight because pursuing Blackfoot would not respect the limits of their enemy's territory.

Well below timber line, on a south-facing slope where he would get the sun, he denned up in a clump of balsam, breaking off some branches and covering himself with them to mitigate the early morning chill. He had not eaten for something like forty-eight hours.

That night he dropped down into the valley of the Yellowstone proper. It was cloudy and the late-rising, waning moon gave little light. As he felt his way from tree to tree, the glimmer of the river on his right guided him. His feet, now that he was down off the rocks, were mending and he stopped frequently to bathe them in the streams which crossed his path. Around his waist he had knotted and twisted a belt of lithe willow and from it hung a small branch of balsam to protect his groin.

On this night, his third away from the Missouri, Colter estimated that he had travelled another fifteen miles, leaving a hundred and seventy between him and Lisa's fort.

Colter, in his fourth day without food, was alert for that last hope of all — a porcupine. A porcupine would be food. True, he lacked flint and steel to make a fire, but, dismem-

bering it with a sharp piece of rock, he would wolf its back
-haunches raw. More than once he had tasted its fat white
flesh, flavoured with the inner bark of pine and spruce it
fed upon.

Colter's thoughts rambled on, keeping pace with his feet
as he beat his way down the valley. Though he was growing
weaker and several times had pulled himself up in his tracks
when he staggered, he had put thirty miles behind him by
nightfall. He again covered himself with branches and, though
his teeth clicked in the cold, he dozed a few hours in a cave
under the roots of a wind-toppled pine tree.

About midnight he was awakened by a stir in the forest
behind him. As he stood up he saw in the dim light of the
moon the upper branches of a forty-foot spruce tree trembling as though they had a vibrant life of their own. A porcupine was up there, feeding.

Colter determined on a desperate proceeding. Naked
though he was, he would climb the tree. Chasing the porcupine to the very treetop, he would shake it loose or somehow
get his hand under its unprotected belly and toss it to the
ground, where, descending quickly, he would smash in its
head with a club or rock. He might get a few quills in his
hand — but what were a few quills to a man faint with hunger
and a hundred and forty miles from human habitation?

More than "a few quills" were waiting for Colter up the
tree, and the porcupine came within an ace of exacting from
him the vengeance which he had denied the Blackfoot. As
he climbed, the porcupine at first climbed higher. Then when
Colter was about thirty feet from the ground and could
almost touch him, he backed down, slapping his wicked
barbed tail from side to side. So rapid was his descent that
in the darkness Colter had virtually to let go and slide down
the trunk and through the yielding branches.

When Colter hit the ground, his right hand and forearm
were studded with quills and the porcupine, with its promise of meat, was again high up in the spruce tree. Colter now
knew he could not catch it.

The quill of the porcupine is hollow and its point is barbed
so that it tends to work inward from the skin it penetrates.
Colter, pulling at the quills, broke them off, leaving the barbs
imbedded. His arm felt as though it were being stung by a

thousand ants.

By nightfall the forearm was red and swollen, and by morning the inflammation had reached his shoulder. On this, the fifth day, still more than a hundred miles from Lisa's fort, he came upon a pealike plant — *Psoralea esculenta* — whose tuberous root was eaten by the Crows. He dug up the root with his fingers and ravenously ate it. Its slight, pulpy sustenance was to carry him to his journey's end.

For a day and a night it snowed lightly, the flakes melting on his body and adding to his misery. Out of the snow, fifty yards behind him, a black timber wolf appeared, dogging his steps. He kept his distance, stopping when Colter stopped, proceeding when Colter did. To Colter's fevered eye his form, looming in the snow, was that of a monster. But the wolf was merely curious and, making no effort to attack, followed him to the fort's clearing.

Eight days after he had won his race with the Blackfoot, Colter stood outside Manuel Lisa's gate at the mouth of the Bighorn. In those eight days he had hidden from Indians, starved, lived on roots and, naked and barefoot, covered two hundred miles of rough mountain country. Twenty-five miles a day, under the best of conditions, is a good average for mountain travel.

Those in the fort at first did not recognize him. "John Colter," he croaked. He repeated his name when they continued to stare at him, unbelieving.

Colter stayed with Lisa until he went downstream to the Hidatsa village on the Missouri. From there he undertook his last expedition, guiding the party of Menard and Henry to Three Forks. After five men had been lost in a fight with the Blackfoot, Colter exclaimed that he had had enough of Indians and mountains. He was then thirty-five years old.

He retired and took up a farm near the present town of Dundee on the Missouri — probably on the land warrant issued to him as part of his pay by Lewis and Clark. He married a girl called "Sally," last name unknown. When he died of jaundice in November, 1813, Colter, according to the *Louisiana Gazette*, St. Louis, December 11, 1813, left an estate of $229.41.

He left more than that — an estate not to be assessed in money. In August, 1934 the "Colter Stone" was presented to the museum of Grand Teton Park. The stone, its weathering attesting to its age, had been found on the site of old Henry's Fort, near St. Anthony, Idaho. This was country Colter visited during his 1807-08 expedition to the Crows from Lisa's fort at the mouth of the Bighorn on the Yellowstone. The stone is rough lava, three inches thick and uneven. On one side is inscribed "1808." On the other, the name "John Colter" is still legible.

Grey Owl

"Old" MacNamara and Albert Johnson were misanthropes. For them the wilderness, though in the end it failed them, offered an escape from organized society. However, the wilderness can also be made a stage whereon a man may strut and masquerade and have half a world for his audience.

Because of this, on the morning of April 13, 1938, as the sun topped spruce and pine-clad ridges and shed its wan light on still-unleafed poplars in the draws between them, in a hospital ward in the town of Prince Albert in northern Saskatchewan, stricken with pneumonia and brought in a few days before by horse-sleigh from his cabin on Lake Ajawaan, miles to the northwest, a man was dying who had never, in fact, been born.

Yet his death was to be newspaper copy, much of it front-page, throughout the English-speaking world and to spark a controversy between two continents which continued long after his uneasy bones had been laid into the cold earth of his adopted country.

For the man who turned his face to the wall that early spring morning in the Prince Albert hospital, while beaver slapped their tails on the waters outside his now deserted cabin and while the loon cried mournfully from across the lake, was a "best seller," the author of *Men of the Last*

Frontier, Pilgrims of the Wild, Tales of an Empty Cabin, Sajo and Her Beaver People — books urging game conservation, tolerance towards the Indian, narrating the story of the beaver and of man's life along the waterways and in the forests of northern Canada. They had gone through many printings, sold in the tens of thousands in Canada, the United States, and the British Isles.

The newspapers of April 13, 1938, and in the days and weeks which followed, told of a man, six feet two in his moccasins, long, plaited black hair tied in a thong behind his head, dressed in buckskin, who had been wined and dined in London as an emissary of the Northland — and, though the papers said nothing of this, surfeited with the rich food before him, had been hungry for the bannock and grease of an Indian tepee. Blood brother of the Ojibways, the forest-dwelling people of Québec and Ontario, initiated into their tribe by age-old ritual, he had been received by the then ruling monarch of Great Britain, King George VI, and, on leaving, had addressed the King as a "brother."

Acclaimed as the saviour of the beaver from extinction — no one has a better right to the title — he had stood before thousands upon British public platforms, bemused, blinking, in the glare of a hard-won renown. On his way to that renown he had stood most of one night, snow-blind, unable to make a fire, in a raging storm beneath a spruce tree. He had, another time, been so famished that he had eaten with gusto, entrails and all, the sinewy and stinking carcass of a marten rotting in its trap. He had been found in the heat of an Ontario summer day, unconscious, overcome by stomach fever, lying below the railroad track, his swollen face covered by flies, and was nursed back to health by a passing prospector. Again — as though an ember glowed within him which men would not see extinguished — a forest ranger had come upon him by the winter trail when his feet were half frozen, his body comatose with subzero cold, and strapped him behind a dog team and taken him to a cabin's warmth and shelter.

The man who died that morning in Prince Albert, who was, quite literally, a "self-made" man and who, as the records show, had had four wives and was probably a three-time bigamist, was a self-styled halfbreed called Wa-Sha-

Quon-Asin, or Grey Owl. At the time of his Canadian natur-
alization in Prince Albert in 1934 he gave his birthplace as
"near Hermosillo, on an Indian encampment in the State of
Sonora." His mother, he said, was an Apache and his father
a Scotsman named McNeill.

It was on Grey Owl's death that another figure, that of
Archie Belaney, a forgotten man for more than twenty years,
emerged from the shadows and, speaking through the voice
of a maiden lady in Hastings, a seacoast town in the south of
England, revealed that all the details submitted by Grey
Owl on taking out his papers, excepting only the date of his
birth, were spurious and unfounded. Thereby was exposed
one of the most amazing stories of imposture of the past half-
century — amazing in its range because of his lonely and
perfect duplicity. Far from having been born near Hermosillo, Sonora, Grey Owl had not even seen the place and was
no more related to an Apache mother than he was kin to
Florence Nightingale. As for the Scots father — he was but a
figment to account for the pair of blue eyes, an incongruity
steadily gleaming out of his tanned features, which Grey Owl
felt himself constantly bound to explain.

Despite those blue eyes, and with the aid of a fictitious
miscengenation and the inspiration of a vision which neither
hardship nor personal disaster could erase from before him,
Grey Owl had beguiled royalty, hoodwinked peer and com-
moner, buffaloed his publishers and public. Even his wives,
it seems, were not party to his secret. Ready to be photo-
graphed at the drop of a hat in full regalia, an eagle's feather
in his hair, a tomahawk in his hand, he was a poseur, a fake,
a hoax — and a dedicated man. His was a masquerade which
lasted over two decades — but one purely beneficent in its
purpose and effects. He not only impersonated an Indian, he
became one to such an extent that his true identity was lost
in the process. Until, finally, he *believed* himself to be one.
He was a man with a message. Only by being an Indian could
he speak forthrightly for them and for their "little people,"
the beaver.

Archie Belaney, who, resurrected from musty file and
anecdote, uncovered Grey Owl's deception and his histrionic
achievement, was born in Hastings, England, September 18,
1888. Lovat Dickson, English publisher and intimate of Grey

Owl, verified the circumstances, to his own surprise and discomfiture, soon after the death of his best-selling author. Archie Belaney was a solitary boy, intense in his fondness for Indian games. He was brought up by his two aunts, Carrie and Ada Belaney, sisters of his father, George, who, because of his drinking habits, had been sent away from England on a remittance when Archie was only two, by Mrs. Julia Belaney, Archie's windowed and well-to-do grandmother. George Belaney, the remittance man, lived with the Indians somewhere in North America — at least Archie was so led to believe by his mother, Kitty, whom he was occasionally permitted to see. Of Kitty, the outsider, whose family name is given differently as "Cox" or "Morris," little is known. George had brought her home with him from the United States, but whether she was American or English in origin is unknown.

Archie played his Indian games in defiance of his aunts and grandmother. They were a pretense, undertaken to fit him to go out and seek his father — a pretense which became the core and substance of his later being.

He was a boy who was born to live his dream, and when he was only sixteen, over his aunts' protests, he sailed away from Liverpool for Halifax to follow after the father of whom he had no memory. Archie would find a father — though not the one he set out to look for. He would find him around a campfire, shadows dancing against the forest gloom, uttering incantations in an alien tongue, man in his speech, ghost in his movements. Archie would find, too, in his escape from matriarchy, the country he had read about in James Fenimore Cooper, the woods and rivers and portages, and because he had to listen to the pleading of a full-blooded and beautiful Iroquois girl he would leave a name upon the land. Archie was coming, not to conquer the wilderness, but to be conquered by it.

However, when he landed, grey-shrouded Halifax, with the foghorns moaning, seemed a poor beginning for a schoolboy's odyssey. Archie's aunts had given him five pounds above his passage money. This took him to Toronto. He got a job there as a clerk in a dry-goods store — poor stuff this for a young man who wanted to run with the Indians, hunt moose, and tramp the snowshoe trail!

But that summer of 1904 in Toronto was no ordinary summer. A word was in the air, a magic word — silver! Someone up North, so the story went, had thrown his pick away in anger. Falling, it had nicked a rock and laid bare a fabulous vein of the metal close to the town of Cobalt on the new Temiskaming and Northern Ontario Railroad. With hundreds of others, Archie packed his suitcase and, in city clothes, set his face northward.

Days later, discovering that the turbulent frontier had no time for a green hand fresh out from England, penniless, hungry, footsore, he was counting the ties back along the way he had come, the drab prospect of another job behind another counter in Toronto before him. The day was hot, hotter than any English day. Mosquitoes pestered him. "Bulldogs" drew blood with their bites. Up his nose he breathed little "no-see-'ums."

To add to his troubles Archie had cramps — his first piece of luck in a new land. When a train bore down upon him where the rails curved along the rocky shore of Lake Temiskaming, dysentery had so taken its toll that he was barely strong enough to move out of its path. He rolled down the embankment and lay senseless by the waters of the lake. There a prospector and guide, Jesse Hood, paddling by with his two Indian helpers, saw him. Hood brushed the flies off Archie's red, bloated face, lifted him into the canoe, and brought him into camp.

He did more than that: he let Archie stay on and learn the rudiments of handling a birch-bark canoe from Michelle, the young Ojibway helper. Archie took to the work so well and with such eagerness that within two years he found himself hired out as a guide in summer and fall and mail carrier in the winter in the little hunting and trapping centre of Temagami, on the lake of the same name westward from Temiskaming. This was not bad progress at all for a raw, but apt, English boy.

It was there that, now in the summer of 1909, Maude Leopold, a "lady typist" in the office of the Temagami Steamboat and Hotel Company, was aroused one morning from her machine by shouts from the lake. Through the window at her elbow she saw seven or eight canoes, their paddlers churning the green waters as they bore down upon the landing below her. These were Ojibways, quiet and decorous people, who often came to town for supplies from their encampment at Bear Island, some miles up the lake. But, though this was her first summer in the North, Miss Leopold realized that what she saw approaching was to be no usual trading visit. These Indians, the tails of their red and purple headbands trailing in the wind, were on more angry business.

With others from the office Miss Leopold hurried outdoors. Only then did she observe, under the shadow of the hills, that one paddler was well out in front of the main body. The others were pursuing him and he was thrusting his bobbing craft with all his force of arm and body across the choppy waters to the haven of the landing.

Because of his long, plaited hair, his fringed skin clothing, she thought at first that, like those in his wake, he was an Indian. In a moment, however, when he turned to look back, she recognized Archie Belaney. She knew Archie by sight well enough. Because of what he wore, his reticence, his preference for their company, he was frequently mistaken for an Indian by outsiders. He did not seem to mind, and encouraged the notion by his failure to deny it. High cheekbones, a long, straight nose, a wide mouth, with thin, uncurving lips, added to the illusion. His blue eyes and a speech in which the accent still lingered attested to his real origin. Just out of his teens, but tall, robust, burned brown by sun and wind, he appeared to be five or six years older.

Miss Leopold — who, more than forty years later, was living in Castleton, Ontario — breathed easier. Like some others, she did not approve of Archie. She regarded him as pretty much of a "loafer" — between trips as a guide he was necessarily idle about the town. Nor could she condone his liking the unconventional society of Indians. That Bear Island lay on his winter mail run was small excuse. She had even heard talk that he had a girl up there waiting for him in a bark tepee. . . . For what was happening now, he had only himself to blame.

Archie, despite his utmost efforts, did not make it to the landing. Overtaken, surrounded by brandished paddles and amid threat and exhortation, he was compelled to beach his canoe a few hundred feet up the lake.

That evening in the office of Arthur Stevens, Justice of the Peace, he married Angele Uguna, an Ojibway maiden of Bear Island with whom he had tarried while carrying the mail the previous winter — and who had been in one of the pursuing canoes. Miss Maude Leopold had been witness to a "shotgun" wedding, North-American-Indian style. As for Archie — after all, he needed peace along his mail run and to be assured that his sleigh dogs would not begin suddenly to die from frozen titbits picked up along the trail.

For all that, this was more than a mere "shotgun" wedding or the making of another young Englishman into a "squaw man." On this summer morning Archie Belaney had been pursued across Lake Temagami not so much by a group of irate Ojibways as by the dark emissaries of his destiny. Without Angele he might have stayed on at Temagami and, in time, become one of its more competent professional guides. But his enforced marriage shook him up, interrupted his routine, partially cut him off from the bachelor gatherings of the town. Nor was he exactly *persona grata* at Bear Island.

He and Angele lived for a while in a cabin beyond the town limits. Archie did not stay long. Marriage, instead of binding him to the place, propelled him away from it. Even before their baby girl was born, he left Angele, who returned to Bear Island — and Archie, unwittingly, took his first step on the pilgrimage which was to leave his name as a legend on the land he walked.

Since his arrival in Canada he had sent only one postcard home to England. Now he turned his back on Temagami and set out westward for Biscotasing, a trappers' rendezvous he had heard of near the height of land between the Great Lakes to the south and James Bay, the lower reach of Hudson Bay, to the north. Had he been obeying the lines of a script written for him he could not have made a choice more likely to serve the end of what he was eventually to become. For here, at Bisco, he tried on tentatively the disguise he was to wear for two decades, to make known on two continents, and which he was not to put aside until he breathed a last sigh on a spring morning in faraway Prince Albert, Saskatchewan.

At Bisco, in those days, trappers, hunters, traders, rivermen, and forest rangers from the lusty Spanish, Ground Hog, and Mississagi rivers met, pitched their tents beside the lake, drank, fought, feasted, and danced to whining fiddles in the spring on their coming out of the bush and in the fall before going back into it. In 1909-10 it offered a spectacle as close as anything remaining in North America to the gatherings of mountain men below the Rockies in the previous century. To Archie, able in canoe and on snowshoe, on his way to being a skilled hunter and trapper, it presented the challenge which had brought him across the ocean. In Bisco there were no half measures. A man had to "cut the buck" or get out.

Here were men, white, Indian, and halfbreed, some of whom could paddle seventy-five miles in a day and make a carry of five hundred pounds across a portage. Above a few of the foreheads that Archie saw were shallow indentations where the pressing tumpline had sunk into the bone. Here the Hudson's Bay Company — the "HBC" or the "Here-Before-Christers" — the oldest company in the world, chartered in London in 1670 for "trading out of Hudson Bay," had long ago established a post. Fur brigades used to arrive at this little lake settlement with its thirty-odd log houses, its two churches, its Company store, from Moose Factory, from Old Green Lake, Mozaboang, Flying Post, and Fort Mattagami, heralded by the dip of paddles, by drum and fife in the summer and by the tinkle of harness bells in the winter. Algonquin, Cree, and Ojibway came in to trade pelts from the forest.

At Bisco, Archie listened to Nu-Tache-Wan-Asee, "Man Who Plays in the Rapids"; to "Mister Musho," an old scar-faced Indian; to Boyd Mathewson, Charlie Dougal, Red Landreville, Billy Mitchell and Jimmy L'Espagnol and others who were to teach him some of what they knew.

But, old-timers that they were, these men were at first puzzled by the stranger in their midst. Sure, his clothes were Indian-made (Angele Uguna had made them). He was dark, like an Indian. He did not toe out in his moccasins — this making for a longer stride than the average white man takes. Archie had learned well from Michelle, Jesse Hood's Ojibway helper, and from the Ojibways on Bear Isand. But how about those blue eyes and that "limey" accent? Who was this fellow, anyway, hanging about the Company post and asking questions about the country?

Archie sensed the distrust. Around the campfire he had an answer: he dropped a remark about Buffalo Bill. And what did *he* know of Buffalo Bill?

"My father," Archie said in his clipped speech, "used to travel with him. Got in trouble, my old man did, with an Apache woman down in Sonora." Archie paused, looked around.

"That's in the Southwest," he added. "I was the trouble."

His father had taken him when he was a boy on tour to England and left him there with an aunt, his father's aunt, for a season. "Ahnt" was Archie's pronunciation of the word.

"I took the old lady's name," he concluded.

He had accounted for everything — the name of Archie Belaney on his trapper's licence, the blue eyes, the "limey" accent — and also for any ineptitude he might display in his new surroundings. Perhaps it was a form of revenge for the matriarch-ruled days of his boyhood, a revolt against the aunts and grandmother who had scorned his Indian games and wanted him to grow up to be a good commuter like all boys of his "class." As for his father, his real father, George Belaney, the remittance man — Archie was beginning to see that he had never been in search of him so much as in search of the place where he had imagined him to be. He was there now, in Bisco, gateway to primeval forest and brawling waters.

And if any of those who heard his tale outside the Company post or across the campfire — for it was often told — grasped that they were hearing the first spoken lines of a consummate actor they said nothing about it then — and little long years after. It made small difference to them. As Archie was to write, in Bisco it was not a man's personal history that was important. It was his knowledge of geography. These men, he wrote, believed that men are born equal and that it is up to each one to maintain his status. If he wanted to be a halfbreed, it was all right with them — but he would have to accept what went with it.

This truth Archie confronted a few months later when he was thrown out of a "blind pig" for being an "Indian." This was a personal triumph but a moral defeat. It was already a tenet of his, held to even more doggedly as time went on, that an Indian had the same rights as the next man. One of these was to stand up and buy a drink. Indians, the barkeeper pointed out, as wards of the government, were not allowed to drink in public places and if Archie was not an Indian then he, the barkeeper, had never seen one. Archie, pride forbidding him to say that he was not an Indian, pointed out that a "blind pig," being against the law, was hardly a "public place."

The altercation took place at a whistle stop some thirty miles down the line from Bisco. In the "blind pig," Archie was later to relate, there were, besides himself and the heavy-set bartender, two loggers sitting at a table and a constable of the Mounted Police on his way to Bisco. He was a young man with pink cheeks, newly in the Force, and was not drinking but merely keeping warm and passing the time until the local came by to take him to his destination.

When Archie was tossed out into the chill spring thaw by the bartender and the two loggers, the policeman took no part in the brief affray.

However, Archie picked himself up from the moist ground and coming back into the bar threw the knife carried in his belt humming into the pine-panelled wall by the bartender's left ear. . . . When the train for Bisco was flagged down that night, a somewhat damaged Archie boarded it with the young constable. In Bisco, where the Hudson's Bay factor was also the magistrate, he would be charged with attempted assault with a deadly weapon. The new member of the Mounted took his duty so seriously that, as Archie sat beside him in the day coach, he handcuffed his own left wrist to the prisoner's right.

After half an hour or so Archie turned his head to the toilet at the end of the car. He and the constable walked back to it. It was small. Two men could hardly stand up in it. Besides, Archie had to sit and to have the use of his right hand. The constable removed the handcuff, reminding him to leave the door ajar. Archie entered. Soon the toilet was flushed, the door clicked shut and was locked. The constable, the empty handcuff dangling from his wrist, heard the crash of breaking glass.

By the time he had pulled the emergency cord and the train had stopped and the conductor came running up, they were half a mile beyond where Archie had slipped through the window and rolled onto the right of way. The train, after a short pause, left a very lonely constable trying to track an elusive and knife-throwing "Indian" in the dark. By the next morning, when he had walked on blistered feet the dozen-odd miles to Bisco, Archie, the Hudson's Bay factor, and a crowd of grinning rivermen were waiting to give him welcome. The constable did not press his charge.

But Archie, though he might pass among men for a half-breed or even an Indian, had to do with another antagonist, one who would accept no counterfeit, the Canadian subzero cold. His travels, the next winter, brought him well east of Bisco, to the borders of Algonquin Park, a game preserve where rifles were forbidden unless officially sealed. Archie, secure in his prowess on snowshoes, let it be known that he would carry an unsealed rifle sixty miles across the park. The temperature, when he set out, was about thirty below.

He almost made good his boast. However, a few miles from his journey's end, he committed two blunders where not even one is allowed. Following the waterways, the winter highway of the forest, he failed to test a stretch of uneasy ice with a pole. He stepped into an air hole, a common hazard, where a warm spring bubbles or where the stream, flowing too swiftly to freeze, is covered only by a dome of snow. Archie pulled himself out of the trap, wet to the knees. Stubborn, he did not stop to make a fire, the smoke of which might reveal his presence to the park rangers, whom he was attempting to outwit. He would "tough it out" for the six or eight miles to the park boundary, where he would find shelter. This was his second and almost fatal error. An Indian, patient in hunt and travel, would have taken no such chance.

A ranger, advised of Archie's overland trip, had cut his snowshoe trail some miles back and now overtook him where he had fallen, unable to walk farther, feet encased in balls of ice, fingers too numb to whittle shavings or strike a match, his body lethargic with cold and his mind wandering. Archie spent weeks recovering. He had learned the hard way that the Canadian winter is a cold and excessive mistress.

When the war came in 1914, he was back in Bisco and, caught up in the mood of the men around him, enlisted. Because he showed himself to be a dead shot and further-more had declared that he was a halfbreed, he served as a sniper. He was gassed, and wounded in the foot, recuperating at his aunts' house in Hastings. There, though he had not divorced Angele Uguna, he married Constance Holmes, an English girl whom he had known when he was a boy. When she would not go with him to Canada, Archie sailed without her. Embittered, soured by the slaughter of the war, he returned to Bisco to take up where he had left off in 1914. Nearing thirty now, he was brooding and short-spoken, shunning more than ever the white man's company.

A man can never go back. At Bisco most of the old, familiar faces were gone, scattered by the war, lost in its trenches. A new railroad had been built through Archie's old trapping grounds and homesteaders pecked at its meagre soil. Nor was he, himself, the man he had been before. His wounded foot gave out on the trail. Frequently he had to lay up at an Ojibway encampment on the Mississagi River, where the women tended and fed him. He lived and hunted with the tribe, spoke their language, wore their clothes. Archie Belaney the Englishman had virtually ceased to exist.

One night, crossing a lake shortly before the spring break-up — night travel was indicated because of the firmer snow — Archie noticed that the dark line of forest half a mile to his right, a few minutes before plainly discernible under the waning moon, was growing indistinct. He shook his head, blinked his eyes. His eyes smarted as if hot sand were under the lids.

He bent low against the cold wind blowing down from Hudson Bay and tramped on. Soon the farther shore on his left, two miles away, faded into formless grey. He could see just straight ahead. He looked down at his buckskin shirt. It was white, yet against his cheek no snow was falling. He looked inside his shirt. Here, too, it was white. His eyes pained, streamed with water. Archie was snowblind.

Off to the right he could hear the wind, risen to half a gale, roaring in the timber. Only in the sanctuary of the timber would he avoid the white death, closing in like four walls around him. He stumbled towards the timber, guided by his ears, tripped on his snowshoes, got up, staggered on, hands out — stretched for the touch of a friendly branch. His feet came loose from the snowshoes, which, held only by their lampwick bindings, dragged at his ankles. He floundered, crawled towards the sound of the forest like a wounded animal towards its burrow.

The rest of the night he stood in the loneliness of darkness beneath a spruce tree, shivering, frightened as he had never been before, blind and unable to make a fire.

Then hours later, in the morning and in the twilight of returning vision, a fire burned before him — but not one that he had made. Earlier a voice had spoken to him. "I am Ne-Ganikabo," it said in Ojibway. "I will make a fire."

Ne-Ganikabo . . . "The One Who Stands First. . . ." Archie, wincing, turning away from the flame, remembered the name and the man. Ne-Ganikabo was so old that he seemed to be of another race and age. White hair framed his lean, mahogany-coloured face. He carried an ancient muzzle-loading gun, a sharply ground hand axe, and a medicine pouch decorated with porcupine quills and containing bony relics. He was still a fabulous hunter and a leader among the Ojibway people.

For four years Archie studied under Ne-Ganikabo, the student under the master. With all he had learned he was but a beginner beside his mentor, moving ghostlike through the trees. Archie learned to judge ice by the sound of an iron-shod pole and to keep his direction in the forest at night when no star showed and with no trail to guide his feet. No small undertaking this, as anyone who has tried it knows. A torch will help along a trail, but where there is no trail a man will tend to walk in the dim circle just beyond its light. Archie learned to follow a month-old snowed-in moose trail by peeling off his mittens and digging carefully down to feel the hidden outline of the hoof. It would be broader in the direction the moose had been travelling. This barehanded feat in subzero cold, requiring up to fifteen minutes of concentration, was no mere academic exercise because the moose, upon which Archie and the Ojibways depended for food and clothing, might have "yarded" with his fellows only a mile away and after a month or more still be there.

At the end of four years Archie had, so to speak, passed his written tests and as a skilled hunter and trapper now contributed to the strength of the tribe. With Ne-Ganikabo, who was the closest to a father he had ever had, standing as his sponsor, he appeared one night before a leaping fire in a forest clearing to receive his "oral" — in other words, to be adopted by the Ojibways as a blood brother, from one of whose other bands he had fled across Lake Temagami so long ago. To the chant of "Hi-Heeh, Hi-He, Ho, Hi-He, Ha!" repeated to the point of hypnotism, he was named, "Wa-Sha-Quon-Asin" or "Grey Owl," "Shining Beak, the Night Traveller." It was the "Ph.D." of the wilderness. The boy who had played Indian games in the woods outside of Hastings, England, could ask no more.

But he did. He wanted more than he had been given, more than he had yet found. He wanted to see new country, the age-old quest of trapper and trader. It was on his way there, travelling north and east, that he crossed again Lake Temagami and on the *Temagami Belle* met an Iroquois girl from Matawawa, on the Ottawa River, whose pleased promptings were to make the name of "Grey Owl" a long-remembered one and to leave it written large in the annals of the outdoors.

Anahareo was a slim, dark-haired lass with a willowy figure, wearing high boots and breeches and a khaki shirt open at her warm brown throat. When he saw her on the deck of the *Temagami Belle*, Archie wasted no time in introducing himself. "Grey Owl," he said in English, "but they call me 'Archie.'"

Anahareo, who was going to a tourist camp to work as a waitress for the summer, lifted her head to appraise this tall, dark, buckskin-clad man with the plaited hair and the telltale blue eyes. "Why," she asked, "if your name is 'Grey Owl,' do they call you 'Archie'?"

Archie looked out across the lake. Maybe he recalled another girl, Angele Uguna, still living there at Bear Island. To Anahareo he said, in good Canadian idiom, "Well — see? — I had a Scotsman for a father, a long way from here." Soon she had his history, the background he had evolved for himself: the Apache mother, the deserts of the Southwest, Buffalo Bill, and all the rest of it, including his blood brothership with the Ojibways. Archie, when the occasion arose, was not backward in speaking of himself.

Before they left the steamer, he learned that Anahareo was called "Pony" for short. In the fall of 1927, after delays and many letters, she journeyed north to meet him at the flag stop of Doucet on the Trans-Continental line in Québec. In her luggage she had two portentous volumes: a book on *The Power of the Will* and another entitled *The Irving Writing System*.

She became Archie's third wife and went to live with him in the cabin he had built on a nearby lake. This dusky-skinned beauty was no butterfly. She could snowshoe, swing an axe, make a fire, put up a tent, and carry a load on the trail. But, raised on the lower Ottawa River, near the centres of civilization, she used lipstick, liked pretty clothes, and was partial to the radio. Archie held out against the radio. Along with others of his kind, he believed that it heated up the air, "so that on account of some gigolo with corrugate hair singing . . . in Montreal or Los Angeles a bunch of good men had bad snowshoeing all winter."

Defeated on this point, Anahareo — after all she was an Iroquois, in whose councils women had always held a high place — was obdurate in another. She would not sit alone in the cabin. She would accompany Archie on his trapline.

She did — and he was amazed by her reactions. A trapped lynx, whose killing he had muffed with his axe, emitting a woman-like scream of agony, crawled towards her for protection, and as he administered the final death stroke Anahareo turned away, shuddered, cried out. Death to the lynx was life to Archie. It was his living — and Anahareo's. Men trapped to live. They trapped lynx, marten, fisher, fox, weasel — and, above all, the beaver. True, behind them they left desolation: beaver villages empty, houses ruined, dams destroyed, lakes and ponds drained. Archie did not relish the suffering he inflicted. But that was how it had to be. An Iroquois, such as Anahareo, should be the first to understand. . . .

The climax came in the spring. It had been a poor winter for fur and prices were low. Because of that, Archie undertook a spring beaver hunt. It was against his grain. Always, following Indian practice, he had trapped beaver under ice in the winter before the young were born. Now, in early May, he would be taking the grown beaver, leaving the young to perish in the lodge. There was only one lodge on his lake. His first "set" yielded three drowned beaver. The mother was missing and a trap unaccounted for. The two remaining kittens could be heard crying in their wattled house. All one day and part of the next Archie and Anahareo searched for the mother. Hers was the most valuable pelt. At last they gave up. But let Archie, or rather Grey Owl, tell it:

"So we turned to go, finally and for good. As we were leaving I heard behind me a light splash, and looking back saw what appeared to be a muskrat lying on top of the water along side of the house. . . . I threw up my gun, and standing in the canoe to get a better aim, prepared to shoot. At that distance a man could never miss and my finger was about to press the trigger when the creature gave a low cry, and at the same instant I saw, right in my line of fire, another who gave out the same peculiar call. . . . they were young beaver! I lowered my gun and said:

"'There are your kittens.'

"The instinct of a woman spoke out at once.

"'Let us save them,' cried Anahareo, excitedly, and then in a lower voice, 'It is up to us after what we've done.'

"And truly what had been done here looked now to be an act of brutal savagery. And with some confused thought of giving back what I had taken, some dim idea of atonement, I answered:

"'Yes, we have to. Let's take them home.' It seemed the only fitting thing to do."

Here in simple words, Biblical in their effect, a man un-tutored in the art of writing tells of his own conversion. From now on Archie would continue for a while to trap and hunt — but he would trap and hunt no more beaver. He gave Anahareo his word and stuck to it. Hunger might be outside the door — as was to occur the next winter — and across the lake from the cabin, a beaver colony whose pelts would pay for food, but he would not harm them.

To the two young beaver, captured near Doucet, Québec, Archie and Anahareo gave the names of "McGinnis" and "McGinty." The newcomers, weighing only half a pound each at first — at maturity they would scale seventy — raised on diluted canned milk and later the inner bark of poplar saplings, their natural food, had wills of their own. They were no ordinary pets. Soon they took over the cabin, building their own house within it, usurping the bed, so that the right-ful owners slept upon the floor, cutting down the table to see what was on top of it. They were, indeed, "little people," standing up to wring out their coats when coming back from a dip in the lake, chattering, hands on each other's shoulder, like little old men speaking English in a foreign tongue. Archie — his wife, Anahareo, long ago had succumbed — felt himself coming under their spell and resisted, feeling that to give in would be "unmanly." But not for long. Slowly he and Anahareo conceived the idea that they would be the instruments of saving this furred race from the doom that was falling upon it.

To that end, hearing of a likely place near Cabano, in the Temiscouta region on the south shore of the St. Lawrence in Québec, where with native beaver and their two young ones they might found a colony of their own, they left Doucet.

That next winter they built a cabin on Birch Lake, forty miles from Cabano, living on the grubstake advanced by a kindly French Canadian storekeeper. Archie was to pay it back with a winter fox hunt. But he discovered to his dismay that this southern country was so trapped over that barely a fox remained. On the lake a beaver colony stood. He and Anahareo might be hungry in the spring with the hunt over and no money to buy groceries — but Archie, encouraged by the girl beside him, stood by his resolve. No beaver!

It was then that, desperate, with no trapline to run — a strong man, the use of his one talent "taboo" — in lantern-light with Anahareo's *The Irving Writing System* beside him — she had, in her hurry at leaving home to marry him, mistaken it for a course in embroidery — he sat down and wrote an article for *Country Life* in England, using the beaver kittens, McGinnis and McGinty, as his protagonists. He sold this, his first article — sold it to a magazine published for red-coated fox hunters and tweed-jacketed bird watchers. Sold it and signed it "Grey Owl." And paid for his grubstake.

That spring he and Anahareo moved by toboggan closer in to town, transporting the two beavers in the stove, out of which they could not gnaw their way. At the new camp McGinnis and McGinty swam away and disappeared. They were never seen again.

Soon he had two others: "Jelly Roll," the female; and "Rawhide," the male. The next winter, at the urging of *Country Life*, still with his manual on writing handy, he wrote *Men of the Last Frontier*, a book on his early days as trapper and hunter.

The notices given it in the press, along with the local notoriety of a man and woman who shared their house with beavers, brought "Grey Owl" to the attention of the National Parks Service of Canada. They made a film record of his unique establishment, put him on their payroll, took him and Anahareo and Jelly Roll and Rawhide to Prince Albert National Park in Saskatchewan, and fixed them up in a cabin on Lake Ajawaan.

Until this move — it was at the beginning of the Great Depression, which darkened the early thirties — Archie had conducted his masquerade for the benefit of a few hundred backwoodsmen, hunters, trappers and traders. Now the years of practice in appearing to be what he was not bore fruit and were given a purpose and direction which earlier he could not have foreseen. He was stepping before a larger audience, which, if less critical, would also be less indulgent. Grey Owl became known to the Canadian public as an Indian who had appeared from the Southwest and had taken on the preservation of the beaver as his lifework.

At first he carried on his campaign from Lake Ajawaan, assisted by the Canadian park authorities. The beaver were going, he pointed out, and with them a way of life. With beaver there was lake, marshland and greenery, and moose and other game that thrived upon it. Without them the country was going to waste. Bands of Indians were starving, their lands eroded and ruined, bereft of fur and meat. This was not a mere local problem. It was national in scope. The spring beaver hunt with its destructions and cruelties must be done away with. Beaver must be trapped, yes, but in the proper season, under ice and in the winter. First of all, to regain their numbers they must be protected. Today, more than four decades after Grey Owl began his crusade, the dwindling beaver population of Canada, then in many former rich hunting grounds counted in dozens only, has risen to the tens and hundreds of thousands, and a corps of technicians, travelling by canoe, horse, and plane, and aided by local trappers and Indians, watch over them and transplant them from areas where they are overcrowded to others where their skilled engineering is needed. Hunting and fishing, valuable tourist assets, have prospered with the comeback of the beaver.

It was as the advocate of such a programme, as a representative of Canada's native people, whose voice he had become, and as an author of still another book, *Pilgrims of the Wild* — the story of his and Anahareo's adventures with their young beaver — that Grey Owl, leaving behind his wife and their newly-born baby daughter, went to England in the fall of 1935. He arrived in style on the *Empress of Britain* and was met by a crowd of reporters. The emigrant boy of thirty years before had been invited by his publisher, Lovat Dickson, to deliver a series of lectures.

How did he feel, this English boy, returning in Indian regalia, to the land of his birth? The answer is, he did not feel anything at all — that is, as a former emigrant boy. Listen to him as he rises for the first time to address an audience in London. See him standing there, alone in the light, feather in his long, plaited black hair, buckskin fringes trembling on his broad shoulders as he moves cautiously on soft moccasins, blue eyes staring from a brown, sharp-featured face. His voice rings out, vibrant, filling the packed hall. "I am Wa-Sha-Quon-Asin," he intones, "Grey Owl, a North American Indian. I come from far across the western ocean, from a land of illimitable forests, great lakes, and rushing rivers, to tell you something of this land of mystery and its inhabitants, that you may know us all a little better . . ." And so on and so on.

An actor? Of course. Playing a part? He was living it. He *was* Grey Owl. No Indian would speak of "illimitable forests." He would take them for granted. Few white men would have the effrontery to use "us" in such a context. But the speaker was neither red nor white. He was Grey Owl, Archie Belaney's imaginary man. And not only had Archie created a character to suit the part. He had even created a country for him. The term "Grey Owl country," a nebulous region of forest and stream in the Canadian hinterland, was already in common use.

However, before he got his protégé on to the public stage, Lovat Dickson had a problem on his hands. This man, so far as he knew, was a halfbreed trapper with a literary streak who had turned from trapping beaver to saving them. At the first press conference in London, arranged to put this angle of the story across, Grey Owl seized a photographer, threatening to tear him limb from limb. The photograher had wanted to take a picture showing Grey Owl with a specimen of London's fauna. In other words, fondling a cabby's horse.

Two nights before his opening lecture at the Polytechnic, at Grey Owl's insistence, he and Dickson drove out of London and made camp, tent and all, on the edge of Epping Forest. Grey Owl, himself, was playing at being an "Indian." There, over the fire, he recounted to Dickson the plight of a "halfbreed," accepted by neither of the races to which he pertained.

On this and a subsequent tour in 1937 he gave his lectures, spoke in London, in provincial seats and in Hastings, where he was born. In Hastings he asked anyone present by the name of "Belaney" to see him when he had finished. Of that interview the world was to hear less than a year later.

Grey Owl was entertained by Lord Sempill at Grosvenor House. During the meal he tried to retain his butter dish after the main course, forcefully withholding it from the waiter. It was grease and he longed for the grease and bannock of the trail. He remembered, too, regarding the sumptuous spread before him, the spring day his cache had been washed away and he had dined on a trapped marten's carcass and another time when he had been so hungry that he had eaten the entrails of a grouse, acting as scavenger to that "tidy eater," the grey owl, whose name he bore. Not many had suffered so to be an imposter — nor gained so much from it.

At Buckingham Palace, Grey Owl appeared before the King and Queen and the royal family. Most of them had read his books. Leaving, he spoke to King George VI, Protector of the Faith, Emperor of India, as a "brother" and reminded him that, as sovereign of Canada, he but held in trust its natural riches for the Indians, the rightful heirs.

Returning across the Atlantic, the royal imprimatur upon his imposture, Grey Owl spoke in the United States and in Massey Hall in Toronto — in Toronto, where he had begun his Canadian career behind a dry-goods counter. Everywhere he went now, newspapermen followed. His life had become a public spectacle. Even so, his disguise remained invulnerable. He went about in it, the saving of the beaver the overriding theme of all he wrote or said.

Back at Prince Albert National Park that April of 1938 perhaps he felt it slipping from his shoulders. His task was almost done: the beaver were on the way back. Life had long been a struggle merely to live — travel, hardship, endurance against wind and cold and in plunging waters. It was the journey that he cherished, not its destination. Now what he had fought for, food and meat and drink, were his for the asking. In a way, he had ceased to function. And in the bottle, to which, in later years, he had turned more frequently, he found only another bottom.

Anahareo, probably because of this, had left him, with their daughter Dawn. At his death — there is no record of his ever having obtained a divorce — he was married to Yvonne Perrier, a French Canadian girl with Indian blood.

Now fifty years old, Grey Owl went back to his cabin on Lake Ajawaan, outside the town of Prince Albert. Yvonne, his fourth wife, was recovering in the provincial capital of Regina from an illness. And, at first, on that April day by Lake Ajawaan, it did not seem that death was there with him. The beavers, Jelly Roll and Rawhide, could be heard busy in their mud hut, which filled a side of the cabin. Squirrels and whiskey-jacks came to his call. A bull moose, a friend of four years, stood on the edge of the clearing to welcome him back. On the lake the ice was breaking up. The sap was rising in the trees and the sweet, deeply remembered smell of spring was in the air. All around him life was stirring, but before Grey Owl's eyes was a dimness and on his body a faintness he could not shake off. He lifted the receiver of the park telephone and called a neighbouring ranger. Four days later he was dead of pneumonia in Prince Albert.

It was then that, the news cabled across the ocean, a reporter in Hastings recalled that when Grey Owl was there he had asked to speak to anyone by the name of "Belaney" in his audience. He went out to interview Miss Ada Belaney. "Of course, Grey Owl was my nephew," she said. "He was raised right here, in this very town." Constance Holmes, Archie's second wife, confirmed the statement. There was no question, she added, of his having had Indian blood in him. He was English, through and through.

And so the story bit by bit was unravelled, amid claim and

counterclaim, editorial, article and interview, until the fully documented figure of Archibald Stansfeld Belaney, born in Hastings, September 18, 1888, stepped out to take a post-humous bow — the artist in imposture, a wry grin on his face as he confronted the world, which, for a worthy purpose, he had so long deceived.

Grey Owl lives on in his books and as a legend and in the happy slap of beaver tails on northern waters. It was not he, but Archie Belaney whom they buried on a knoll near the cabin by Lake Ajawaan. The preacher who presided was a prudent man. He took from Archie his buckskin clothes and moccasins and eagle feather and put upon him a blue serge suit, shoes, white shirt, and stiff collar lest, last irony of all, imposter to the end, lest he arose in the full panoply of the wilderness to confuse his Maker.

The Little Bear
That Climbs Trees

On an early October day a forty-five-year-old prisoner
stood trial for his life in the Assizes at the Court House on
Georgia Street, Vancouver, British Columbia. Like Almighty
Voice, he was an Indian, wore moose-hide moccasins, and
was over six feet tall. Again, like Almighty Voice, he had
been hunted by the authorities through a northern wilderness
and now waited for their judgement. Unlike Almighty Voice,
he had given himself up voluntarily.

Under his frayed, much-worn mackinaw shirt the chest was
deep, the shoulders broad and sloping. Despite his three
months behind prison bars his skin still was swarthy, but
pallor showed in the hollows under his cheekbones. He wore
a black mustache, a rarity among his people. More remark-
able were his eyes, sombre and hooded like an owl's.

Like a man in darkness, he looked out from them on the
crowded courtroom before witnesses were called — at judge
and eminent counsel and carefully selected jury — strangers,
except for one man, speaking another language than his own.
In their hands his fate reposed. A reporter for the *Vancouver
Daily Province* noted his "alert eyes" and his face, "grim
and expressionless."

His name was Simon Gun-an-noot, a Kispiox Indian from
the upper Skeena River country five hundred miles north of

Vancouver, and his presence in the dock was the sequel to one of the longest and most baffling manhunts in Canadian criminal annals. It began on the afternoon of June 19, 1908, at the village of Kispiox near the juncture of the Kispiox River with the Skeena, which empties into the Pacific by the port of Prince Rupert, a hundred miles to the west. The manhunt ended thirteen years later, on the evening of June 24, 1919, when Gun-an-noot walked out of the forest and gave himself up to the law.

Today fishermen reach the Kispiox after a few hours' plane flight from Vancouver, and one of them, in October, 1954, took from its swift-flowing waters the world's largest sport-caught steelhead. In 1906, however, it was a journey of five days by coastal steamer and river packet to Hazelton, where the Skeena and the Bulkley valleys join a few miles below Kispiox village.

During Gun-an-noot's thirteen years of outlawry in the wilderness the Grand Trunk Pacific had been pushed through to Prince Rupert, linking Hazelton to the "outside." This was the second Canadian railroad to extend to the Pacific, the first being the Canadian Pacific, which laid steel into Port Moody, near the present city of Vancouver, in 1885.

On his emergence from exile Gun-an-noot saw his first train. The Great War had been fought and won and the German Kaiser banished to a woodlot in Holland. In Russia the Czar and his family had been "liquidated" and a strange breed of men, the "Bolsheviki," had taken over in his stead. Brown and Alcock had flown the Atlantic. On city streets in North America the motorcar had largely replaced the horse and women's skirt lengths were soon to rise from below their ankles to their knees.

In those days the jurisdiction of the Mounted Police did not extend west beyond the height of land in the Rockies. The government of British Columbia prosecuted the search for Gun-an-noot.

Over the years it had spent more than one hundred thousand dollars to flush him from his hiding place, and its agents, including Pinkerton detectives brought in from New York, had covered thousands of leagues through jungle-like mountain country. An unlooked-for result of this exhaustive effort was to be the indictment, if only at the bar of public opinion, of the person who had, in the first place, instigated it: British Columbia Provincial Police Constable James E. Kirby of Hazelton and, later, of Smithers, up the Bulkley River. Another result, more lasting, was to make a name, little known at the beginning of the search, into a byword for human endurance and cunning and to give, to the man who bore it, a mountain as a monument.

Nor did the passing of thirteen years, nor the evidence produced at the trial in Vancouver, resolve the mystery which had haunted the case from the beginning: the mystery of the four almost identical bullet holes.

Gun-an-noot, when he surrendered, had not fired a single shot in his own defence. Almighty Voice gave up his life in blood and strife. Gun-an-noot's life, in contrast, with the things that for him made that life worth living, was taken from him gradually, whittled away by the slow attrition of the years. In the Vancouver courtroom opposing counsel contended for a life already doomed.

Gun-an-noot's ordeal — that of being an invisible man before the law for thirteen years — had its beginnings on a trail above the Skeena. There, soon after dawn on the morning of June 19, 1906, two men were lashing their horses into a gallop. They were a mile apart and rode in opposite directions.

One man with a torn and broken finger rode south towards Hazelton, where he hoped to have it dressed at the hospital before setting out to the north with a pack train. The other, his partner, rode north to Haguilite, the Indian reserve on the Kispiox, to gather in the horses and make ready for the journey.

The men were Alex McIntosh and Max Leclaire, both in their late twenties. Scotch, French Canadian, and Cree Indian blood flowed in their veins from their forebears who had come west with the early fur traders. McIntosh and Leclaire, hiring out as guides and packers to hunters and prospectors into the far reaches of the upper Skeena, were continuing the traditions of their kind in a country little changed from what it had always been.

As well as being business partners, they were closely coupled by the bond of the bottle and had spent the dark hours preceding their diverging rides along the Skeena at the

Two-Mile House, a recently opened saloon and eating place between Hazelton and Haguilite, and a half hour's ride from either. A fifteen-year-old Indian boy, Peter Barney, tending cows, saw them leave together. Then they parted.

These two men, riding away from one another along the river trail under the timbered mountains, shared a still further and more drastic bond than that of the bottle: crouched in a willow bush, or prone behind a log, rifle in hand, Death this morning waited for each of them. Two reports, a mile apart, echoed up against the mountains, stilling the song of birds. Then, after a minute, the birds resumed their song and the river's hum once more filled the valley.

In each case the victim, riding loosely in the halfbreed style, leaned forward over the saddle-horn as his horse galloped beneath him. In each case the deadly marksman waited until the rider had passed. Then, in the split moment when the mounted man was outlined against the sky, he had shot him from below, low in the back, the bullet passing upward through the body.

John Boyd, a squat, dark-visaged Babine Indian from the lake district to the north and east, coming into Hazelton for supplies, found the first body, that of Alec McIntosh, while the dew was fresh upon the grass in which it lay. McIntosh was on his back, arms and legs extended. His face was swollen and his shirt stained with blood. Boyd noticed that the little finger of his right hand − the injury which had put him on the trail to Hazelton − was torn. A bullet had entered his back about two inches to the right of his spine just under the twelfth rib and emerged an inch below the collarbone, two inches to the left of the chest's centre line. A post-mortem was to reveal that in its course it had penetrated the diaphragm, ruptured a lung, and severed the main artery of the heart.

The remains of McIntosh's partner, Max Leclaire, were to be discovered, farther up the trail, barely an hour later and shortly before nine o'clock. Leclaire had been shot low in the back, two inches to the *left* of the spine. The bullet had come out below the collarbone, two inches to the *right* of the chest's centre line, ripping the heart to shreds in its course.

By each corpse, lines trailing and coat hard-caked with sweat, a saddled horse was grazing.

McIntosh and Leclaire, partners in life, were also partners in death. Riding at a gallop, stooped in the saddle, they had received virtually identical wounds, each from below and each slanting diagonally upward through the body, one from right to left and the other from left to right.

The victims being a mile apart when they were toppled from their horses at about the same time, the same man could not be responsible for the double crime. But it was also unlikely that two separate men would have inflicted wounds so similar. The question was to receive little scrutiny and was never answered, nor were the bullets or their cartridge cases recovered.

A horseman — and every man for miles around worked with horses — would ask another question: how was it that the horses had not shied at the scent of a killer so close beside the trail? It was determined afterwards by the angle of the bullet's course that in each instance the killer was not more than ten or twenty feet from the rider and the wind which might have favoured him with McIntosh would have been against him with Leclaire.

John Boyd, the Babine Indian, when he hurried into Hazelton with his news, was troubled with no such speculation. He had seen only one man dead, Alec McIntosh.

Hazelton in those days, strung out along the north bank of the Skeena, numbered two hundred people living in log cabins. There were also the barracks of the British Columbia Provincial Police, a Hudson's Bay Company's white-clayed trading post, a church, the hospital, and the house of its doctor, H. C. Wrinch, in later years a well-known and highly respected man in his profession.

Boyd went at once to the police barracks. There, over his morning coffee, Constable James E. Kirby listened to his tale. Kirby, to be described in the Vancouver courtroom as a man "whose mentality was exhausted as soon as he had seized upon one idea," strapped on his revolver, saddled his horse, and rode up the trail with Boyd. He immediately recognized the body of Alec McIntosh. On and off for a dozen years McIntosh had been his guest in the local jail charged with bootlegging, creating a public disturbance or molesting the native women.

He brought the body in, draped over the saddle of the

dead man's pinto horse. *Rigor mortis* had not yet set in.

Soon a report reached town of another body, farther up the trail towards Haguilite. Now accompanied by Dr. Wrinch, Kirby rode forth again to retrieve the morning's second bloody harvest, the mortal remains of Max Leclaire. Leclaire also had a police record.

By the time of the inquest, called for that afternoon by Edward H. Hicks Beach, the town coroner, Dr. Wrinch, in his post-mortems, had fixed the manner, cause, and approximate hour of the twin murders. He said the two men had probably died within minutes of each other.

About twenty witnesses appeared: Kispiox Indians, half-breed and white-skinned trappers and hunters and hangers-on, men who had been with or seen McIntosh and Leclaire during the previous twenty-four hours. The picture which their testimony produced was that of an all-night drunk at the Two-Mile House between Hazelton and Haguilite. In the proceedings, which left the premises disordered with blood spattered on the walls and floor, McIntosh and Leclaire had been prominent. Two full-blood Kispiox Indians had also shared the limelight — Simon Gun-an-noot and his brother-in-law, Peter Hi-man-dan. Neither of them was present at the inquest.

Gun-an-noot, thirty-two years old, educated by Catholic priests, was a distinguished character in the valley. His physical stature and his thin black mustache marked him in any gathering. He weighed two hundred pounds and had been seen to stun an ox with his fist. His muscles were like springs and he moved with a cougar's grace. Besides that, he had the reputation of being able to walk faster, shoot straighter and fight better than any other man in the upper Skeena region. But he was an advocate of peace, even in his drinking.

Above all, Gun-an-noot prided himself on his family. His young wife was pretty, slight of figure, with dark dancing eyes. They had two children, a girl and a boy. The boy was still a baby, carried on his mother's back, swathed in moss in a board cradle. They lived at Kispiox village on the Haguilite reserve, half an hour's ride from the Two-Mile House. There they owned a small store. When the police subsequently took it over, its contents were assessed at two hundred dollars. During Gun-an-noot's absence on his trapline in the winter, or prospecting in the summer, his wife managed the store. This sharing of business responsibility by an Indian with his wife was as unusual as was his setting of himself up as a store-keeper. The Gun-an-noots were saving money because they were ambitious for their children and planned to hire a tutor so that their young ones would speak perfect English and learn to live in the white man's way.

"Gun-an-noot" is a transliteration of "Zghum-min-hoot," or "the Little Bear That Climbs Trees," as the bearer of the name was known among the Kispiox tribe, an offshoot of the great Carrier nation, which, before the white man's coming, controlled the central interior of what is now British Columbia. They were given their name by the early traders because of a peculiar habit of their widows. This was to save a few bones from their husbands' cremations and carry them for two or three years in a pouch hung from their waists.

As a child, Gun-an-noot had learned what it is to be linked to the word "murder." One day he and his younger brother and a few neighbouring children had been playing with a loaded musket. The brother pulled the trigger and, seeing that he had killed one of his playmates, ran away into the forest. Before the bereaved and outraged parents, summoned by the shot and the cries of the children, Gun-an-noot stood his ground — though he was aware that he might be held hostage for his brother's wrong.

The father of the dead child said to Gun-an-noot, "We will not take you. There is murder in your blood. Instead your family will pay us your height in blankets."

A few days before the murders along the Skeena River trail Gun-an-noot had sold his winter catch of fur. An astute trader, he had bargained until he got a fair price at the trading post in Hazelton. He had appeared at the Two-Mile House the night before the inquest to celebrate the deal by having a few drinks with "the boys." It was against the law to serve liquor to Indians. However, the portly proprietor, a Mr. Cameron, who had lately come from parts unknown, had lenient views and believed that a man with money, whatever the colour of his skin, should be allowed to spend it. Gun-an-noot, like many big men, held his liquor well. This night his very sobriety was to tell against him. Stacked behind the bar was a .30-.30 rifle. It belonged to a man named Charles

Fulmore, who, taken with premature hunger, went into the kitchen about midnight to prepare breakfast. When the subject of marksmanship came up, Gun-an-noot took the rifle and a lantern and, with a few cronies, went outside. Hanging the lantern in a tree, he turned and walked thirty paces away from it. He now asked to be blindfolded. When this was done he faced the tree and put four of the six shots through the lantern, smashing it and dousing the flame. Back in the bar he paid Cameron for the lantern and returned the rifle to its place. During the early morning hours someone stole Fulmore's rifle — but not Gun-an-noot, who was to leave the Two-Mile House empty-handed. Someone else needed a rifle an hour or two before McIntosh and Leclaire were murdered.

Most of the witnesses at the inquest were suffering from the pervasive hangover but, though the evidence they gave was confused on some points, they agreed that soon after midnight when he had come back into the bar Gun-an-noot had "words" with McIntosh. Until now, money in his pocket from his fur sale, Gun-an-noot had "stood" most of the drinks, McIntosh and Leclaire partaking liberally of them. Suddenly McIntosh, who was notoriously tight-fisted, called for "drinks on the house."

Gun-an-noot chided him and, laughing, said to those at the bar, "Mac is opening up his heart." McIntosh, perceiving the taunt, replied that he could buy more than drinks with his money. Someone asked him, "What, for instance?"

"Women . . . they all have their price." And looking at Gun-an-noot, "Yes, even your Christian squaw."

McIntosh, a man who became mean after a few drinks, must have known that this was dangerous ground. Gun-an-noot was a Catholic and his wife a staunch worker for the Church among her people.

McIntosh, stocky, well built, hard from a rigorous life in the mountains, nevertheless was choosing an opponent who outweighed him by fifty pounds, the champion fighter and outdoorsman of the Skeena Valley. The enmity between the two was not new. McIntosh, as a halfbreed, was fully accepted neither by the Kispiox Indians nor the white settlers. He envied Gun-an-noot his assured standing among both, and if he could challenge or humiliate the other would raise himself in his own esteem.

Now he said, emphasizing his words, "Sure — any one of them on the reserve can be bought. I know because I've done it — and Mrs. Gun-an-noot, too."

There was a roar as from a wounded grizzly. Gun-an-noot picked McIntosh up and hurled him, like a sack of flour, into a corner of the bar. Leclaire, McIntosh's partner, leaped upon Gun-an-noot's back and was pulled off by Peter Hi-ma-dan, the Indian's brother-in-law. The fight became general and was broken up only when Fulmore, Richard Hamilton, a mail driver from the Cariboo, and Cameron, the barkeeper, forced Gun-an-noot and Hi-ma-dan to the door. Furniture had been smashed, McIntosh's finger ripped and broken, and Gun-an-noot's nose bloodied.

At the door, going out with Hi-ma-dan — like himself, unarmed — Gun-an-noot swung about and shouted to McIntosh, "Someday I'll fix you, good!" It was not a mere drunken threat. Everyone at the inquest testified that the two Kispiox Indians were sober, as distinct from the rest of the crowd, excepting the three who had pushed them to the door. A drunken man could not have shot the flame from a lantern blindfolded — nor, for that matter, could many men who were completely sober.

This sobriety was regarded as highly incriminating. Drunken men, so it was decided at the inquest, could not have fired the shots which dispatched McIntosh and Leclaire from their world of brawls and petty misdemeanours. Sober men must, therefore, have committed the crime — and Gun-an-noot and his brother-in-law were sober.

The logic was unsound, but convincing if it were assumed that the cause of the two deaths was rooted in the disturbance at the Two-Mile House. There for all to hear, Gun-an-noot had avowed that he would "fix" McIntosh. Peter Hi-ma-dan was his companion — and a few short hours later McIntosh and his partner were found dead upon the trail. Had the records of McIntosh and Leclaire been searched they might have revealed that the two men had enemies present the night before their deaths who might have taken this opportunity to pay off old grudges. Constable Kirby, the chief policeman involved, made no such search.

Finally settling the guilt of Gun-an-noot and Hi-ma-dan was their failure to appear at the inquest. All others for whom word had gone out appeared. In the clouded circumstances the jury brought down its fateful verdict: "We, having heard the evidence relating to the above case, have come to the conclusion that Alec McIntosh was killed by a gunshot wound on the morning of the 19th inst. between Two-Mile creek and the hospital are agreed that it was a case of wilful murder by a person of the name of Simon Gun-an-noot (Indian) of Kispiox village."

In the second verdict, concerning the death of Max Leclaire, Peter Hi-ma-dan was associated with his brother-in-law as an accomplice. A reward of five hundred dollars was posted for the arrest of either man.

Immediately after the inquest Cameron, the saloonkeeper, vanished and was never seen again on the upper Skeena. It would seem to be highly suspicious that a man would so readily abandon a business he had but lately established. No notice was taken of it. More than thirteen years later Constable Kirby was to admit in the courthouse in Vancouver that "Gun-an-noot was the only one I looked for."

On the other hand, Kirby's preoccupation with Gun-an-noot was in keeping with popular opinion. Renegades though they were, McIntosh and Leclaire had relatives and friends who were so convinced of the Indians' guilt that they threatened a lynching when they found them. Others now remembered that Gun-an-noot had become "overbearing" and asked by what right he alone among the Indians had set himself as a storekeeper. Gun-an-noot, they said, had been getting "too big for his boots." Under the pressure Kirby could not be idle. He had to act.

His first move was to confine Nah-gun, Gun-an-noot's aged father, in the Hazelton jail. This was the procedure adopted by Sergeant Colebrook with Sounding Sky, father of Almighty Voice. Knowing the close bonds between the two, Kirby thought that the arrest would bring Gun-an-noot in to face his accusers. In charge of the jail he put a boastful and garrulous deputy, "Windy" Johnson.

Wily old Nah-gun was not the sort to remain behind bars. Allowed to exercise in the log stockade adjoining the jail, he soon discovered that the outhouse, though entered from the inside, was built outside the walls. He also discovered that two of its boards were loose. The third evening, he escaped into the mountains, probably pulling up his trousers as he ran. His jailer from then on, no longer so boastful, was known as "Silent" Johnson.

Meanwhile Gun-an-noot and Hi-ma-dan had taken to the hills. In later years Gun-an-noot said that he had wanted to attend the inquest. His father, Nah-gun, who before Kirby took him in had gone out into the forest to visit his son, advised him not to come in. Feeling ran too high, he said. It would be wiser for Gun-an-noot to disappear for a while until tempers cooled. This was especially so because he was an Indian. Gun-an-noot, he added, had no reason to take seriously McIntosh's accusation against his wife. Everyone knew that she had been faithful.

Before he left, Gun-an-noot shot the five horses in his corral to deprive his pursuers of their use. He knew that he and Hi-ma-dan could move more quickly on foot —and, besides, hoofmarks would betray where they had gone.

The upper Skeena is sometimes referred to as the "northern tropics." Devil's club, salal, thick-growing alder, and willow crowd its valleys, and tight forests of spruce clothe its mountainous slopes. If a horse strayed from the beaten way, a new trail had to be cut for it. Further, horses must stop to feed. A man in prime condition would soon leave his mounted pursuer behind, travelling days without halt and shedding, with moccasined feet, hardly a trace of his passage.

To Constable Kirby, armed with a warrant and supported by a group of sworn deputies, Gun-an-noot's wife denied knowledge of her husband's whereabouts. Doubtless she spoke the truth.

Days are long in the North in June, and Kirby and his followers pushed their search into the evening, fording the Kispiox on their horses. There they heard howling in the distance. In a forest clearing they came upon fourteen dogs tied to trees. They were pack animals Gun-an-noot used on his winter trapline, and he had tied them up, guessing where Kirby would ford the river and knowing that their howling would distract the constable and his men from his trail. Kirby returned with the dogs to Kispiox village.

This set the pattern of a fantastic pursuit of a will-o'-the-wisp that was to endure for the next thirteen years. Gun-an-noot, during the first night, slipped back to his house to learn from his wife that he was charged with murder. Leaving, prepared for a long absence, he took with him two pairs of snowshoes. Before they met again, his young wife, who would wait for him through the years, would be middle-aged, his children would be adolescent, and he himself would be a man old beyond his time and looking towards the grave.

Until that far date in the future — June 24, 1919 — Gun-an-noot became a phantom, a frequenter of a strange, shadowed land. He was forever across another river, behind another ridge or beyond a farther mountain. He and Peter Hi-ma-dan — who, in 1910, was to die of pneumonia along a winter trail — travelled light with blankets, a tea billy and rifles. They lived off a country where rabbits, grouse, deer and moose usually were plentiful. The police, on the other hand, were burdened with the conventional impediments — tents and grub boxes packed on horses. In the winter their time away from base would be limited by what they could carry on their backs. In addition, Gun-an-noot was in home territory. Here, over the passes, along the creeks, he had trapped and hunted since a boy with his father as mentor.

The upper Skeena, north from Hazelton, may be likened to a great fir tree fallen into the mountains. Innumerable branches, or side streams, join with the parent trunk. The tip, or headwaters, lies up against the source of the west-flowing Stikine and close to Telegraph Creek. Beyond are Dease Lake and the Atlin country. To the northeast is the Finlay, which, joining with the Parsnip, empties eastward through the Rocky Mountains as the Peace, the only river on the continent which, rising on their western slope, breaks eastward through them. A lower branch of the Skeena bends southwest to drain ninety-five-mile-long Babine Lake. South and east of Babine Lake are the headwaters of the Nechako, a far-western reach of the mighty Fraser. This was the territory — ten thousand square miles of muskeg, forest, canyon, plateau and mountain slope — which, for more than a decade, was to be the hideout of "the Little Bear That Climbs Trees."

Reports came in that he had been seen in the Yukon, in the Atlin country and on the head of the Finlay. None of them proved valid when, after weeks, and sometimes months of toil, they were followed up.

Within a year the case had attracted more than local

attention — though the outside public had other significant affairs before it. The "horseless carriage," for example. In the summer of 1906, Vancouver papers played up the names of J. S. Rear and W. H. Kimpton, who had bought a "Model K," thirty-horsepower, four-cylinder car in Seattle and driven the hundred and fifty miles north to the Canadian city in fourteen hours. On the way they passed through "swamps and wallows."

The British Columbia government, however, could not neglect its task on the upper Skeena. A murder charge could not be lightly dropped, nor possible criminals permitted to run at large to encourage others. This latter point was especially relevant in the developing North. Rumours grew that the Skeena was a lawless region. Prospectors and settlers were turning away from it in 1907.

In that summer the government called in two men from Pinkerton's National Detective Agency in New York at a cost of fifteen thousand dollars. Possibly professional pride forbade their calling upon the Northwest Mounted Police, which now, as the Royal Canadian Mounted Police, patrols the province.

The Pinkerton men went north to Hazelton. The agency has no present record of their journey, nor of what two New Yorkers felt when they looked out on the northern forest. Perhaps they merely hummed the appropriate tune, "My Pretty Red Wing," a currently popular song. When they returned in the fall, apparently without sifting the evidence of the inquest, the two fugitives were still free.

In November, Provincial Constable Otway Wilkie from Vancouver led a party of four into the wilderness. Winter was selected as a propitious season, for the valleys would be more open when the trees and bushes had shed their leaves and a man would leave snowshoe tracks when he travelled. By pack horse and raft Wilkie moved two tons of supplies from Hazelton two hundred miles north to Bear Lake and put up a winter camp. From it they scouted the Sustut, Otseka and Ingenika; the Kettle, the Omineca and the farthest fringes of the upper Skeena, all within the limits of what was to become known as "Gun-an-noot country." In their travels they passed the peak shown today on the map as "Mount Gun-an-noot."

In dead winter they covered hundreds of miles, breaking their snowshoes in down-timber, losing their dogs, and returning to camp half starved and nearly frozen. They saw no sign of Gun-an-noot — but Gun-an-noot, as he revealed later, saw them. On a cold December day he and Peter Hi-ma-dan were returning in late afternoon down a box canyon on the headwaters of the Skeena, where they had set rabbit snares. Suddenly Peter, who was leading, put up his hand and pointed. Wilkie and another man, heads down, carrying packs, were approaching the entrance to the canyon from the right. The hunted men knew the two belonged to Wilkie's party and Wilkie later confirmed that he was one of them. Probably less than a hundred men were trapping on the Skeena that winter. It was the business of Gun-an-noot to know the territory of each of them. The movement of Wilkie's party was the winter's gossip, and news of their approach always preceded their arrival. Indian trappers passed it on to Gun-an-noot. In another fifty yards Wilkie would cross the incoming snowshoe trail of Gun-an-noot and Peter. The two Indians, in a blind canyon whose walls they could not scale, would be trapped.

Peter dropped behind a rock, raised his rifle, and aimed it at Wilkie. Quickly Gun-an-noot crouched beside him and, putting his thumb under the hammer, whispered to his partner to wait. He was astute. Had he pushed the barrel of the rifle upward the pressure on Peter's finger might have triggered it. The mere movement probably would have revealed their presence to the watchful Wilkie.

It was near twilight. Apparently Wilkie thought it was time to return to camp. At any rate, after a few more steps, he and his companion paused and talked. With a final glance up the canyon — and within a dozen paces of the snowshoe track which through months of bitter cold they had been seeking and as close as that to likely death from a .30-.30 bullet — they turned back upon their trail and disappeared into the forest.

From that day on, Gun-an-noot seldom lost track of the Wilkie party. Shadowed, he became the shadower, careful always to move so that his snowshoe tracks would not be crossed by those who regarded themselves as his pursuers. The white men stayed low in the valleys. The Indians travelled high, as is the habit of native hunters who must command the country to live.

The winter of 1907-08 was severe with heavy snow. In mid-February, Gun-an-noot and Peter were in a cave without fire on the slope of Gun-an-noot mountain watching Wilkie's main camp beside the river half a mile below them. The hunting had been poor. Moose, deer, even grouse and rabbits seemed to have fled the land. The outlaws were starved and half frozen, and on this morning were considering surrender as an alternative to their desperate plight.

As a rule when Wilkie went out on patrol, at least one man remained to guard the camp. On this morning the entire group of five set out under heavy packs. Wilkie had decided to call off the manhunt, leaving behind him a well-stocked cache of bacon, flour, tea, beans, rice and sugar. Gun-an-noot and Peter, suspecting a trap, waited until the next morning before going down to avail themselves of the good things so providentially offered. Ironically these supplies, left behind by those sent out to apprehend them, carried the Indians through the critical days of their indecision and well on into spring. Gun-an-noot was to say that had Wilkie not come out after him he and Peter would have had to come in and give themselves up in February, 1908. It was a turning point. From that time on his material fortunes improved.

After 1910, when Peter Hi-ma-dan had died, Gun-an-noot, now alone, was in touch with George Biernes, a government packer on the Telegraph Creek trail to the Yukon. This trail had been part of an ambitious project to stretch a telegraph line between New York and London by way of Alaska, the Bering Strait, Siberia and St. Petersburg. The undertaking was abandoned on the laying of the Atlantic cable in 1865, but the trail which had been cut through northern British Columbia has been kept open until the present day.

Biernes and Gun-an-noot had often hunted together, and a meeting between them on familiar territory came naturally. Gun-an-noot knew that the police had closed his store and confiscated its stock — this though they had still to prove that he was a criminal. Fearing that his wife and children might be in want, he showed Biernes a cache where he would leave the fur he trapped. Biernes would sell the fur and deliver the proceeds to Mrs. Gun-an-noot. Throughout his long exile Gun-an-noot cared for his family. More than that, he commissioned Biernes to hire a missionary named Thorkerson to tutor his children. Biernes observed that Gun-an-noot's concern was not for himself but for those dependent upon him and that he was haggard with worry for them.

In the late spring of 1918, R. T. Hawkins of the Yukon Telegraph Line met Gun-an-noot on the head of the Stikine. Gun-an-noot was hungry for companionship and he showed that he was familiar with Hawkins' movements since the latter had come into the country and aware of what was happening within a radius of a hundred miles. Gun-an-noot exchanged a haunch of caribou meat for beans and bacon.

Hawkins urged him to surrender, telling him that the government would provide counsel. Gun-an-noot replied that when he had two thousand dollars he would come in and pay his own way.

The next summer Gun-an-noot walked into the camp of Mr. and Mrs. Campbell Johnston of Vancouver, who were investigating the Ground Hog coal felds northwest of Hazelton. When they, too, tried to convince him to stand trial, he answered as he had to Hawkins.

Although his head now bore a price of a thousand dollars, none of the several people from outside who met him, nor any of the many trappers and prospectors who knew his whereabouts, attempted to turn him in. Sentiment, against him in the beginning, was turning strongly in his favour. The current opinion was that even if he had shot McIntosh or Leclaire the world was well rid of their carcasses. Gun-an-noot, always evading those sent to capture him, and at the same time providing for his family, had become a living, almost a cherished legend. Informers, on whom police depend in such a manhunt, "clammed up."

All this while, of course, the Provincial Police had not been inactive. Other "bean-pot brigades" on a less ambitious scale than Wilkie's had taken to the trail in the summer months, his experience having discouraged further winter forays. These parties came back with strange tales. They woke in the morning and missed a pound of tea, a bag of sugar, or a tin of syrup. Replacing what had been taken, they often found a brace of grouse or a cut of venison. In that nettled and forested country where a man, at times, could not see beyond an arm's length, they swore that more than once when they paused for rest they had heard a breathing beside them in the thicket. Gun-an-noot chose carefully those before whom he appeared. To others he was still "the invisible man."

Now, beyond his ken, a catastrophe was brewing which for four years would make him forgotten as well as invisible. Over the seas the German Kaiser was preparing for war, and until after the Armistice, November 11, 1918, the search for Gun-an-noot was suspended, though nominally it remained in effect.

However, unless death itself intervenes, a murder warrant, even one of thirteen years' standing, must be served if the law of the land is to have meaning and if the police are to retain their authority. Accordingly, in the late spring of 1919, John Kelly, now Chief Constable at Hazelton, made ready for another expedition into the wilderness.

However, a more effective force was at work. Biernes — who died, seventy years old, in 1953 on his ranch in the Kispiox Valley — had not lost touch with the wanted man and had now interested a Vancouver lawyer, Stuart Henderson, in the case. Henderson, born in Scotland in 1864, the son of a stonecutter, since coming to British Columbia as a young man had made a name for himself in criminal law as the champion of the "underdog." He went north to meet Gun-an-noot.

Biernes, after many failures, had persuaded Gun-an-noot to come to an abandoned cabin five miles outside of Kispiox village at noon on July 24. He met Henderson in Hazelton and rode out with him to the meeting place, leading a horse for Gun-an-noot. Their horses tied to trees outside, for four hours they waited inside the cabin, behind the open door. Henderson was impatient and about to stand up to leave when, silent as a shadow, Gun-an-noot stood in the doorway. He had walked sixty miles that day to his appointment.

The three men talked until dusk. Gun-an-noot was afraid of the "white man's justice." Henderson assured him that he would have a fair trial. Biernes told him that his wife was not well and that she needed him. Almost reluctantly Gun-an-noot agreed to give himself up — but only when he had made sure that Biernes could advance Henderson two thousand dollars saved from the sale of fur trapped during his years of outlawry.

They had ridden three miles downriver towards Hazelton when Gun-an-noot, who was last, pulled up his horse. He stared long and silently at the mountains. Then he dropped his head, wheeled his horse and, at a walk, proceeded back whence they had come. He could not face the prospect of giving up his hazardous freedom for months behind prison bars.

Biernes, who knew his man, called after him tauntingly, "You are afraid. I did not think Simon Gun-an-noot would be afraid."

Henderson, following the cue, said loudly to Biernes, "I have wasted too much time already on this case. I would not have come at all if I had known that Gun-an-noot would be afraid."

They said no more and continued on towards Hazelton. Within half a mile they were overtaken by galloping hooves. Gun-an-noot followed them without a word into Hazelton. "The Little Bear That Climbs Trees" had climbed high enough. It was time to come down. In Hazelton he insisted on going alone to the police barracks.

Chief Constable Kelly, who had been put on the alert by Biernes, was waiting at his desk. Gun-an-noot walked in. He said, "I am Simon Gun-an-noot. I come to give myself in."

It was Kelly's first glimpse of the notorious fugitive. Now, instinctively, his eyes turned from the tall, travel-worn figure before him to three rifles in a rack on the wall.

Gun-an-noot, watching, said, "You don't want to be 'fraid of me. You never saw me before, but I know you − and I could have shot you many times out on the trail."

Put behind bars, under restraint for the first time in his life, Gun-an-noot sat down on the bench and cold sweat so drenched his clothes that they had to be changed.

Remanded to a higher court, he was taken south to Vancouver and lodged in Oakalla prison until October 7, when he faced the jury at the Assizes Court on Georgia Street.

Interest was intense, and line-ups formed before the court's doors were open. Nevertheless, Gun-an-noot's trial did not make the front page. The *Vancouver Daily Province* devoted its headlines to "the imminent collapse" of Bolshevism, the illness of U.S. President Woodrow Wilson, the

Japanese threat to Asia, and to a Robert Leeson, sourdough, then on his way to Ulster to claim the estate of the Earl of Milltown. The postbellum year of 1919 was the dawn of the short-skirted flapper's era.

Gun-an-noot's concern, however, did not extend beyond the courtroom, and his world was confined within its walls. Plucked from his ancestral home in the North, instead of the murmur of mountain rivers he listened to the drone of voices disputing his fate and instead of the creak of wind-blown trees, or the lonely howl of the timber wolf, he heard behind the courthouse on Robson Street the backfiring of automobiles and the clang of streetcar bells. All his life he had been independent, asking no one's help, and free to roam where his fancy led. Now his every movement was dictated to him and the question of whether he would live or die was with judge and jury, men whom he had never seen before. Small wonder that his eyes were "alert" as he tried to follow the intricacies of legal procedure in which he was ensnared like a blind man in a tight growth of tall willows.

The Crown prosecutor in the trial was Alex Henderson, K.C., who had been a student at Osgoode Hall in Toronto with his opponent, Stuart Henderson. Unknown to him, among the spectators was a law student, H. E. M. Bradshaw, who was to inherit his practice. The prosecutor, a former athlete, was red-cheeked and stocky and wore pince-nez. In contrast, counsel for the defence was tall and spare and, as he leaned forward to make a point with the jury, had a "hawklike"aspect. Mr. Justice Gregory presided.

Gun-an-noot was here charged with a single crime, the murder of Alec McIntosh. That McIntosh had been murdered was not contested by the Defence. In the circumstances, suicide was ruled out and no justification for the killing was alleged to support the lesser charges of manslaughter. The question was, did the evidence as adduced condemn to death the man at the bar, Simon Gun-an-noot, Indian, of Kispiox village?

Most of the witnesses called thirteen years earlier had attended the Hazelton inquest into the deaths of McIntosh and Max Leclaire. The years had mellowed them and they were now markedly favourable to Gun-an-noot. An exception was James. E. Kirby, constable at Hazelton in 1906, whose professional reputation was at stake.

Under cross-examination by Stuart Henderson he said that he had known the murdered man, Alec McIntosh, since 1893 and had jailed him many times. On the other hand, he admitted that the accused's reputation had been good, "for an Indian, very good."

He had protested against the issuance of a licence for the Two-Mile House, where the trouble began before the murder. "I predicted it would develop into a tough place – and it did," said Kirby.

When he came upon McIntosh's body he had not been able to find the spot from which the shot had been fired "because the ground was spongy and the tracks had disappeared." Defence counsel suggested that, on the contrary, the soft ground would have yielded up the tracks had he searched diligently.

He had arrested Nah-gun, Gun-an-noot's father, because he was on his way to Kispiox village, where he lived. "If that was a suspicious action on the part of Nah-gun, a lot of us might be arrested," commented Stuart Henderson.

Cameron, the innkeeper, had been summoned the day after the inquest, charged with selling liquor to Indians. He did not appear. The witness, however, would not grant that he had "disappeared," although he had not set eyes on him since.

Stuart Henderson, after stating that Cameron might have had to pay a small fine for his offence in serving liquor to an Indian, said to Kirby, "Do you expect the Court to believe that that alone was sufficent reason to account for his flight and for him to give up the Two-Mile House, which he had so recently opened and in which he had invested money?" To the rhetorical question the policeman made no reply.

Referring to Kirby's denial that Cameron had "disappeared," defence counsel asked, "Then why did you say that Simon Gun-an-noot had disappeared?

"Because I searched for him."

"Then there was just a hunt for one man, not an investigation of the state of affairs?"

"I was hunting for just one man."

"Your mind was made up that Simon was guilty?"

"He was the only one I looked for," replied Kirby.

Dr. H. C. Wrinch, who had performed the post-mortem, testified that McIntosh had been dead "two or three hours" when he saw the body soon after nine in the morning. The bullet that killed him had been fired "from a distance of from ten to twenty feet," and the dead man, perhaps knowing that he was in danger, "must have been leaning far forward in the saddle as he galloped for his life." The killer had possibly been kneeling or lying down.

Peter Barney, who as a fifteen-year-old boy had seen McIntosh and Leclaire ride off in different directions while he was herding cows the morning of June 19, 1906, declared under cross-examination that he had also seen Gun-an-noot.

Mr. Justice Gregory interrupted the examination to ask the witness if Gun-an-noot, who left the Two-Mile House before McIntosh, had taken the same direction as the murdered man. Barney said, "They rode off in opposite directions."

The trial lasted three days. Stuart Henderson called no witnesses, resting his defence upon cross-examination of those called by the Crown. Nor did he ask Gun-an-noot to testify on his own behalf, thereby denying to the Crown the right to cross-examine the prisoner. Alex Henderson, as a prosecuting attorney, was noted for his ability to trip a witness on his own words.

Summing up for the Defence on October 9, the last day of the trial, Stuart Henderson pointed out to the jury that the Crown had not succeeded in placing Gun-an-noot at the scene of the crime. "The Crown's own witness," he declared, "Peter Barney, has testified that, on leaving the inn, Gun-an-noot rode in one direction and McIntosh in another." Further, the dead man trifled with native women. He would have many enemies who might well have taken advantage of his altercation with Gun-an-noot to put the blame for the crime on the accused. They had heard that Cameron, the innkeeper, had fled the country the day after the inquest. Probably others had vanished whose trails the police had likewise failed to follow. Here he turned and, pointing to Kirby, stigmatized him as a man whose mind had room for "only one idea at a time." Trials such as this were held because the police often arrested the wrong man. In conclusion he stated, "The prisoner has already been punished for a crime he did not commit by thirteen years of exile in a harsh northern wilderness. Throughout that time he provided for his family. He endured his exile because he was afraid that he would not receive justice in a white man's courtroom. It remains with you, the jury, to prove to him that his fears were groundless."

Alex Henderson, the Crown prosecutor, taking over from his friend — outside the courtroom they were intimate — derided his description of the prisoner's "exile." "This 'harsh northern wilderness,'" he said, "is, in reality, a hunter's paradise where game abounds. It has been the home of Gun-an-noot's people for hundreds of years. Put him down in the city and he might starve, but up there where he was born, where he knows every trail and every river, he lived like a wilderness prince." The prisoner, he insisted, had indicted himself. An innocent man would long ago have come in to confront his accusers.

Charging the jury, Mr. Justice Gregory advised them that the accused did not have to prove himself innocent. The Crown must show that he was guilty. On the circumstantial evidence — and no other had been brought before the Court — the rule was that "such evidence must not only be consistent with the accused's guilt but" — and he put heavy stress upon the second point — "inconsistent with any other conclusion."

After deliberating fifteen minutes the jury acquitted the prisoner. The charge relating to the murder of Leclaire was withdrawn as it rested on evidence already given — and, because only the one murder was considered, the mystery of the matching bullet holes in the two bodies was not discussed.

Gun-an-noot was free to return to his Northland, to the smell of campfire smoke and the roar of lordly rivers. But he was now a broken, beaten man. During thirteen years of banishment he had seen his hope of raising his family in the white man's way denied by the white man's law. Even deeper than the mark of the thirteen years was the one left by the months in prison and the harassment of legal procedure. Pronounced "not guilty" by the court, he was a man branded in his own eyes by what he had borne to regain a freedom that was his by heritage. Leaving the dock, he collapsed and spent a month in the hospital to recover.

In late November he went back to the upper Skeena. There

his father, old Nah-gun, was dying. He asked to be buried on the shore of Bowser Lake, sixty miles north into the mountains from Kispiox village. There he had been a boy and there he had taught Gun-an-noot to hunt. Gun-an-noot in the spring carried him in on his back, dug into the ground, and left him at peace under the budding poplar leaves.

That fall he and George Biernes, as further payment of a debt, took Stuart Henderson, his able defender, on a hunting trip. The burden of the trip fell on Biernes. Gun-an-noot, the man who had never before yielded first place on the trail, complained of being "tired."

When the hunt was over, the man with whose name he was now linked in legal history, had gone south with his moose head and his bear hide, Gun-an-noot confided in Biernes that he would hunt no more. To his wife and children he said that he must tend more carefully his father's grave.

A few years later he walked into Bowser Lake, caught pneumonia and died. He lies there today by his father's side. His secret, if he had one, was buried with him. Simon Gun-an-noot, Indian, of Kispiox village at last was beyond the reach of the white man's law.

The Grass Man and Walker among Trees

Until quite recent years two obscure and little-known peaks, Mount Hooker and Mount Brown, were, even by experts in the field, thought to be the highest on the North American continent south of the Yukon and Alaska and north of Mexico. Others, also familiar with the Rockies, contended that no such peaks existed.

Looming over the Hudson's Bay Company's old fur trail at Athabaska Pass, where it drops down to the Big Bend of the Columbia, their heights above the sea were set at 15,700 and 16,000 feet respectively. The controversy was not finally settled until the summer of 1920, when the Inter-Provincial (Alberta-British Columbia) Boundary Survey Commission cut them down to size, establishing the height of Mount Hooker as only 10,782 feet and that of Mount Brown as 9,156 feet.

The myth of their supremacy began as far back as 1827, when fur brigades, with the creak of runners on brittle snow, the crack of whips, and the imprecations of French Canadian and Métis drivers, regularly crossed the Athabaska Pass on their journeys between Hudson Bay and the mouth of the Columbia, a distance of nearly three thousand miles. With one of these brigades in the spring of that year travelled a young Scottish botanist, son of a stonemason, who made the first ascent of Mount Brown — indeed, the first recorded ascent in the Canadian Rockies — and, on his return to the old country, published his mistaken findings to the world. They were accepted and for generations appeared on maps of the British Admiralty, on maps in general, and in textbooks throughout the world.

The young Scotsman who had come around the Horn on this, his first voyage to western North America, and who was to suffer a grisly death in an animal pit in the then Sandwich Islands a few years later, is a forgotten man today though he has left his name on the land. The tree named after him, the Douglas fir, being the most merchantable timber in the Northwest, stands on mountain slopes from northern British Columbia south to New Mexico. The same young botanist was responsible for the fact that the first discovery of gold in California was made *in England* in 1831. It was found on the roots of trees which, during a subsequent sojourn on the West Coast, he sent back to the Horticultural Society of London.

David Douglas — not to be confused with the Sir James Douglas who became the first Governor of British Columbia in 1858 — was born June 25, 1799, in the town of Old Scone, now abandoned except for its castle, but once the site of the crowning of Scottish kings. When he was twelve years old he quit school and went to work as an assistant gardener on the nearby estate of the Earl of Mansfield. He had already taken to the collection of plants and seeds as a hobby, gathering them in solitary walks through the rugged countryside, developing qualities of independence and observation which were to stand him in good stead in the mountains of the Far West. He was also a studious reader of botanical works, so much so that by 1820 he was able to join the staff of the Botanical Gardens in Glasgow. Here he attended lectures given by a famous professor of botany from the city's university, William Jackson Hooken, whose name Douglas was later to hang upon a Rocky Mountain peak.

In the spring of 1823 he went to London and joined the Horticultural Society on the recommendation of Professor Hooker. That August, the directors sent him on a four-month collecting expedition to the eastern United States — no small tribute to a man, only twenty-four years old, who had been in their employ less than half a year. His real life, however, began after his return when in the succeeding July he set out, via Cape Horn, in the Hudson's Bay Company's ship *William and Ann* for the Company's post near the mouth of the Columbia, where he arrived April 12, 1825. The Horticultural Society had put him under "the protection" of the great fur-trading company because their posts were the only permanent bases in the western wilderness. The Hudson's Bay Company had absorbed the Northwesters, their rivals, in 1821, and now held the Oregon territory in common with the Americans, following the Treaty of Ghent of 1818.

At the HBC post, Fort Vancouver, a hundred miles up the river, where he was to pass the next twenty-three months botanizing in the valley of the lower Columbia, Douglas won and kept the valuable friendship of Chief Factor Dr. John McLoughlin, who put horses and guides at his disposal and even lent him his favourite saddle horse. McLoughlin, a generous man to all wayfarers, was to be designated as "the very Christ of Northwest occupation" by the most noted of western historians, Hubert Howe Bancroft.

David Douglas, the first white man other than trader or hunter to visit this territory, was, in those days, shy and diffident, though he later became quickly outspoken and on one occasion was to denounce the men of the HBC, his benefactors, as having "no interest above a beaver skin." A contemporary said of him a few years later when he was thirty-one, "a fair, florid, partially bald Scotsman of medium stature and gentlemanly address, about forty-eight years of age." By then a rigorous life in a hard country had taken its toll and Douglas, his eyes weakened by snow blindness, had lost part of his sight.

He left Fort Vancouver for far-off Hudson Bay on March 20, 1827, travelling with the annual express on the journey which was to bring him to the foot of Mount Brown. His companions, and the Indians, now knew him as "the grass man." He called himself only "a culler of weeds."

The party, in command of a company clerk, Edward Ermatinger, a year older than Douglas, travelled upriver in two flat-bottomed Columbia river boats with pointed prows, each propelled by paddles in the hands of seven singing, roistering voyageurs. The young botanist jotted down in his diary that these men made light of hardship. Any one of them who complained was dubbed a "pork eater" — a term of denigration in the mouths of those whose pride it was to live off the chase.

Douglas walked some of the way along the riverbank, gathering seeds and plants to add to the collection he had with him. At Fort Colville on April 12 the brigade split up and Douglas proceeded north with Ermatinger and the boat crew of four French Canadians and three Iroquois Indians. Lining their boat though the perilous Dalles de Mort — "Rapids of Death" — they reached the outlet of the Canoe River at the Big Bend of the Columbia on April 27. From here, at the Big Bend, where the river rounds the northern-most point of the Selkirk range, they could look south, between that range and the Rockies, towards its source in a little lake one degree north of the present border. They left their boat, tied on snowshoes, hoisted sixty-pound packs, and began the ascent to Athabaska Pass.

The snow was soft and heavy and so deep that it often covered the blazes on the trees, more than shoulder-height above the ground, making the trail difficult to follow. The Wood River, along which the trail ran, was open and its icy waters frequently had to be forded. The cold was not severe, never reaching more than a degree or two below zero at night. During the day it thawed, impeding travel. Camp was made around a fire supported by green logs of spruce or bal-sam to keep it from sinking into the snow. Boughs of the same trees were laid for sleeping, sodden clothes hung out on branches to dry. Unused to snowshoes, Douglas, several times a night had to spring from his blankets and put weight on his feet to relieve the cramps in the back of his thighs, known among voyageurs as *mal de raquette*. These cramps are caused by the burden of snow on the snowshoe, which, in soft going, a man lifts with every step he takes, thus pulling the muscles at the back of his thighs.

On the morning of May 1, after the usual pre-dawn start, the little party camped a few hundred yards to the west of Athabaska Pass. From here Douglas ascended Mount Brown and, unwittingly, made himself the father of a legend. His diary for the day reads:

After breakfast, about one o'clock, being well refreshed, I set out with the view of ascending what appeared to be the highest peak on the north or left-hand side. The height from its apparent base exceeds 6,000 feet, 17,000 feet above the level of the sea.

After passing over the lower ridge of about 200 feet, by far the most difficult and fatiguing part, on snowshoes, there was a crust on the snow, over which I walked with the greatest ease. A few mosses and lichens, Andreai and Jungermanniae, were seen. At the elevation of 4,800 feet vegetation no longer exists — not so much as a lichen of any kind to be seen, 1,200 feet of eternal ice. The view from the summit is of that cast too awful to afford pleasure — nothing as far as the eye can reach in every direction by mountains towering above each other, rugged beyond all description; the dazzling reflection from the snow, the heavenly arena of the solid glacier, and the rainbow-like tints of its shattered fragments, together with the enormous icicles suspended from the perpendicular rocks; the majestic but terrible avalanche hurtling down from the southerly exposed rocks producing a crash, and groans through the distant valleys, only equalled by an earthquake. Such gives us a sense of the stupendous and wondrous works of the Almighty. This peak, the highest yet known in the northern continent of America, I felt a sincere pleasure in naming Mount Brown, in honour of R. Brown, Esq., the illustrious botanist, no less distinguished by the amiable qualities of his refined mind. A little to the south is one nearly the same height, rising more into a sharp point, which I named Mount Hooker, in honour of my early patron the enlightened and learned Professor of Botany in the University of Glasgow, Dr. Hooker, to whose kindness I, in a great measure, owe my success hitherto in life, and I feel exceedingly glad of an opportunity for recording a simple but sincere token of my kindest regard for him and respect for his profound talents. I was not on this mountain. Menziesia, Andromeda hypnoides, Gentiana, Lycopodium alpinum, Salix herbacea, Empetrum, and Juncus biglumis and triglumis were among the last of Phanerogamous plants observed.

Wednesday, 2nd — At three o'clock I felt the cold so much, the thermometer stood at only 2° below zero, that I was obliged to rise and enliven the fire and have myself comfortably warmed before starting. Through 300 yards of gradually rising open low pine wood we passed, and about the same distance of open ground took us to the basin of this mighty river, a circular small lake, 20 yards in diameter, in the centre of the valley, with a small outlet at the west end — namely, the Columbia; and a small outlet at the east end — namely, one of the branches of the Athabasca which must be considered one of the tributaries of the McKenzie River.

This is not the only fact of two opposite streams flowing from the same lake.

This, the "Committee Punchbowl," is considered the half-way house. We were glad the more laborious and arduous part of the journey was done. The little stream Athabasca, over which we conveniently stepped, soon assumed a considerable size, and was dashed over cascades and formed cauldrons of limestone and basalt seven miles below the pass; like the tributaries of the Columbia on the west side, the Athabasca widens to a narrow lake and has a much greater descent than the Columbia. At this point the snow was nearly gone, and the temperature greatly increased. Many of the mountains on the right are at all seasons capped with glacier. At ten we stayed to breakfast fifteen miles from the ridge, where we remained four hours. The thermometer this morning stood at 2° below zero, and at 2 p.m. at 57°. We found it dreadfully oppressive. (pp. 71-72.)

There are two main points of interest in the above diary entries. One is Douglas' estimate of the heights of Mounts Brown and Hooker and the second, his mention of the Committee's Punchbowl.

As his biographer, Athelstan George Harvey, points out in his thoughtful *Douglas of the Fir*, his mistake was in believing that at Athabaska Pass he stood at about 12,000 feet above the sea. Travel over the pass virtually ceased in 1846, when the Northwest Boundary Commission settled on the 49th parallel as the dividing line between the United States and Canada, depriving the HBC of its stake in the Oregon Territory. Years before that, settlement had deeply encrouched upon the fur trader's domain. The HBC turned to what is now central and western British Columbia, reached by way of the Peace River canyon and Yellowhead Pass to the south of Peace River.

Athabaska Pass is, in fact, only 5,700 feet high. This was not definitely established, however, until 1893, when A. P. Coleman, geology professor of the University of Toronto, wishing to settle the controversy, led a party on to the headwaters of the river. He climbed Mount Brown and set its height at 9,365 feet. Nevertheless, many people still cherished the earlier myth, questioning whether Coleman had found the right pass. The Inter-Provincial Boundary Commission settled all doubts in 1920.

Harvey, in his biography, shows that many other travellers through the Canadian Rockies have overestimated the mountains' height, even years after Douglas had passed through them, and that before Douglas, David Thompson, who discovered the pass for the Northwesters in 1811, thought the Rockies to be "higher than the Himalayas." Thompson, the first white man to follow the Columbia from its source to the sea, who explored the vast watersheds of the Peace and the Saskatchewan, making maps as he travelled, has been called "the greatest land cartographer who ever lived." Douglas lacked instruments to correct his impressions, based upon the currently accepted altitude of Athabaska Pass. His estimate of the heights of the two peaks above the pass, as distinct from above the sea, are close to the reality. The persistence of the myth is due to the Canadian Rockies being unknown territory until 1885 to few men except fur traders, whose sole interest in mountains was to pass through them. In that year the Canadian Pacific Railway was thrust through the Rockies.

In his second entry Douglas describes the Committee's Punchbowl, but omits the reason for its name. In dead winter brigades of dog teams stopped by it and, because it was the highest point in their journey, broached a keg of rum. Many stories have come down of riotous parties staged around its frozen surface and voyageurs who, crazed with fear as they looked up at the peaks shouldering the starry sky, fell howling into the stunted timber, whence later they crawled back to the campfire or were rescued by their less intoxicated companions. Because of these alpine orgies George Simpson, a governor of the Hudson's Bay Company, crossing the pass westward two years previous to Douglas' journey, gave the tarn its name. "Committee" refers to the Company's governing body.

This little mountain lake, feeding two oceans, the Pacific, and the Arctic, was not the only phenomenon of its sort in the Rockies. Less than a hundred miles to the south were the two-hunded-mile-square Columbia ice-fields which drained through the Columbia to the Pacific, through the North Saskatchewan to Hudson Bay and the Atlantic and through the Athabaska to the Arctic. The Miette River, which Douglas and his party, descending the Athabaska on foot, reached on

May 4, as late as 1910 flowed into the Pacific by way of Yellowhead Lake and the Fraser, and the Arctic by way of the Athabaska. Today it flows only into the Athabaska. Taking two canoes from the Company's cache at the mouth of the Miette, where the present-day town of Jasper stands, the express continued down the Athabaska two hundred miles to Fort Assiniboine and then walked overland to Fort Edmonton on the North Saskatchewan, more than another hundred miles. There, on May 21, Douglas was welcomed by Chief Factor John Rowand. His diary for Wednesday, May 23, treating of a "Calumet" or golden eagle, reads:

A fine young Calumet Eagle, two years old, sex unknown, I had off Mr. Rowand; brought from the Cootanie lands situated in the bosom of the Rocky Mountains near the headwaters of the Saskatchewan River. His plumage is much destroyed by the boys, who had deprived him of those in the tail that were just coming to their true colour. Many strange stories are told of this bird as to strength and ferocity, such as carrying off young deer entire, killing full-grown long-tailed deer, and so on. Certain it is, he is both powerful and ferocious. I have seen all other birds leave their prey on his approach, manifesting the utmost terror. By most of the tribes the tail feathers are highly prized for adorning their war-caps and other garments. The pipestem is also decorated with them, hence comes the name. Abundant at all seasons in the Rocky Mountains, and in winter a few are seen on the mountainous country south of the Columbia on the coast. Are caught as follows: A deep pit is dug in the ground, covered over with small sticks, straw, grass, and a thin covering of earth, in which the hunter takes his seat; a large piece of flesh is placed above, having a string tied to it, the other end held in the hand of the person below. The bird on eyeing the prey instantly descends, and while his talons are fastened in the flesh the hunter pulls bird and flesh into the pit. Scarcely an instance is known of failing in the hunt. Its ferocity is equal to the grisly bear's; will die before he loses his prey. The hunter covers his hands and arms with sleeves of strong deerskin leather for the purpose of preventing him from being injured by his claws. They build in the most inaccessible clefts of the rocks; have two young at a time, being found in June and July. This one had been taken only a few days after hatching and is now docile. The boys who have been in the habit of teasing him for some time past have ruffled his temper, I took and caged him with some difficulty. Had a fresh box made for seeds and another for my journals, portfolio, and sundry articles. Could find no lock to put on it. The river here is broad, four hundred yards, high, clayey, and muddy banks, water muddy. Coal is found in abundance. (pp. 268-69.)

Leaving the hospitality of Fort Edmonton behind him — its people gave a dance in his honour — Douglas descended the North Saskatchewan by riverboat with the express. Eventually — after a side trip to Fort Garry, near the present site of Winnipeg, Manitoba, where he spent a month botanizing — he reached Hudson Bay at York Factory on August 20. He was dismayed to learn that his golden eagle, sent on in advance with the main party, had strangled itself on its leash. His precious seeds and bulbs, however, which he had packed with such care, and carried across a continent, were in good condition.

Douglas sailed on the Company's ship, *The Prince of Wales*, on September 15, 1827. After a fast passage he landed in England on October 11. He was not a well man. While waiting to sail from Hudson Bay he had rowed out with some others to visit his ship. In the bay, because of the shallow water, ships stand well offshore. A sudden squall blew the small boat out to sea. They were tossed about, drenched in rain, for two nights and a day before they could return to land. As a result of this experience Douglas kept to his bunk for most of the voyage and was still not fully recovered when he came into home waters.

He had gone out from England a youth. He returned, at twenty-eight, a true veteran of the western wilderness — a mountain man used to sleeping under a tree, rifle at his side. He felt out of place in the crowded London streets, and as he shouldered his way through the mob his memory called him back to the wide, unpeopled lands that so recently he had known.

He could recall a day in southern Oregon during his search for the sugar pine. A she-grizzly had crossed his path and now rose up to protect her young. Douglas was alone and in the saddle. Horses are inordinately fearful of bear or moose smell. However, Douglas was astride the horse of Dr. McLoughlin, chief factor at Fort Vancouver, no ordinary animal and one that had been taught to "stand" under gunfire.

Douglas rode up to within twenty yards of the grizzly. His first ball, not truly aimed, killed a cub. With the second he mortally wounded — or so he believed — the mother, who retreated into the bush. Douglas, when he returned to camp, made a present of the dead cub to an Indian with whom he was travelling.

The event was hardly a sporting one and it can only be hoped that the mother recovered and found her other young. However, it required a raw courage. Few men armed with a modern rifle and ammunition would dare approach so close to a grizzly and her cubs, and it would be an exceptional horse that would permit one of them to do so.

Douglas found his sugar pine of which he had heard from the Indians, who esteemed its seed as a delicacy. The finding nearly cost him his life. His diary of Thursday, October 26, 1826, reads:

> Weather dull and cloudy. When my people in England are made acquainted with my travels, they may perhaps think I have told them nothing but my miseries. That may be correct, but I now know that such objects as I am in quest of are not obtained without a share of labour, anxiety of mind, and sometimes risk of personal safety. I left my camp this morning at daylight on an excursion, leaving my guide to take care of the camp and horses until my return in the evening, when I found everything as I wished; in the interval he had dried my wet paper as I desired him. About an hour's walk from my camp I was met by an Indian, who on discovering me strung his bow and placed on his left arm a sleeve of racoon-skin and stood ready on the defence. As I was well convinced this was prompted through fear, he never before having seen such a being, I laid my gun at my feet on the ground and waved my hand for him to come to me, which he did with great caution. I made him place his bow and quiver beside my gun, and then struck a light and gave him to smoke a few beads. With my pencil I made a rough sketch of the cone and pine I wanted and showed him it, when he instantly pointed to the hills about fifteen or twenty miles to the south. As I wanted to go in that direction, he seemingly with much good-will went with me. At Midday I reached my long-wished *Pinus* (called by the Umpqua tribe Natele), and lost no time in examining and endeavouring to collect specimens and seeds. New or strange things seldom fail to make great impressions, and often at first we are liable to over-rate them; and lest I should never see my friends to tell them verbally of this most beautiful and im-

mensely large tree, I now state the dimensions of the largest
one I could find that was blown down by the wind: Three feet
from the ground, 57 feet 9 inches in circumference; 134
feet from the ground, 17 feet 5 inches; extreme length, 215
feet. The trees are remarkably straight; bark uncommonly
smooth for such large timber, of a whitish or light brown
colour; and yields a great quantity of gum of a bright amber
colour. The large trees are destitute of branches, generally
for two-thirds the length of the tree; branches pendulous, and
the cones hanging from their points like small sugar-loaves in
a grocer's shop, it being only on the very largest trees that
cones are seen, and the putting myself in possession of three
cones (all I could) nearly brought my life to an end. Being
unable to climb or hew down any, I took my gun and was
busy clipping them from the branches with ball when eight
Indians came at the report of my gun. They were all painted
with red earth, armed with bows, arrows, spears of bone, and
flint knives, and seemed to me anything but friendly. I endeavoured to explain to them what I wanted and they seemed
satisfied and sat down to smoke, but had no sooner done so
than I perceived one string his bow and another sharpen his
flint knife with a pair of wooden pincers and hang it on the
wrist of the righthand, which gave me ample testimony of
their inclination. To save myself I could not do by flight, and
without any hesitation I went backwards six paces and cocked
my gun, and then pulled from my belt one of my pistols,
which I held in my left hand. I was determined to fight for
life. As I as much as possible endeavoured to preserve my
coolness and perhaps did so, I stood eight or ten minutes
looking at them and they at me without a word passing, till
one at last, who seemed to be the leader, made a sign for
tobacco, which I said they should get on condition of going
and fetching me some cones. They went, and as soon as out
of sight I picked up my three cones and a few twigs, and
made a quick retreat to my camp, which I gained at dusk.
(pp. 229-30.)

Douglas' mind might have ranged still further back in time
to July 19, 1825:

Today I visited Cockqua, the principal chief of the Che-
nooks and Chochalii tribes, who is exceedingly fond of all the
chiefs that come from King George — words which they learn
from Broughton, of Vancouver expedition, and other com-
manders of English ships. His acquaintance I previously had.
He imitates all European manners; immediately after saluting
me with "clachouie," their word for "friend," or "How are
you?" and a shake of his hand, water was brought immediately
for me to wash, and a fire kindled. He then carried me to one

of his large canoes, in which lay a sturgeon 10 feet long, 3 at the thickest part in circumference, weighing probably about 400 to 500 lb., to choose what part should be cooked for me. I gave him the preference as to knowledge about the savoury mouthfuls, which he took as a great compliment. In justice to my Indian friend, I cannot but say he afforded me the most comfortable meal I had had for a considerable time before, from the spine and head of the fish. A tent was left here, which could not be carried further, in which I slept. He was at war with the Cladsap tribe, inhabitants of the opposite banks of the river, and that night expected an attack which was not made. He pressed me hard to sleep in his lodge lest anything should befall me: this offer I would have most gladly accepted, but as fear should never be shown I slept in my tent fifty yards from the village. In the evening about 300 men danced the war dance and sang several death songs. The description would occupy too much time. In the morning he said I was a great chief, for I was not afraid of the Cladsaps. One of his men, with not a little self-consequence, showed me his skill with the bow and arrow, and then with the gun. He passed arrows through a small hoop of grass 6 inches in diameter, thrown in the air a considerable height by another person; with his rifle he placed a ball within an inch of the mark at the distance of 110 yards. He said no chief from King George could shoot like him, neither could they sing the death song nor dance the war dance. Of shooting on the wing they have no idea. A large species of eagle, Falco Leucocephala, was perched on a dead stump close to the village; I charged my gun with swan shot, walked up to within forty-five yards of the bird, threw a stone to raise him, and when flying brought him down. This had the desired effect: many of them placed their right hands on their mouths — the token for astonishment or dread. This fellow had still a little confidence in his abilities and offered me a shot at his hat; he threw it up and I carried the whole of the crown away, leaving only the brim. Great value was then laid on my gun and high offers made. My fame was sounded through the camp. Cockqua said "Cladsap cannot shoot like you." I find it to be the utmost value to bring down a bird flying when going near the lodges, at the same time taking care to make it appear as a little thing and as if you were not observed. (pp. 137-38.)

During his twenty-three-month stay at Fort Vancouver on the Columbia, Douglas had shipped home numerous packets of seeds, bulbs, and cuttings. Among the seeds were those of the tree to be named after him, the lumbering of which more than a century later was measured annually in the hundreds of millions of dollars. Of this noble tree — its seeds were already sprouting in the gardens of the Horticultural Society in London — he writes:

Tree remarkably tall, unusually straight, having the pyramidal form peculiar to the *Abies* tribe of Pines. The trees which are interspersed in groups or standing solitary in dry upland, thin, gravelly soils or on rocky situations, are thickly clad to the very ground with widespreading pendent branches, and from the gigantic size which they attain in such places and from the compact habit uniformly preserved they form one of the most striking and truly graceful objects in Nature. Those on the other hand which are in the dense gloomy forests, two-thirds of which are composed of this species, are more than usually straight, the trunks being destitute of branches to the height of 100 feet to 140 feet, being in many places so close together that they naturally prune themselves, and in the almost impenetrable parts where they stand at an average distance of five square feet, they frequently attain a greater height and do not exceed even 18 inches in diameter close to the ground. In such places some arrive at a magnitude exceeded by few if any trees in the world generally 20 to 30 feet apart. The actual measurement of the largest was of the following dimensions: entire length 227 feet, 48 feet in circumference 3 feet above the ground, 7½ feet in circumference 159 feet from the ground.

Some few even exceed that girth, but such trees do not carry their proportionate thickness to such a vast height as that above mentioned. Behind Fort George, near the confluence of the Columbia River, the old establishment of the Honourable the Hudson's Bay Company, there stands a *stump* of this species which measures in circumference 48 feet, 3 feet above the ground, without its bark. The tree was burned down to give place to a more useful vegetable, namely potatoes.

On a low estimation the average size may be given at 6 feet diameter, and 160 high. The young trees have a thin, smooth, pale whitish-green bark covered with a profusion of small blisters like *P. balsamea* or Balm of Gilead Fir, which, when broken, yield a limpid oil fluid possessing a fragrant and very peculiar odour, and which, after a few days' exposure to the action of the atmosphere, acquires a hard brittle consistence like other rosins, assuming a pale amber colour. The bark of the aged trees is rough, rotten, and corky, the pores smaller and containing less rosin, and in the most aged, 4 to 22 inches thick, greatly divided by deep fissures.

Douglas, the stonemason's son, who left school at the age of twelve, now in London consorted with the learned and the noble, his fame firmly based upon his travels and his botanical discoveries. Nevertheless, for two years he importuned his superiors to send him again to the Columbia. To prepare for his next adventure he studied astronomy and navigation.

He sailed again on the last day of October, 1829, rounded the Horn, touched at Honolulu, and arrived at Fort Vancouver on June 3, 1830. He spent the next three years travelling by schooner between the Columbia and California and in a disastrous expedition to New Caledonia, now north-central British Columbia.

In California, where he spent most of 1831-32, passing from Monterey, his port of disembarkation from the north, along the Camino Real from one Franciscan mission to another, he journeyed as far north as San Francisco and the Sacramento Valley. It was doubtless from this latter region that he sent to England the roots on which flecks of gold were found. The Californians knew of the gold, but did not encourage its exploitation. The holy fathers looked askance at any large influx of people into their tranquil, sun-blessed territory, and the Spanish soldiers, who in an earlier century had plundered Mexico, in California were too lazy to wash or dig for the precious metal.

While in California, Douglas received a letter from Baron Wrangel of Alaska, asking him to visit the Russian-owned province and pass on from there to Siberia and cross Asia and Europe on his return to England. On October 14, 1832, the indomitable Scotsman arrived back on the Columbia to put the project into effect. Unable to secure a northward passage by ship, he set out from Fort Vancouver in the spring of 1833. A man named Johnson, an old seaman, was with him as a servant. Travelling with the New Caledonia brigade by boat and pack train, they crossed from the watershed of the Columbia onto that of the Fraser and reached Fort George on the latter river's upper waters late in May. From there Douglas and Johnson went on west to Fort St. James, arriving early in June.

Between them and Alaska lay hundreds of miles of trackless jungle-like forest, towering mountains, and raging rivers. The prospect for two lone men was appalling, and, reluctantly, Douglas turned back from it, accepting his first defeat.

Coming down the Fraser on their return to Fort Vancouver, the canoe was overturned in rapids below Fort George.

Johnson made it safely to shore, but Douglas was tossed about in a whirlpool for more than an hour before being washed upon the river's bank. Reoutfitting themselves at Fort George, they reached the mouth of the Columbia in August after a few stops along the way in the interests of botany.

Late in October, Douglas sailed on his last long voyage. He took ship for Honolulu, where, by way of San Francisco, he landed on December 23, 1833. He planned to study the exuberant flora of the islands and then to return to England with his specimens.

During the next six months Douglas explored the islands, passing by schooner from one to the other. His first feat was to ascend with a party of natives Mauna Kea in Hawaii, 13,784 feet, highest island mountain in the world. With the barometric instruments he now carried with him he set its height at 13,851 feet, a fractional difference from its true height of 13,784. He little knew that on this, his outstanding climb, he stood more than four thousand feet above the summit of Mount Brown on Athabaska Pass. Wind and snow aggravated his failing vision and on his descent he applied opium to ease the pain in his eyeballs.

By early July, 1834 he was ready to take passage home and set out alone to cross from northern Hawaii to the port of Hilo to the south, where he expected to find his ship, a distance of about a hundred miles. The trail led over mountains. The morning of July 12, Douglas had breakfast with one, Gurney, a rancher who warned him that the natives had dug pits farther along the trail. These they had covered with branches and fern growth in the hope of entrapping the wild cattle which roamed the forest.

A few hours later two natives, travelling north, noticed a piece of cloth by one of the pits, the farthest from the rancher's hut. The pit was open. Inside the pit was a wild bullock, raging-mad and foaming at the mouth. Under the hooves of the bullock, a mangled thing of horror was what remained of the body of David Douglas, aged thirty-five, botanist and "grass man," native of Scotland, lover of trees, gatherer of seeds and of the world's far flowers, follower of rivers, and climber of mountains.

His biographer, Harvey, is of the opinion that, after passing safely the two pits, which were undisturbed, Douglas, upon approaching the open one, had been drawn to it by naural curiosity. His eyesight being poor, he had stepped too close and the ground had given way beneath his feet. When Gurney, the rancher, heard the dire news from the two natives, he went to the pit, shot the bullock, and extricated the two bodies. He wrapped that of Douglas in a bullock hide, hired natives to carry it to the seashore, whence it was taken by outrigger canoe to Hilo and, finally, north to Honolulu. There David Douglas, in a ceremony attended by officers of a visiting warship, H.M.S. *Challenger*, was buried in the cemetery of the native church.

In his thirty-five years he had made three crossings of the North Atlantic, twice rounded Cape Horn, and travelled a good twenty thousand miles by canoe, riverboat, saddle horse, and by his own two legs in the wildest parts of North America. He had explored and climbed in the Sandwich, or Hawaiian, Islands. In London he had walked as an equal with the mighty.

David Douglas, whose name still stands towering on western mountain slopes, died young, but the years he lived were long, long years.

Shwat
The End of Tzouhalem

In the mellow light of an autumn moon a bit more than a hundred years ago, a young man of the Cowichan Indian tribe stood alone on the shore of a rocky inlet in the southeast corner of Vancouver Island off the coast of what is known as British Columbia.

The water of the inlet was calm and on it floated the body of a girl, long black hair spread out fanwise about her head. Earlier in the evening the young man in his search had come upon a small cedar dugout washed up on a shingle beach a mile or so to the north.

The girl in the inlet lay supine and floated unnaturally high in the water. So clear was the moonlight that it showed her closed eyes, as though she slept, rocked in the slow swells which, telling of the expanse beyond the inlet, caressed her brown breasts and firm, round thighs.

Beneath her, reaching up from the dark depths, sinuous, snake-like forms writhed and twisted. The watcher on the shore recognized them as strands of kelp. The girl's body rested on a bed of kelp and so lay lightly upon the water's surface.

The young man waded into the cold water up to his shoulders. He took hold of a strand of the kelp and pulled it towards him until he could lift the girl free. Then he carried her ashore and over the rocks to the edge of the forest. There he laid her down upon a couch of moss and broke branches from a balsam tree and covered her over — all but the upturned feet. Stubbornly the toes broke through the balsam boughs, commanding attention.

He bent to look more closely. He saw that the soles of the feet were black and charred, as if they had been slowly roasted. Feeling them, he noticed that in places the flesh was gone and under the instep his fingers touched exposed tendons.

He straightened up and, stepping to the head of the body, pushed aside the balsam to reveal the girl's face in the moonlight. He looked down on the smooth, high cheekbones, the eyelids and the lashes in eternal sleep. Then once more he covered the face with boughs.

The girl was sixteen years old, and she was his bride of three months before.

For two nights and two days the young man waited beside her body in the sheltered inlet. Outside the waters were dangerous, controlled by a hunchback, Tzouhalem, a man whose twenty-year record of pillage, rape, murder, and torture is probably unequalled on the West Coast north of the Tropics. At one time, with confederates, he held under siege the entrenched forces of the mighty Hudson's Bay Company.

To return to Comiaken, his village at the head of Cowichan Bay, the young widower would have to pass close to Kwa-tas — "the Lookout Place" — a grass-topped point of rock where Tzouhalem, when not on a savage foray, was encamped. Coming down the bay the night before, the bereaved one had drifted in his dugout silently by the point under a clouded moon.

Therefore he now waited until, after forty-eight hours, with a shift of wind to the south, storm clouds blew up. When the rain came, he carried the dead girl to his dugout, beached a few yards up the inlet. He put her gently down under the thwarts, shoved the dugout into the water, and paddled home six miles up the bay, safe in the stormy darkness from Tzouhalem and his band of marauders. The next day, amid the lamentations of many mourners, the girl, in a cedar box, knees folded up against her shoulders as tribal ritual demanded, was buried outside the village.

Old men of the Cowichan tribe, who have had the story from their fathers, mothers, aunts or uncles, still tell of the girl lying with closed eyes on the bed of kelp just beyond the lower reaches of the bay on which they live. When, in their recital, they refer to Tzouhalem, who was the cause of her death, they lower their voices and shake their heads. "He was a bad man," they will say, "bad all the way through. He had no good in him."

Almighty Voice and Gun-an-noot, "the Little Bear That Climbs Trees," had outlawry imposed upon them. Before the crimes of which they were accused, but never convicted, both had been law-abiding and were individuals of outstanding merit in their communities. Pursued by the white man's police, each had been befriended by his own people. The thoughtless words of a police corporal had goaded Almighty Voice into his flight from the law. Incriminating circumstances had turned Gun-an-noot towards the same desperate course.

Tzouhalem, on the other hand, was one who from his middle years dedicated himself to crime and violence. His chosen victims were his blood brothers, the Cowichans, and their young women.

The Cowichans, brown-skinned and stocky, with a Mongolian cast to their features, are part of the widespread Salishan group which inhabit the southern coast and interior of British Columbia and extend southward into the state of Washington. Crossing over from the mainland centuries ago in dugouts shaped from cedar logs, they became known by the name they gave to the valley on Vancouver Island, where they settled. "Cowichan" means "Land Warmed by the Sun." Opening to the south and east, the valley is said to have the most salubrious climate in all of Canada. The fishing in its bay and river is known to sportsmen across the continent.

Like Gun-an-noot, Tzouhalem has left his name on a mountain. Mount Tzouhalem lifts its rocky and fir-clad slopes sixteen hundred feet above Cowichan Bay. In its shadow, along the shores of the bay, the Cowichans catch crabs and dig clams as their forefathers did. They spear salmon from the banks of the Cowichan River and go to sea in power-driven commercial fishing boats.

They are not apt to forget the name of Tzouhalem. Walking, or driving their battered cars into the nearby town of Duncan, where, attracted by the climate, retired Englishmen from all parts of the world have come to sit out their final days, they follow the five-mile-long Tzouhalem Road. In the town they gather in the beer parlour of the Tzouhalem Hotel. There, in a guttural, sibilant tongue, the young men discuss logging wages, fishing conditions, and the current gossip, while the old men stare into their beer, lost in the shade of days that are no more.

On the far side of a low hill, across the railroad tracks from the Tzouhalem Hotel, is a fuel-gas store. Where the store now stands, Tzouhalem was born in the last decade of the eighteenth century. He was about sixty years old when, in 1854, a woman held his arms as her husband split his head open with a Hudson's Bay Company axe.

There were years of blood and treachery on the northwest Pacific coast, and the deeds of Tzouhalem must be judged within the context of his times. From the Queen Charlotte Islands, three hundred miles to the north, the warlike Haidas made raids into Cowichan Bay, crossing sixty miles of open sound and then travelling through the protected waters between Vancouver Island and the mainland. Their seagoing dugouts, with soaring and sculptured prows, often measured sixty feet in length and carried thirteen paddlers each. They were armed with spears, clubs and axe-flint knives. The Cowichans lived in small villages around the bay and up the river.

Off one of these the enemy canoes, four or five in number, would appear silently out of the dawnlight. The Haidas had foraged south for slaves. Before the villagers were properly roused from sleep, the northerners had seized their captives, killing those who stood in their way, pushed their canoes back into the water, and were paddling north to their home waters. In their turn, the Cowichans raided the communities across the straits on the mainland, up the Fraser River, and along the shores of Puget Sound.

Young Adam Horne of the Hudson's Bay Company was witness to a raid by the Haidas in May, 1856. In a dugout which "rode the water like a duck," he led a party of five a

hundred miles north of Fort Victoria to a place called Qualicum, today a fishing resort and the site of rich men's homes.
From Qualicum he was to find a trail across the island to the
west coast.

Just below Qualicum he and his little party camped in
a protected cove. They made no fire for they feared the
natives. Near dawn Horne was awakened by the Iroquois
canoe man who was with him. Crouched in the timber, they
watched a shadowy fleet of northern canoes, which they
were later able to identify as those of the Haidas, entering
the creek north of them leading to the village of the Quali-
cums. Soon columns of smoke were rising above the village.
It was not until noon that the Haida war canoes emerged
from the creek. The jubilant warriors were whooping. Several
of them stood upright, and from their hands, held by the
hair, dangled human heads. A gale was blowing from the
south. The Haidas hoisted reed-mat sails, and the canoes —
their bottoms oiled to speed them through the water — fled
north before the wind.

Later that day, Horne and his company visited the Qualicum village. They saw the blackened timber of burned houses
and more than a score of mutilated bodies. Only one old
woman, grievously wounded by a spear, survived. Before she
died she told them, through Horne's interpreter, that most
of her people had been killed in their sleep, women and
children and men. The Haidas had taken away with them
as slaves two young women, four little girls, and two older
boys.

The caste system prevailed on this part of the Pacific coast
and slaves were a form of wealth. They were used as servants
and, in the ritual of a crude and sadistic form of "conspicu-
ous consumption," were sometimes thrown alive into the
hole dug for the raising of a totem pole or for the decorated
corner post of a chief's house. The pole or post was then
pushed down upon the screaming victim.

Behind the villages rose the mountains, sombre with rain
forest, their upper reaches frequently shrouded by mist for
days or weeks. There, in the gloom of Douglas fir, hemlock,
and cedar, and in the untrodden recesses of the high valleys,
strange, mystic beings held court and played with the des-
tinies of men. Chief among these was Thunderbird. Thought

to be a representation of the now nearly extinct Siberian eagle, the largest of its kind, Thunderbird had dominion over earth, water and air. From the mountaintops he could swoop down and lift a whale from the sea in his talons. His outspread wings cast a shadow between the sky and the world below and their movement caused the thunder to roll. From his eyes lightning flashed and rain was shed by his feathers from the lake he carried on his back. Symbolic of man's relation with this spirit-creature world and looming out of the forest dusk above his villages were the totem poles. These gigantic wooden sculptures had genealogical or heraldic meaning expressed by piling human and animal figures one on top of the other. Today they are prized exhibits in leading metropolitan museums.

Into this land of myth, of mountains, of forest and turbulent sea, where native tribes warred among themselves, the white man appeared as early as 1774 — and his coming was but another mystery. The natives did not understand whence he came, nor yet the hunger for sea otter skins which brought him to their country.

This marine animal's range was limited to a few islands in the far-north Pacific and to two off the coast of California. In his migrations between the two localities he became the prey of the Nootkas, a tribe on the west coast of Vancouver Island who coursed the sea in cedar dugouts. Often they found the mother lying on her back in a bed of kelp, with her young cradled in her arms. Although the sea otter, which weighs up to eighty pounds, bore only one pup a year, the species existed in untold thousands two centuries ago. In one day two Russian sailors clubbed to death seven thousand on one small island. The dense, lustrous fur was at one time the most valuable in the world, a single pelt bringing $1,703 in 1910 in the London market. Vicious hunting has reduced the immense herds to some three thousand survivors. Today these are protected by international treaty.

In the late eighteenth century, when the white man arrived off the north Pacific coast, the rich reward of their fur awaited him. He came in tall ships with billowing sails and the natives spoke of him as "one who builds houses on the sea."

Juan Pérez, a Spaniard, stood off the Queen Charlotte

Islands on July 18, 1774, and claimed possession of the coast for Spain. Twenty-five years later the Russians established themselves at Sitka, Alaska.

Following Pérez, James Cook, the famous English navigator, anchored in Nootka Sound on the west coast of Vancouver Island in the spring of 1778 and began the trade in sea otter pelts for which China was then the main market. The Americans, under Captains Kendrick and Gray, arrived in 1788. They, with the British, were to share the trade of the coast after the ousting of the Spanish at the signing of the Nootka Convention in London on October 28, 1790.

Tzouhalem, born only a few years later, entered into troubled times. The age-old rivalries among the many coastal tribes continued. The Haidas, the Nootkas, the Kwakiutls, the Salish and their offshoot, the Cowichans, each had its own language and its separate territory. They offered no common front to the white man, whose trading practices were to disrupt their primitive economy, whose liquor and disease were to shatter their health and decimate their numbers, and whose priests and ministers of the gospel, belittling their beliefs and mocking their ceremonies, were slowly to undermine their faith in themselves as people. Tzouhalem, entering manhood, looked out on a shadowed future, and his life became a revenge upon the society which bore him into the world, a stunted man.

He was born a hunchback to parents of lowly stock. Though they were not slaves, they had no place in the hierarchy of the Cowichans, and their dwelling, instead of being a part of one of the "long-houses" with carved and painted corner posts, was probably an "illihie," a tepee-like affair of bark and boughs.

Some of these long-houses of the Coast were three hundred feet in length and ninety feet wide. The posts and rafters which supported them were cedar, and the walls and roofs were of cedar "shakes." Reed mats lined the walls and were hung out at intervals at right angles to them to divide the house into family compartments. Family organization was matrilineal, descent being through the mother, and the husband, in theory, only a visitor at the hearthside. In fact, as hunter and fisherman, he was the provider and the number of wives he could support was the measure of his prowess.

167

At the end of the drear winter months of rain, the Cowichans and other West Coast tribes held their initiation rites in a long-house specially designated for the occasion. Presumably, soon after reaching puberty, Tzouhalem attended one of these nocturnal ceremonies —ceremonies which, little changed, have continued into the present day.

Tzouhalem, as a young coastal Indian, also fasted and endured a solitary vigil to seek a vision of his guardian spirit — the eagle, the snake, the raven. He came out of the forest after his fasting, in charge of two or more older men, to join in an initiation dance in the long-house — a dance whose essential aesthetic and spiritual qualities were not measured by flesh torn and blood spilled, as in the Sun Dance of the Plains Indians.

One such dance — one of many held by the Cowichans during the season — took place early in a recent March, when the frogs in the sloughs behind the long-house began their first timid croaking. The long-house, set within a grove of tall Douglas firs, was in the village of Klem-klem on a branch of the Cowichan River, a half-mile from the bay.

Inside the house masked figures draped in skins, furs and feathers, fanged like bears, beaked like birds, deer hooves clicking at their ankles — the young men who that night were to dance their way into manhood — circled slowly about the two fires of high-built fir logs. Sparks rose into the dusk, where beams supported the peaked roof of cedar shakes and through the vent holes streamed into the cloud-topped darkness. Beaver-tooth rattles hissed and drums throbbed. The drums were of deer hide stretched taut over the burned-out butts of cedar logs and their beat, echoed up against the slopes of Mount Tzouhalem, three miles distant to the north, was a tremor of the ground itself, a murmurous thunder from underfoot.

Mingling with the crackling of burning logs, the sibilant rattles and the pulsing drums, up-borne upon the assembled sound like waves upon the water, was the chant of the old men and the old women. They sat back from the fires on a bench behind a hand-hewn plank serving them as a table on which they beat with sticks in counterrhythm to their song. Above them, in staggered rows, sat their kinsmen and guests invited from other villages, two to three hundred in number, intent and dusky faces showing briefly in a sudden flare-up from the burning logs.

"Oo-oo-ah, Ah-ah-oh, Oo-oo-ah, Ah-ah-oh" was the chant of the old people as they hit with their sticks the long plank at knee level in front of them. The chant was redundant, persistent, yearning. Through it they were reaching deep, deep into the past, into their far away and long ago. They were calling to other old men, to other old women, to their ancestral ghosts, who, before coming to the island, had wandered the timbered valleys of the mainland, who had threaded their way south through the icy mountains of the North and who, before that, around yak-dung campfires on the gusty plains of Asia, had, with similar chants, invoked the phantoms of a past even more remote and in a land still farther away.

The old people also called to Grandfather Coyote, to Raven, whose voice inhabits the forest's dark places, to Whale, who knows the depths of the ocean, and to Thunderbird himself. Each young man had his own song and danced his own dance. He rose to dance and sing, often foaming at the mouth, when he felt that "power" had come into him from his clamourous surroundings.

The old men and women had learned the song of the young man and, while he danced before them, they called upon their ancestors and upon the spirits of the forest that his "power" might enable him to become a man. On occasion during the ceremonies, because the Cowichans are a matriarchal group, an old woman would move out and stand between the two fires and recite the genealogy of the young man about to dance. Her voice had much the same cadence, and the repetition of names much the same mesmeric effect — seeming to carry the listener out of and beyond the walls around him — as the intoned announcements of train stops by the dispatcher in New York City's Grand Central Station.

Tzouhalem, after thus achieving manhood's estate, became — as his later exploits were to prove — a man of strength, unusual sexual vigour and, despite his deformity, commanding presence. His deformity, indeed, may well have assisted him in his rise to stature. Physical peculiarities were, at times, a mark of distinction among the West Coast tribes and shed a protective aura about their bearer. Even though his parents held no exalted place in the closely knit tribal structure, Tzouhalem, if only because of the hump on his back, might have assumed a position of authority among the Cowichans, had he stayed with them.

However, he was a marked individual, by temperament as well as by physique. Primitive man, as distinct from his civilized counterpart, has a collective conscience and accepts without question the various "taboos" imposed upon his behaviour. Tzouhalem's independent nature rebelled against this tight discipline of communal living where, except for his song and dance, each man shared what he had with those about him. At any rate, he left his people and for years he was a wanderer. Some of those years he spent with the Songhees, his later allies against the Hudson's Bay Company. They lived thirty miles down-island from his village of Comiaken, and through them he had his first contact with the white men, trading up from the south.

After twenty years, about 1835, when he was forty, he returned up Cowichan Bay, but not to his village. With a few Cowichan followers, like himself estranged from their people, he established a base at Kwa-tas, today known as "Green Point," downstream from it, where the Cowichan River falls into the bay.

Backed by the timbered mountain which in after years was to bear his name, from here he dominated the river traffic, essential to the Cowichans, who lived off the sea. Dugouts, returning upstream, were robbed of their catches of clams, oysters or salmon, or their owners were wantonly shot at. Tzouhalem and his men had muskets procured in trade from the Songhees or white traders. These were as yet a novelty to the Cowichans, who had had less contact with the outside world.

So far, like others of his kind, Tzouhalem was only exacting tribute from those who passed his way. He showed his true colours a year or two later, soon after a visit to the village of Comiaken, where he went protected by his armed band or "gang" of eight or ten men. The villagers received him with kindness because they wanted peace and to end the trouble on the river.

Tzouhalem admired a carved and painted totemic door-post of one of the communal houses in which the aristocracy of the village lived. He said he would like to have a few posts of the same order about his "illihie" on Green Point and inquired after the man who had carved it. When Loo-ha, the young sculptor, was brought forth — he had been a child when Tzouhalem had set out on his wandering twenty years and more before — he was invited to Green Point. Tzouhalem would have his men bring down cedar logs from the forest and Loo-ha would carve them.

The sculptor accepted the offer. For payment he was to receive a musket and balls and powder. His mistake was that he brought with him in his dugout the comely Talkanaat, his young wife. Tzouhalem had still to make his reputation as a debaucher of young women. The girl's eyes danced with the excitement of the outing, her black hair shone with fish oil, and the knee-length garment she wore was woven from the inner bark of the cedar tree and the long wool of the Rocky Mountain goat. Wool was an item of trade with the mainland, there being no wild goat on the island. The natives' only domestic animal at this time was a small dog. Like the Chinese, they considered its flesh a delicacy.

Loo-ha and his wife were fed smoked clam and salmon and the boiled roots of camas lily and given a brush shelter to themselves. For weeks the sculptor worked outside Tzouhalem's "illihie" and completed many poles with totemic designs to the liking of his host. Planted in the ground, they were about ten feet high. Tzouhalem had exacted an unusual requirement. It was that the tip of each pole be pointed.

One afternoon, Loo-ha looked up and asked for his wife who had not been far from him. One of Tzouhalem's men pointed to the edge of the forest and smiled. Loo-ha observed that Tzouhalem himself was not on hand and recalled that he had not seen him since the last pole had been put in the ground.

He laid aside his stone chisel, dusted his hands and rose to go in search of Talkanaat. Strong hands detained him. When he struggled and cried out, he was bound to one of the poles he had carved. While he tried to burst the ropes of cedar which held him, Tzouhalem's men beat drums.

Over the beat of the drums, Loo-ha heard a woman scream in the forest. At last Talkanaat came out, running towards him. She was pursued by Tzouhalem, who, back twisted under its unnatural hump, seemed to progress sideways, like a crab.

Before Talkanaat could reach her husband, one of Tzouhalem's men stepped forth and held her. Tzouhalem came up, panting. He laughed and spat at the bound and impotent Loo-ha. Then he turned to the wife, struggling in the arms of his follower, and ripped her garment from her. The sun glowing upon her brown young flesh, she was flung upon the ground. There, among the grasses, in full sight of her husband, while one man pinned her arms and two others her thrashing legs, Tzouhalem, in a half circle of beating drums, mingled his shadow with that of the girl and performed his outrage.

When he rose from his pleasure, adjusting his breechclout, Loo-ha was foaming at the mouth. He swore that, as he lived, he would kill the man who had defiled his wife. "Swallower of darkness," he shouted, "spawn of the dunghill whose filth you eat, may your organs one day be cut from you and, while you watch, slowly roasted and then given to the village dogs to devour."

Below the point is a flat. The tide, well out, was turning. Tzouhalem listened quietly to the raving of Loo-ha, then ordered his men to take the captive and stake him on the flat to await the incoming tide. It was a slow death in the evening, the water lapping up to the victim's lips and receding, literally a death by inches. The twilight rang with the cries of Talkanaat, herself bound to a pole to watch her husband's torture. In the morning the body was recovered. The sculptor's head was cut off and spiked upon the first of the poles he had carved for Tzouhalem. It was the forerunner of many others to follow.

That night, Talkanaat crawled from the "illihie" to escape through the forest to the village from the man she now knew as a monster. She was caught and hauled back, and over the coals of the campfire the soles of her feet were carefully toasted — a refinement of the widely known "bastinado," in which torture the small bones of the victim's instep are shattered with rods. She would still be able to crawl, but never again to walk with the stride of a young woman. She was as good as tethered to the "illihie."

Equivalent forms of maiming were known in other parts

of the West. Alexander Henry, a trader of the Northwesters stationed on the North Saskatchewan in 1806, noted in his diary that a Cree Indian, L'Hiver, had cut the heel tendons of his wife to keep her from "gadding about" while he was absent on the hunt.

Perhaps Tzouhalem's acts of sadism against the young sculptor and his wife were premeditated. After all, he had ordered that the tips of the posts about the "illihie" be sharp ones. Yet it would seem he bore no grudge against the unwitting Loo-ha and Talkanaat as individuals. His history was to show that his malice was turned towards mankind itself. Of humble birth, self-banished from his people, somewhere in his wanderings he had become an apostle of violence. However, violence alone would not distinguish him in a region and an era of violence, when the whole and intricate tribal culture of the Pacific slope was breaking under the impact of the white man's coming.

It was the motive behind his violence, and the means that his violence took, which marked Tzouhalem. Unable, or unwilling, to achieve position within his tribe, he proceeded to achieve it without. "They" had house posts in the village. Therefore he would have poles outside his "illihie." "Theirs" were topped by totemic crests. His would be topped by human heads. Beheading their men, taking their women, he set out to avenge himself upon those who, as he thought, had denied him. A man's prestige as hunter and provider was reflected by the number of women he had. Tzouhalem, then, would have more than any other. Others might waste time in wooing. He would seize. That those for miles around might know when a new woman came to his bed, his men, surrounding the "illihie" on these connubial occasions, beat on their drums of fire-hollowed logs and deerskin. Tzouhalem was an abnormal man and he lived in times of abnormal change for his people.

The Cowichans, who in those days numbered about five thousand — today their population is less than half — were dispersed in various communities. A village such as Comiaken, of no more than sixty people, could not easily resist a sudden raid by a well-armed and disciplined band. On the two occasions when the villages joined against him and tore down his "illihie," Tzouhalem and his men retreated up the mountain behind his camp. There, in rock caves, with ball and powder, they were impregnable to assault by flint-tipped spear and bow and arrow. When the cry died down, they returned to the point and rebuilt the "illihie."

Again the outlaw was undoubtedly a man of "power" in the eyes of his superstitious victims and antagonists — "power," that mysterious emanation or force of being which came to a man from the "medicine" he had made, from the particular animal which was his tutelary spirit — Tzouhalem's is not known — or even from a peculiar hump on his back. Modern man attributes power to what is within him. Primitive man attributes his version of it to what comes to him from without.

How many women Tzouhalem enticed into his camp, seized from passing dugouts, or carried off by raiding a sleeping village, no one knows exactly. Thirty to forty is a common guess. Others, whose soles he did not have to scorch to keep in camp, were doubtless attracted to him now that he had become a man of "power." The number of men he killed by his own hand, or by his direct order, would be much in excess of this. They were killed by stealth or after capture, for, with one recorded exception, he avoided pitched battles.

Tzouhalem did not operate only in and around Cowichan Bay. After women, head-hunting was his lifework — the more restrained practice of scalp-taking being unknown on the West Coast. For this purpose, with pillage as a side line, he and his stalwarts paddled in their open, forty-foot-long dugouts as far south as today's Tacoma, a journey of a hundred and forty miles across the Strait of Juan de Fuca, and down the coast, the strait notorious for its tide rips, strong winds, and sudden storms. On other occasions, still hunting heads, Tzouhalem crossed the strait and travelled a hundred miles up the Fraser. That he and his small force repeatedly came back with trophies to adorn the poles outside the "illihie" on Green Point attests to his ability as an early-day "commando." Swarms of carrion crows cleaned the skulls of flesh, leaving the grinning, bony masks to stare down at, and intimidate, all who used the waterway to the upstream villages.

The northern Kwakiutl and Haida, the most warlike people on the Coast — to whose districts Tzouhalem wisely made no approach — at times took their women with them on their raids. Tzouhalem often did the same. The women cooked and made camp. At other times on going away he turned them loose, leaving them to make their way as best they could on crippled feet back to their homes. They would soon be replaced. Many died in their servitude and were buried on the Point. As recently as 1947, R. G. Gore-Langton, a retired Englishman, who then owned the property of the Point, dug up several small brown skulls while he was digging a basement for his house.

The zenith of Tzouhalem's career was attained in the spring of 1844.

By this time the Hudson's Bay Company had built its Fort Camosun on the southern tip of Vancouver Island, the present site of Victoria, capital of British Columbia. In the spring of 1844 a shipload of cattle was imported from Mexico. They were to provide meat and work as draught animals in the fields around the fort.

A. Begg, in his *History of British Columbia*, published at the turn of the century, quoting from the journal of twenty-six-year-old Roderick Finlayson, the Company's factor, relates that Tzouhalem and his band, after travelling the thirty miles from Green Point, raided the cattle, killing several, and then invested the fort. They were assisted by a group of Songhees under the chief, Tsililtchach.

When Finlayson, "the young, fair-haired chief," as the Songhees knew him, came out to protest, through an interpreter, Tzouhalem, taking equal rank with the chief, replied, "Those animals yours? Did you make them? They are of the land, like the deer. What nature sends us, we slay and eat." Part of the conversation was conducted in "Chinook," the trading language of the Coast, a mixture of English, French Canadian and Salishan. Nor was Tzouhalem's comparison to deer farfetched. The cattle, coming from Mexico, were small and lean and their behaviour was "sprightly."

The renegade Cowichan leader made another point. The cattle were used for hauling. That, he said, was the proper function of women. The native women might become rebellious, saying that they were forced to do an animal's work.

Finlayson answered that the cattle had been brought "from beyond the seas" and that they were being used for what they were intended. He warned that unless Tzouhalem made restitution for those he had killed, the gate of the fort would be closed against him and he would be denied the trade for which, presumably, he and his men had made their journey.

"Close the gate!" shouted Tzouhalem. "We lived here before without you. Do you think that now we will perish?" Finlayson withdrew behind the walls of the fort. He had barely a score of dependable men under his command — English and Scotch storekeepers and carpenters and a few French Canadian voyageurs.

Tzouhalem and his Songhee allies numbered about a hundred, and for two days they held the fort under siege. However, their musket balls merely bounced off its logs and in their inexperience in this form of warfare it did not occur to them to set it afire.

Finlayson bravely stepped forth once more and called for a parley. He pointed out to Tzouhalem that muskets could not prevail against the fort. Further, he said, he had within the fort that which could make kindling of the Songhee village across the narrow inlet. Tzouhalem was unbelieving.

When Finlayson retired again into the fort he turned his nine-pounder against the Songhee village and reduced to splinters one of the cedar long-houses. It was a measure he had reserved to the last because, for reasons of trade, he did not wish to incur the enmity of his neighbours.

Luckily, the house being empty — he had given warning — no one was hurt, but the demonstration persuaded the Songhee chief that things had gone far enough. He and Tzouhalem came forward and in their turn asked for a parley. At their request, to convince their still hostile followers, Finlayson aimed his field gun at a dugout and blasted it out of the water.

Terms were made. The two Indian leaders agreed to hand over otter and mink skins to the value of the destroyed cattle. In return, they were given tobacco and shot and powder. The next day, Tzouhalem and his men paddled back to Green Point.

For another ten years he was to continue his programme of head-hunting, rape and plunder. It was near the end of this period that he took the girl whose body was found by her husband floating on a bed of kelp in an inlet at the foot of Cowichan Bay. Tzouhalem had come upon her while she was digging for camas root, a potato-like bulb, beyond the edge of her village of Comiaken.

Despite the fact that the soles of her feet, following custom, had been scorched after her capture, the girl contrived to steal away from the "illihie" at night and crawl down the beach to a small dugout. Wind and tide were against her and, unable to make her way upstream to the village, she was blown down the bay.

Days later, her husband, having heard of her escape, set out to find her. Likely her dugout had been overturned in a tide rip and, being washed away from it, she shed her clothes in the struggle to reach shore. The Cowichans were not swimmers and the temperature of these waters, even in summer, is about 45 degrees. The girl had little chance of survival. A wave lifted her and left her body upon the kelp.

The nemesis of Tzouhalem was a lone woman digging clams at low tide on Kuyper Island one summer day in 1854. Kuyper Island is down the bay, around Separation Point and north through Sansom Narrows — a distance of fifteen miles from the "illihie" on Green Point.

On this day Tzouhalem was unaccountably alone. Possibly, in the light of his past record, he had become careless.

At any rate, when he saw the woman, bent to her task, he beached his dugout and, in his forthright way, made for her. The woman, whose name was Shwat, dropped her basket, half filled with clams, and holding tight to her shovel-like clam-digging stick, ran yelling up the path to her cabin. Tzouhalem confidently followed.

Inside the cabin the woman, a singularly lusty wench, fought against him and continued to call for her husband, who, as it happened, was not far away, gathering firewood. He came running at her summons.

When he arrived at the cabin door, Shwat had pinned Tzouhalem's arms to the log wall with her clam-digging stick. The husband, Ben-wah, wasted no time. Raising the two-and-a-half-pound Hudson's Bay Company axe, with which he had been cutting wood, he split the intruder's skull wide open. When Tzouhalem fell, to make doubly sure, Ben-wah beheaded him, in keeping with the usual practice of his victim.

Then the man and woman, recognizing who lay dead at their feet and fearing for what they had done, fled the blood-spattered cabin.

In a few days Tzouhalem's men, in a long dugout, came by for the remains of their leader. Tzouhalem may have left word with them of where on this, his last voyage, he was going or Ben-wah, the husband, recovering from his fright, may have boasted of his deed around a village fire. At all events, it was a deed which had wings and would not long be unknown.

Tzouhalem's men laid his body in the dugout.

On the return, as they rounded the headland after passing though Sansom Narrows and could see up Cowichan Bay, they were appalled to observe a tremor in the headless trunk at their knees. Slowly it rose to a sitting position. Slowly it turned in the dugout and slowly it lifted an arm to point towards the "illihie" below the mountain four miles away on "Kwa-tas." Then before their staring eyes it subsided into its former repose.

To doubt that this happened — that Tzouhalem's corpse rose and gestured — would be to doubt the word of Johnny Bear, an eighty-year-old Cowichan of Duncan, short, solidly built, with bristling white mustache and a voice that resounds like a foghorn. He had the story direct from his father, whose cousin was in the dugout conveying the body homeward.

Today Tzouhalem's headless skeleton lies in a cave, sealed with boulders, on the slope of the mountain which is his monument. Somehow it seems fitting that the woman-avenger whose struggles availed to put it there went by the simple and compelling name of "Shwat." Tzouhalem's broken skull is said to be in tribal hands, and closely guarded.

I Look Upward and See the Mountain

The traveller, male, about fifty, westbound on a freight locomotive out of Jasper, Alberta, one morning in late May, 1927, had the name of Jan Van Empel, and a more improbable physical specimen of a wildernesss, or mountain man perhaps did not exist between Alaska and New Mexico. He had seen Alaska. Death waited for him in New Mexico.

Van Empel was of medium height, broad of hip and shoulder, and, though not fat, he was overweight. He was splay-footed and wore a full, flaxen beard. The beard and his weary eyes, hung with pouches, looking out at the world through steel-rimmed spectacles, gave him the air of a St. Bernard dog groggily coming back to life after a week-long binge on the monastery's brandy. His clothes — a brown tweed jacket, a blue flannel shirt and loose black tie, grey flannel trousers — draped his frame as though he had, somehow, struggled into them from below.

Yet Van Empel was as truly a wilderness man as any who have gone before him in these pages. David Douglas devoted himself to the search for seeds, roots, and grasses. Van Empel's life was a quest for mountains. This May morning his destination was Mount Robson, across the divide in British Columbia, where he would find more of them. Behind Mount Robson he would also undergo an experience worthy to be set beside any of those he had heard recounted by others of the outdoors fraternity.

Van Empel had seen a good many mountains in his time. Born in Holland — he still spoke with a heavy Dutch accent — he had emigrated at an early age to New York City. There, while working as caretaker, night watchman or day labourer, he studied art. Later he made a living as a commercial artist. It was not until he was past forty that, like Gauguin, he was able to pursue the unlikely task that for years had been before him, a man with his roots in a European tide flat. Gauguin left Paris for the South Seas. Van Empel left New York City for Alaska. As well as his oils, brushes, easel and palette, he took with him his well-thumbed Schopenhauer.

In Alaska, at Sitka and elsewhere, he painted the mountains, the inlets, the glaciers, the old Russian churches with the shadowy figures of Indians passing into them. He painted in crude strokes, heavily and in perspective, so that his canvases took on depth and drew the observer's eye up dim valleys and far into groves of shrouded trees.

Returning to the United States, he held exhibits in New York City and Boston. With money in his pocket, he turned west again, this time to the Canadian Rockies, and arrived in Jasper in late November. There he rented a one-room shack in the south end of the town. His became a lonely figure as, during the winter, wearing a warm mackinaw and muskrat cap with untied side flaps, sketchbook under his arm, he plodded through the snow, climbed the hills and tramped the frozen Miette River putting down on paper the shapes of mountains which, later in his shack, he would transmute to oil and canvas.

The townspeople — railroaders, merchants, game wardens, hunters and trappers — did not take kindly to him. They worked for their daily bread, whereas Van Empel merely "idled." The citizens of Lucerne had regarded "Old" Mac-Namara as an eccentric, a miser and, rightly enough, a misanthrope. Jasper looked upon Van Empel, set down for no apparent reason in their midst, as being at least "peculiar." When for days he did not emerge from his shack, the little frame structure under its plume of blue smoke assumed a sinister quality, as if within its walls a wizard were brewing enchantments against those around him. When he showed a few of his paintings in the local drugstore, the town took umbrage. Painting from the window of his shack, the artist had put a tilted outhouse well into the foreground of a town scene, snow-covered mountains looming above. Several of the townspeople pointed out to him that most of the houses now had septic tanks and that the showing of outhouses would offend the summer tourists. "Ya, maybe that is so," said Van Empel, standing beside his creation, "but the outhouse is there, so I paint it." Then, as was his habit before making a point, he inclined his head, pulled at his beard and, shaking an admonitory forefinger, added, "You show me just how to make a painting of this, what do you call it? This septic tank, then I will make one for you."

Now in the locomotive cab Van Empel was headed west away from the town and its complainers. The cab was crowded. At the right, hand on the throttle, head out of the window, was Sam Sliter, rotund, red-faced, a seasoned "hog-head." The fireman was Sammy Fellows, sallow-cheeked and slight. With his right foot on the floor board of the coal tender, his left depressing the lever which opened the devouring red maw under the locomotive's belly, he shovelled coal steadily as they climbed up the Miette Valley towards Yellowhead Pass. The head-end brakeman sat at the window to the left.

Van Empel stood, balancing as best he could in the swaying cab. His packsack with extra clothes and socks, his paints and palette were at his feet and his right arm was wrapped around his beloved easel. He reflected that he might have made an easier journey had he taken the passenger later in the day. However, Sam Sliter, whom he had frequently met in the beer parlour of the Athabaska Hotel, hearing that he was going to Mount Robson, had invited him, strictly against company regulations, to make the trip by locomotive. Van Empel had accepted for "the experience."

At Geikie, halfway to Yellowhead Pass, Sliter turned and shouted to him that, if he wished, he could clamber out the front window and along the running board and seat himself on the "pilot" above the cowcatcher. Handing over his easel to the brakeman, Van Empel gingerly made the experiment, holding onto the handrail, sensing the hot pressure of the boiler as he edged forward along its side. On the pilot he tucked his legs under him, and wind parting his beard, was borne west through the mountains, a goggle-eyed statue on a platform of iron.

Passing the summit of Yellowhead, 3,720 feet, the lowest rail crossing of the Rockies, he was conscious, as the train hit the downgrade, of the immensity which pushed him on — of the pounding locomotive and of the forty cars behind it, carrying coal, cattle, wheat and merchandise for the western coast. At the mile board west of Lucerne, Sliter, back in the cab, pulled the cord above his head and the locomotive uttered its metallic roar, almost lifting Van Empel in fright from his seat.

Settling back, observing the blue lines of the rails winding before him through the mountains — the locomotive did not so much pass over them as it seemed to drag them under its hungry wheels and consume them — he was aware of himself as only a piece of vulnerable flesh set in the forefront of a pulsing iron monster. At any moment, rounding a curve, he might see a boulder on the track which, riding up the cow-catcher, could crush him against the boiler front, for this was spring, the time of slides in the mountains. Instead, crossing the Fraser above the Grantbrook, up which "Old" Mac-Namara had once run his trapline, and turning west into a "cut," he saw, a hundred yards down the right of way, a full-grown grizzly bear walking upgrade towards the approaching train, his head swinging lazily from side to side.

Suddenly aware of what was roaring down upon him, the bear reared up as though to dispute the locomotive's passage. Sam Sliter had seen the grizzly, too. The locomotive howled. The grizzly for a second stood irresolute, amazed at this affront to his dignity, forepaws crossed below his chest, stubby ears twitching. Then he dropped to all fours, turned tail, and fled down the track, the thick fur on his shoulders gleaming in the sun, rising and falling to his long, loping stride. As the gap closed between them, the locomotive gave voice once more. The grizzly, after one agonized backward glance, lengthened his stride, his whole body quivering with the effort. He did not take to the timber. The westward track offered easier going, nor would it occur to him that the locomotive pursuing him along the rails could not leave them to pursue him through the bush. For the same reason horses and moose, especially at night when they are caught in the headlight's glare, are frequent casualties of the right of way.

The locomotive was slowly gaining on the bear, although Van Empel doubted that Sliter would actually run him down. Indeed, he felt the locomotive slowing as the engineer applied the air. The grizzly was by now going all out, his feet kicking up pebbles from between the ties. At a curve, where the tracks turned back towards the Fraser, he continued straight on, up a steep gravel cut-bank, his hind claws reaching for his ears. The locomotive gave a final blast to speed him on his way, and Van Empel, looking back as he vanished overhead among a climp of poplars, wished him full joy of the mountains to which he was returning.

At Red Pass, a junction point where a branch line runs west to Prince Rupert and the mainline swings southwest to Vancouver, the train pulled up for water and "orders." Here, too, the Fraser falls out of Moose Lake and into its series of canyons below Mount Robson.

Van Empel got down from his perch on the "pilot," stretched, and walked back to rejoin Sam Sliter in the cab. "Ever been as close as that to a grizzly before?" Sliter asked him. "We were going twenty miles an hour."

"Ya, in the zoo in New York, but then I never thought I would someday be chasing one of them through the mountains."

Forty minutes later Sliter stopped the train at Mount Robson Station. Van Empel climbed down the iron-runged ladder. Handing down to him his pack and easel, Sliter pointed to the trail leading to the Hargreaves ranch, half a mile below the railroad.

Alone on the platform — the freight train's whistle, sounding far down the line, was a fragment of nostalgia floating for a few seconds on the mountain air — Van Empel confronted the summer's challenge lifting to the northward. "Giant among giants, immeasurably supreme," Mount Robson stood solitary, shouldering the sky. To the west was the white spire of Mount Whitehorn. To the east the long, icy ridge of Mount Resplendent. Up high the prevailing west wind blew, and from the peaks trailing banners of snow reached eastward.

Few mountain spectacles match that of Mount Robson

seen from the southward on a clear day. Most of the world's great mountains rise from plateaus, but not Mount Robson. Almost thirteen thousand feet high, it rises sheer and lonely from a valley floor of not more than three thousand, presenting a precipitous front of ten thousand feet. Eternal snow crowns its summit. Glaciers, like hoary and intertwined beards, hang upon its chest. Up these glaciers lies "the road to the sky," according to a legend of the Shuswap Indians, who lived below the mountain until the white man came.

Buttresses of ribbed blue rock, copper-stained, based upon the valley floor, sustain the glaciers. The peak has been climbed several times. Weather, and not technical difficulties, is the conditioning factor. Gale-like winds and avalanches defend its upper approaches. Even as Van Empel watched, snow on its crest, built into an overhang by the western wind and weakened by the noonday sun, crumbled and fell away. The slide swept down the icy slopes in towering billows, as if the mountain had breathed and emitted its breath in ominous gusts of snow dust. It was an act of silence. Van Empel waited for the avalanche's roar, the voice of angry mountains. No sound came to him. Although Robson, in the pellucid air, seemed so close that he could reach out and put his hand upon it, he knew that it was about eight miles distant.

"Avalanche" is from the Swiss-French word *avaler*, "to descend into the valley," an apt word, concise, born from the routine of a mountain people. And Van Empel gazed, spellbound, as the tons of snow and ice spilled over Robson's rocky cliffs into the timber below, part of the mountain making its descent into the valley. Walking down the trail to the ranch house, inhaling the pungent scent of the towering balm of Gilead trees through which he passed, he shook his head. Avalanches were not in his line. He was not a climber. He was an artist, a lowly petitioner from mankind, seeking not the mountain's conquest, but in their obdurate rock and ice the truth that drew men to them. He was but another of those pilgrims who, since the dawn of history, have come to the mountains to search for what they would never find. The record Van Empel made of his pilgrimage hangs today on the walls of private homes and museums across Canada and the United States.

What was the "truth" that men looked for in mountains? Van Empel found it hard to define. During the month he spent at the Hargreaves' ranch in the wide valley below Mount Robson he would try to explain the nature of his quest to his host and the two or three ranch hands who might, at times, come to watch him at his easel which he had set up in the open. The easel was a folding tripod affair, its legs about five feet long. A ledge or "step" between two of them supported his canvas.

Pointing to the image of Robson slowly taking form beneath his brush, he would say, as if addressing a student audience, "This mountain here now" — and he would make a curving gesture with his right thumb as though to impress it deeper into the canvas — "is not the mountain you see. It is another mountain completely. That is because each man sees his own mountain. A hunter now, if he looks up there at the mountain, he looks at the gullies or the alplands, where he expects to see game, maybe a bear or a mountain goat. The climber, he looks for something else. He looks for a way up the mountain. For him the mountain is something to stamp beneath his feet. But me, an artist, I look for what is inside the mountain, something that is like a magnet and draws me to it. The mountain as a force, that is what I want people to feel when they look at what I have done."

Then he would shrug his shoulders and add, "But I cannot say it in words. After all, I can only paint. I am a man with my feet in the mud. Still, I look upward and see the mountain against the sky. That I would show, too, mankind bound to the earth and aspiring to the stars."

The response to Van Empel's dissertations, except for a shuffling of feet, was never marked. After all, his audience was that of men who had lived all their lives among mountains. In their eyes he was only a sojourner, a man who was passing through.

Roy Hargreaves, for instance, in a sense was apprenticed to Mount Robson. He was one of four brothers who, before World War I, had come north with their father from the mountains of Oregon. After the war, in which Roy had served, they made a clearing in the forest below Mount Robson Station, built the ranch house of logs and cedar shakes with corrals and stables to care for fifty head of horses, and set themselves up in the outfitting business. In time George and Frank, the older brothers, moved away to Starvation Flats, farther down the valley, though for a while they continued to help with the summer's tourist traffic. Jack, the youngest, married and went to live in Jasper. Since the summer of 1925 and until the present day Roy and his wife, Sophia, have managed the outfit on their own.

In the fall Roy and his men take out hunting parties into the Smoky River country beyond Mount Robson, During the summer they take tourists from Mount Robson Station by saddle horse on the daylong journey to the cabins at Berg Lake at the foot of the mountain's northern slope. Late in June, Van Empel set out for Berg Lake, his stretched canvases — which had come by express from Jasper — carefully tied on the top of a pack-horse's load. George, the oldest of the Hargreaves "boys," a man in his forties, was his guide. Van Empel, who could not afford the usual tourist tariff, was to be a guest at Berg Lake during the summer, a courtesy accorded him through the good offices of Walter S. Thompson, then publicity director of the Canadian National Railways.

The trail from the ranch house leads down to the Fraser and to the bridge across it, where the river foams through a canyon, and then onto a green poplar-studded flat. From the flat it snakes through a silent cedar forest, emerging onto the pebbled shore of Kinney Lake, close under the cliffs of Mount Robson. Here, as Van Empel passed, awkward in the unaccustomed saddle, small avalanches were falling every few minutes, the snow turning to water on the sun-heated rock.

Crossing Whitehorn Creek, above Kinney Lake, George Hargreaves, riding ahead and leading the pack pony, turned in his saddle and pointed to a little bird of dark plumage perched on a rock. "That's a water ouzel," he said. He went on to explain that even in winter the bird inhabited mountain streams where rapids, or an underground spring, kept them open. The water ouzel was a diver, a swimmer under water, living off the vegetable matter carried by swift water. "Yes," George said, "I've watched one of those water ouzels on a very cold day. He was standing on only one foot. He hit the rock he was standing on with his beak. A spark flew up and he warmed his other foot with it. Then he put that foot down, hit the rock again with his beak, and warmed the foot he had been standing on."

"Of course," George added, "that was on a mighty cold day."

"I will remember. It was very cold that day," Van Empel replied.

They were now riding through the Valley of a Thousand Falls. Here innumerable streams of water from the melting ice fields below Mount Whitehorn vanished into mist before reaching the valley floor. As they climbed the "Flying Trestle," where the trail led over to platforms built into the precipice, Van Empel's face was washed by the spray from Emperor Falls. Leaving the falls behind, he followed George Hargreaves and the pack-horse on to the shingle flats of Berg Lake, source of the north fork of the Fraser. This is drear alpine country, almost at the edge of the timber. Over the divide to the east the water drains into the Arctic.

Van Empel, in his journey, had made a half circle around the base of Mount Robson. The peak still reared above him but, whereas from the south it had been a monolith, here it was a gleaming, icy blade against the setting sun. A piece of ice the size of a two-storey house breaking loose from the glacier on its northern face fell with the sound of thunder into Berg Lake. Minutes later the swell laved the hooves of Van Empel's horse where the trail hugged the water's edge.

Van Empel was given a small cabin to himself and for the next two months he painted mountains and observed people. Most of the tourists were middle-aged and from the United States. The young lacked the time or had not made the money. Middle-aged, the tourists were for the most part of middle means. The wealthy generally hired their own outfits, guides, horse wranglers and cooks, and went farther back into the mountains. Man and woman, with an exception here and there, came to Berg Lake Chalet wearing khaki breeches and shirts, high-laced boots with upturned toes, uniformed for their holiday as though, if necessary, they were prepared to do battle for it. Van Empel disdained them for their cameras. The purpose of their stay in the mountains seemed to be to use up film and to litter trails and the chalet clearing with small yellow cardboard boxes and tinfoil. Memory of where they had been, perception of what they saw were both provided for them, factory-made, in a black package hung from their necks, strapped to their bellies, stowed away in their pockets, to be taken out or banished at their will. Under the peaks, whose summits sparkled with sun-kindled fire, they played bridge before the fireplace in the chalet. Van Empel shied away from the tourists, who, for their part, regarded askance his bearded, unkempt appearance. He preferred the company of the guides, who spent their time in service to the mountains, as, when the day's work was done, they squatted by the campfire. Their talk was of horses, trails and river crossings, and now and again, of people.

Some of the guides were from Jasper, where during the winter they worked as firemen or brakemen on the "spare board" of the railroad. From them Van Empel heard the story of Mr. A. and Mrs. B. He had heard it before. All of Jasper knew it. As he listened he pictured the little town as he had seen it on a spring evening from a hilltop, its houses with red roofs, its trim streets lined with poplars, and beyond it, far to the south, the ice fields at the head of the Athabaska River glowing blue and green and pink in the sunset like a sudden garden in the sky. However, the drama of Mr. A. and Mrs. B. — as they are still above the ground they must remain anonymous — though it had springlike connotations, reached its climax one cold December night when a blizzard roamed the valley and the town huddled under a canopy of snow.

Mr. A., a burly man in middle-age, was said to have had at one time a good law practice in the town of Saskatoon on the prairies. He had taken to drink and had lost, in sequence, his reputation, his practice and his wife. From Saskatoon he had drifted from place to place, finally coming to Jasper, where he did not so much practice law as suggest, in his indolence, to prospective clients where, in Edmonton or other parts, competent legal advice might be had. His income came from collecting insurance premiums, witnessing documents and from small speculations in mining stocks. By the winter of 1926-27 he had settled down with a "housekeeper" and moved into a pink stucco house not far from Van Empel's shack. Van Empel recalled the housekeeper as a florid-faced woman — the colour of her grey-streaked hair matching that of Mr. A.'s drooping mustache — who seemed to be forever beating a rug out of an open window.

Before Mr. A. took up with his "housekeeper," however, his ways had been more devious, as came to light on the December night when the blizzard blew. Mr. A. had passed the first part of the night between the sheets with Mrs. B. Mrs. B.'s husband at that time was "hoghead" on the time freight, a steady run between Jasper and Edson, the next divisional point to the east. Like many engineers, Mr. B. played a few special trills on the locomotive whistle at the mile board to acquaint his wife with his coming. This, as circumstances demanded, might be taken as a hint to have a meal ready or simply, to avoid embarrassment, as a warning that her husband would soon be home. In Jasper, where many husbands were regularly absent from their wives for twenty-four hours or more, these shrill announcements of arrival piercing the frosty air at a time caused behind masked windows quick stirrings and excited whispers which presaged an imminent departure as often as they did the preparation of a late supper. Then the wife who had not swept the new fall of snow from her back steps would be up early in the morning with the broom.

On this particular night, Mr. B. had been remiss and forgotten to give his usual signal or his wife, deep in the mysteries of Mr. A.'s embrace, had failed to hear it above the howl of the blizzard. So it came about that Mr. A. lit on the back porch just as Mr. B.'s footsteps crunched on the front one. The night was bitter. The snow was two feet deep. Mr. A.'s clothes, all of them, even to the suspensory he wore because of his varicocele, were in the warm bedroom he had left. He could not walk up the street, across the town, naked. Aside from his being seen, his feet would freeze. He waited, teeth chattering, on the porch against the wall, listening to Mr. B.'s enraged denunciation and the long wails of Mrs. B. from within.

After a few minutes a window in the side of the house opened. An object, two objects, thumped into the snow. The window closed. Mr. A. put his head around the corner of the porch, his breath rising yellow against the light from the window. He stepped down into the searing chill of knee-deep snow. There he found his shoes and socks. The shoes were filled with snow. He emptied them and put them on and waited hopefully beneath the window, like a shorn, shivering and hungry Airedale for another bone. His long red woollen underwear and his trousers came next. He had to sit down on the steps, remove his shoes to pull them on. Snowflakes melting on his bare shoulders, he cursed and mumbled, half perishing with cold, until his shirt, tie, vest, jacket, hat and buffalo-hide coat were flung into the snowbank. When, his shirttail hanging out, his hat askew on his head, one arm through an overcoat sleeve, he was groping his way through the trees, the window opened once again. As it slammed disdainfully shut with an echo which shook him to his foot soles, Mr. A. discovered at his toes, its belt and strands suggesting a snake strangely writhing on the snow, the outlines of his suspensory. He picked it up and went home a chastened man, it was to be supposed, to his room across the town.

Nor was the incident one to cause a rift between him and Mr. B. Formerly known to one another only by sight and name, sharing a further acquaintance, as it were by proxy, they had, it now appeared, sufficient in common to establish the basis of friendship. At any rate, Van Empel had seen them frequently together in the town beer parlour.

The morning after the campfire discussion of the affair between Mr. A. and Mrs. B. — most of the men accepted the story at face value, though a few questioned some of its details — Van Empel set off with his sketchbook to walk a few miles down the Smoky. This river, tributary to the Arctic-flowing Peace, rises in Lake Adolphus just over the divide to the east of Berg Lake.

It was now late August and a touch of fall was in the air. In the timber wind sorrowed, and overhead clouds lay low against the peaks. Near noon Van Empel found himself in a clearing, a deserted cabin at is lower end. To his left rose a sheer rock wall and to his right the river murmured.

The cabin was without a door, and he stepped inside. Against the far wall a crude bunk slumped, the willows that had formed its "springs" littered over the earthen floor. Firewood and kindling were on the top of the round-bellied stove, where they would be secure from pack rats. Such places where man once had lived, but lived no more, strangely fascinated him. Turning to go outside, he saw that one of the logs abutting on the doorway had been blazed flat with an axe at eye level. On the blaze, written in crude letters with a pencil, he read, "Frank, I've gone on down-valley with the horses." Mystery shrouded the words. Who had "gone on down-valley," and on what dim mission? He felt a companionship with this other, nameless pilgrim seeking his destiny in the mountains.

Stepping over the threshold and pausing for a final backward look into the cabin, Van Empel sensed that he was no longer alone in the clearing. He "froze" and, listening, at first heard nothing but the ceaseless flow of the river and the moan of the wind in the spruce trees. Then it seemed he heard a whimpering from behind the cabin. It was like a child's muted sob — a child incongruously lost in the forest and wanting his way home. Putting his head around the corner of the cabin towards the source of the sound, Van Empel saw only a mass of upended roots where the wind, months or years before, had toppled over a balsam tree.

Hearing a twig break, he swung quickly about, to confront a grizzly bear at the upper end of the clearing, about sixty feet distant. He was soon to learn that it was a she-grizzly and one of unusual qualities. Head held low, she regarded him with red-rimmed, myopic eyes, from under the hump of her shoulders. Her lip curled to show yellow fangs. Retreat into the cabin where he would be trapped being out of the question, and the rock wall above it cutting off his escape in that direction, Van Empel began to walk in a half circle away from the bear and towards the river. Uttering a deep growl, she moved to intercept him. When he stood his ground she reared up, immense in the forest gloom.

Van Empel, now a thoroughly frightened man, felt as if hair were lifting along the ridge of his spine. He attempted again to approach the river, having the notion that if he could wade it and put it between himself and the grizzly he would be safe. The she-bear, again on all fours, cut him off, yet she did not come closer. He thought of climbing a tree. However, he was not built as a tree climber. Besides that, the branches on the trees near at hand began high up, beyond his reach. Instead he backed towards the mass of upended roots behind the cabin. The grizzly, rather than trying to head him off, followed, but kept her distance. When he paused, she followed suit.

Now he heard again, but more distinctly, the childlike whimper he had heard before. Taking his eyes from the grizzly and staring into the roots that reared shoulder-high beside him, he saw a cub, a small one born the previous winter, dangling with his hind foot caught in a crotch, his paws barely an inch above the mossy ground. The cub had perhaps run along the trunk of the fallen tree, climbed into the roots, missed his footing, and become entangled in them. He could not climb back, nor by himself could he free his foot, nor could his mother do it for him.

Van Empel, so close to the cub that he might have touched it, looked towards the mother. She no longer snarled, but seemed to be watching him expectantly. It was, he said later, as though she had herded him towards her young one with what vague hope in her animal mind only God would know. She had done this despite her instinctive fear of mankind. Bears have notoriously poor vision and depend upon their keen sense of smell. Yet in the man-tainted air she did not run away nor charge to the rescue of her cub. She waited.

It is not unknown for animals of the wild to come to man in their distress. There is the age-old story of Androcles and the lion which limped up to him with a thorn in its paw. Deer and antelope have joined pack trains when too closely hunted by wolves or coyotes. In her book *Sierra Outpost*, Lila Lofberg relates that a female coyote, its forefoot mangled and torn from being caught in a trap, dragged itself one winter day to the Lofbergs' cabin on Florence Lake, California. For three weeks the coyote lay in a shed, the door of which was left open, while her foot mended. She ate the food the Lofbergs brought to her.

Van Empel of course realized only that he was in a serious situation. In any case, the she-bear had not suffered injury. It was her cub that was in trouble, and he knew that it would be the utmost folly to go between the she-bear and her cub. Bears on occasion desert their young. Usually, though, they are quick and ruthless in their defence.

The bear looked at Van Empel with a puckered brow. Suddenly it appeared that in the forest shade a community of interest had been established between them. His fear vanished. He knew what he had to do.

He forced his way into the tangle of roots, keeping the cub between him and the mother. The cub's whimper became a bawl. "B-a-a, b-a-a," he cried for his mother. He weighed no more than twenty pounds, his heavy fur fallen forward along his back. Van Empel seized him by the hind leg from which he hung, lifted him quickly and dropped him to the ground. He fell with a squawl. The mother rushed towards him, throwing up a spray of moss as she slid to a halt, only twenty feet away. The cub scampered to her. She reared up enfolding him in her arms. Her upper lip curled. If bears can smile, she smiled.

Van Empel stepped over the tree trunk behind the root and walked towards the river. Slowly she turned, still upraised, and now made no attempt to deter him. He looked back and saw a wilderness mother, wind trumpeting overhead, clutching her babe to her breast. It would be one of his finest paintings, he thought, if he could put it down on canvas. He would show that life, all life, is infinitely precious. It was a conception which was persistently to elude him.

Time was growing short for the Dutch-born artist. Leaving the Rockies in the fall of 1927, he sold a collection of his paintings to the Canadian National Railways. Some of them hung for years on the log walls of Jasper Park Lodge. They were destroyed by fire in the summer of 1954.

He sold others in the eastern United States and Canada. Late in 1930, Van Empel set out from Boston to motor to Mexico. He had in mind the province of Sonora. He was in a road accident in New Mexico, suffered a broken leg, and died from an embolism in December, still in quest of mountains.

The
Tepee

I went into that valley, tributary to the Athabaska, to look at the timber. It was not big timber. Timber does not grow big on the Arctic slope of the Rockies. It was big enough though, and clean, the branches beginning high up, tall, lean, black lodgepole pines, with the hard look of hunger on them — hundreds of them, thousands of them, rank after rank by the river, column after column coming down to it.

I am a short man, thick in the calf and forearm, deep in the chest, among those trees, slim and aspiring, I felt smaller and shorter than ever. I walked so that scarcely a pine needle creaked under my hobnailed boots — carefully as a child who searches for God in an empty church I walked, wondering what lumber the timber would yield for poles and railroad ties.

That was the idea we had, my partner and I, to float logs down the river in the spring to the tie camp on the railroad. It was September and my partner had not come with me. He had gone into Edmonton to see his girl. Bruce had no notion of who his girl was, or where she lived, or if she had brown eyes or blue. The less of her he knew, the easier she could be found. He was to return in October, by which time I would have looked over the timber and picked a site for the cabin we were to build. We would take out the logs for poles and ties in the winter, skid them down to the river over the snow to be ready for the breakup in April.

I had been in the valley three weeks or more when I saw fresh, unshod hoof marks on the trail above my camp. My roan saddle-horse and the two pack-horses were shod. I knew the tracks of each of them. These tracks I found were strange. It was in the afternoon and I was riding my roan bareback, driving the other two horses before me along a ridge of willow which led into the timber and towards a meadow I had found two days before. Feed in that valley was scant. I had to drive my horses a mile before turning them loose to graze.

The number of strange tracks showed there were six or seven head of horses ahead of me — and only just ahead, for, dropping from the ridge and crossing a small stream, I saw water still seeping into those tracks along its edge. Probably too, being unshod, they were Indian ponies. Bands of Cree Indians moved along that eastern slope of the Rockies, between the railroad and their hunting and trapping grounds at Grande Cache on the Smokey. I knew them, had worked with them on fall hunting parties, had visited with them in their tepees.

We were only a few yards from the timber when I saw the woman. She came out of it riding a small, wild-eyed pinto. She sat him close as a burr, holding with a high hand the lines of her rawhide bridle. She wore buck-skin trousers, not fringed, but fitting her leg tightly, and a man's blue woollen shirt open at the throat.

She came onto me suddenly, with no warning at all, so that my roan jumped, hardened his muscles, as she swung off the trail to let me by. She appeared, passed, left me twisting on my horse, staring at her back, before a word had gone from my lips or my tongue had formed a word to greet her. She came so near that the breath of her passage brushed me and I felt hard earth on my shin, spattered from her horses' hooves. Her long black hair was free and flowed back until her forehead shone in the evening light. Her eyes, squeezed into slits against the sun, gave no sign of having seen me. Only her nostril, like a small autumn leaf fingered by the wind, flinched as she went by. She passed me as though I were a stump and she a woman riding on a fateful mission.

I watched her blue shirt vanish towards the river, her appearance in itself an act of disappearance. She would not go far. She had brought her horses upstream to loose them in the meadow. She was going back now to her camp and it would not be distant from my own. I saw her ford the river. The gleam of her shirt died before my eyes as she entered the forest on its other side.

A river ran between us. But a river could be forded. It could be crossed on foot on one of the many spruce trees the wind or winter snow had laid across it. The valley, which had been empty, which was wide enough to hold and to shield from each other's eyes, two hostile armies, now with one woman in it was crowded. Our horses fed from the same poor crop of grass. The air I breathed was shared between us. And there would be others too. There would be her husband. Or many others. She might be camped in a tepee with her family. It was that which I set out to learn. Not that, at that moment, I especially desired to. I had enough on my hands to keep me occupied. But she had come close to me, to spatter hard mud on my leg. She had, so to speak, touched me, and I had lived long enough to know that the one escape from woman was to go towards her.

I dismounted, slipped the bridle from my roan, lashed the lines across his long, smooth haunches, sent him and the two pack horses with him, racing up the trail. I returned quickly to my tent in its clearing. There the tea water was boiling on the tin heater stove, but instead of preparing supper, I took down my hunting glasses. I climbed the small rise separating me from a view down the river. From behind some willows I observed the tepee. It was less than half a mile away, a brown, up-ended funnel.

Firewood was stacked neatly beside the closed flap of hairy moose-hide which served for its door. Inside, a fire was burning and grey smoke puffed slowly from the cluster of poles at the tepee's tip. Pitched low and broad in the Indian style, it gave me the impression of having pushed itself up out of the ground while my back was turned. I had, during the day, heard no sounds of arrival, no whinnying of horses, no shouts, no chopping, none of the strife of making camp in the wilderness. It had simply sprouted, as a mushroom would sprout, and seemed as much a part of its surroundings.

The tepee was on a point in the river commanding a view upstream and down. When a man stepped out its door, he held the valley in his vision. The dark forest opened two arms about it and beside it grew a young poplar tree, its leaves already scorched yellow by the frost. Above, a mountain rose. It rose in ledges and great hanging cliffs. It thrust itself urgently up out of the earth and was still shaking from its shoulders rocks and struggling timber and white cascades of water whose rumble reached me where I stood.

I took my glasses from their case, sat down, putting my elbows on my knees, holding the glasses steady to examine more closely what was before me. At first the yellow poplar tree filled the lens, flaring like flame from the soil. Leaves dropped about its roots shed a glow upon the ground.

Dusk was in the valley, but the sun, topping the western range, held the tepee, the poplar tree, the narrow point of shingle jutting into the river, in a pool of light.

The woman's pinto horse was tethered downstream on a goose grass flat. As I watched, the haired flap of the tepee was pushed back and the woman emerged. She had tied her hair with a red ribbon. She began to carry firewood inside. The glasses brought her near to me so that when she bent over I saw the hang of her brown, heavy breasts. I saw the pebbles pressing against her moccasined feet and, glinting in the sun's light, what might have been a gold ring on her finger. Once coming out, she straightened and looked up the valley, into my eyes as it were, and she seemed so close to me that I expected her lips to open and speak my name. I slipped lower until I was lying flat on the ground. When I raised myself again, she was gone. The flap of the tepee closed. Smoke swirled more heavily from the tepee top.

I lay there until all the stars were out, until, one by one, they vanished behind a storm cloud rising in the east. I waited. I supposed her man would be about. But I had seen no one but her. I heard no voices. In the tepee for a while the fire burned and between the black lines of the poles a woman's form was outlined on the canvas, grotesque and slow moving, as if a giant winged bat, half-stupefied with smoke, fluttered between the walls. The fire inside died down.

I heard the river throbbing in the dark. At first a gentle

flow of streaming waters. Then an endless advance and an endless receding of ripples over shallows and the beat of the conflict filled the night, fell against my ears so that I no longer knew if it was the river I listened to, or the throb of my heart, or the throb of a woman's heart lying like mine close against the ground and echoing from the stolid rock of mountains.

I crossed the river on a spruce log and walked towards the tepee, at first no more than a ghostly blur in my vision. No stir came from within it. No sputter of a half extinguished fire. I thought, "Perhaps she has gone."

When I came closer I smelled dried hides and old wood smoke and grease burned on the fire. I knocked the back of my hand against the flap of moose-hide.

"Hello!" I said. I paused. I hit the flap again. "Hello! Hello!" I said. "May I come in?" The wind ran through the dry leaves of the poplar tree beside me.

I reached my hand in front of me and my fingers ran against coarse new wood. I pulled them back, startled at the palpable shape of an opened doorway. I put forth my hand again. I shoved it in and knocked a piece of wood from about my shoulder level into the tepee, rolling it into the coals of the fire.

A wall of wood prevented my entrance. She had piled firewood from inside before the doorway and fortified herself against me.

I commenced to unbuild what she had done. One by one I took those slim pieces of wood and laid them outside by the wall of the tepee. I worked with care, with precision, feeling myself involved with her in a deep scheme of silence. Not one of those pieces of wood should fall from my hands to disturb the spell. And while I worked I heard the mutter of the river, closer, and closer behind me, until at last in the dark my feet felt wet with its water.

I removed the last stick of firewood. I entered. The flap dropped behind me. I turned, fumbled with its cord, but my fingers failed to tie the knot to hold it to its pole.

The coal still gleamed red in the fireplace made of a circle of stones on the ground, and rain tapped on the canvas above me. After the rain would come the snow. Soon snow would lie over all the mountains.

I sat down by the wall of the tepee. I leaned over, stirred with a piece of kindling the coals of the fire until a flame leaped up, lighted the woman's face where she waited under a robe of grey marmot skins across from me. For some time she did not speak.

Finally she said, "You were slow. I have been waiting." I told her I had taken my time. For one thing I hadn't been sure that she was alone.

"Oh, yes," she said, "I am alone."

She reached up and touched a fringed shirt of caribouhide, worn almost black from use, which hung from the stub of a branch on the slanted pole above her.

"He has gone down to the railroad. Maybe he will come back tomorrow and maybe not until one or two days later," she said.

"Who's gone down to the railroad? Who's coming back?" I asked.

"Felix," she said. "My husband — with a pack-horse for some flour and tea. Then he will look for a place with better feed. He always takes good care of the horses." She drew in her breath. "He is a very strong man," she said. "I have seen him lift a horse on his shoulders."

A mountain cayuse weighs six or seven hundred pounds. The feat was one to be regarded with respect.

"He sounds like quite a fellow," I said. "Does he do that very often?"

She shook her head. "No, not very often. Just when he feels good and there are people around . . . But I knew before he came back you would be down to see me."

"You did, eh?"

"You were behind the willow bushes watching me," she said. "The sun flashed on your hunting glasses."

"Then why did you pile your firewood in the door of the tepee?"

She turned her head and looked up into the night through the funnel above us, where the wind whined through the tapering tepee poles. She put the back of her hand across her mouth and dug her teeth into its flesh. Her cheeks creased and hid her eyes in their folds. She tossed on the bed and giggled, lying on her back, moving her black head of hair from side to side. Her knees rose up under the robe of skins.

They spread and came together, then spread again.

One of her legs escaped from its covering, knee and thigh rising, brown and smooth and glistening as with oil in the firelight, round and firm, commanding as the shape of my desire.

The edge of the marmot robe rell between her knees. I saw that she lay naked.

As I went towards her, around the edge of the fire, I thought of her working in the narrow tepee, piling those sticks of wood by the door one by one above the other, and realized what I had sensed before, that it had been no more than a gesture, the gesture of a woman who in another place would have hid her face behind a shawl, have drawn the curtain across her window, have said that she was busy and would I come around another day.

Later I learned her name was Marie Lapierre. Marie and Felix Lapierre — names not without their brave connotations. They recalled the days when French voyageurs and Scottish traders of the great fur companies travelled through the country with flags and sound of harness bells, with drums and bugles, and mixed their blood with that of the native Cree Indians, as if so to atone for the ingenious rascality of their trading.

Marie and her husband had arrived, only the day before, from somewhere close to the Peace river in the North. The season was now too advanced for them to return with their horses and they would stay in the valley for the winter. After all it mattered little where they were, so long as the woods gave cover for game and fur. They were vagrant as a puff of wind and came and went for no more apparent reason. They were not seeking life, nor fleeing from it, nor interested in building a larger tepee than their neighbours. They lived by what they had, and not, in the white man's way, for what they lacked. The future did not intrude into their present, but their life-long present endured into the future. They had rifles, traps and horses, and the skill to use them.

The next day I settled on a cabin site for my partner and myself. I cleared a bit of ground and cut a few logs for the cabin. Snow had fallen lightly during the early morning and, coming back to my tent, I saw Marie's small footprints among my own. Before entering the tent, she had carefully circled it, as though stalking a piece of game. She had taken a few pounds of flour from the bag hung from the ridge-pole at the back and emptied about half of my tea from its tin.

Two nights later Felix Lapierre returned and came to see me.

It was late, after eight o'clock, when I saw his portentous form against my tent. The moon was out and the canvas above me so drenched with light that it seemed, when he touched it, it would commence to drip and the drops to hiss upon the low, round stove, glowing and panting with its heat in a corner by the door.

Felix threw back the flap and, awaiting no invitation, seated himself on a grub box just inside. He took papers and tobacco from his vest pocket and set to rolling himself a smoke. I watched him from where I lay on my blankets, head upon my pack-sack. He was a tall man, broad shouldered. A stronger man than I was. His black hair, its tips appearing silvered in the moonlight filtering through the canvas, hung down over his eyes. From behind it, his face looked out — the driven, hollow-cheeked face of a man who has travelled far through the mountains.

Then he dropped his eyes to his task, where his long fingers weaved and coaxed until suddenly from among them the cigarette emerged, completed as by sleight of hand.

I lifted myself and sat with my arms buckled over my knees.

"Well," I said, "you got through all right."

"Sure, I always get through," he said. He spoke to me in English — English learned in some mission school, at the foot of a black robed priest. He spoke with caution, correctly, and in monotone.

After a minute, he asked, "She has been around, eh?"

"Who?"

"Her down there at the tepee. My wife."

I told him I had seen her three or four days before when I was putting my horses up into the meadow. "She rode by me," I said. This, at least, was literal truth.

Felix said, "Usually she stops to talk."

A puff of smoke from his mouth spread along the canvas wall. From under it he stared at me coldly and, as it were, slowly — the gaze of an ancestry foreign to my own, of blood and hunger, hunt and knife, of forest and hill, stream and lake. I wondered how much he knew, and if he did not know, what he would do when he did know. Marie — she needed to tell him nothing. The marks of my hobnailed boots, in three nights of going and coming in the snow about the tepee, would speak a logic of their own. There was, further, my remark about his "getting through." It had hardly passed unnoticed.

For what must have been a minute he stared at me. We did not speak. The stillness was a third self in the tent. Through it our eyes became locked in a contest of wills. Then I glanced quickly, as with stealth, to my left. There, within arm reach of Felix, my rifle in its scabbard rested against a pile of horse blankets. Ashes fell and settled in the stove.

His eyes followed mine. He dragged deeply on his cigarette, took it from his mouth. As he exhaled, the smoke spread along the canvas wall, lay for a while long and flat beneath the shadow of the pine tree branch moving forth and back in the night wind. I waited for what he would say.

"You have found good feed for your horses?" he asked me quietly, studying his cigarette stub, flicking it from the end of his thumb against the stove. It was a conventional question.

"Pretty good feed," I said.

He half rose, as if about to leave, thought better of it, and settled himself again on the grub box.

He said, "She told me." Then after a pause, he added, "About you and her." It seemed he smiled, or perhaps it was a mere curl of his lip, but I caught a glimpse of white teeth like a light that glimmered and dimmed in his mouth. Marie had told him — Marie, who with her careful speech, her tossing head, stayed with me less as a woman than as a place where I had been.

I failed to answer him, not knowing what answer to give.

He stood up. I rose quickly to stand beside him. In the narrow tent we were so close that our chests almost touched, and feeling his breath warm upon my forehead I was aware of fear, wondering what he might do. He was a strong man. He had lifted a horse on his back.

He held out his hand. "I am not mad," he said.

We shook hands. His was the wide, sinewy hand of the horseman. Taking me by surprise, he tightened his grip around my knuckles, bore upon them with a pressure I could not resist. The joints cracked. I lowered my elbow, bent my knee to relieve the pain rising as sound to my lips.

"No," he said, without relaxing his grip. "I am not mad. This winter I will camp here or up the valley where the feed is better for my horses. I will be away a lot of the time on my trapping line. You and my wife . . . it will be all right, see?"

Then he let go, turned, ducked out the tent flap and was gone, having shown me the contempt of his strength and the disdain of his charity. From the doorway I watched him go along the ridge and down it, wading through the willows that in the moonlight rose around him, around his legs, his hips, his shoulders until at last, when against the gleaming river his head dropped from view, it was as though he had walked down among the roots, under the faded grasses, into the earth to which he was closer neighbour than I.

Trees Are Lonely Company

It has been an open fall — but now, in mid-November, in
the valley of the Moose, wind blew, snow flew — and with
every stride he made, downriver towards the railroad, Jake
Iverson, the burly, black-bearded trapper, was remembering
the green grass. Green as springtime it had been, up there
around the pool.

Breaking trail ahead, legs, snowshoes, swinging from his
hips in tireless rhythm, was Felix Lemprière, also a trapper
and a guide. Behind Jake, rifle ready in the crook of his arm,
came Corporal Dallison of the Royal Canadian Mounted
Police. Last in the procession was a big, wolf-like dog, ears
laid back, tail held level and uncurving.

Heads down, wordless, the three men pushed through the
storm. Sometimes a moosehide mittened hand would reach
out, as if the ever shifting, ever receding snow were a curtain
which, by a gesture, could be parted. Breaths rose, mingled,
and were whipped away by the wind.

Incident by incident, timed to the creak of snowshoes,
Jake recalled again what had brought him to where he was
with a rifle pointed hot against him. It was the green grass.
That was what "they" would be asking — why had he failed
to notice the green growing grass? A mountain man, and he
had failed to heed the grass when it was green . . .

There, in the upper valley, five days ago, all the willows had long ago shed their leaves. Even those around the pool were barren and the grass everywhere was scorched yellow by the frost. All the grass, that is, except the grass on the water's edge by the pool. That had been green, green as grass in May. And he had seen that it was green, although, at the time, he had paid it small attention. He had been busy and moving around a lot.

Nor was it as if he knew the river well. His cabin and Clem's, his partner's, was away back, a week's travel back on the Muddy. Usually, they came up the Muddy, down the Jackpine, up the Smokey and over the summit behind Mount Robson to reach the railroad. On this occasion, they had turned off from the Smokey over Moose Pass. Jake had not been along there for four or five years. But Clem had wanted to learn about the country, so they had come over the pass, down the Moose.

And anyway, not giving full notice to the green grass — that was no sign there was anything wrong, Jake argued to himself. Look, another man, less sharp, would have taken the money. It came to just over eleven dollars — a five, two twos, a couple of ones and some coppers. No silver, just the coppers. Not enough to be much good to anyone. Not enough to buy a winter's grubstake. And that's what they were coming out for, two trappers coming down the river to Red Pass to buy their grub. Of course, Tom Boylan, the storekeeper there, would have "staked" them, so the money wasn't so important after all.

If he had taken the money, he would have committed theft. And "they" would never pin a theft on him —not on old Jake Iverson, "Wilderness Jake," thirty years in the mountains and on speaking terms with most of the trees along the windings of every creek from the mouth of the Canoe at the Big Bend in British Columbia, north to where the Smokey joins the Arctic-flowing Peace in Alberta. Jake could even address some of the trees by name, like Jessie, for instance, the lone-growing birch by the footlog over Chatterbox creek. Roots washed by the stream, she reminded him of a maiden, expecially in the spring when her leaves were newly out, a maiden touching toes to the water. And there was Natalie, a school-marm tree, standing on the edge of Starvation Flats.

Up on the North Forks, where Whitehorn creek empties into it, was old Maude. Shutting his eyes, he could still hear her groan, and her old joints creak, when the wind blew down from the icefields. There were many other trees, with names, and nameless. But none of them, he repeated to himself, when he spoke had ever answered him back.

Naturally, being the man he was, and with all those trees in the Moose valley peering over his shoulder, he wasn't going to take Clem's money. "Clem Rawlings" was the full name, a lean young man with red hair and a moustache not so red as his hair. He was a fast traveller, proud of his long toes and high arched feet. He never wore boots. He wore moose-hide moccasins. Clem had been a great one too for writing letters which he carried down with him when they came out to the railroad, letters to correspondence schools. One day he wanted to be a salesman and the next he was set to pull up stakes and become a blacksmith. He wasn't content to be just a trapper. It used to trouble Jake's nerves at times, in the cabin or around the campfire, the way Clem would talk of what he was going to do with himself. At other times they both became sullen and unspeaking. They had lived together so closely that each had become his companion's conscience and until one could speak only if he reviled the other.

Even so, Jake wouldn't take Clem's money. No one would ever be able to say that old Jake was a thief or that he spent what was not his own. So, instead of lifting the money, he had stuffed stones into the pockets on top of it and tied the trouser cuffs with rope and unbuckled the belt around Clem's waist and shoved more stones into the trouser tops and buckled them tight again.

He did not search the pockets of the mackinaw or shirt. They held papers, envelopes from Clem's letter writing. The shirt, like the woollen underwear, was red. Clem believed that red kept out the cold. No, Jake let the shirt and mackinaw be. Then he dragged Clem across the clearing. One of the socks, trailing through the hot coals of the campfire, began to smoke. He dragged Clem across the clearing and through the low fringe of willows to the clay bank of the river and slipped him into the pool made by a back eddy. It took all his strength for the stones added weight to Clem's small, wiry body, so that Jake was scarcely aware of the grass among the willow roots, the grass which ran around the water's lip like a half circle of low burning green flame. Clem, his flat, pale eyes staring, mouth open as if he shouted, sank feet first. As he went down, his long red hair streamed from his scalp, as though a breeze blew up from below him. Afterwards, bubbles rose to the surface. Jake strained to see, but he could not see bottom, nor where Clem lay, through the clear, swirling water. The pool was very deep.

Jake dropped Clem's rifle in after him. This gave him pain because it was a good rifle, a .303 Savage with a telescope sight. But it was Clem's rifle, as the money was his and Jake would not use it. Going back to the campfire, he gathered up Clem's bedroll, pack-sack and the snowshoes he had been toting on his back against the coming of snow. Because this stuff would not easily sink, he cached it in the bush, under a log and dead branches, half a mile back from the trail. Returning, he scattered the bough bed, and swept up with a spruce branch, obliterating from the clearing all traces of the morning's business.

It was now coming on to noon and he was tired from what he had done. Before pulling out, he sat against a stump to have a smoke, staring down the valley. It was a calm, blue mountain morning and he could see as far as to where the valley narrowed and between two tall peaks, that were like a gateway, fell into the Fraser along which the railroad ran. During the night it had snowed. Though the snow, failing a wind, still clung to spruce and balsam on the slopes, the sun had thawed it in the valley bottom. That was all to the good, Jake considered. The thaw would dim his and Clem's tracks, the tracks of two men, coming down the river. Not that anyone would have been apt to see them. Except for grizzly hunters in the spring, few people travelled the trail up the Moose.

Out in midstream, as he watched, cakes of ice were floating down from the headwaters. Any day now, with a quick drop in temperature, which would occur if the snow held off, ice would bind the river. Of course, he had small cause for worry. A body weighted with stones, like Clem's, would not likely rise to the surface, ice or no ice. For all that, the ice, and snow upon the ice, would be a seal upon his efforts.

Jake was mulling this over, ready to knock out his pipe and be on his way, when, still looking down the river, he saw what sent a chill clean through him and made bristle of the hair upon the nape of his neck. Only a quarter of a mile away, coming around a bend, he saw a policeman. He knew it was a policeman, a Mounted Policeman at that, by the muskrat cap he was wearing with the flaps tied up and the yellow striped breeches. Another man was with him. They were afoot, rifles in their hands, snowshoes tied upon their packs.

At first Jake would not accept the evidence of his eyes. He rubbed them until the tears ran. He thought that he was already shaking hands with the willows. That was an idea Clem had had — that if a man stayed out too long in the mountains, he would surely go out to shake hands with the willows. Damn Clem. Damn him and his ideas. Why wouldn't Clem leave him alone?

If it hadnt been for his ideas . . . Still, it wasn't only his ideas. Sure, he talked a lot about them. He'd talk when Jake was tired after a day on the trail and the fire in the stove had burned down and the logs of the cabin were cracking in the cold. Jake might doze off for a few minutes and wake up and Clem continued to talk. He read magazines and newspapers, hid them in his pack when they were coming in from the railroad. That used to make Jake angry, for they had all they could do to pack in the grub they needed. It was in the magazines that Clem found the correspondence school advertisements which he wrote away about. His pockets were always full of papers, envelopes, pencils. He never studied, because by the time he got back an application form from one outfit to make him a salesman, he was in touch with another one that was going to show him how to be a mechanic.

But it was what he read in the magazine articles that he liked to talk about at night. The night before the last one, when they were sitting around their fire on the far side of Moose Pass on Calumet creek, he was talking about penguins. He had read that there were penguins on some place called the Falkland Islands. He was all set to go down to the Coast and sign on a ship so that he could see the penguins. On his way back, he was going to stop off in South America and go up in the high mountains there and trap chinchillas. Lots of money in chinchillas, he told Jake, as if Jake didn't know. But the money was in raising them, not in trapping them. Jake had had to listen, though all the while he knew Clem would do nothing about what he was talking about. No, he would stay and trap marten and lynx and silver fox, if they were lucky and trapped anything at all. You don't get rich being a trapper.

Sometimes when Clem was talking, Jake in impatience would rise up in the middle of one of his sentences and go out of the cabin, or leave the warm circle of the campfire, to walk in the forest among his friends, the trees. He would look up at them, at their heads, proud against the stars, nodding now here, now there, in guarded converse of their own. He would listen, half afraid of what he might hear. When no word came to him, he would return, relieved, soothed, to find Clem asleep or, more likely, still awake and ready to go on talking about his plans and ideas. It wasn't his ideas alone. It was more than that. Perhaps it was just the way they met up, a bit more than two years before. It was as though Clem had been sent, as though "they" had sent him, although Jake did not get to figuring along that line until some time later. Clem appeared beside his campfire one evening up on Sheep creek which flows into the Smokey. Walked out of the bush, stood beside the fire and there he was — a little fellow with moose-hide moccasins, red shirt, red hair, reddish moustache, pale blue eyes. He had a rifle, a bedroll, a pot, but no frying pan. He was travelling south, living off the country. His father, he said, was a homesteader down at Hudson Hope below the canyon on the Peace. Probably Clem had been reading and Hudson Hope was too small to hold him. So he started south to the railroad through the mountains. Only, he didn't go on farther south. Not then. He moved in with Jake to his cabin on the Muddy. Nothing was said. It was just taken for granted. At first it sat well. Jake had been alone so long, it seemed it would be good to have a partner for a change. Trees make a lonely sort of company.

Clem was young, not more than twenty-five, and he weighed no more than a hundred and thirty — Jake topped the scales at two hundred — but he was a moose for work and for travel. He took over the cooking, baked cakes and bread in place of bannock, roasted the meat instead of frying it. On the trail he carried the heavier pack. He got into camp before Jake and, when Jake pulled in, the spruce boughs were laid for the bed, wood cut for the night, supper hot and ready to be eaten. That's the way it was, day after day, night after night for the better part of two years until, finally, it began to get Jake down. He commenced to feel old. He felt he wasn't carrying as much, travelling as fast, working as hard as he should. Of course, when a man is over fifty, he has to expect to slow down a bit, but he doesn't want to have to remember it every waking hour of the day.

This Clem with his red hair, and those flat, blue eyes — they seemed to have no lashes — who never tired, was like Jake had been in his youth — first into camp, carrying the heaviest load. When Jake faced him across the campfire, it was as if he regarded himself of thirty years before and if Clem looked at him and grinned, Jake knew he was making fun, telling him he wasn't the man he used to be. Clem was doing what he did to show that the older man could do it no more. Even his ideas — these things he talked about — Jake had had ideas too. He had been going to see the world, but he had learned that the world was wide, a wide, wide place. He had put off from month to month, from year to year, what he was to do and each year, though maybe he was in a different valley, he was doing what he had been doing before — making snares for rabbits, notching trees for marten traps, canning moose or caribou for his winter's meat.

But it was when they came out to town, out to Red Pass on the railroad; that Jake became really suspicious. Clem went off talking to people — to railroaders, to other trappers, to strangers. Then it occurred to Jake that "they" had sent Clem up to spy. Sure, he had appeared from the other direction — from the north. That was probably part of the scheme, trying to fool old Jake. Jake, trusting no one, least of all the bankers in town, kept his money, more than a thousand dollars in five and ten dollar bills rolled in a yellow slicker, cached beyond the clearing of his cabin on the Muddy in a hole in a rock wall, plugged with a stone. No one knew where it was but himself. Clem never knew, or so Jake had thought. Jake went out there only when Clem was away hunting or running the trap-line. When snow was on the ground, he would approach the cache by indirection so that, though it was only half a mile back from the cabin, to reach it he would often travel four or five miles over muskeg, through forest and along frozen streams. Not so much as a blaze marked the spot. Well, maybe "they" were after the money. Maybe they just wanted to watch old Jake, see what he was up to and they had picked Clem for the job.

At any rate, if he was watching Jake, Jake was watching him. That's the way it was this last night when they camped beside the backwater on the Moose, two days' journey up from the railroad, going into town for their grub. They had finished supper. They were drinking their tea and Clem was still talking about those God-forsaken penguins on the Falkland Islands. Jake bore it as long as he could. Then he rose and once more walked out among the trees, a little distance back from the fire. These, in the Moose valley, were stranger trees. He did not know their names. Yet he spoke a word. As he lifted his head to listen, it seemed to him that in response, up there in the thousand-needled branches, there was movement, a rustling, something less than sound, the echo of a whisper, a sigh that might have been his name.

He felt gooseflesh climb upon his shoulders. The next minute, in the chill night, he was sweating. Fearful of showing his back to the darkness, he retreated in slow, careful steps backward to the fire. In its welcome light, he turned about, confronting Clem who looked up to regard him — as it appeared to Jake — in a peculiar manner. Jake straddled his legs, wiped a hand across his forehead.

Clem, sitting with his back against a spruce tree, now glanced away and up towards the mountains. It was quiet, just the fire purring, the river flowing, the earth rolling beneath the stars.

Then Clem stared at Jake again, in the same peculiar manner, wrinkling his brows. In a moment he had spoken. For no reason at all, he declared to Jake, who stood above him across the campfire, "You know," he said, "a man has to be out here only so long until he begins to shake hands with the willows." He said nothing about the trees and the ghosts within them. He was too wise for that.

He spoke once more, to ask without warning, "Know what

I would do if I had a thousand dollars?"

Suddenly, in a flash of flame behind his eyes, the entire progress of events became apparent to Jake: why Clem had stumbled on to his camp that day on Sheep creek, why Clem had been trying to run him into the ground by making him travel faster than was his wont and why, in Red Pass, Clem was constantly whispering about him to strangers. Clem had discovered where the thousand odd dollars were hidden behind the cabin on the Muddy. Otherwise, why should he have said "a thousand dollars," no more, no less? He had discovered the money, but he had been afraid to take it for if he had had it on him, he would not have spoken as he did. No — he was waiting for his chance, biding his time.

A thousand dollars — a lonely lifetime's savings, every penny earned from trap-line, lumber-camp or mine. It was the dust of the years, watered with sweat and heavy with toil.

If Clem had been slower in saying what he did, if Jake had had a chance to think some more, or if he had not been standing with his partner squatting vulnerable across the fire, or if, though no wind blew, the murmur of the forest from behind him had not risen until it was a roar between his ears . . . As it was, Jake acted in self-defence and in the only fashion that he knew. He did not hesitate. He sprang, his boots scattering hot coals into Clem's face, and his fingers, those long fingers, strong as spruce roots, were around the other's throat. Soon, rolling into the fire, Jake smelt scorched woollen clothing. Then he felt the pulse in Clem's throat, beating against his fingertips like a marten's heart, but slower, when, bending over the trap, he squeezed in the chest, squeezed out the life, gently so as not to injure the fur. He had not meant to hang on so long as he had. He had merely intended to teach Clem a lesson, to teach him to keep his nose out of another man's affairs. But when he loosened his grip, Clem did not move, he did not speak, although his lips were parted as if he tried to. He lay there all night long. A light scuff of snow fell upon his cheeks, his open eyes. It did not melt. Jake sat by the fire and listened. He heard only the stilled tumult of the mountains. It was as if a great shout had come out of them and he waited, listening for the echo. It never came though, later, he was to start up from sleep, believing that he was about to hear it.

He did not touch Clem again until the morning. He had done what he had had to do. It had been himself or Clem. Now, by noon, he had finished with his task when, coming up the trail towards him, he saw the policeman and the other man. It was no vision, he realized, after rubbing his eyes. They were real enough, coming around the bend a quarter of a mile away. Jake had no time to jump the trail and take to the bush. His fire was still smoking, his gear was about it — but with no sign of anything that had belonged to Clem. Then, growing calmer, he thought that if "they" were after him, they would get him, no mistake about it. But why should they be after him? What did any of them know about him and Clem? No one could be asking questions as soon as this. He had met Mounted Policemen on the trail before. He had met them down the Smokey, checking up on the Indians at Grande Cache. Also, sometimes they came in after poachers. Jasper Park, a Dominion government game preserve, was just to the east of Moose valley.

Jake recognized the man with the policeman. He was Félix Lemprière, a French-Canadian, thickset man, wearing a buck-skin shirt, a tall black hat and a purple neckerchief. Soon he and the policeman were sitting around the fire which Jake had built up for them, eating their lunch of bully beef, bread and tea. With them was the big, wolf-like dog. He sat back a bit, panting, tongue lolling. The dog seemed to smile, as if he knew everything that Jake did and a bit more besides. But then, Jake figured, dogs don't talk.

The Mounted Policeman asked Jake a surprising question. He was young. He was new to that reach of country. Jake had not seen him before. He had only one eye, a black patch over the other one, the left one. The good eye was brown and it seemed to size Jake up, cool and steady, like an eye along a rifle barrel. Squatted on a log, he looked up, holding his tin mug in his hand, his breath puffing from his mouth in the cold air as if he were slowly burning up inside. He looked up at Jake and said, "I'm Corporal Dallison. I suppose you're Clem Rawlings?"

Jake, Clem Rawlings? Clem was so close to him, right at his elbow, so to speak, beyond the unleafed willows that, if it hadn't been for the water in his ears, he might have heard what was said. However, Clem wasn't listening anymore, Jake had not let Felix, the French-Canadian, go down to the pool for water for the tea. No, he had grabbed the billy and gone himself but, though he had had no breakfast, he drank none of the tea when it was made. Now, as the Corporal spoke, Felix sat on his heels looking into the fire. Felix and Jake had not spoken. They knew one another. They had met in Red Pass and along the trail. When there was need to speak, they would speak. If Felix had not been there, Jake might have permitted the Corporal to go on believing that he, Jake Iverson, was Clem Rawlings. The notion came to him, but he let it drop.

"No," he said, "Clem's my partner. I'm Jake Iverson."

"Oh!" the Corporal said, biting off a chunk of bread, "They told me there were two of you up here, but farther on, I thought . . . down the Smokey. I didn't know which was which."

Jake thought he should explain about Clem and why he was not with him. "He's gone over the head of Terrace creek," he said, nodding up the river. He was thankful again for the night's light fall of snow and the morning's thaw. The tracks of two men coming down would not show. "Up Terrace," he said, "and down the glacier to the summit behind Mount Robson. From there he told me he was crossing over the shoulder of Mount Whitehorn to the Swiftwater. He'll be coming down the Swiftwater about now and I'm on my way to Red Pass to meet him. We're going to stock up on grub."

"Lots of snow up high where he's gone. No good for glacier travel," Felix said, shaking his head.

"That's what I told him," Jake said, continuing to address the Corporal. "I told him he'd come to a bad end travelling alone across the ice. But he wanted to see the country, so he took his snowshoes and he's gone. that's how he is — bull-headed. You can't tell him nothing."

See? Jake was playing it crafty. If, later on, they went to look for Clem, they would go looking over the glacier and the high country behind Mount Robson. Wise old Jake. A man who wasn't lucid, bright as a dollar, would hardly have thought of that.

The Corporal and Felix sat around the fire a while longer. They talked about the weather and of how late the snow was in coming to the valley. The Corporal was not travelling to Grande Cache. No, he said, his lone eye impaling Jake upon its gaze as if the old trapper were a fly upon a pin, he was out to check up on poachers who had been taking fur out of Jasper Park, the game preserve over the divide to the east. Jake assured him that he and Clem did all their trapping on the Muddy, miles distant to the north and west. But the Corporal's words brought a half smile to his bearded lips. Felix, the man travelling with the Corporal, was the best-known poacher in the country and it was him the Corporal had selected as his guide. Felix lifted a wary eye to Jake. Jake said nothing. Old Jake knew when to keep his mouth shut.

The dog was there too, bedded down now, chin on paws, but his eyes were open and seemed never to leave Jake's face. Jake was worried about the dog. If he got to frisking about, he might find Clem's bedroll and pack-sack only half a mile back in the bush and begin a yapping.

But the dog stayed by Felix, his master, and in a few minutes Felix and the Corporal fixed up their packs and were on their way up the valley. In a few days they would return down the Moose, or perhaps down the Snake Indian and come out in Alberta. It would depend upon snow conditions.

When the sounds of their going had perished and Jake was shuffling around the fire, something caused him to look behind. The dog stood on the edge of the clearing, one fore-paw lifted, staring at him with black eyes large enough to put on the fire and boil moose meat in. Jake picked up a stick and threw it. The dog ran up the trail with a yelp, tail sucked under his belly.

Jake's plans were vague. Red Pass was two days' journey distant. When he arrived, he would have a likely tale to tell the boys in the beer parlour. Instead of sitting, as usual, by himself in the corner, he would join the group at the big table in the centre of the room. There he would say that he was concerned about Clem and would have to go up the Swiftwater to look for him. He would go in over the divides, far back from the Smokey where the Corporal might be, to his cabin in the Muddy. Then, with his thousand dollars, he would come down again, hop a freight at a lonely siding and go down to the Coast. From Vancouver, he would slip across the border to Seattle. Or he might simply head north, farther and farther into the mountains. No reason for alarm or hurry. It would be weeks, possibly months, before they set out to search for him or Clem.

But now, before starting downriver to Red Pass — he had told the Corporal that he was going there, and there he would have to go — he had a final job to do. The dog had made him apprehensive and, leaving the campfire, he went into the bush, picked up Clem's bedroll, pack-sack and snowshoes from where they were cached and carried them still farther back. He carried them to a rock slide, buried them under rocks. No dog nor man would find them there. It was the last move required to lock the door behind him.

It was dark when he returned to the campfire. In the dark it would be a bother to break camp, so he cut more wood, went upstream for his water and cooked a meal of bannock and bacon, rolled up in his blankets, slept the night. He was secure now. He could rest.

The morning broke bitter cold. No snow, no wind, but the heavy frost had come. The murmur of the sluggish river was distant because brittle ice had formed along its edges and only in midstream was it flowing freely. The chatter of a nearby creek was stilled. A weird, half-silence gripped the land as though God's fist had closed upon it.

But through the fringe of barren, frosted willows, Jake, rising from his blankets, saw the glint of open water with mist upon it. The pool had not frozen, though it was stirred by no strong current.

Strange that there was no ice upon the pool in whose depths rested the body and all the dreams of Clem, his partner. Then, pulling on his trousers, his boots, breath sifting grey from his nostrils, and parting the willows to look more closely, Jake saw again the green grass around the water's lip, and understood. The pool had not frozen, perhaps during the entire winter it would not freeze, because within it, bubbling up, was a warm spring of water. This kept the neighbouring grasses green. Such pools were not uncommon in the mountains. In winter, snowshoeing up the rivers, a man had to be on guard against them. Still, he sensed that it was a long and sorry chance which had guided him to such a spot with Clem's body.

The snow would come and fall upon the ice which already half rimmed the pool. The waters of the pool would remain clear and open.

Under Jake's nose, pushed through the willows, a piece of paper floated. He leaned over, picked it up, took it with him as he turned to make his morning's fire. It was a sodden fragment of envelope, the pencil marks upon it now illegible from their long soaking, which, somehow released from the pocket of Clem's shirt or mackinaw, had risen to the surface. Doubtless, it had been addressed to one of the correspondence schools to which he had the habit of writing.

After gulping his breakfast, Jake returned to the pool. He gazed upon its placidity for long minutes before he saw the patch of wool, shredded from red underwear or shirt, which had lodged among willow roots. He picked it up and put it in the fire. He wondered — the phenomenon might be caused merely by the action of the water, or a mink, having swum under the ice from up or down the river, might be working down there in the pool, tearing at Clem's clothes to reach the white flesh beneath them. The belly was what it would go for.

Jake could not leave the pool — it seemed he would stay by it forever — while these grisly remnants of memory, of what had once been a man, were throughout the day, slowly and inexorably, upborne to his view. The Corporal and Felix might return this way. They would go to the pool for water for their tea. What they would find there would give them pause, cause them to think, to put two and two together. Jake cursed the green grass. On another part of the river, what was here revealed to sight, would have been hidden beneath ice and beneath snow, when the snow came. He cursed the thousand dollars behind his cabin on the Muddy. Yet he was thankful that, though his fear of the dog, and the need of burying Clem's gear farther from the trail, he had come back to filch from the pool this testimony of guilt.

He crouched in the willows for hours, body benumbed, eyes transfixed by the water's promise. Mechanically, as a piece of paper, a tatter of wool, a corner of a handkerchief, floated to the surface, he reached out for it with a branch of spruce, ground it in his fist, stuffed it in his pocket.

When night came and he could not see, he dozed by his

fire and in the morning resumed his watch. Snow fell. It fell upon the forest and the willows and upon Jake's shoulders. It lay white upon the ice on the pool's rim. Into the pool each flake settled with a slight hiss and melted.

From the pool, steam rose as though in its warm depths, a man still breathed.

Jake, eyes wide and glaring, crouched beside the pool, heedless to snow, to cold, to time that was passing. When the snow ceased and the clouds lifted and the late sun shone up on the snow pink mountains, the pool was red, red as blood, lapping at his toes, and he could no longer see what floated there upon it.

It was then, or a day later, or two — he could not be certain, for time was absent with all timely things — that on their way back to the railroad, the Corporal and Felix Lemprière, ghostlike and wavering figures, were with him around the campfire and that he was pointing to the pool and babbling, "Blood. All of it, blood, Clem's blood."

Jake did that because now there was no cause for pretending. He had his wits about him. What he could see, the Corporal could see — though the Corporal at first, and until Jake led him back to the rockslide where he uncovered Clem's buried gear, was unbelieving.

Afterwards, seeing the big wolf-like dog, facing him by the campfire, Jake sprang to throttle him with his bare hands. Felix and the Corporal held him off.

Then Felix, under Jake's direction, sank a fishhook into the pool and pulled up a piece of Clem's trouser leg. Later the pool would be dragged with heavier tackle.

That was how it happened that, each bending his head to the driving snow, Jake had come down the Moose between the Corporal and the French-Canadian, the dog following behind.

Several times he had stopped to explain to the Corporal about the thousand dollars and of how Clem, with his fast travelling and nosing into his business, had persecuted him and to affirm that he, Jake, had done in self-defence only what any other man, with the same savvy, would have done. The Corporal had nodded in apparent agreement.

He and Felix had stood aside quietly too when Jake once stepped from the trail, took off his cap and bowed to a school-marm tree which, it seemed, he had met on his last trip down the Moose long ago. After speaking, Jake listened. Five nights before, as Clem's body lay beside the campfire, likewise he had listened, because at that time it was as though a great shout had come out of the mountains and he had waited to hear its echo. Now he thought, again he was about to hear that echo — from a tall spruce beyond the school-marm tree where the wind, in great gusts of snow, troubled the dark forest.

Jake shook his head. He turned down the trail, behind Felix, followed by the Corporal and the dog. This he could not explain to the Corporal — that Clem's voice was up there in the tree tops, calling to him, but in the howl of wind and groan of forest he could not distinguish what Clem was saying.

Nearing the railroad, though the snow still flew, it appeared to Jake that the green grass along the edge of the pool, now grew taller. It reached his knees, his waist, and higher, to engulf him. He put out a hand to fend it from his face.

Yet, as he stepped from the trail, climbed the embankment to stand upon the grade, the scene of where he was, was clear before him: the twin blue rails hurrying away to converge in the distance, the telegraph poles, weary with their burden, staggering into the storm. Instinctively, he dropped to one knee to untie a snowshoe, for here, between and beside the rails, the snow was packed and shallow and three men could walk abreast down the line and into Red Pass round the bend.

The Corporal, as if casually, knelt beside him. There was a quick click of metal. When Jake rose, his right wrist was handcuffed to the Corporal's left.

The three men, the prisoner in the middle, the dog behind, walked west down the track. They turned their backs upon the Moose where the legions of the wind howled and stamped and on whose upper reaches, into a pool half rimmed with grass, snowflakes fell and melted.

The Warning

Hank Dugald had been squatting on his heel against the jack-pine stump for several minutes before he noticed the squirrel. This was unusual, because Hank had been a trapper along that western slope of the Rockies for most of his fifty years. As a rule, his senses were alert and his eyes quick to detect any movement in the forest where he made his living.

However, the squirrel, head down on the trunk of the Douglas fir — only ten feet above the ground and thirty feet or so away from Hank — had not moved at all, except for a nervous twitch of its tail. And besides, Hank had been looking beyond the fir tree to the cold gleam of railroad tracks in the valley below him and to the green section house and the red water tank.

Nearer to him, under the wooded hill where the Hoona river broke out of the mountains, was a tent, with four horses grazing nearby. It was this that had caught his attention, for in the door of the tent stood a man in the brown jacket and the blue yellow striped breeches of the Royal Canadian Mounted Police. Probably a constable and his helper on census patrol, checking up on the number of trappers and half-breed hunters in the region, Hank said to himself.

But staring at the tent, so unexpectedly pitched in his

path, he began to mumble and to curse softly. Involuntarily, he shifted slightly the .30-30 rifle laid across his lap.

Now the squirrel chattered and inched farther down the tree trunk. The sudden noisy rattle so close at hand gave Hank a start, but only for a moment. His mind returned to what was before him in the valley and to the trail going north along the Hoona behind him. Up north, on the head-waters of the Hoona, was his sod roofed cabin. For four days and three nights now, he had fled away from it down river toward the south.

He had made no fire during the nights. Nor had he during the day always followed the trail on the hard clay of the river bank. He had kept back from the river when he could, floundering knee deep through lush beaver meadows, picking his way over rock slides, pushing through green-leafed willows whose branches reached out as if to detain him in his flight. And with each step he tried to assure himself, over and over again, that what he had done back there on the headwaters was only what any other man would have done under the circumstances. A man had a right to defend what was his own.

And anyway, the fellow had been a breed. Hank distrusted the half-breeds, those living remnants of the fur-trading days. They were "different." They lived in tepees, moving here and there as occasion or fancy prompted them, restless as cloud shadows upon the land. They never settled down as people should.

Four days ago one of them, Joe Plant from over on the Arctic divide, had come into Hank's wilderness and had actually invaded his cabin. The door had not been locked. Hank, who trusted no town banker — nor, for that matter, any other man — had close to five hundred dollars rolled in a yellow slicker and buried beneath his bunk, and he knew better than to do that which would arouse suspicion. In the mountains, a locked door was an open invitation to pillage.

Night after night Hank would unearth his money, spread it out on the blankets after covering the window, and count it over in the candlelight to be certain that not a single bill was missing. He was not a miser. He was merely prudently on guard to see that no one filched from him what was his own, what had become his only love and life itself.

The afternoon four days ago, when he had surprised Joe

Plant, Hank had been out cruising a side valley of his next winter's trap-line. As he entered the cabin, Joe, a slim young man, was on hands and knees reaching under the bunk. Hank roared, grabbed him by his purple shirt and jerked him to his feet. Young Plant said he had come to borrow tea. He and his people, pulling in from the north earlier in the day, were camped a mile away. Finding no one at home, he had sat down to fill his pipe and wait. The stove was still warm. He knew that Hank would soon return. Then, somehow, as he was filling it, the pipe had slipped from his fingers and rolled under the bunk.

Hank had not believed a word of it. He had always regarded the Plants as a shiftless crew. Tea? Instead of tea, they needed a lesson. So, when Joe Plant left, Hank picked up his rifle and set out after him, angling through the forest to intercept the trail the other would take.

As Plant emerged on to a rock bluff over the river, Hank was behind him and on higher ground. He raised the rifle, aiming just over the crown of Plant's black hat. The bullet, so close to him that he would feel its wind, would warn him to stay out of other people's cabins. At the instant Hank's finger squeezed the trigger, Plant, in his stride, stepped on a piece of down timber, lifting himself up a foot or more. The rifle cracked. The black hat flew off. The young man threw up his arms and fell forward off the bluff into the river, fifty feet below. The shot which was to be only a warning had caught him square between the shoulder blades.

Hank was appalled. He walked over to the bluff and looked down. A brown hand, lodged between two boulders, showed from the white-toothed waters, as though in death Joe Plant still clung to life.

Hank's stomach chilled. He raced back to his cabin. Overturning the bunk, he discovered young Plant's stubby pipe. The earth above the cache of dollars was undisturbed. Hank dug up the money, stuffed food and a blanket into his pack sack and lit out for the railroad, four days south down the Hoona. The other Plants might have heard the shot. Or perhaps, when they went to look for their missing kinsman they would come upon the hand, upraised from the wrath of waters . . .

Even now, with nearly a hundred miles behind him, his

back was uneasy as he looked at the tent so freshly, so grimly planted where the Hoona joined the main valley. The constable in the doorway was staring up the Hoona — staring, so it appeared to Hank, into his very eyes, though he knew that he could not be seen through the trees.

Again he noticed the squirrel, still head down on the tall fir tree. And now it seemed to him that the river, with its many branches down which he had travelled, was itself like a giant fir tree fallen into the mountains. And, like the squirrel, he had come down it nearly to its roots, where it was set in a mightier valley.

And all this while, since its first chattering, the squirrel had not moved. Its moist, twitching nose pointed to the grass at the foot of the tree. There, in the grass, Hank detected for the first time a stir and a whisper of movement — in the grass a weasel waited for its prey. While Hank had been sitting silent and immobile, the squirrel and the weasel had shaped their fateful meeting at the foot of the Douglas fir. To go back up the tree, the squirrel would have to turn — and in the moment of its turning the weasel, swift as daylight, inescapable as conscience, would have it by the throat. Death for the squirrel was life for the weasel.

Hank's finger crept to the safety catch of his rifle. He took a final look at the railroad tracks. That had been his idea . . . to hop a freight and lose himself in the city on the Coast. But he had not counted on the police being here to meet him. Yet he could not return up the Hoona. There the Plants waited. They would hunt him down.

Like the squirrel on the tree trunk, Hank on the river trail dared not go back and feared to go down. If the constable did not know today, tomorrow or the next day the Plants would tell him. While Hank was hopping from one slow freight to another, the police — more relentless in pursuit than all the Plants or the three tribes of weasels — would be after him. The telegraph would catch him before he reached the Coast.

He chose the easy way.

Slowly he lifted his rifle and fired. The report echoed through the hills, and at the foot of the fir tree blood stained the grasses as the weasel squirmed and died.

When the constable rode up the trail towards him, Hank's face was tilted to the blue sky. He was listening to the squirrel, chattering its message of release from the top-most limb of the fir tree.

At the constable's first words, he roused himself, his thoughts suddenly returning to the headwaters of the Hoona and to the figure of a young man, arms outflung, on the bluff above the river. "I just meant to warn him," he mumbled to the constable. "Not to hurt him, see? Just to tell him to keep away, to keep away from the cabin."

The Stranger

The stranger had a low, assured and rather sing-song voice — quite the sort of voice one associates with the foothill country of Alberta where horses and cattle range and the life of men is to tend them, often to sing to soothe them or merely to remain awake in the saddle.

He approached us in the early morning as we smoked our cigarettes after breakfast around our camp fire below Brulé Mountain. It was in June. We had nearly a hundred head of horses there with us, held in the pasture for the night between the bars three miles below on the trail, and the high, giant rock ridge to the south over which we would pass at the beginning of our long day's journey. We were moving the horses from their winter range on the head of the Solomon up to Jasper where, during the summer, they would be used to take eastern tourists, tourists from the British Isles, California and others of the world's far places, over the mountain trails. Pete, the ranch foreman, and I had passed three weeks of hard riding, gathering them in the high valleys, cutting out the poor ones, driving those we needed into pastures and corrals. They were soft-footed after their winter in the snow, still unshod, round bellied and sleek on lush spring grass — and our job was to lead and drive them fifty miles through the mountains, across rivers and through muskegs, over rocks and through pine forests where the ground was carpeted with needles, and deliver them, forty tons or more of horseflesh on the hoof, safely to our boss for their summer's work.

We were short-handed. There were only the two of us. We had use for another man.

Above our small camp fire, its flames at times blown flat upon the ground by the wind, rose the ridge, running down off Brulé Mountain, to the wide, grey waters of the Athabaska, the Cree Indians' "river of reeds" and the farthest southern reach of the Arctic watershed in North America. The ridge had no name, but it was a dangerous part of the spring horse drive. It was a shoulder of the mountain perhaps six hunderd feet high and the trail swung up it in a series of switchbacks no wider than and as precarious as a set of tilted pantry shelves. From only half a mile down the valley there appeared to be no trail at all, only dark rock with here and there a bush or stunted spruce upon its slope.

The previous spring we had lost a mare in the crossing, an old and sure-footed mare. The horses, strung out in single file, pushed too hard from behind, had bunched. She missed her footing, slid on the slippery black earth only inches deep over the rock framework of the mountain. She jumped the line of horses on the switchback below her. Her front legs buckled. She rolled end over end, like a cartwheel, to land with a broken back in the down-timber at the foot of the hill. Pete had had to go back and kill her with his saddle axe.

Since then, he carried a rifle.

His was the burden of taking the horses through to Jasper and to him was the credit of having brought them through the winter. All winter he rode the range alone bucking snow up to his horse's knees and bitter north winds studded with snow that ripped the breath from his mouth. Yearlings and mares with sucking colts too weak to paw through to the grass on hillsides, he drove during the early spring into the corrals by the ranch house and fed, or, failing that, packed feed out to them. Every sleek round belly we had with us was a tribute to his judgement as a horseman and his strength and courage as a rider.

He was a lean red-faced man in his forties, bald-headed, with blue eyes cold and flat as pieces of ice. He was given to sudden bursts of anger when his neck and ears would flush with blood — yet with a horse his voice never rose above a murmur. He wore a ten gallon hat. Years before his knees had suffered a permanent disagreement and were no longer on intimate terms. Standing, he looked as though he were about to jump, and walking, jolting his body, it seemed he was shaking his baggy trousers down and would only by luck arrive at the most casual of destinations without social disaster.

He rode a rangy roan gelding which, along with my buckskin, had been picketed near our camp during the night. We had already saddled them for the day's ride and Pete was rising, bridle in hand, when the stranger appeared before us.

He stepped from the spruce trees behind us so quietly, so suddenly that I had the impression he had been there in the shadows watching us for minutes, perhaps close to us the whole night through while we lay on the ground, rolled in our blankets.

"Hallo!" he said, in that low voice, lingering over his words. "You fellows figuring on pulling out?"

We looked around, startled. He was a tall man, past his youth, thin shanked, hatless. Masses of blond hair fell down over his brow. The corners of his tight lips drooped and the stain of chewing tobacco was squeezed from them. His ears were large and stuck out from his head, seemed to bend forward in a great effort of listening for our words enclosing his small, brown, withered face, his speech, like a set of parentheses.

Pete, gaining his feet, said, "No, we're just going to sit here and watch the grass grow."

"Now," said the stranger, "I wasn't figuring that." He straddled his long legs as though he felt the earth lurch beneath him and sought to set himself more securely upon it. "No," he went on, "I didn't figure that. With all these horses around, I figured you were travellers — like I am too, in a way of speaking, just travelling."

"From the prairies?" I asked him.

He turned to me, slowly and deliberately, twisting his body on his narrow hips. I saw his eyes circled with coal dust. And when I noticed his hollow cheeks, his chin with its stubble of beard, it was as though he had no eyes at all, but only the dark sockets — for the man was hungry and from his face the eager skull looked out. I guessed he had come in from the prairies riding a freight train — the railroad was a bare two hundred yards below our camp running between the horse trail and the river up to Jasper.

"Yes, a traveller from the prairies," he continued. "That's what I told the brakeman when he put me off the train at Entrance, down the line there twelve or fifteen miles. Since then, I've been walking, counting the ties. They've sure used a lot of ties to make this here railroad, put a bit too close together for a man with legs like mine. I had a good ride as far as Entrance though, sitting in the open door of an empty box car. I told the brakeman I was a traveller. A tourist, I said, come to see the mountain scenery. That's what they wanted up here, I asked him, wasn't it? They write books about tourists coming to the mountains. He was a funny fellow, that brakeman. He kicked me off just the same. That was last night. He said he was afriad on a freight train I wouldn't find the comfort I needed. He said I might complain and cause them trouble. Besides, tourists, he said, travelled on tickets, not on box cars."

The stranger smiled, showing us a few worn yellow teeth. He squatted on his heels, cupping his chin in a long fingered hand.

"A ticket," he said, "that's what he thought you needed to enjoy the mountain scenery. There's lots of scenery in these parts all right. A man gets a crick in his neck looking at it." He lifted his head to the mountains around. "It makes a man hungry just to see it. I guess it's the hungriest scenery I ever did see."

Pete, standing above us, his bridle with the silver rosettes slung over his shoulder, kicked the fire, threw a piece of wood on it, moved the tea-billy closer.

"We've grub here," he said, "if you're hungry — but we haven't much time. We're in a hurry."

"I don't want you boys to think I came by here looking for a hand-out," said the stranger. "I could do with a mite to eat all right. But I'm not really hungry. Why I had a bit of supper night before last in Edson, down the line. A farmer there . . ."

I fried him bacon, baked him bannock, poured him tea.

While he wolfed his food, leaning back against a tree, he asked us where we were taking the horses. We told him.

"Jasper!" he exclaimed. "Now that's the place I was aiming to go myself. I figured there might be work there for a man who was handy with a rope and knew how to put his hand on a strange cayuse."

"You been around horses much?" Pete asked him.

"Sure. That's what I want — work with horses. You see, I've had some hard luck — well, when you see a man without his hat, you know he's had hard luck."

The stranger at our campfire assured us that, in his younger days, he had ridden the range and we had no good cause to doubt him — he had the hands, the easy speech, the indolent grace of body. Since then, he had taken up a homestead in the foothills and one night it had burned before his eyes. He referred to it in passing, as to something of no concern at all — so far away, so long ago, it might have been a small misfortune of his grandmother in her youth.

But even then, I think, Pete distrusted him. "I thought you said you came from the prairies?" he said.

"That's right, the prairies or the foothills. It's all the same. This homestead of mine . . . well, a creek came down there out of the hills and my place right by it where it flowed out onto the plains."

Pete seemed unconvinced. He was moving away to his horse when the stranger, raising his voice, said, "That's what I was figuring when I heard your horse bells away down the track and walked up here from the railroad. I thought, well, here's my chance. Men with horses. Perhaps they'll take me along with them for a day's travel. Maybe I'll even get as far as Jasper, might even find a job with the outfit . . ."

Pete glanced at me. I suppose I nodded. We could do with another man to help us with the horses. We had an old saddle we were taking up to Jasper to be mended and a hackamore bridle could be made with a bit of rope. While the stranger and I packed up and he watched me throw the packs on the pony, but failed to lend a hand, Pete went out and dropped his rope over a young sorrel mare, saddled her, knotted a hackamore and fitted it to her head and mouth.

"I don't know about the job," he said, addressing the stranger, "but you can ride with us into Jasper, if you've a mind to. You can help with the horses. We don't want them to string out too much or to bunch up too much on the trail — especially going up there." He pointed to the ridge, a half mile or more away across the flat.

The stranger ran his eyes along the upflung arm and when they met the ridge they opened wide, revealing their whites, unsoiled but astonished, in his tanned and coal-streaked face.

Grey, tattered bits of mist blew up against the ridge.

"You take horses up there?" he asked.

"That's where the trail goes," Pete said. "A man has to follow the trail."

"Jimminy, that's a tough looking place for horses."

"You're not scared, are you?" Pete studied him closely.

"No. I ain't skeered none." He wagged his head and spat a long stream of tobacco juice on a wild rose nodding in the wind at his feet. I believe he had eaten his breakfast with the chew of tobacco tucked in his cheek.

"Say," Pete added suddenly, "those are hard looking boots to ride a horse with."

Instead of our high-heeled, sharp-toed, soft leather riding gaiters — Pete's a special handmade pair — the stranger wore a wide-toed snoutish boot made for walking in soft loam and mud, a farmer's boot. I wondered how he would get them into the stirrup, or getting them in, if he would be able to get them out again. He glanced down, waggled them, spread them, so that they seemed to look back at him and grin.

"They're all I got," he said. "They're the only ones I have."

"I never seen a horseman wearing a pair of rafts on his feet before," Pete commented.

We measured the stirrup leathers to the stranger's arm. We tightened the cinch for him. We cared for him as if he were a pilgrim and a tourist. Pete told him to be easy on the mare's mouth. "She's a good little horse," he said, "but she has a tender mouth and that hackamore may bother her a bit. Ride her with a loose line and you'll be all right."

We gave the stranger the lines and stepped back to let him climb into the saddle. He tried to mount facing in the same direction as the horse, his right hand on her rump like a man climbing stairs two at a time. We knew then he was a raw hand with horses and I wondered about the tale he had told of wanting to swing a rope in Jasper and his homestead burning — every word he had spoken I doubted. But we didn't wish him hurt, so I held the mare's head while he set himself in the saddle.

Under him the mare was nervous. She sucked her tail between her legs. Her head went down. We thought she was about to buck. Instead, she stood and trembled.

"Easy," Pete said, "easy, girl." He rubbed her nose, patted her neck.

"Don't move around in that saddle so much," he said looking up. "You're not on a homestead. You're in a saddle. A man would think you had ants in your trousers."

Pete was a bit concerned. Afterwards he told me he realized then the best thing to do would be to leave the stranger and let him catch the next freight train to wherever he was going. But we had gone too far. We had the mare saddled and him sitting in the saddle. Besides, he was a pair of hands that we could use.

During the night some of our horses had strayed high on the hillsides grazing. We rode up to drive them down. Our extra hand stayed down on the flat, riding in a circle, trying to keep them in a herd as we hazed them down, jumping windfall and crashing through willow bushes. When his mare broke into a trot, his feet went out, his arms went up, his blue mackinaw shirt billowed, his fair hair flopped on his forehead, his big ears seemed to wag — so that he resembled a man attempting flight. W were worried and then we laughed about it, thinking of how sore he would be when he arrived at Jasper.

"He'll be so wore down, he'll be riding on his shoulder blades," Pete said wrinkling his red face and removing his hat to polish his bald head with a green bandanna handkerchief.

It was eight o'clock before we had all the horses down on the flats. We untied the pack-horse and set him loose with the rest. I rode to the south end of the clearing to lead the string up the trail and over the ridge. Pete rode in the rear where there was the most riding to do, taking care that none of the horses cut back through the timber. We put the stranger pretty well in the middle. There, all he had to do was to keep pace with me ahead of him, prevent the thirty-five or forty head of horses between us from lagging.

As we lined out into a gallop, heading for the foot of the ridge, Pete and I began to shout and sing with the feel of the wind in our faces, the strength of long muscles between our thighs. The stranger was silent and looking back I saw he was pulling leather, grasping the saddle-horn, his face white and taut, his big boots swinging in the stirrups as though he were trying to cast them off.

The horses were running free, manes and tails flowing, kicking, snorting, whinnying, searching for their companions of the winter range, for a familiar scent, a remembered face or whatever it is one horse looks for in another that he wants for travelling company.

We reached the foot of the ridge in a flurry of dust and a thunder of sound. I lowered my head to pass through some tall willows and set myself forward in the saddle to help my horse on the climb. He settled to a walk. He was a good size for a buck-skin. He had a black stripe down his back, a black tail, a black mane curved over the arch of his neck. He went along carefully picking his steps, clicking his teeth against his curb bit, flicking his small, pointed ears and nodding his head as if our progress were a sort of endless affirmation.

The trail was so narrow that as we climbed my riding gaiter brushed the grass and bushes on the upper side and the slope was so steep that grass, growing in patches of dark earth, hung down of its own weight, clean as though combed and ruffled ever so slightly by the wind. Behind me I heard the horses. I heard the thudding of their hooves on the flat, the cracking and bending of the willows as they bunched where the trail commenced to climb, their deeper breathing, and now and then, a cough as they lowered their heads to the ascent. On the hillside they were following slowly in single file. That was what we wanted. There was no room for crowding.

On the hillside I swung first to the left, then doubled along the switchback to the right. As I climbed, the mist gone now with the heat of the sun, the valley grew below me. I saw the fields near the ranch house, six miles away, sprinkled with the green dust of new hay and beyond them, the rounded foothills, spruce on their ridges and the light green of poplars in their draws. The Athabaska river was wide and quiescent as a lake, snow-topped mountains beyond it. Beside it, the railroad ran in twin black lines of haste — the railroad that brought tourists and strangers into the mountains, that led west to the Pacific and east across the continent to the Atlantic.

Soon, I saw off the toe of my gaiter the tips of the poplar and pine trees on the flat below and, stretching through them, the shining brown and black and golden string of horses like the twitching back of a great and sinuous beast slowly burrowing into the hill. I turned and swung again across the hillside. I saw Pete riding back and forth across the trail, hazing the horses along and from where I was, two hundred feet above, it appeared that he was being swung by the glossy line of flesh and bone and hide, as if he and his roan horse were the tip of an indolently flexing tail, still remaining half nerveless on the flat, but being drawn gradually and surely into the hill below me. Now and again, I heard him shout and saw faint dust rise from his horses hooves.

The stranger was already on the hill going in the same direction as myself, but with a line of horses heading the other way above him. He was at the low end of one length of trail, I, at the high end of another. We had three lengths of trail between us. It was a great thousand footed monster I led up the hill.

I waved to the stranger. "How's it going?" I called.

He looked up. He had both his hands on his saddle-horn, the knuckles white, his lines knotted beneath them. He slightly lifted his hand as though he were about to wave it to me, then replaced it again on the horn. He half-opened his mouth to smile or speak, but he didn't smile and he didn't speak. He didn't look up and he didn't look down. He had his eyes on his horse's head. Then he and the horse, as the trail turned again, disappeared behind an outcrop of rock. For a moment I saw only his great forward bending ears that seemed to rise above his head. He came out from the rock, his shoulders and head in full view, legs hidden by the bulge of the hill, moving up and down to his horse's stride as if he were a man on stilts. And always between us, the horses, the rumps of horses, the withers, the manes, the fidgetting ears or only a brown eye catching a glint of the sun.

I was almost to the top of the ridge taking the last switchback that led to the summit when I noticed the horses bunched several turns below me. The man from the prairies had pulled up and stopped and Pete at the foot of the hill, unable to see him, was shoving the string along.

"Hi!" I shouted, "what are you doing?"

Up to me the stranger turned a face shrivelled with fright.

"I'm going back," he said, "back, back . . . to the ground."

I called to him that he couldn't. I waved my arms. I pointed to the horses on the trail behind him that he couldn't pass.

It was too late. He tried to dismount, but his left stirrup was down the hill and he lost his nerve. He pulled savagely on his hackamore bridle and the sorrel mare, in her time a first-rate cow-pony — she could turn on a dime — pivoted beneath him, pattering forefeet pointed down the slope, her head low, her toffee coloured tail bowed between her legs. Then I had to move along for horses were coming up behind me.

When I next saw the stranger, he was heading down the trail, facing into the up-coming line of horses, trying to drive them back. They reared away from him and were pushed on towards him by the weight of numbers from below.

A big black slipped from his footing, dragging his haunches at first along the ground, his forefeet braced as he tried to hold himself against the hill. Then, as he slipped farther and farther down, closer to the horses on the switchback below him, he straightened out, crossed them in a soaring leap, fell, rolled, slid three hundred feet to the rocks and down timber at the foot of the ridge. I heard him hit, but I could no longer see him. That was the beginning. The long and orderly procession of horses hesitated, smelled terror in the air. Some succeeded in turning back or in holding themselves to the trail. Others seemed to be snatched from it, glossy rumps or bellies flashing in the sun, appearing below me for a moment, crashing down the slope. An avalanche of horse-flesh, tons of horseflesh, were pushed down the mountain side, vanished as dust and rocks and splinters of old logs settled. Pete, who by this time was out on the flats again, told me later that all those manes and tails had in a vague way the semblance of brown rushing water. All the horses seemed bays. Many of them appeared to leave the trail and throw themselves down the hill for no more reason than that they saw the others doing it — as if among them existed a compact for destruction. It had the appearance of sound — the shape of tumult — but what he remembered was sudden silence.

The surprising part of it was the number of horses to reach the bottom of the hill safely. Fifty or sixty head were on the switchbacks between the stranger and Pete, and of these at least thirty left the trail. Some scrambled back again, while others tobogganed down on their haunches and were perhaps pillowed below by those before them on the rocks and among the harsh dead timber.

The stranger's mare was one of those to make the descent whole. I saw her running, full out, tail streaming behind, her rider bent low over her neck. I am not sure yet whether she ran away with him or whether he set her on the run to flee the scene of his weakness, his failure and his folly.

I saw Pete, off his horse now, his hands lifted over his head, make a few stumbling steps after him. Then he showed his face to the hill and what was there before him, dashed his hat to the ground, jumped on it, danced up and down in anger and bewilderment. In a minute, slowly, head down, he went to his horse, tied it to a tree and took his rifle from the scabbard. He had work to do.

I could not descend to him until I had cleared the horses off the trail below me, pausing to feed with no one to drive them on. I took my horse to the top of the ridge and went back on foot and chased them to the summit. Grass was there and a small lake where they would stay and graze.

From the foot of the ridge where Pete was working, I heard a rifle shot. He was shooting the injured horses, a long break between each shot. He would want to be close to put the bullet in the right place, square between the eyes. I counted nine shots. On the flat I saw a brown pinto kicking against his bowels wrapped around his hind leg, jerking them from his belly. Closer in where I could not see, I heard a horse's wild piercing scream. It made my stomach ache to think of those horses, like the brown pinto, with old stumps run through their guts, with legs broken, wedged between rocks as large as a section labourer's house. I was slower to drop down the hill than I might have been.

I heard no more shots and wondered if Pete, running out

of ammunition, were using his axe, stunning them between the eyes, or bringing it down over the eye or between the ears where the bone is softer.

Far down the valley a pillar of black smoke travelled toward us. The westbound passenger was due. The whistle of its locomotive sounded mournfully through the hills as though it were lost, seeking a way through the mountains to the sea.

Down off the ridge I found that Pete had had to kill fourteen horses. Later, their bodies would have to be buried. What had happened would be the talk of the countryside. It would follow Pete wherever he went as a horseman. The hill, so long unnamed, would have its name.

He sat beneath a pine, head between his knees. He did not look up as I approached. He was sweating. His shoulders shook. His ears were red enough to bleed.

I told him I was going after the man from the prairies, the stranger. At the mention of him, Pete spat.

"I ought to have aimed the rifle," he said, "when he came down off the hill."

Above us and around us horses peacefully grazed, clipping the hillside grass. At the foot of the ridge, crows gathered, cawing.

I rode after the stranger, but I did not come upon him. We did not see him again. I found the sorrel mare, coloured a dark bay with sweat, dragging her bridle lines on the trail to the main range five miles back from the railroad.

When, days later, we reached Jasper, we heard something of what had happened to the man from the prairies whose words we had doubted, but whose hands we had trusted to help us up the hill. It may have been a chipmunk or a rabbit or the smell of a bear in the bush that, while he was riding hell-bent-for-leather along the trail, making for Entrance where the valley breaks out from the mountains, frightened the sorrel mare. At any rate, she shied, jolting him out of the saddle and when the big toe of his boot caught in the stirrup, she dragged him through the timber. Before his foot came free, she smashed him against a tree.

It took him three days to crawl the five or six miles to the railroad through a rocky draw, across down timber and through picket-like close ranked second growth pine. He had a broken left hip and couldn't move very fast. He shoved himself with his right knee and right elbow until each became a bleeding stump. After that, he literally dragged himself by his hands, by his fingers, almost by his lips and teeth, pulling grass out by the roots, taking hold of bushes and small trunks of trees, anything to give him purchase on the ground.

A freight train stopped and they picked him up when they saw him lying close by the track on the right of way. He was in a high fever, one of his hands festered with porcupine quills, and so exhausted he couldn't say at first who he was or where he came from. Shirt and trousers were rags that didn't clothe, but merely hung upon him. His shoulders and stomach were covered with matted blood and dust and leaves and grass.

The freight train took him east out of the mountains to Edson where for three months he lay in the public ward of the hospital.

He had been thrown from the mare near a creek, Solomon creek, and it was only by following the creek, he said, and having its water to drink that he was able to reach the railroad at all.

Pete regrets that. He says there used to be such clear, sweet water in Solomon creek.

The White Horse

When a man is packing in the mountains it is a good rule to have in his outfit a white horse. In the evening, at the end of the day's travel, the horses are turned loose to graze and at sun-up the packer goes out on foot to drive them in to camp. A white horse can be seen far away on a side hill or among the willows on the flats or showing for a moment deep in the timber when the bays, roans, blacks or buck-skins, making up the rest of the bunch, stand hidden. Without having to follow tracks, to listen for the always elusive sound of a bell, the packer sees at once where some, at least, of his horses are, rounds them up and brings them in.

Yet on the morning that Nick Durban decided that his white packhorse, Bedford, was lost, this very whiteness was a disadvantage. It was in early March, and windless, after a snowfall. Nick's cabin, from which in the winters he trapped, was on a rise above the forks of the Little Hay, between the foothills and the first range of the Rockies. As he stood on his snowshoes outside its door, bundled in mackinaw jacket and trousers, beaver cap, moose-hide mitts and moccasins, snow was everywhere about him. It was on the branches of the pine trees and on the spruce and balsam high upon the mountain sides. It lay heavy on the ice-filled creek and spread white and dazzling across the meadows, bright enough to blister the eyes. The whole world, it appeared to Nick, must be one white ball whirling around the silver sun. A white horse would melt into it like a handful of flour. His bones, flesh and hair would dissolve, would perish, would be absorbed by the translucent day.

The tracks Bedford had made had been filled in by fresh snow, dusted over by the wind and for a week he had not been in his lean-to shelter against the cabin where Nick, on the other side of the log wall, could hear his warm breathing and the crunch of his hooves on the frosty ground. But until now, the fourth morning that, neglecting his marten traps, he had set out to look for the white horse, Nick had assured himself that Bedford was not lost. He h..d merely strayed. In his search, extending over those four days, Nick had circled the meadows, followed the creeks to their head and returned in the late afternoons, his snowshoe trail stretching like a pattern of lace from his feet, and from his door in the morning seen again the cold mist lying in the draws, as if it were his breath left there the previous day in his passing.

Only one place remained to him to go — the bench directly behind and above the cabin, six miles distant beyond muskeg and brule. It was called the High Valley for some reason that Nick could never understand for it was no more than a sloping tangle of jack-pine and down-timber.

Yet, on the whole, poor though the name might be, he was glad that it had one. It was more home-like and warmer to have names about. In the valley only the creek was named and one mountain, called Black Mountain. All the hills were nameless. Even the pass which Nick crossed several times a year, leading into town and the railroad, was without a proper name. On the town side it was known as the "pass to the Little Hay" and on its north side the few trappers and homesteaders who used it, referred to it as the "pass to town." The matter had been discussed between Nick and his good friend Olaf, the Swede, who ran a trap-line farther down the Little Hay. Olaf had said that in the old country all such places had names, but he did not see how, in these foothills a pass, especially a low, gentle pass, that had no name, would acquire one.

The High Valley — that was different. It had had a name

longer than anyone could remember, and it was up there that the white horse, wandering from the cabin, might have gone for shelter or to rustle food. Nick, crossing the meadow from his cabin, now climbed up after him, snow boiling about his legs, his snowshoes sunk in the snow until he seemed to be walking on his knees. It was very cold. The air scorched his nostrils, his breath hissed from his lips and icicles hung from his grey moustache and beaded upon his brows.

He saw wolf tracks — five sets of them, a litter hunting with their dam and farther on a moose had broken trail for him up a tilted forest aisle.

As he went along he recalled trips he and Bedford had made together when they both were young and, looking back, those years were green, the valleys green, veined with sparkling streams of water, and in them grass grew bunched and strong and thick . . . His memory took him as far as the early days when the railroad came to the mountains. It was at that time, about 1908, that Nick had set himself up as a packer. He had had his own string of horses and packed supplies to a survey camp from Edson at the end of steel in Alberta. He packed through the foothills into the Athabaska valley, up against the Rocky Mountains where the blue glaciers glimmered. Sometimes when he had dumped his loads and unsaddled his horses, the surveyor, a Mr. Bedford, asked him into his tent for a glass of whiskey.

Mr. Bedford — Nick doubted that he had a first name — was a tall, spare Englishman from between whose sallow cheeks a sharp, red nose showed as a chronic inflammation. Often, coming in from the wind, his eyes watered, as if, in truth, it pained him. Each day after his work on the line, Mr. Bedford, returning to camp, removed his soiled clothes and took a bath in a tin tub made ready for him on the creek bank. Then he dressed in a black suit, white shirt and black bow tie, silk socks and patent leather shoes and walked forth and back before his tent, polishing his eyeglasses, whose long, black ribbon was looped about his neck. He ate his supper, brought by the chainman (who had already filled his bathtub), the youngest member of the party, off a folding table covered with white oilcloth and put by his tent door. All of this impressed Nick as an unqualified achievement for a man living under canvas. The detail upon which afterwards he most remarked, however, was the silk handkerchief Mr. Bedford on these occasions wore tucked up his sleeve. Until then Nick had seen only two things come out of a sleeve — a hand, and, now and again, a card.

It was following this year's work that his bay mare dropped the dappled colt, which as the years passed was to turn white and to which, in tribute to their association, Nick gave Mr. Bedford's name. The colt was long in the leg, high withered, with one blue eye. After his weaning he developed into a solitary beast, feeding a bit away from the herd on the side hill, a habit which finally determined his naming.

In time Mr. Bedford and other surveyors concluded their tasks and went away. The railroad hammered its way along the trail they had blazed. Soon trains howled through the Athabaska valley. Nick, resenting the intrusion, drew back into the northern hills, built his cabin and laid out his trapline. For a while he kept his six head of horses, using them on hunting trips in the fall. As the years passed, these long trips became less frequent. His horses fell away. One of them he sold to a homesteader over the divide. One of them the wolves ran down. The others foundered in the snow, or purged with new spring grass, lay down in weakness and failed to rise from some south facing hollow.

At last only Bedford remained. Foaled in the foothills, he outlived the others brought in from the plains. Nick was able to remember it was thirty years, half a lifetime, since Bedford had been a colt. They had grown old side by side, but it seemed that the white horse had aged two years to his one, so that now, at thirty, he was about to leave off where his owner, as a packer, had begun.

For Bedford, probably the oldest horse on the Athabaska watershed — Nick knew of no other surviving from construction days — had not been worked for many years. He had been loose to graze. With age his joints had stiffened and his tendons could be heard snapping when he walked. Usually he stayed close at hand — the feed was good and he had had it all to himself — dozing in the sun or under the shed built for him against the cabin. From long standing the horn of his hooves grew long, forcing him back on his fetlocks. His teeth had worn down and long pieces of grass and even of willow showed in his dung, swallowed whole and passed undigested.

By those dried piles of dung, found along the creek or on a gravel bar in the creek or in the willows where the horse had gone to escape the flies or among the timber where the rain or wind had urged him, Nick more than once had paused to shake his head, part in dismay and part in anger. They gave him hurt within his entrails, as if the failure, of which they were evidence, were his own. Age was the portion shared by him with the white horse. It was age which over the period of years had cut down the length of his trap-line from eighty miles to sixty, from sixty to forty, from forty to thirty, until now, on his weekly rounds, he travelled only twenty miles to clean his traps.

They had come a long journey together — yet the horse, whose wants foretold the journey's end, was at the same time the one abiding link with its beginning, with the early days, with youth, when Nick in a crimson shirt rode at the head of his pack outfit and drank whiskey with Mr. Bedford and climbed all day hunting and never knew what it was to have to stop for breath on a hill slope or to be tired coming into camp with a haunch of meat over his shoulder.

More recently there had been the trips into town with the fur catch. Nick did not ride Bedford. Bedford was a pack horse and had not been broken to ride and now he was too old to pack. Nick packed the fur on his own back. He saddled the white horse and led him with a fancy Indian bridle over the pass and down the thirty miles of trail, taken in easy stages, to the railroad. Some people laughed at that. In town the boys threw stones, shouting that the old man was afraid to ride the old horse. Nick spat on the rutted road, shook his fist at them. After all, a man with self-respect did not go to town without a horse, or bring his horse in naked, or try to break to ride a horse as old as Bedford.

Afterwards, were the summer evenings at the cabin on the Little Hay. At supper Bedford put his head through the open window, shutting out the sunset, bringing an early dusk indoors. His flaring nostrils blew crumbs from the table top or he gathered up with his awkward lips the oatmeal spread there for him or nibbled at a piece of bannock set out to cool. Sometimes he nuzzled the tobacco can, which held sugar, and upset it. They had had words over that. Nick had even raised his voice. Then Bedford withdrew, walking stiffly down to the meadow where, belly deep in grass, he looked up and nickered.

The sun had passed its height when Nick, climbing through the snow from his cabin, pausing every few minutes to draw wind, now came upon him in the High Valley. Bedford was in a clump of second growth jack-pine, their trunks laced with old, fallen logs, as securely corralled as he had ever been. His lower jaw had dropped, showing the yellow discs of his teeth and, though one ear was cocked, his blue eye was glazed and drowsy. Robed and bearded with snow, he sat on his haunches, his shoulder leaned against a tree. His gaunt rib cage bulged, the ribs wide-spaced with his years, and standing beside him, Nick kicked at a white mound pile of dung. The horse had been caught there for some days, nibbling at bark and dry twigs, too weak to paw down to the scarce, pale grass or yet to force his way out over the down timber. The cold had hamstrung him and his back legs had collapsed. He was frozen stiff and solid.

Nick slipped his hands from the mitts which, suspended by a cord from around his neck, fell and slapped against his thighs. He stepped forward and while with his right hand he patted the horse's withers, trying to smooth the rigid, up-standing fur, and pinched the gristle under the roots of the mane, he held his left hand, cupped as with sugar or oatmeal, up to the mouth, against the chill, breathless nostrils. Snow dropped from the horse's mane into rounded, silent pits by his snowshoes. The snow lay around Bedford, lapping at his flanks, like a slow and ever rising flood. It lay over all the hills and all the mountains, deeper and heavier than a man had thought for, farther than his eyes had ever seen. Nick walked upon it on his snowshoes and beneath its surface Bedford was already sinking. On it the sun threw their shadows, merged them in a dark and inky pool. He put his head closer to the horse. He said a word and went away, downhill over the broken trail to his cabin, settling his webbed feet with care, aware of the depths which sustained them.

After a time, crossing a creek bed, he stood to listen,

hearing water under the ice beneath his snowshoes, pulsing against his foot soles. He waited, attentive to the soft, lively sound of spring. Here, lower in the valley, it had thawed at noonday and now at evening a light crust had formed on the snow. Later, when he could already see the fork of the valley, and up to his left the pass to town, the pass without a name, Nick heard very clearly and near to him the clang of a bell, as though a horse, sheltered by the spruce tree over yonder, had tossed his head. He went on, knowing that no horse bell was within a hundred miles and that a man, alone, heard what he most wants to hear.

Before entering his cabin, he hesitated at the foot of the rise on which it rested, measuring again its lines and worth. It was a well-built cabin, logs securely housed and chinked, roof dry and firm beneath the burden of snow. It would last a long time yet, beaten by the drifts upon its hill top.

In the cabin Nick lit the lantern and hung it from the beam. Making a fire in the stove, he went over to his bunk and rolled back the blankets and mattress, revealing the old newspapers he had put there to keep out the draft. They were the back pages, the pages of the want-ads, for experience had taught him that their close-set type was the warmest. Headlines let in the air. Here among the little words, where men sought jobs, offered their small goods for sale, made inquiry for friends and relatives and for things lost, he found the help he needed.

He studied two sorts of notices, one under "In Memoriam" and the other under "Lost and Found." He preferred the "Lost and Found," liking the idea of posting a reward to indicate you had lost what was important, what was of real value, what you could hardly get along without.

After supper he searched the cabin for his glasses, finding them on the shelf behind the mirror. They were steel-rimmed and hooked behind his ears. Probably they were quite unlike the glasses Mr. Bedford, the railroad surveyor, had worn, lacking, as they did, the long, black ribbon. Still, they served the same purpose, because with their steel rims around his eyes, Nick was disposed for figuring and working with a pencil.

He knocked the end from a prune box and brought it to the table, smoothing its surface with his axe blade until it was white and pleasing to the touch. He took the lantern down, set it by the teapot and began to carve with his knife on the prune box end, referring in his progress to the want-ad sections of the newspapers, frequently removing his glasses to see better what he was doing. Afterwards, he blacked the letters in with pencil. As the fire in the stove burned low, his fingers grew numb and his pipe perished in his breath, puffed against the lantern.

When he had finished he put on his mackinaw and mitts and beaver cap. Outside, he stood looking for a minute at the failing moon. He hoisted his pack-sack, picked up his axe and snowshoed eight miles down to the fork in the trail on the way to town. With his axe he cut away the lower branches of a lone standing spruce tree, and blazed flat a section of its trunk. It was a winter blaze above the level of a man's head when the snow had melted into the ground. He nailed the sign there, so placed that it would be seen by anyone coming up or going down the trail.

He stepped back to regard his completed work, stamping his feet, blowing on his fingertips where the frosty steel of the nails had burned. The sign read: "Lost — a white horse named Bedford. The owner offers a reward." At the bottom he carved his own name — "Nick Durban."

During the coming months at least half a dozen men would see the sign and read it. They would be trappers going out with their furs in the spring from the country more to the north, or coming in with supplies in the summer and fall. Each of them would see it twice.

Olaf, the Swede, who was his friend, and who travelled on skiis he had hewed and whittled from birch wood, would read it, looking up, stroking his black beard which lay like a young fir tree on his barrelled chest. "By Yimminy, a good horse, a fine horse," he would say, wagging his head, spitting a shaft of brown snooze into the snow. It was Olaf who had taught Bedford to eat bannock. Each visit he made to Nick's cabin he brought a round brown bannock specially baked for the occasion.

And Fred Brewster, the guide and outfitter, would be passing through on his regular hunting party in the fall. He would see the sign, read it aloud to his tourists, who were rich people from the East, and tell them about Bedford.

They would know then, all of them, that he was a good horse. If he had not been a good horse, his owner would not have offered a reward.

These men who were neighbours would understand. They would not go to look for the white horse. They had seen him in his age. They would know that if Nick could not find his horse, then Bedford was where no one would find him again.

Nick returned to his cabin tramping his shadow into the dawn's golden snow. From up toward the High Valley he heard a wolf howl, and then another, and his flesh winced and the pit of his stomach chilled for he knew that they had found Bedford.

Later in the month, the thaws having come, he decided to go into town. Formerly he had waited until most of the snow had seeped into the ground so that the white horse could go more easily with him. Now he travelled alone, taking with him on his back his fur catch, the pelts of marten and weasel and those of two silver fox trapped high in the timber.

Approaching the trail forks where he had hung the sign, his pace quickened. By the tree he paused. Someone had been there before him. Brown snooze juice was spattered on the snow. Under the sign was a pattern of ski tracks where Olaf had stopped to read. He had stood there, shaking his head, stroking his beard. Then he had gone down valley, along the other fork of the trail, back to his cabin. It was all there, clear as writing, in the snow. The tracks were three or four days old, their outlines rounded, made before the thaw.

One new set of sharper tracks cut across them, leading up towards the pass. Olaf, apparently, had come this far on his way to town. At the spruce tree he had turned back. Perhaps he had forgotten something at his cabin ten miles down the trail. Then, after a day or two, he had set out again. This time he had not stopped at the sign.

Nick followed on his snowshoes the trail Olaf had broken towards the pass. As he rose above the timber, nearing the summit of the pass, he saw what at first seemed to be a marker Olaf had planted in the snow to mark the trail. Soon he saw that it was too tall, too heavy and that it stood not on the trail, nor beside it, but twenty-five or thirty feet above, close to a wall or rock. Nor was it just one post. It was two, buttressed with stones from a nearby slide. They supported a frame two feet high and three feet wide. Within the frame spruce saplings, peeled of their bark and steamed, had been bent and nailed to form letters.

Nick blinked his eyes, rubbed them, trying to make out the words the letters formed. There were two words, the longer one above the lower. In a minute or two, against the rough, rock wall behind, they joined, coming alive before him. They spelled "Bedford Pass."

Nick shuffled his shoulders under his pack, stood on one foot and then the other as though the ground beneath his feet were hot. Olaf, who made his own skiis, had understood. He had read the sign in the trail forks, had gone back to his cabin to cut and peel and steam and bend and nail the spruce saplings within their frame. He had carried them up to the pass, cut posts from two four inch jack-pine and wired the frame to them. Chips and bark were scattered in his many angled ski tracks. His job completed, he had continued on his way into town.

Like the passes in the old country Olaf came from, the pass now had its name. "A pass has its name," Olaf had said. "No one gives one to it." Nick recalled their conversation of long ago.

He went carefully over the letters, one by one, to be sure that the name was correctly spelled. He would have liked the "B" to have been a bit larger. Still, the name would stand there for months, for many years, high on the pass between land and sky. Hunting parties and tourists would see it. People would ask how the pass got its name. Someone would tell them about Bedford, the white horse, the last horse left in the valley from the early days.

Afterwards, the time would come when no one would remember. It would be a name, as the High Valley was a name. Maybe the wind blowing hard from down the valley, or merely a moose or caribou in early September rubbing the velvet from his antlers, would push the posts down. Then the name would sink into the earth and become part of it.

Nick, the first man to cross Bedford Pass, pointed his snowshoes down hill to town and the railroad where Olaf had gone before him. Bedford was now a name. The wolves would not have him. He would outlast flesh and bone and hide and hair. He would endure so long as men climbed rivers to their source and spoke into the wind the pass's name they travelled.

The Bride's Crossing

I, Felix Lemprière, beat my fist upon my chest.

Of course, Sergeant Tatlow — Sergeant Tatlow of the Royal Canadian Mounted Police — does not see me do so, nor does he hear the sound, although this is deep and, to me, like the rolling of a distant drum.

The sergeant does not see nor hear me because he is still a mile away, riding up the valley to my cabin. From the cabin door, a few moments ago, I saw his scarlet jacket spotted against the light green leaves of a grove of poplar trees. For the moment I did not see the horse beneath him — the tall bay with the blazed face — because the sergeant, following the trail, dropped from the poplars into the thick-growing willows of the valley bottom. The willows reached to his waist so that he seemed to be wading through them on legs longer than a man's legs or to be upheld and borne along by an invisible and mighty hand. His approach, armed with the law, fills the narrow valley with threat, throws a gloom upon it, like that of the dark cloud which goes before the storm. Yet Sergeant Tatlow — and that it is the sergeant from Brulé on the railroad fifteen miles away, I have no doubt, for his is the only scarlet jacket for miles around — the sergeant and I are old friends. Twice we have hunted together the mountain sheep. He is a patient hunter, a deadly shot. Still, for all that, always behind him is the law — the law which, like a wide-flowing river with hidden fords, bears some men up, casts others down.

I have now walked around behind the cabin and stand between the cabin and the corrals. Marie has walked with me — Marie Sangré, the daughter of old Pierre. As I am about to beat my chest again, she puts a finger to her lip. My fist unclenches. My hand falls to my side.

Then I commence to tell her what I have told her before. The words, repeated, give me the courage I need. And I speak quickly as it appears that we have little time. Already it is late afternoon, an afternoon in early June when the mountains rise blue and the waters run lusty and at timberline the golden-crowned sparrow calls to his mate. This evening, this very evening, before the sun goes down, Marie and I are to be married. The priest has come and in the clearing before the cabin walks forth and back, head down, lips moving, as he reads his breviary. Also in the clearing several tepees have been set up and their smoke floats grey above the spruce forest, for many friends and relatives have arrived to witness the wedding. This, as the saying goes, is a day of days, a day of a great gathering of people from near and far, from Solomon creek and the Grande Cache and the Athabaska valley. They number twenty, possibly even twenty-five. Never before on the Calling river have so many come together for such an occasion.

So I tell Marie again that, whatever happens, we will be married. Not all the constables, corporals, sergeants, inspectors and superintendents in western Canada, with their horses, will prevent our marriage. I am about to add, "not even God Himself," when I remember the priest and am silent. The priest has ridden in from the railroad on an old plough-horse, cassock kilted about his knees, because no church is nearer than Edson, one hundred miles out in the foothills.

But I am silent not only on account of the priest who paces on the far side of the cabin. I am silent most of all for lack of words. I think to myself, "Sure, we will be married, maybe, and then on this, our wedding night, when we were to ride up the new trail to the meadow by the stream where the caribou come down to drink, by which I would make camp and spread balsam boughs for our bed — tonight, instead of that, Marie will be alone and I will ride down to the railroad with the sergeant." This is what is in my mind for I know the law is not for me and mine. No, the law is for the red-headed man on the buck-skin mare who has sent the sergeant riding towards my cabin. So, at least, it seems to me.

Suddenly, in anger, I turn to Marie to speak this that is in me. Marie, who is only to my shoudler, takes my arm, squeezes it for me to be quiet and we walk side by side, to and fro, on the hard ground behind the cabin. After a few steps, I speak again, slowly now, almost with caution. Who is the sergeant, I ask, and what have I done that he should come between us? Is the man with the buck-skin mare a good man and worth the trouble he is causing? And I — what have I done that is wrong, that another man in my place would not have done?

It is true that the sergeant, with whom I have travelled in the hills, is a good man. Still, he has his duty. He is a big man, too, with a big chest, but not a chest so big as mine. True, instead of my purple silken shirt, he wears his jacket with gleaming buttons, breeches with yellow stripes instead of mackinaw trousers and boots with spurs instead of soft moccasins.

For all that, I am Felix Lemprière, I tell Marie, as she is Marie Sangré, whose great-great-grandfathers, French and Iroquois, long before the railroad or the Mounted Police were dreamed of, came by canoe and dog-team with the early traders and stayed to live here below the mountains, to marry the native Cree women, to hunt and fish and trap and guide, to ride proudly on horses and, later, to learn English from the priests and white settlers. We are a small people, a few hundred, but no man commands us. Each of us has his horses, his snowshoes, his trap-line, his rifle. Our life is a shadow that passes in sunlight, without hurt to what is around it. Yet the sergeant, my friend, with the law in his hand, is already close to my cabin.

What is it that I have done? I turn Marie's face gently so that she looks up the Calling river flowing by my cabin. Up there for three miles, hemmed in by river, walled by mountain, the hunting trail plows through muskeg where pack-horses sink and flounder and lose their shoes between sunken, grasping roots. During the hunting season, it has long been a horror of mud and pot-holes, of wearied horses and cursing men.

So, what have I done? I have done what no one else has done, though many others from down the river use the north-going trail by my cabin. I have, as they say, studied the situation, considered it from many angles and, during the two months of April and May just past, with the help of Marie's father, old man Pierre and his brother, Samuel, have thrown a log bridge across the river below my cabin and cut a trail up the other bank where, because it is a west-facing slope, the ground is drier. By this means, the trail avoids the muskeg entirely. Certainly, the bridge is narrow. It leans upstream and then downstream. It bends in the middle where old Pierre, a man wise in building, persuaded us to buttress it on a mid-stream rock. The bridge has no rails, no planking and the chinks between the three logs — three logs laid lengthwise, a set on each side of the mid-stream rock — are packed with moss. But it is a bridge, and it spans the white teeth of rapids where no horse could ford or swim. No man on horseback has yet crossed the bridge — this new bridge which, though half a mile below my cabin and on Crown land, I regard as my own because I and my people have built it.

I admit, without further words, that the idea of the bridge was not mine at the beginning. No, it was the idea of an English lord, a stranger, a man from over the seas. Him, last year in September, I took hunting into the sheep country beyond the head of Calling river. A very rich man, his family had made their money by collecting bird dung on the west coast of South America and selling it at high profit. This I have from Fred Brewster, a neighbour, himself a very great hunter, who recommended me to the English lord. No matter — the English lord was one given to thought and when, sheep, moose and caribou heads tied upon our packs, we returned down river from our hunt and for two hours wallowed through the muskeg just above my cabin, on reaching the corrals where we unpacked, he drew me aside. Like the horses, we were mud-spattered, sweating, and tired. More than that, the English lord was angry. "Felix," he said to me, "there should be a law against it — against a piece of trail such as that. Since there is no law, you might build a bridge." Then, standing on the little knoll in front of my cabin door, pointing downstream, he showed me where to build the bridge.

All that winter, that is to say, last winter, I reflected upon what the English lord had said to me. In the spring I rode north to the Grande Cache on the Smokey and talked to Pierre Sangré. So, in early April he and his brother, Samuel, came down to help me. Marie came with them to tend the fire and cook in the tepee. Between Marie and me, nothing had been arranged, but everything was understood. I had known her when she was but a girl, playing by the river with a doll made of feathers and rabbit skin stuffed with grass. Now that she was a young woman it was assumed, even without the words being spoken, that when her father returned north, she would remain with me. We would be married when the bridge had been completed. Life is not always gay and this would be a celebration, a double celebration, and one of note in the foothills.

Across that bridge, although yesterday its building was finished, no one so far has gone on horseback — as I have already stated. I do not deny that two mornings ago, a man tried to cross with his horse. His name is Cal Stubbins, a newcomer, a poacher who takes fur from the traps of others, the red-headed man from five miles down the river. While we worked on the bridge in May, several times he rode up, watched us, spat and rode away. Though he, too, travels the northern trail, he made no offer to help. A lazy man, I thought, one who probably can sleep with his boots on, upright in a chair. But his skin is light and freckled, his eyes pale blue. My people's skin is brown and their eyes are dark.

Two mornings ago early, when I happened to be alone on the bridge, shaving bark from the logs with my axe, he came again, this time with a friend from the city, a pack-horse following between them. They were on their way up the river to fish. As Stubbins spurred his buck-skin mare forward towards the bridge, she snorted, shied at the smell of fresh-cut timber. There, the river surging below, I braced my legs and faced him. I would not let him pass. The bridge, so to speak, was not yet officially open. First there was a ceremony, an important ceremony, to be performed — of which, naturally, I said nothing to Stubbins.

He dismounted, dropped his lines, came to me, shoved his chest against me. Again, it was a big chest. Still, not so big as mine. I noticed whiskey on his breath and dropped the head of my double-bitted axe to the log on which I stood. Had he asked me, I would have explained to him why, in the circumstances, he would have to wait another day or two before taking horses across the bridge. He asked nothing. He said to me, "Out of the way. We're going across."

Then, before I had had time to reply, he turned his head back over his shoulder. There on the rise of land, outlined against a white cloud, was Marie standing on the trail leading down to the bridge. She wore moccasins, fringed, moose-hide leggings, a blue woollen shirt open at the throat and had her black, glossy hair tied back with a blue ribbon. She was as beautiful, it seemed to me, as a young birch tree which, by a stream, sheds light by the dark forest. Stubbins' blue eyes turned from her to me.

"So," he said to me, "tough guy, eh?" He put his hand out to shove me aside, repeating as he did so, "Tough, eh? Showing off for your half-breed squaw . . ."

After that, after those words, I remember little. I remember nothing at all until, lying flat on the bridge, I looked down and saw the red head of Stubbins bobbing in the green swirl of a backwater and farther away his black hat bouncing on the river current. I wondered, how did Cal Stubbins get away down there — Cal Stubbins who had wanted to use a bridge he had not helped to build so that he and his friend would not become bogged in muskeg on their fishing expedition? Then on my shoulder I felt a touch. "Come," said Marie. "Let him be — see, he is climbing up the clay bank." Marie hid her face behind her hand. She was laughing.

I inquired why she was laughing. "It is because," she said, "when you threw him off the bridge, I saw the soles of his riding gaiters and they were new and still very white and as he fell, his arms reached out for the water as though he were thirsty."

It appeared to me that all of this was hardly a cause for laughter. I was sure of it when, Stubbins, shaking and dripping wet, climbed on his buck-skin mare and, his head raised arrogantly above me, exclaimed hoarsely, "You'll hear more about this, Mr. Felix Lemprière. Oh, I know your name all right. So will Sergeant Tatlow down at Brulé."

Stubbins and his friend from the city, before whom he had been humbled, did not go fishing — they might still have taken the old trail by my cabin through the muskeg. Instead, they turned back down the river the way they had come.

Now, two days later, on this day that was to be our wedding day, with Sergeant Tatlow only a few hundred yards away, facing Marie behind my cabin, holding her by the shoulders, I ask her, "Why did I turn Stubbins back from the bridge?" She smiles. She looks away. She knows well why I turned him back. I turned him back, I tell her, because it had been decided that she would be the first to cross the new bridge on the white two-year-old which this spring I have broken.. She will cross the bridge this evening of our wedding. Her father and her Uncle Samuel will follow. After them will come myself and the priest, then the other people, and we will be married by the pool fringed with quivering poplars on the far side of the river. The bridge in days to come will be a mark upon the land, a sign to men who travel. It will be known as "The Bride's Crossing" and the day, our wedding day, that Marie on the white two year old rode across it, will be remembered. A small thing, you think, and unnecessary that there should be such occasion in the opening of a log bridge at the foot of the mountains? Then, do not forget the cold, the snow, the wail of the winter's blizzard and long nights by lonely campfires on the trapline and you will understand, perhaps, that at times an event, a festival even, is required to give light and push back the darkness of the year.

Such, at any rate, is our plan for the wedding, but as I speak to Marie and hold her closer to me, I hear the thud of hooves, the tinkle of spurs, the heavy breathing of a horse. Sergeant Tatlow, because Cal Stubbins has gone down to see him, has arrived at the cabin. It is not a trifling matter, I think, to have thrown a man from a bridge into a river. But what else, at the time, was there to do? The law — I know nothing of the law, except that it is made far away by men whose eyes are blue like those of Stubbins and whose way of life is not my own.

Marie lifts one foot in its pliant moccasin, puts it behind the other knee. She touches a finger to my throat. Then she grasps my shirt, pulls herself tightly to me. "Sergeant Tatlow," she says, "has come because he has heard we are to be married. See, he wears his dress uniform. That is why he has come. He is your friend and you are to be married." She nods.

She tells me that I should now go around to the front of the cabin and meet the sergeant. I reply that the sergeant may come to where I am. Marie leaves me. I walk over to the corrals.

Four horses are there behind the bars: two pintos, my clean-legged roan saddle-horse and the white two-year-old which is Marie's to take her over the bridge. I speak, hold out my hand. The white horse, with his pink nostrils, nuzzles it. I could mount my roan, ride away, but that would mean that I would leave Marie.

In a few minutes the sergeant is beside me — an older man than I am, and not so tall and with a brown moustache. Because he is not so tall as I am, his eyes do not meet my own. They look above my head as though, when he spoke, he spoke to another who is behind and over-tops me. Then he looks away — at the white horse, up the valley, at the mountains. His moustache twitches, as if he were about to smile. Of that I am not sure for, under the moustache, I cannot see the corners of his mouth. He comes at once to the point.

He says, "Felix, I hear you have been obstructing the Queen's highway. More than that. I am told you used violence."

I do not comprehend. There is no highway nearer than that beyond the railroad and across the Athabaska valley, almost twenty miles away. The sergeant continues to speak. A trail through the foothills or the mountains, he tells me, is like a highway. All men are free to use it. By building the bridge, I improved the highway but I did not, therefore, make it my own. Nor is the bridge my own for it rests on Crown land and is made of Crown timber.

"Suppose," the sergeant says, "a tree had fallen across the trail or across a road. You cut through the tree, cleared the way and then stood, axe in hand, defying any one to pass? An offence, Felix. A fine, at least, possibly imprisonment if you threatened with your axe."

I bow my head. I listen. "But I did not raise my axe," I reply. "I dropped its head to the deck of the bridge."

"Oh?" Sergeant Tatlow jerks his head sideways. Apparently he had heard differently.

"And provocation," he asks me. "Did Stubbins threaten you?"

"No, but Marie, she was there . . ." For an instant, I am tempted to describe to the sergeant how she looked, uplifted against the white cloud, as though she were not on the earth at all but floating above it. The effort is beyond me. I repeat, "Marie — and he called her, he said . . ."

The sergeant raises his hand. "Never mind," he says, "I think I can guess the rest . . . and then you threw him into the water?"

There is no purpose in denying what I had done and what I would probably do again. The sergeant, my friend of the hunting trail, has a heavy hand. It claps me on the shoulder. "Good man," he says. "I might have done the same myself. It may be a lesson for him — and for others like him who forget that . . . well, that men are men."

Then his tone changes. "I might have done the same," he adds, "in your position. I do not know. I know only that you, Felix Lemprière, must come with me to stand before the magistrate at Brulé, charged with doing bodily harm and with obstructing by violence the Queen's highway."

I gasp, although what he has said is only what I feared he would say. "Brulé?" I ask. "And now, at once?"

From beyond the cabin we hear laughter, a phrase of song. Already the celebration of the wedding is beginning. The sergeant listens. He is not deaf, nor has he been blind to the tepees pitched before the cabin, nor to the priest walking in the clearing.

He turns to me. "Well, maybe not tonight. Maybe a week from now. I will arrange a postponement if you promise, on your word, to come down a week today."

I promise.

He takes my arm. "And do not worry too much," he tells me. "The magistrate, Mr. Falder, knows Cal Stubbins, knows him too well on his record as a poacher. Your word about the axe should stand against his. There may be a fine, a small fine . . ."

I smile. I am ready, I am able, even eager, to pay a fine. It is worth it to have seen Marie's face as Cal Stubbins pulled himself from the river.

"But the bridge, Felix," the sergeant is saying, "it is for any who wish to use it. It must be open tonight, by midnight, at the latest." He pulls his moustache with gloved fingers and his teeth show beneath it.

Tonight . . . Midnight . . . I wonder if the sergeant, before coming out to the corrals to speak to me, has had a word with the priest or with Marie and learned about the wedding because it is accepted by me, by all of us, that the bridge and the new trail are to be open this evening as soon as Marie has ridden on her white horse across the river.

Passing around the cabin I say to the sergeant, "The law . . . it is beyond me. I do not understand it." I am thinking of the business of the Queen's highway.

"The law," he replies, "is what men make it."

Now from in front of the cabin we see the priest and all the people going towards the bridge where they will wait. They are a group of many colours, of buck-skins, mackinaws, red and purple sashes and shawls flowing in the breeze so that there in the sunset they are like a garden of tall growing flowers which mysteriously moves down to the river.

From her tepee, beside her father, Marie steps freshly dressed in white — in a white, beaded suit of bleached caribou hide, with white moccasins on her little feet and with a white scarf tossed carelessly over her black head of hair, and framing her brown oval face.

She runs towards us, her scarf trailing behind and the sergeant, studying the priest and all the people, turns to me and asks, "The best man — who is the best man?"

I bridle. My fist rises to beat my chest for I look around and I see no man in all the valley who is a better man than myself unless, indeed, it be the sergeant and, naturally, the priest. But Marie has overheard. She beckons to me. I go. Standing on tiptoe, leaning against me, she speaks softly, her breath warm on my ear. Listening, I realize I had not quite understood the sergeant's question about "the best man."

I leave Marie and return to his side. I say, "Perhaps . . ."

He answers, "Of course, Felix, for me — for a friend it is a high honour to be the 'best man' at your wedding."

So it is that, the sun low in the mountains and the shadows long about us, I wait with Marie and her father and her Uncle Samuel and the priest and the great congregation of people, at least twenty-five in number, and many more, counting the children, while the sergeant, as my best man, goes to the corral to saddle the white two-year-old on which my bride is to ride over the bridge to the pool on the far side of the river where, in the whispering shade of the poplar trees, we will be married.

Ito Fujika, the Trapper

These days, seeing the name of Japan in the newspapers or occasionally hearing news of Japan over the radio, the people of Red Pass remember Ito Fujika, the trapper.

Ito, like many of his countrymen, had been a fisherman off Lulu Island on the coast of British Columbia. Two years before the war in the Pacific, wearying of the drudgery and the constant toil at the nets, he left his boat and took a train east to the Rocky Mountains, getting down at Red Pass where he planned to set himself up as a trapper. Before coming to Canada, he had trapped fur for the Emperor's Manchurian troops. He had also trapped out of his native town of Miyanoshita and now in the Rockies wished to return to his former way of living.

The people of Red Pass, a small town on the upper Fraser river, recall particularly the times when, down from his trap-line, he used to sit in the beer parlour, having left his pack in the hotel room, the cheap room at the end of the hall near the toilet. They remember Ito as he sits alone and sips his one glass of beer until closing time at ten o'clock at night.

The men at other tables regard him a bit askance. They speak of him in undertones. He is like a brown wooden image, half-human in size, propped over there in the corner. The forehead protrudes. The eyes shift. Once in a while the white teeth show, as if inside of him a light flickered and was dimmed. The beer in the glass on the table, close to his chest, diminishes slowly, as by a process of osmosis, for no one notices that he raises it to his lips. There is stealth, they think, even in his drinking in a public place. Undoubtedly, though, he is alive. Life is in him. But what form of life? And what is life? Idaho Pete, a big American, himself a trapper, asks the question — naturally not aloud, to be overheard. He considers a marten in the trap, still alive. You bend over it. You put your hand around it, feeling the quick beat of the heart. Your fingers tighten until the ribs bend and break. The beat of the heart ceases. Life was there and life is gone. What is gone and where? It is a gentle way to kill, for it protects the fur from blemish. Yet is death ever gentle? Idaho Pete turns to his neighbour, forgetting death, life and Ito Fujika. He recalls the day he and his partner were drunk on the head of Calling river and chased an Indian from his trap-line.

Ito, arriving at Red Pass in November, had come ready for cold weather. He had bought a muskrat cap whose untied flaps hung loose about his ears. His grey coat was knee length. On his feet he wore overshoes. It was not a conventional outfit for mountain travel, but it kept Ito warm. And at Red Pass, he realized he had come to the place he sought. Here were the mountains, higher than those around Miyanoshita, and, as at Miyanoshita, the sound of falling water. Across the lake was the green forest.

Shortly before six in the afternoon, Ito showed himself in the log cabin which was Mr. Scroggins' store. He was polite. His English was good. He replied, when asked, that he was going trapping and wanted food, and a pack-sack to carry it in.

Mr. Scroggins, who was tall, pale and excessively lean — Ito was puzzled that one should be so lean when food was stacked around him on the shelves — had a cuspidor behind the counter. He leaned over it and spat before studying again the man before him.

"Where do you figure on going trapping?" he asked.

Ito made a gesture with his arm towards the door, indicating the lake, beyond it the gap through the mountains. "Up there," he said, "and build a cabin."

"You had better wait until tomorrow," Mr. Scroggins said, as he went about closing the store. That night Ito sat under a spruce tree at the east end of the town. He caught two trout with the line and hook and piece of red flannel he always had with him and ate them raw.

In the morning he came again to the store.

"You won't have to build a cabin," Mr. Scroggins told him. "There's one up there already."

Ito bowed his head, smiled. He wrung his hands. If there was a cabin up there already, he suggested, then someone else must be trapping in that part of the country?

"Someone else was," Mr. Scroggins said. "He isn't trapping there anymore. He's gone away."

It was in this fashion that Ito came into possession of John Flaherty's cabin. The cabin, being built on Crown land, was there for anyone to use it. Ito did not know this and was convinced of his bargain when Mr. Scroggins threw in the entire outfit — traps, two axes, pots and pans, sleeping bag — of Mr. Flaherty who had left for elsewhere. Mr. Flaherty, a man of temperament, had not done well in his trapping and one by one had surrendered his belongings to Mr. Scroggins whom he owed for a year's grubstake. Ito paid for the outfit more than twice its worth when new, taking three hundred dollars from a belt about his middle. Again, he was in ignorance and was pleased at the charity offered him, a newcomer of alien race.

The cabin was no more than a day's travel into the hills. Ito made several round trips to carry in his equipment and grub. On the last trip he carried in, strapped to his pack-board, the Number 6 trap. This was a bear-trap, weighing about forty pounds, of which he was proud.

The cabin itself was hardly a basis for this emotion, being no more than a lean-to against a cliff. During cold weather it frosted at night and sweated when the stove was lit by day. In the thaws the roof leaked. Still, for all that, Ito was happy, having owned nothing of the sort so substantial in his life. He laid out his trap-line, following, to some extent, Mr. Flaherty's old blazes. In town in December he bought heavier socks, moose-hide moccasins and a pair of snowshoes. He retained the long grey coat and tied the flaps of the fur cap under his chin.

Ito's success as a trapper that first winter was not marked. His traps yielded a marten, three weasels, a mangy fox. The lack was due partly to ineptitude, but mostly to the valley, close to the railroad, having been pretty well cleaned of fur. Notwithstanding, the fur he caught gave him sensuous delight. He knew that it would become a portion of a woman's garment and touching it felt that he was in a way touching the women of this strange land who would wear it. These caresses became a secret ecstasy, consummated in the lantern light of the wind-battered cabin.

In the spring, when the snow had seeped into the ground, but before the willows were leafed, he set out the bear-trap above the cabin at the foot of a slide. Just beyond it he put his bait, a slab of rancid bacon. Four or five days later, returning to the trap, he found, clamped within its jagged jaws, the forepaw and arm of a grizzly bear. Tendons, ripped from the shoulder, hung from the upthrust arm. The grizzly, great in strength and rage, had broken away. That, however, was not Ito's fault, nor did it denote a failure of the trap called "Number 6." The trap had held. The weakness was in the bear himself. If his arm had been as strong as the trap his sixty-pound hide would now have been in Ito's keeping.

When he next went down to Red Pass he took the arm and paw with him to demonstrate that he, Ito Fujika, formerly a catcher of small fur in Japan, had trapped a grizzly bear, the mighty animal of the Rockies. He laid the hairy and frozen limb on the counter of Mr. Scroggins' store and was astonished when a woman customer ran out screaming and when Mr. Scroggins seized the trophy, strode to the door and thew it across the road.

Aside from such small affairs and the occasion when, on the edge of town, bowing to impulse, he was discovered trying to strangle the schoolteacher's Airedale, Ito got on well with the people. In the summer he worked on the railroad section gang and was accounted a good worker. After the snow flew again, he appeared and reappeared from his trapline, walking across the frozen lake, his feet deep-sunk on their snowshoes, so that he seemed to be walking on his knees. On the coldest day he would come in smiling, washing his mittened hands — not as the other men, whose understanding of the country and unconfessed affection for it, permitted them to curse the wind and snow and the awful silence which was about them like the threat of a word unuttered.

The night in late February when Idaho Pete crossed the floor of the beer parlour to Ito Fujika's table, it was cold outside and still. Now and again the logs of the building cracked, as if that cold and stillness bore upon it.

Idaho Pete — who had never been in Idaho, but who, coming from the States, had been given his name because he talked of it as the state where one day he would like to "settle" — explained, before leaving those at his own table, that he was inclined "for a bit of fun with the little Jap."

"Well, Fuzzy," he said, seating himself by Ito, "how's tricks?"

Ito receded deeper into his corner. His muskrat cap was on the chair beside him and his close cropped hair stood stiff as quills.

His teeth flashed. He made a sound. He lisped, nodding his head to lend emphasis to his good will.

Idaho Pete leaned closer. "They tell me," he said, "that fur is running good up in that valley of yours." He twisted in his chair to wink at his friends.

Ito said nothing.

"Well, Fuzzy," the other continued, "I figure I need a change of scenery. Things are awful dull out on my trap-line. Maybe in a day or two I will be up there to call on you and if I like the look of things, I'll be there to stay. See?"

Ito uttered one word: "No!"

He uttered it without thinking, instinctively. His cabin, his traps, his trails to be given up to another man? He said "No!" again, more softly.

Idaho Pete shrugged his broad shoulders, blinked his eyes. He turned to the table he had left. "He says 'No!'" he shouted across the room. He laughed. His drinking companions laughed. Idaho Pete slapped the table so that Ito's glass jumped, fell to the floor, shattered.

Idaho Pete rose. He said from his height, "I'll be seeing

you, brown eyes. Watch for me. I'll wear a red mackinaw so you'll be sure to know me when I come up the trail."

Ito sat for a few minutes, listening to the other table. "He believed me!" Idaho Pete said. Then there was more laughter. Someone else said, "Why that country was cleaned out years ago. No white man — remember Flaherty had to clear out. Only a Jap could make a living up there." They laughed again. They were laughing at him — at Ito Fujika who had ancestors, at Ito Fujika, son of the Emperor, to whom they were properly servants. They laughed at Ito Fujika, who now owned his cabin in the mountains.

The next morning Ito left the hotel earlier than was his custom, without breakfast, while it was still dark. Soon after noon he reached his cabin.

When the next day he had set the bear-trap — the Number 6 trap, the one which had wrenched the arm from the grizzly bear — he returned to Red Pass. He had set the trap two miles below his cabin in a depression in the trail where anyone, travelling into the cabin from the railroad, would have to pass. He had sunk it in the snow, dusted snow over the marks of his work. Now, as he neared the town, snow fell in slow, wide flakes from the heavy sky, a final seal upon his efforts.

Ito had come to a decision. He would go down to the Coast to visit his cousin. He mentioned this to Mr. Scroggins in the afternoon. He would wait in town overnight for the train.

Walking about the town, observing the snowfall, he reasoned that if, in his absence, the big man in the red mackinaw became entangled in the trap, Ito Fujika could not be blamed. Ito Fujika was absent on family business. Perhaps, not expecting to be back until the spring, he had put out the trap there on the chance of catching a bear when his fur was prime. That is to say, when the bear was fresh from his den. At any rate, no one had a right to go up to his cabin when the owner was not at home. The trap, indeed, was no more than a lock upon the cabin door.

It was probable too that weeks would pass before anyone learned of what had taken place. The wide jaws of the trap would seize the man just below the knee. They would crush the bone. If he freed himself, which was not likely, for a lever was required to pry those jaws apart, where would he go, and how far could he go in deep snow with a shattered leg and in cold which split trees and caused the very lake to groan? Drowsy with pain and cold, he would fall asleep. He would not awaken.

When someone passed by, or when word, in its mysterious course, reached the town, he, Ito, would be far away, possibly in the United States — for means existed of crossing the border — or with the fishing fleet in Alaskan waters.

Ito, of course, regretted the necessity of leaving. He would have preferred to be on hand when the trap was sprung, out of view among the spruce trees above it, watching. When he thought of the scene, the red mackinaw like a huge spot of blood on the snow, his skin tightened, his scalp puckered, a tingling and a warmth suffused his limbs, his breath came quickly.

No one passing him now as he walked towards the beer parlour in the twilight, seeing him smile and nod, would have guessed at this hatred which he had for the big man in the red mackinaw. He felt himself surrounded by big men, by coarse laughter, by big feet waiting to trample upon him, by big hands eager to take from him, as from his people, everything that they had. The man in the red mackinaw was the type of all he feared. He went to the beer parlour, not because he wished to meet Idaho Pete again, but to nurture hatred for him and also because it was wise to be seen by as many as possible a days travel from his cabin.

In the beer parlour, before Idaho Pete had appeared, Ito was restless. He drank his glass of beer. Without thought, he had a second. From that it was easy to go on to the third, and after the third to another.

When Idao Pete came in, it seemed to Ito, his vision not as steady as it was before, that they were acquaintances of long standing. Idaho Pete stood for a half a minute inside the door, feet apart, hands in his pockets, hat cocked back from his forehead, looking about the smoky room. Ito recalled then foreigners he had seen on the streets in Tokyo, Idaho Pete's eyes were cold, blue, assured like those of a man on a hilltop. He walked to the table where his friends were sitting. Seated, he glanced at Ito. He winked. Ito's neck was scalded with a hot rush of blood. He smiled at Idaho Pete, ran his tongue around his lips.

He could not look at the other man without thinking of the trap under its blanket of snow on the trail. Thinking of the trap, he questioned if it were set in exactly the right place, if there might be a chance of a man passing without stepping on its sensitive pawl, if, in other words, it were set in the narrowest part of the trail. It seemed now that it would have been wise to have put the trap just a bit higher where the ground sloped more sharply away to the valley. This was the last touch that was needed. If he hurried, and was without the encumbrance of a pack, he decided he would have time to go up there and still return to take the next afternoon's train — if he hurried, if he used the darkness.

Ito left the beer parlour through the side door, swiftly, like a shadow sucked through the wall into the lobby of the hotel. He found his snowshoes, went out, crossed the railroad tracks. There, tying on his snowshoes, he began the crossing of the lake. The wind, newly risen, jolted him, but feeling carefully with his feet he kept to the hard hump of the trail made by his previous crossings. On either side the vast snow-field stretched away, like mist waiting to engulf him. The wind, shifting to the east, was sharp enought to peel flesh from bone.

For hours, having crossed the lake, Ito struggled and panted upwards in the timber. His chest heaved, his heart pounded, and his head, with the beer he had drunk, was as in a vise of steel. Here in the forest where the snow was softer he floundered off the trail, ran his face against trees, caught his webbed snowshoes in the branches of fallen logs, fell and got to his feet. Darkness was the always yielding wall against which he pressed.

Lost in the furious treadmill of the night, in the frozen mountains whose valleys, he sensed, were made for giants to walk in, he commenced to wonder how far he had come, if he were close to the trap or still miles from it. Soon each step was taken in apprehension of the hungry jaws hidden ahead underneath the snow. It was even possible, he reasoned, that wandering from the trail in the dark and back onto it, he had passed the trap. Ahead of him, now it was also behind.

He stopped. His mind urged him on, but his vulnerable legs faltered, refused, remaining unmoving in the snow. He looked down, and in the darkness, unable to see his feet,

was overcome with dizziness, like a man who fronts an abyss.
Sweat broke out over Ito's body, coursed down the small of
his back, and his racing blood made the roar of a waterfall
between his ears.

He thought he would find a stick, a sapling, to prod the
snow before him. He held out his arm, took a step. He
touched a young balsam. He tried to bend its trunk, to break
it off. It was young enough to bend, too old and strong to
break. He wrestled with it, fought its roots. His fury mounted
against this thing which gave and would not yield. He sobbed.
Foam flew from his lips. He took out his knife, hacked at the
thin trunk. In final impatience, he climbed into its branches
until his weight bent its tip into the snow. There, leaning on
it, he began to whittle again at the trunk. Slowly, as if with
a will of its own, with a strength beyond his strength —
already numbed with cold — the balsam slipped from his
grasp. Suddenly it flew upright, intent on its business of
growing, slapping him across the face, throwing him on his
back in the snow.

Ito did not at once get up. He was tired, his energies were
spent. He thought he would rest a minute, pillowed on the
snow. He shivered, his teeth chattered, his breath hissed
faintly in the snow. He curled his knees into his chest, his
head fell onto his arm and Ito was asleep.

He was still asleep when, six weeks later, a sergeant of the
provincial police came up to investigate the cause of his
absence, for Ito had left his pack-sack and trail axe uncalled
for, and at the hotel they were not sure whether he had gone
to the Coast or returned to his trap-line. The thaw had come
and the sergeant, before reaching him, had found the Number
6 trap revealed through the snow on the trail. He sprang it,
hooked it on the branch of a tree. Ito had circled the trap
and was above it. What was left of him, a pair of martens
having been to him before the sergeant, was only a hundred
yards from his cabin door.

Today in Red Pass, some people will still tell you of Ito
Fujika, the trapper, who was new to the mountains, and who
set a beartrap in dead winter and then grew weary and slept
on the way back to his cabin. Others, for no cause that they
can state, at mention of his name will wag a head, spit and
walk away.

A
Mountain Journey

Dave Conroy, whose breath had hung stubby icicles on his moustache, paused upon the very summit of the pass. He tucked his ski poles under his arms, leaned upon them, sinking their discs into the creaking snow, and while he rested there panting, the cold was an old man's fingers feeling craftily through his clothes.

He was tired. He was so tired that his mouth was dry with the taste of salt. He was more tired than he had any right to be, and Hoodoo cabin on Hoodoo creek, where he could pass the night, was still five miles away. It was downhill now though, downhill all the way. For the first time during the long day he could stand back on his skiis and let them carry him where he wished to go. Since daylight he had come twenty miles and climbed four thousand feet from the lower Smokey to the pass. On his shoulders he had lifted upwards with him at every step his pack of food for another five days on the trail, his blankets, axe and fifty pounds of fur for the market — the result of six weeks' trapping on the head of the Jackpine. At every step too, he had broken trail and his skiis had sunk a foot in the new snow, white and soft as flour.

He knew as he stood on the summit that he should have made camp two miles back in the timber and crossed the divide in the morning. Back there he had passed a fine spruce tree, its wide branches sweeping low, so that close against its trunk, cradled in its roots, he had seen the brown mossy ground where no snow had fallen and where he might have made his fire and spread his blankets. That tree, like a strong and lonely woman, called to his weary body to stop. But two hours of daylight remained and he went on.

He thought that if he had waited another two weeks to come out, till March, the snow would have had a crust for travelling, the days would have been longer, the cold less severe. Anyway, a man was a fool to travel alone in the mountains, especially with a heavy pack, bucking a fresh fall of snow. A man when he was alone would travel too far. He would travel till he could travel no more, for the mere sake of travelling, when a day or two's delay in the time of his arrival made no difference at all.

Still, the worst was over. It was downgrade now to the railroad, eighty miles of trail along the Snake Indian river with cabins to put up at every night. No more siwashing under trees, burrowing four feet down in the snow for a place to sleep, with a snow-covered tree sweating in the heat of his fire, dripping water on his neck and dampening his blankets. Not that under such conditions a man slept very much. It was too cold. If he slept, his fire slept with him. It was better to stay awake, his blankets over his shoulders, and a pile of wood handy at his elbow.

Up there on the pass it was very still. No wind blew and his breath rose white and yellow before him. His heart thumped and hissed in his breast, and the silence about him as he listened became a roar as if it were the roar of the grey earth rolling on through space and time. Behind him his ski trail stretched a few feet, two black lines with the webbed marks of his ski poles pacing beside them. Mist, like the shadow of universal darkness on the treeless summit, moved about him, searched every crevice of the mountain land, roamed in great billows, formed in the blindness and suffering of eternal homelessness.

Conroy turned his skiis down the slope before him. He was beginning to feel like a ghost on an abandoned planet and he wanted to see the works of man about him once again. He longed for the sight of a cabin, a clearing in the forest, yellow flaming blazes on trees beside the trail. Snow, flung up by the prow of his skiis, pattered lightly against his thighs and as he hummed downwards he thought of supper — brown curled bacon, brown bannock, rice with butter melting on it, tea red and strong as rum.

The rolling alplands, a white sea frozen into weary immobility, became a broken parkland and he made long sweeping turns around clumps of spruce and balsam. Dark green trees came out of the thinning mist towards him, touched him with outflung branches, passed in a flutter and flurry of snow-dust. The cold wind against his face, the loud wind howling in crescendo by his ears, the flow of wind that pressed his trousers tight against his legs, gave him back strength as he exulted in the rush of his descent. Tears smarted in his eyes and through them he saw the landscape opaque and blurred as though it were vibrating to the speed of his passage.

He swung to the right in a wide telemark that threw snow in his face, swept down an open meadowland where the black tips of willows showed between two walls of timber, dropped off a cutbank to the frozen river, glanced a moment over his shoulder at the curved beauty of his ski trail on the hill above, curved and smooth and thin, like the tracing of a pen upon the snow.

And as he looked back, while still sliding forward with the momentum of his descent, the ice broke beneath him. It broke with a low muffled reverberation, startling as if the river had spoken. The snow rifted about him, the points of his skiis dropped down. He was thrown forward and to save himself from falling on his face plunged down his hands. His pack slipped forward upon the back of his head and held him. The river was shallow and his hands rested on its gravelled bottom. He saw the snow melt around his wrists and flow into the top of his mittens, searing the flesh of his wrists like flame. He saw dark water streaming in furrows by his wrists and before he staggered upright again heard water tinkling over pebbles, murmuring, protesting, running downhill between ice and pebbles to the Arctic Ocean.

Conroy was too weak to rise beneath the pack. He rolled over upon his side, slipped the thongs of the ski poles from his wrists, dropped his pack on the snow beside him, raised himself and lifted his skiis from the water. Water had seeped down his socks into his boots and his feet were cold and clammy.

He had fallen into an air hole. Probably a warm spring entered into the river nearby and above it the ice was thin. That was a peril of winter travel. But the rivers, levelled with ice and snow, were the winter highways of the mountains, and a man, when he could, travelled along them in preference to breaking a heavy trail in the timber.

Conroy unclamped his skiis, upended them, and stood knee deep in the snow. Already the water on them had crusted into ice. He took off his sodden mittens, opened his clasp-knife, and tried to scrape the ice from the skiis' running surface. He knew what he should do. He should stop, make a fire, dry his hands and feet, change his socks and mittens. But it was late. It would mean siwashing for another night underneath a tree. A biting wind was driving the mist back up the valley and the sun westering behind the ranges threw long feeble shadows across the snow. He was less than three miles from the cabin, and the promise of its warmth and comfort would not let him stop.

He wriggled his toes in his boots. They were cold, but perhaps, he thought, not wet. Only his ankles and heels seemed wet. If he hurried he could make it. He slammed his right foot back into his ski iron, bent down to clamp it to his ski, but his fingers already were numbed with the cold. He rose again, thrashed his arms about his shoulders, bringing the blood tingling to their tips, opened his pack sack and found a pair of woollen inner mitts. He would have to get along without the moose-hide outers. They were already frozen stiff and he put them into his pack.

His skiis clamped to his feet at last, he hoisted his pack, took his poles and started off, hunching his toes to keep the circulation going. Ice on the bottom of the skiis dragged heavily in the snow, but he fought against it, pushing on his poles, knowing that speed was his one means of escape from the cold hand of wilderness that pressed against his back.

The long white avenue of the river opened before him, lined on either side by tall spruce trees. The wind was rising with the sundown. It whipped snow against his face, cut through the weave of his woollen mitts, set the forest moaning beside him. He bent his head against it, his eyes on the black tapering points of his skiis, ducking and dodging through the snow. It was as though he were engaged in some fantastic pursuit with those ski points always just beyond him, their tight cheeks pulled back into a cadaverous grin.

His shoulder muscles, as he lunged against the ski poles, bulged as though they would burst their skin, ached until their pain became a cry within him. His legs moving back and forth beneath him seemed tireless. They could go on forever and he no longer knew whether he could stop them. The pain in his shoulders was the only reality of his existence and his body was no more than the shape of agony and effort crawling through the twilight, across the long shadows of spruce trees laid upon the snow.

He came up from the river through the timber into the cabin clearing. But no log walls rose to greet him. No closed door waited for his touch to open. He stood in the middle of the clearing where the cabin had been, hemmed about by swaying pine trees, pine trees that swayed as the wind sighed through them. Snow, as if it had garnered light from the day, cast upwards a shadowless glow and Conroy saw close to him the black butts of congregated logs, a corner of the cabin, draped in white, rising lonely as a monument left by men a hundred years ago.

Since he had passed that way, fire had gutted the cabin. A few log ends remained above ground. It was as though the cabin had subsided into the snow that rose like a slow inundation to cover it. A beggared moon from behind a grey rack of clouds wandered in the sky above the earth's desolation and in its light he perceived on the slope above him, where the fire had leaped from the cabin, stiff, branchless trees, like a parade of skeletons climbing up the mountainside.

The next cabin was at Blue creek, eighteen miles down the river. It was farther than he had strength to go. He would camp here in the clearing where the cabin had been burned. He slipped his pack off and reached toward it for the handle of his axe to cut kindling, making shavings for his fire. His fingers refused to bend. Protected only by the woollen mitts, they were stiff with the cold. He beat his hands about his shoulders, flung his arms in circles, took off his mittens and rubbed his hands together in the snow, but felt no blood pulsing in his fingertips.

He bit his fingers. They were cold and white and unresponsive as a dead man's. His right thumb tingled; when he rubbed his hands across his face, his beard bristled on the palms. It was only his fingers that defied him. He had been a fool. He should have made a fire when he fell through the ice, and should have spent the night three miles up the river under a tree. He had always said that mountain travel was not dangerous if a man knew how to take care of himself. Any man who froze his hands or feet had only himself to blame . . .

As he stood there, stamping on his skiis, his arms flapping at his sides, he remembered Duncan Macdonald, who trapped in the Beaver river country and who had walked thirty miles to the railroad on frozen feet to have them amputated by the doctor. Because he could trap no more, Macdonald had opened a cobbler's shop in Jasper to make boots he could no longer wear himself, and Conroy saw him now at his bench, laughing, not saying anything at all, just laughing, his red face wrinkled as he nodded his heavy bald head and laughed.

Conroy decided that his hands were not frozen, his feet, which he could not longer feel in his boots, not frozen. They were only numb. He needed fire to warm them. Since he could not make kindling, since he could not bend his fingers around the shaft of his axe, he would set a tree afire, he would set the forest in a blaze around him and warm himself in its midst. Small dry twigs under a spruce tree would flame like paper. Putting his left wrist over his right, he forced his right hand into the pocket where he carried his match-safe. He pried it out and it fell into the snow at his feet. He spread his skiis and leaned down to pick it up. He poked his hands into the snow. They were like two sticks of wood on the ends of his arms and shoved the safe deeper and farther from him. He stooped lower still and finally, pressing it between his wrists, filched it out. He held it there before him, at arm's length, a round tin cylinder that contained the red flame and blustering smoke of fire. His right thumb, still moving to his command, pressed it into his palm, but his fingers would not catch it, would not twist it open. They would not bring the match-safe to him. They held it from him. If they would only bend, those fingers. If they would understand when he spoke to them.

He looked about him as if he would find the realities of his situation in the snow at his feet. He was eighty miles from the railroad, a journey of four days. Unable to light a fire, without warmth or food, he would never make it. His fingers were frozen. His feet probably were frozen too. He had one chance. Across the river from Hoodoo creek where he stood, a high pass led over into the Moose river. Frank MacMoran trapped up there and had his cabin on Terrace creek. From Hoodoo creek to Terrace creek was no more than ten miles. If he left his pack behind, he could probably pull through. He had never finished a day in the mountains yet without another ten miles up his sleeve.

His back was wet with sweat from carrying the pack, and he shivered with the cold. The cold was nibbling at him, at his nose, at his cheeks, crawling like a wet thing across his back. He forced his hands into his mittens, shoved them through the thongs of his ski poles and started off. He did not need to grasp the poles tightly. His hands rested upon the thongs which bore the weight he put upon them. His fingers did not pain him. He felt no sensations in them at all and his feet might have been pieces of wood strapped within his ski boots.

He crossed the river and angled up the slope towards the ridge that lay between him and the Moose. When he came out of the timber, the moon threw his shadow on the snow, a shadow faltering and stooped as if at any minute it might leave him, send him on alone to go shadowless through the moonlight. His shadow became a burden, something he pulled beside him in the snow.

He climbed high above the timber. The wind blew before him the long ends of the red neckerchief that he wore tied around the collar of his mackinaw, and near him the moon threw the outlines of a peak black upon the snow, black as ink seeping through the snow. Conroy paused a moment, leaned against a snow bank, sank down into it and rested.

How good to rest! How soft and warm the snow! There was the valley below him, empty in the moonlight — the clearing in the forest, timber that looked small and black as marsh grass. Across from him was a line of peaks thrust up against the sky, notched and jagged as if old bones, half covered with the snow, littered their crests. To his left was the pass, a low saddle in the mountains, where he had crossed in the afternoon.

From below, somewhere in the forest, a wolf howled.

Conroy glanced upwards over his shoulder. He had still six hundred feet to climb to the ridge above the Moose, above the cabin at Terrace creek where MacMoran waited. MacMoran would take him in, feed him, make a fire for him to sit beside. He gathered his muscles together, summoned his strength that was slipping from him like a loosened garment. Then he lay back for another moment, to rest.

When he opened his eyes again, the moon had gone. The red sun, topping the range across the valley, shone upon him. His neckerchief flapped in the wind on the snow beside his cheek. He had slipped lower, fallen over upon his side, his face turned towards the route he had followed where his half-obliterated ski trail led down to the timber, the stunted spruce and balsam that seemed to be on their way towards him.

He heard horse bells. It was winter and no horses were within a hundred miles. He heard streaming river water. He heard a wide brown river running over mossy boulders between low banks of grass and willow. Across the valley he saw a cottage he had never seen before — a white cottage, low roofed, with green trees beside it and an open door.

Then he remembered that he was on his way to MacMoran's cabin on Terrace creek. MacMoran would be waiting for him. He tried to rise, but his arms stayed still at his side. Snow had drifted over them. A weight was on them that he could not lift. They were heavy with the burden of their own inertia. Snow like a blanket covered his body and the wind blew snow against his face.

For a moment he thought again of Macdonald who had brought his frozen feet to the railroad. Macdonald frowned and shook his head, opened his mouth and spoke some words that Conroy could not hear.

They would come and get him, Conroy thought — Macdonald, MacMoran, someone would come and get him. They were camped now down by Hoodoo cabin. They would see his trail and come and get him. He would lie for a while and wait.

Later, the pale cold sun was high in the sky. It shone full upon him. But the light of the sun was dim, as if a brighter light shone from behind it and the sunlight was its shadow. He could not see across the valley now, where the white cottage with the open door and the green trees had been. The world was growing small, dying slowly in the darkness of the sunlight.

The Promised Land

Two men walked between the forest and the city. Before each stretched the narrow road, long and white and true. No trees were by it to give shelter from the sun, nor in the two days' journey was there a bend or hill or gully to confuse the traveller with the distance he had come, nor with that still before him. Over the road the wind blew gentle and cool and now and again the water of a spring bubbled among the rocks and flowed away into the fields where grew the tall, green grass.

One of the men was coming from the forest and so saw only the white towers of the city far away where the road ended. The city, as is the way of cities, was built upon the plains, and when he stopped to rest he thought he heard the hum of life in its buildings, the rumble of cars in the streets and the voices of people as they called to one another by name.

The other man, with the city behind him, saw only the forest where, too, it seemed the road ended. The forest rose before him on hills and beyond the hills were the mountains. He thought of the shade of the trees and the moss beneath them where a man might lie, and of pools and trout and of the peace of mind and quiet of body that would be his. Sometimes along the road he paused to look again towards the forest where these things he sought waited for him.

The two men met early in the morning of the second day when they stood midway between the forest and the city. They stared at one another a time before they spoke. The city man who was short and fat, with a red face and glasses, and the man from the forest who was tall, broad in the shoulders, his face dark and bearded. He had sun and wind wrinkles about his eyes so that he appeared always to be looking into the distance. He carried a pack on his back.

"Well, it's a fine day and a pleasant road," said the man from the city. He lifted his hat and mopped a bald head with his handkerchief.

"God made the day," said the other. "And as for the road, there's good, honest work in it as well. On this road a man can see where he's going. He can see where he came from too, if he's so foolish as to care about it."

"That's what I was wondering," said the man from the city.

"And what were you wondering?"

"I was wondering — well, I see you're from far off — but where could you be going?"

"To the Promised Land, of course," said the man from the forest.

"But that can't be. It is I who am going to the Promised Land and we're going in opposite directions."

"Now, that's good — so you're going to the Promised Land as well. Well, let me tell you this— if you keep along the road the way you're going, you'll come to its end in the evening and all you'll find there will be the forest."

"That's it. That's where I'm going. To the forest."

"And who ever told you," said the man from the forest, "that you'd find the Promised Land among a lot of trees?"

"I wasn't told. I just heard it."

"Well, I'll tell you something, my friend. Don't always believe what you hear. Speech is often only a shield for ignorance."

"That may be," answered the man from the city, "but you're going to the city. And tell me this — who ever told you you'd find the Promised Land in the city?"

"I wasn't told, my friend. I don't believe what people tell me. I read it. I've been reading about it at night in my cabin through last winter and the spring. Only yesterday I realized

I had been living all these years but two days' travel from the Promised Land, and now I've set out for it."

"So you've been reading. That's the trouble. It's a common failing of the day — but I didn't know it had reached to the forest. Before people can read, someone must write and I'll tell you this — the men who write sit behind locked doors and they write because if they come outside and talk no one will listen to them. They put their lies on paper — for with the black words written on it, you can't see the face behind the page. The Promised Land, indeed, and in the city — I've never heard such a story."

"There's certainly something queer about this," said the man from the forest. "Here we are on a good road, an honest road as I have said. We are both going to the same place — yet we go in contrary directions. I go to where the road ends, you to where it begins."

"That is not so," said the other. "The road begins in the city and leads to the forest."

"No, no, not at all. This road begins at the edge of the forest. I saw it there with my own eyes."

"Come," said the little man from the city, jerking his bald head up in the sunlight. "We began by agreeing. Since then we've done nothing but argue. Let us agree on this at least, before we part — each of us is going to the end of the road, but each of us is travelling a different road and each of us is going to a different place, though we call them both by the same name."

"It seems to me," said the man from the forest, "that we may be going to the same place, but we call the place we are going by different names."

"How is that? We both agreed we were going to the Promised Land."

"Yes, but yours is the forest and mine is the city. Perhaps they are both the same place. You see, you don't know the forest and I don't know the city. Yonder looks like a city to me, and yonder to you is a forest. But I have only your word that what I see is a city, and you have only mine for the forest."

They sat down then and smoked their pipes by the side of the road. Each gave to the other his tobacco, the man from the city the tobacco he had bought in a shop and the man from the forest the leaves he had picked wild on the hillside and mixed with the inner bark of the red willow. Each puffed and found the tobacco harsh to his tongue. They agreed it took a while to become used to strange tobacco.

"But tell me," asked the man from the city. "What are you carrying in that pack on your back?"

"Oh, some blankets and deer meat, a pan for cooking and an axe to cut wood for my fire."

"But you won't need all that in the city."

"But man, I've got to sleep and eat."

The other laughed. He said, "I see you are really a very simple fellow. In the city there is all of that you need. There are shops, and places to eat, beds for sleeping and other people to make your fires." He began to tell the man from the forest where he should go, and what he should do when he arrived in the city. He told him of what he would find to eat, the music he could hear and the crowds on the streets in the evening. "There is one restaurant," he said, "down an alley. Two trees grow in front of its door. There is a waitress called 'Anne.' I'll tell you how to go. You follow the main street through the city, till you come to the second turning to the left . . ." He ceased speaking then and for the first time looked back along the road he had come. For a while he was silent. Suddenly he said, rising, "Come, this will never do. If you get me to talking of the city . . . We must be up and on our way. You'll find what you want there. Ask anyone. They'll tell you."

Then he enquired, "But have you any money?"

The man from the forest shook his head.

"Here," said the other, "take these coins. I don't need them now. I'll take your pack. You don't need it either."

Before they separated, the man from the forest turned and asked, "Where are you going to pass the night?"

"Why, under a tree in the forest."

"You don't need to do that. You can have my cabin. I'll tell you how to find it easily . . . after the road there's a creek and by the creek a trail. You'll see blazes on the trees. You follow up the trail and where it forks you take the turn to the right and after a short distance beyond a rocky outcrop you'll see the cabin on a small rise in the forest. There's water just behind it. You'll find the pail inside the door and wood cut for the fire. It's a good cabin of pine logs. I cut them and built it myself. You'll find it tight against the weather. And I left it ready and unlocked for the next man to come by."

"You're a good fellow," said the man from the city. "I'll remember what you tell me, though I still think I'll sleep under a tree. If I had a room in the city, I'd tell you to go there too, but you see I gave the keys back to the landlord. I knew I wouldn't need them again."

Then they parted. The man from the forest, walking to the city, looked back once and saw the sun bright upon the mountains and the forest crowded dark upon the hills. He saw the man from the city, hoist the pack, then after a few steps drop it. It was heavy. He left it and walked along the white road without a backward glance.

"There goes a foolish fellow," thought the man from the forest, as he felt the coins in his pocket.

The next evening the two men met again at the same place, midway between the forest and the city. The man from the forest was now going back to the forest and the man from the city was returning to the city.

As they approached each kept his eyes to the road and each would have passed without speaking — but along the road that was so narrow, that ran so straight between its points, that offered no shortcut or bush where one might dodge, silence would have been dishonest.

So they stopped and, as before, stood for a time without speech. The black hair of the man from the forest was matted. It hung down before his eyes. His brow, once tanned, beneath it seemed grey, as though in the city he had found age. His shirt was torn and bare toes poked through his moccasins. The aspect of the man from the city also had altered. He had a long cut down his cheek from his night in the forest. He had lost his hat and the top of his head was burned red from the sun and the glasses before his eyes were dimmed with the sweat of his travel.

The sun was low in the sky and, as they stopped, their shadows, leaned with the day's journey, stretched out from under them.

"I see," said the man from the forest, "you're leaving the Promised Land and going back to the city."

The man from the city, using his handkerchief to polish his glasses, holding them in his hand and blowing upon them, stood back on his heels and laughed. "And you," he said, "I suppose, you're not going back to the forest?"

"Indeed I am — and as fast as I can get there."

"Then you didn't like the city?"

"The city, my friend, is a funny place. It is not as I imagined it to be at all. No, not at all. It is a different place entirely."

"Perhaps it is yourself. Perhaps the city isn't so different. It may be the change is in yourself," said the man from the city. "The city when I left it, I see now, was a good place to be. At the time I was too blind to see it. In three days it cannot have changed so greatly."

"Well, you may be right," said the other, pushing back his hair from his brow. "Still it seems to me I was misled in what I read about the city — or perhaps in what I read about the Promised Land. But come to think of it, I never read a word about the Promised Land. I never saw the words written, but I've carried them with me since I was a boy and working on my father's homestead far back in the mountains."

"I see," said the man from the city. "I think I understand. It was something the same with me. When I was a boy we played games in the street and one side held the Promised Land and the others, with me to help them, tried to get in. But tell me, and briefly for I am in a hurry and soon it will be dark, what befell you back there in the city?"

"Well, it was like this. When I left you I walked on and on and was well into the city and among its people before I was hungry. The lights were lit in the shop windows. People were in the streets and all of them seemed to be laughing and joking. There was music too. So I went to the restaurant as you told me. I ate there till I was full and before I had finished, people were standing about the table to watch me. They clapped me on the back and urged me to eat some more. They said they had never known a man could be so hungry. Before I left there, they asked me for some of the coins you had given me. I thought it odd they should know you had given me those coins, but they told me it was the custom to surrender coins after eating, so I gave a few of them up. I explained then to the waitress, Anne, that I was going out to see the Promised Land and asked her to come with me. She laughed and sent me on my way. I heard someone shout behind me, 'Ho-ho, so he's going out to see the Promised Land. I wonder where he thinks he'll find it?'"

"A fair was on in the big park by the lake, so I went there. There was a shooting gallery and I won all the prizes. Again a crowd was about me and they said no man had ever shot so well before. But before I left, they asked me for some more of the coins. I dropped my prizes to get the coins from my pocket and before I could stoop to pick them up, someone had snatched them from about my feet and was gone and lost in the darkness."

"I knew then a man needed coins in the city, but there were lots about me who had them, so I didn't worry. I knew I could go up to a man and ask him and he would give them to me, as you had given yours. Yet when I did that, the man nudged his neighbour. He said, 'Look, a big, hulking fellow asking for coins.' 'A big lazy fellow,' they said, 'he should go where they make them.'"

"So after that I wandered about the streets and I was lost, for all the streets were the same, and all the buildings were the same, and all the people had the familiar faces of people I had never seen before. After a time I came to an iron-railed fence and beyond the fence I heard a wolf howling. I asked a man who was passing, what a wolf was doing in the Promised Land."

"'The Promised Land,' he said, 'The Promised Land — why this is a zoo, a place where they keep wild animals for people to look at. If you go around asking such silly questions, my big fellow, you'll find yourself in there and you'll not be able to get out.'"

"Still over the fence I saw some trees where I could sleep and with the wolves howling I knew I would feel close to home. If it wasn't exactly the Promised Land, it was as close as I could come to it. So I climbed over and for a while I slept. Then two men came with round caps on their heads and clubs in their hands. They kicked me and told me to get moving. I got up then and I hit them. One of them clubbed me on the head and early this morning I awoke and I was behind bars. It was as the man on the street had said — I was behind bars. I was in the zoo — or 'the jail,' as they called it — and soon people would be coming by to look at me."

"Then a man with a brown moustache, and brass buttons on his coat, came by and asked me what I was doing in the city. I told him. He took me out of my cage to a high place in the building. He pointed far away to the forest. 'There,' he said, 'that's *your* Promised Land. You should never have left it. Now get out, get back there. If we find you on the streets again tonight, we'll keep you here for good.' I knew then I didn't want to remain in the Promised Land forever."

When the man from the forest had finished, the man from the city said, "That's a story — such a story as I've never heard before. You are a strange fellow — why you didn't see the city at all. Think of going to the city from the forest and passing your time in the zoo!"

He sat down by the road and laughed. "Wolves and zoos and trees, the Promised Land in the city — why the Promised Land was all about you — the speech of your fellow man and his hearing. What more than that could you want? You weren't as I was, out alone in the forest with no one to talk to. When I left you here a day ago on this road, I was happy. I ran so that I would get to the forest quicker. It was still daylight when I reached it. I had forgotten about eating. I saw your cabin and passed it. I knew the Promised Land was not between walls. It was somewhere deeper, hidden far among the trees. When it grew dark, I lay down upon the moss and watched the stars above me. I felt then I was close. It was just beyond a bend in the hills. A few steps farther and I would have found it. But the darkness made me halt. I had no blankets and I became chilled. The moss I lay on was damp. Clouds came and obscured the stars. Far away I heard a stream running. Its sound was like people talking, so I began to make my way towards it. But in the night I couldn't see. I ran my face against a tree branch. I still bear the scratch it gave me. The trees were monsters. They held me. They shoved me. They tossed me from one to the other. I heard things moving in the forest. There were rustles all around me. A mouse ran over my toes. I, too, heard a wolf howl. He was far away, but I was afraid because I knew there were no bars to hold him. You were lucky back there in the zoo. There were bars. I felt hair sprouting on my scalp where I knew there was none at all. If that wolf saw me before I did him, I would be struck dumb. I would never be able to speak another word to mortal man. I heard that somewhere when I was younger. Then I remembered your cabin. I crawled back on my hands and knees. I ran my head against its walls before I found it. I opened the door and locked it behind me. The lock was rusty and I had a fight to shove it home. I lit all your candles. I made a big fire in the stove. I discovered then the books you had there on the shelf — the brown leather books about the city, so I took them down and with the candles around me on the table, I read so that I could forget what was beyond the cabin door, the wolf, the darkness, the silence, the great trees with the moss beneath them, and nowhere the voice of man. When the sun came up I went down the trail to the road. I bent my knees and kissed it for it would bring me back to the city."

After the man from the city had spoken, the man from the forest, standing above him on the road, pulled his beard and said, "Well, I guess we're two peculiar fellows. You think I'm odd because I found the zoo in the city. And it seems to me it's just as queer to go out to the forest and to pass your one night there in a cabin reading in books about the city."

They smoked for a while without talking, each this time with his own tobacco. Then the man from the forest said, "I guess I'll be on my way. The moon's up tonight so it'll be light for travel. And, as for this Promised Land, my friend, I think it's not in the city, nor in the forest — yet in a way of speaking it is. It's the city a man like me sees from the forest, and the forest a man like you sees from behind those great rock walls of your city. It's really in the place from which you see it. It's a part of the forest for me — a part of the city for you. It's sort of a distance between places too, and that's what a road like this is for, to keep them apart. Some say when shadows grow red beards and the sun shines in the dark and bears walk backwards up a mountain . . . well, you see what I mean."

They parted then, the two friends, in the moonlight, one shoving his shadow, now blacked by the moon upon the road, before him towards the forest, the other pulling his behind him to the city — and as they parted they hoped one day to meet again along this road on which each was now returning to his Promised Land.

293

The Love Story of Mr. Alfred Wimple

Mr. Alfred Wimple pushed the pearl push-button on the desk in his office, on the thirty-fifth floor of the Wimple Building in Vancouver, B.C. After a moment the door opened and his secretary came in.

"Winnifred," he said with decision, "take a letter."

She sat beside the desk, crossed her legs, opened her notebook. Winnifred was a tall girl and, sheathed in her black dress, seemed to Mr. Wimple smooth and sinuous as a watersnake. Her black hair was lustrous, her cheeks pallid, her heavy eyes half lidded as though, bowing to his command, she still dreamed of the night. Sometimes Mr. Wimple — a bachelor in his middle thirties — wondered about her nights. He did not know. He held her "at a distance," mindful of his "place," of where such ultimate thoughts might lead. Marriage! He shuddered. No Wimple had ever married beneath him. No Wimple, indeed, had found it possible to do so.

He pulled the long lobe of his right ear, got up, walked around his chair, sat down again.

"Yes?" Winnifred said.

"A letter," he repeated, looking up at the ceiling. "Let's see now — how should we begin?"

In the quietness of the office it was almost as though Mr. Wimple listened for the words he would dictate. And waiting, he was conscious of the activity going on about him — of the other offices in the building, concerned in holding together the nationwide — the internationally linked — Wimple mining and timber and financial interests. Outside the side window of his own office were the blue harbour waters under green, springtime mountains. The harbour was busy. Deep sea ships plodded, ferries bustled, launches scurried over its surface. The boom was on! Already Vancouver boomed! The West Coast boomed! Across the inlet, logs were boomed and the western wind boomed up the channel. Mr. Wimple, leaning back in his chair, felt himself to be caught up in the boom, to be the very focal point through which its force was to be expended. The awareness endured but briefly, being interrupted by Winnifred.

"Perhaps, if you gave me the name," she suggested, referring to his request to "take a letter."

"It's to the Dingle people," Mr. Wimple replied, put out for the moment at having the domain of his far ranging thoughts invaded.

"You mean Jonathan Dingle?"

"Yes, that's right to Jonathan Dingle, the advertising people."

"'Dear Mr. Dingle,'" Winnifred said, to give her employer a start, something to gnaw upon.

"I tell you what," Mr. Wimple said, "you telephone them . . . or better still, go over and see them for me. You can settle it quicker that way."

Winnifred touched a finger to her hair.

"You know which one I mean? The young Mr. Dingle, he's more progressive, not his father." Mr. Wimple regarded his secretary closely.

"Oh, yes, I've met him," she said. "I once did some work for them — that is to say, for his father. It was two years ago, before I came here, when I was modelling for clothes and hair do's. They used a picture of me. It went all over the country." Winnifred's eyes assumed a distant look, as if she tried to recall all the places where her picture had appeared, or as if perhaps, she were remembering her last association with the old Mr. Dingle. It had been on the twelfth floor of a very good hotel in Los Angeles.

"That's it. That's it exactly. That's what I want you to see him about — all over the country," Mr. Wimple exclaimed, slapping his thigh. He would have liked to have slapped Winnifred's too, but restrained himself and coughed lightly instead.

"I don't quite understand," said Winnifred.

"About what?"

"About what I am to see him about."

"It's clear as can be." Mr. Wimple wished that on this morning, of all mornings, Winnifred would not be obtuse. "It's what I say — countrywide. Tell Mr. Dingle I am going to buy a page in all the magazines of nationwide circulation, Canadian, American — both. You know, the slick ones with colour in them."

"But he'll ask me what for — and, my God, Mr. Wimple, it will be expensive. It will cost money."

"Never mind the money." Mr. Wimple patted his pocket. "Tell him it's for my own use. Money is no object. It's for my own purpose, for the general good. Yes — tell him, 'for the general good.' He can be sure of that." Mr. Wimple turned to the front window of his office beyond which, across the shadowed street and one storey higher, was the office of his rival, Daniel Wurpington. He ground his teeth. "Decidedly," he added, facing Winnifred. "Impress upon him, it's for the general good."

Winnifred went towards the office door, juggling the desk lamp gleam upon the sheen of her buttocks.

"That's all I am to say?" she asked, glancing back, a white hand on the door.

"Yes, that's all, and let me know the results this afternoon. It will be enough. Quite enough."

Enough . . . ample, sufficient, quite enough — in fact, too much, Mr. Wimple considered, mindful that Daniel Wurpington had once declared that he made it a habit to keep posted on everything, everything which came out in the big magazines.

He pushed his desk button again. "Make an appointment for me at the photographer's," he said to Winnifred. "Make it for right after lunch — about four o'clock."

Winnifred withdrew.

Mr. Wimple sighed. With his plans approaching a focus, he felt relieved. And after lunch, right after lunch, he was always able to put his best foot foremost — though in a head and shoulder portrait this propensity might not be apparent. Nevertheless, it would be implied. Unlike Daniel Wurpington, Mr. Wimple was not overweight. He stood lightly on his feet, could put one or the other forward at his whim. From the biology he had been taught at college, he knew he was fortunate in his slimness. Obesity was an atavism, a reversion to our ancestors, an unconscious attempt to store up food for the winter. But instead of fasting through the cold months of the year, men such as Daniel used those months as an excuse for increased indulgence. That was why after meals Daniel drowsed. His subconscious induced him to hibernate, yet he could not hibernate because he did not fast. Mr. Wimple regretted that. It would have been pleasant to have had some months of the year at least when the streets were rid of his rival.

Daniel Wurpington, the rival, was a newcomer to the West, one of the "usurpers." He came from the East. It was rumoured that a forebear, advised by his doctor to drink donkey's milk for his health, had bought a pasture on the edge of town. That pasture was now in the centre of an eastern city, its worth computed in millions. With those millions, Daniel, also in his thirties and a contemporary of Mr. Wimple, had come to Vancouver and, immediately after snubbing the latter at his club, had begun to build across from the Wimple building, a higher building, a circumstance which could hardly be "ascribed to chance," nor yet pass unnoticed. In addition to threatening to invade the mining fields and the timber limits of the Wimples, Daniel now wrote poetry and had made for himself a reputation as "the poet of the financial district." No one had seen his verses, thus giving his claim added authority.

Mr. Wimple, on the other hand, descended from a long line of western Wimples, all of them men of vision, if not of purpose: his grandfather, Nathaniel Wimple of Oregon, had invented underwater fins which, when thrust out at right angles from the hulls of sea-going ships, acted as brakes to avoid collisions; his father, Willie Wimple, after making his fortune in lumber, passed his last days at a cavalry stud farm, teaching horses to "gallop in place," and then, by a shift in the rider's balance, to gallop backwards, a manoeuvre calculated to confuse "the enemy." Disregarding the success of his experiment, he one day wandered on to the race course behind an approaching horse and was run down and killed, victim of his own enthusiasm. He left as his last words, whispered into an old army major's hairy ear, "It confirms my theory. It is most confusing." There was further the Uncle Bogley who had gone to India after the first World War in quest of the mongoose. "A rare bird," he had confided to his nephew, "so called because it has only one wing and with that one wing, it flies." After his sailing, Uncle Bogley Wimple slipped forever from the sight of man.

With this record of achievement behind him, sure in the loyalty of Winnifred and of others in his service, but especially in that of Winnifred, Mr. Alfred Wimple, who, if one were lost for a phrase, might have been referred to as the "keystone" of the wide-flung interests which bore his name, confronted with confidence his rival across the street. To the challenge thrown at him, the magazine advertisement was to be a shattering response.

The advertisement, simply stated, was based upon the theory that the terrible in life was the unseen, the yet-to-be-apprehended, the shadow in the fog, not by any means the fog. It was what was unsaid that would say the most, and Daniel Wurpington would suffer its hidden force.

The second Friday in June, Winnifred entered Mr. Wimple's office, to leave upon his desk, opened at the appropriate place, the first magazine to carry the advertisement. It was a magazine with a picture cover. Within its pages boys met girls, husbands returned, wives were made happy, articles were printed on world affairs. Towards its end, in the advertising section, was Mr. Wimple's announcement.

The top half of the page was chaste as a baby's unused diaper. Then in the middle, quite by itself, was his head and shoulders photograph, the one taken immediately after lunch: the head, its tremulous nose suited to any but the most obdurate keyhole, thrown back at a jaunty angle, the eyes spots of light, flat and baleful, the lips slightly parted, as if, a moment before, their possessor had swallowed. It was the head of a man who had something to say, but who kept his confidence. A man, who when need arose, put his best foot forward, who, doubtless, had it forward even now as you looked upon him. Underneath the picture was written, in Mr. Wimple's own firm up and down handwriting, each word underscored: "It is later than it would appear." Only that nothing more. At the bottom of the page, strung across its width, were the words, "Alfred Wimple, Wimple Building, Vancouver."

Mr. Wimple smiled at his image. He took the magazine and walked to the window. There he could see over to Daniel's office in the Wurpington Building. Mr. Wimple stood in full view, unmistakably himself, but the expected Daniel did not appear before him. Observing more intently, Mr. Wimple saw that across the way the shutters were down and the potted blue geraniums, which usually graced the sill, taken indoors. The geraniums were a conceit of his rival, their presence outdoors on the windowsill denoting his own indoors within his office.

Mr. Wimple slapped his thigh so hard that it stung, and he whimpered in delight at his pain. He shook his head. He laughed. "He will know about it," he thought. "He will have seen, someone will have told him, he will have heard a rumour. He will read these words, 'It is later than it would appear.' It is what they fail to state that will be terrible to him. He will guess this is but the beginning, the opening gun, the rain patter on a leaf before the thunderstorm. He will guess that other matters are . . . that other matters are being formulated, pursued, knocked into shape, that a final consummation is not far off. Yes, other matters." He banged his doubled fist into his other palm.

Behind his back, someone had come into his office, now waited by his desk. It was Mr. Brockle from two floors below. He was sixty years old and for forty of those years had been the brains of the Wimple interests. He was a man all of one colour — bristling iron grey hair, grey eyes, grey cheeks, grey suit, grey suede shoes. He stood in the room with hunched shoulders, like a lump of pig-iron, the floor seeming to sag under his weight.

"What is the meaning of this?" he demanded, waving a magazine at Mr. Wimple. It was another magazine, but one of the ten chosen for the three month "institutional campaign."

"Meaning? I think it's plain enough. It was arranged, executed, all of it, by the Dingle people, a thoroughly reputable firm."

"But what does it mean?" Mr. Brockle insisted.

"Just what it says. It could mean nothing else, not very well, could it? 'Later than it would appear' . . . clear enough, isn't it — especially in these days?"

"It can mean all sorts of things," Mr. Brockle said, pushing his leaden face towards Mr. Wimple. "It can mean that there will be a run on the market, a panic . . . everyone unloading our shares."

Just then Winnifred entered. She set a sheaf of telegrams before Mr. Brockle. "They sent them up from below," she said. Mr. Wimple studied the depression between her breasts in the front of her black, silken dress. It was a nest fit for a warrior's head and he at once saw himself on a black horse leading a charge across the plains of Hungary — the Hungarians, he had read, were a race of superb horsemen — and was about to cross over the border into Poland and on to the steppes of Russia when the telephone at his elbow rang. He lifted the receiver. The young Mr. Dingle spoke. "Beautiful!" he shouted. "Beautiful! . . . the response from all over the country and from the United States, England as well. I mean the new advertising campaign. Tremendous!" He hung up abruptly.

Winnifred had departed and Mr. Brockle was reading the telegrams. The first was from the New York financial house, Downbent & Beaton. "Genius," it read, "marvellous achievement your current advertising campaign." That from Woodburn and Cant of the same city said "Unexampled ingenuity." And so on. There were fifteen of them, all in the same mood.

Mr. Brockle flushed. He came around the desk, put his thick stolid hand on Mr. Wimple's shoulder. "Really, my boy," he said, "I did not understand. You are to be felicitated."

For the first time in his life Mr. Wimple's chest strained the buttons of his vest. Tears came to his eyes. He bowed his head, sensing in the vague, uncertain fashion of all former Wimples, that Mr. Brockle's opinion had been changed by the telegrams. This . . . this bestowal of a hand upon his shoulder he had not foreseen. Nor had anyone foreseen such a rise in Wimple stocks and shares and bonds as occurred in ensuing days. Their ascent was headlined in the papers. On its strength, another boom swept the country. "It is the needed shot in the arm," one financial writer wrote. "Those seven words, 'It is later than it would appear,' are gravid with portent for the future of our business structure."

It was an ideal boom. Prices rose, wages did not. Mr. Brockle and, at last, Mr. Wimple himself, were invited to address meetings to explain the phenomenon. Previous to one of those meetings Mr. Wimple stayed late in his office, going over with Winnifred the speech she had prepared for him. He had forgotten to let down the shutters and now, glancing up, saw Daniel Wurpington staring in at him from across the street — not from his own office a floor above, but from another on the same thirty-fifth floor level as Mr. Wimple's. Mr. Wimple started to his feet, ran to the window. Arriving there, he thought he had been mistaken. He saw no sign nor hair of his rival — which was the more reasonable, in as much as it had been reported that Daniel had gone to the country "to think things over." "It was an apparition, an appearance, not a reality," Mr. Wimple promised himself, going back to his desk and Winnifred.

A week after the new boom began, an obscure observer was heard from. He wrote, "There is something unhealthy in the current panic of inflation, as there is ominous in the words which brought it about. I use the word 'panic' advisedly, because, to the experienced eye, only fear can hide behind such hysteria. Instead of being too late to get in, it is, perhaps, already too late to get out."

And these sentences, this paragraph, published in fading ink on perishable paper, a mere whisper in the howl of the gale, notwithstanding, were read, quoted, passed from one hand to another, grew, persisted until they outlasted the very energies which had given them their being, until men muttered that they had been misled, affirmed that they had been deceived, shouted that they had been swindled and all those who had come so gladly in, desired now only to get out. Wimple stocks, shares and bonds were unloaded. They were disowned. They fluttered in the gutters blown by the winds here and there. Mr. Wimple and Mr. Brockle were called "Reds" and "subversive."

Mr. Brockle walked forth and back trying to tear his iron grey hair. His fingers, however, merely slipped from its upstanding bristles. He shook his fist at the ceiling where, above him, Mr. Wimple from his office looked down to the street — for in the tumult Mr. Wimple remained still unaffected. These things would pass, he told himself. Disaster would be averted. So long as Daniel's window over there was shuttered, the geraniums indoors, he knew that he was sound, that he was winning. "He will be at a loss, trying to guess what final blow is still to fall, what else, so to speak, that is to say, in a manner of speaking, is suspended over his head, what else I have up my sleeve," he thought, fingering his elbow through the smooth cloth of his suit. On the street corner far below he saw people, crowds of them, at the newsstand buying magazines. He smiled, complacent.

Mr. Wimple pressed his forehead against the window pane, the better to see into the street. What a crowd about the newsstand!

At that moment the office boy left three magazines upon his desk. Odd, Mr. Wimple thought, that Winnifred had not brought them in as she usually did. Anyway, the Wimple organization functioned. The office boy was still with it.

Mr. Wimple thumbed through one of the magazines. He found his advertisement — "announcement" he preferred to call it. It was on a right hand page. Across from it — across from it, what he saw took his breath, made him gasp, left him weak and trembling, sweating in his foot soles. Across from him was Winnifred — but not the Winnifred he had known, not the Winnifred in the sleek, black dress. Winnifred here reclined on a white satin couch. She was alone. No one was about, not even under the couch, and she was in a pink negligee. She showed so real before him that instinctively his fingers worked as if to pry her loose from the glossy paper.

Panting from his failure, Mr. Wimple drew back, rubbed his brow and pushed the button on his desk.

"Winnifred!" he cried when she came in, "are you a party to this, to this . . ." He spluttered, waved his hands. Then he pointed to the open magazine.

Winnifred stood unmoving. "I had nothing whatever to do with it, Mr. Wimple," she said. "It is from my modelling days, when I was posing for the hair-do. It is one of those pictures bought by Mr. Dingle, the elder. I may say he arranged the pose . . . but it's pretty, don't you think?" She bent over the magazine, lightly tapping a pencil against her teeth.

"Hair-do," said Mr. Wimple, "modelling . . ." He began to cough, grasping his throat, lifting a knee as though he choked.

As his eyes fell again on the page, Winnifred, the real Winnifred, faded from before him. There was only her magazine picture on the desk. He read the inscription beneath it, bordered by blue geraniums:

"It's late in the morning, early afternoon.
What time can it be, if not high noon?"

And below that, at the bottom of the page, were the words, "Daniel Wurpington, Wurpington Building, Vancouver."

Wurpington and Dingle, the advertising man — they had worked together against him. Wurpington would now be established firmly as a poet. Millions would read this verse of his. And he, Alfred Wimple, had paved the way. They had destroyed the value of his "announcement." No face, no matter how forthright, could compete alone with Winnifred's recumbent form — to say nothing of the border of blue geraniums — on the page opposite to it.

Yes, they had plotted to ruin him. It had been Daniel, after all, and not an apparition, regarding him the night he had worked late in his office with Winnifred. And now, over the country, on newsstands, on trains, in boats, in hotels and rooming houses, already perhaps thrown out of a window and trodden into the mud of a nameless lane, he and his secretary, Mr. Wimple and Winnifred, Winnifred, whom he had always kept "at a distance," were on terms most intimate — intimate was hardly the word — terms denoting a thorough understanding with one another. Small wonder that people crowded the newsstand below the window. They would be talking about him, about him and Winnifred, laughing at him, nudging one another as he passed by.

Mr. Wimple's first impulse, when he had somewhat recovered from his shock, was to have all the magazines in town bought up. But he recognized it was too late. It could not now be done.

That night he did not leave the office. He walked the floor, watching the lights of the city, one by one, and in twos and threes, go out around him. Then the dread darkness had him.

And in the morning, early, while he still lay curled on his couch, he heard men talking outside the Wurpington Building. He looked out and saw workmen on stages sandblasting its walls so that their graveyard whiteness would contrast with the dullness of the Wimple Building.

Later, at ten o'clock, after he had called a barber in and been shaved and eaten a light breakfast at his desk, Mr. Wimple met the blue geraniums put once more behind their grill outside Daniel Wurpington's office a floor above his own. Soon Daniel himself stood in the sunny window, in a brown, fuzzy suit, smoking a cigar, his beard, lightly frisked by the wind, hanging on his massive chest like an up-ended and rusted fir tree on an autumn hillside. The smoke of the cigar puffed from its foliage, as though, beneath it, Daniel were slowly consumed by fire. Daniel's hand came through the window, the gesture catching Mr. Wimple by surprise, and his poet's fingers tapped the ash from the cigar. Mr. Wimple saw it fall, light and soft, breaking into separate streams of powder. Daniel nodded stiffly four times, as though someone, to his resentment, had pushed his head from behind. He grinned, showing that his teeth were as newly cleaned as the walls of his building — but by the dentist, definitely by the dentist. Daniel's lips shaped the words. He shouted them across to Mr. Wimple.

"A good man too," he said. "A good dentist. A college man with a degree."

From the street, thirty-five storeys below, Mr. Wimple heard a hubbub of voices. Looking down he saw the people, hundreds of them, their pale faces upturned, shifting, moving, changing place and colour. And from that mass, from that strangeness, from that pallor of anonymity, rose what could only be a cheer. Faint at first, it endured until it hummed organ-like between the two buildings.

Mr. Wimple was shocked, perplexed, rocked back on his heels, searching for its cause. He looked again at Daniel, still in his window, his fingers combing from his beard the blue geranium petals settled there. Mr. Wimple now became fully aware of the secretary at his rival's side, of her fullness as a person. He blinked, he stuttered, he staggered, failing to grasp at once the testimony of his vision.

The secretary was Winnifred. No mistake was possible. The black hair, the reach of cheek, the drowsy eyes, the black dress . . . the black dress, shadowing in its midst the secret of her being, that fountain of hope and hunger, that circled magic, that very flesh of a dream, that pool between her breasts where the sunlight lay warmed by her substance. Winnifred stood shoulder to shoulder with Daniel Wurpington, ready to take dictation from him.

Mr. Wimple's eyes fell to the crowd below, cheering because she had gone over to his rival.

To assure himself that what he saw was so, he ran to his desk and pushed the button on its top. The office boy came in.

"Where is Winnifred?" Mr. Wimple asked.

"She went away," the office boy replied, "with her note-book."

Returning to the window, Mr. Wimple caught Daniel Wurpington in the act of taking a document from her.

"I have a document," he shouted on seeing Mr. Wimple, his words coming clearly across the canyon between them. Winnifred turning her back, he raised his hand in admonition. "A paper of permission, a permit to build," he declaimed. "We are expanding. We are building. We are going up. Ten more storeys to be added to the building." Daniel bent his head out the window, gazing up to where the new storeys would be. "Tenants," he said in a choking voice, "and new business. It is demanded."

Mr. Wimple smiled. This was what he had expected. The obvious, not the subtle, or the inexplicable . . . the club and not the rapier. And with the obvious Mr. Wimple felt himself equipped to deal. He laughed. In sudden ardour he shook his head until his teeth chattered. He too raised his hand.

"We also," he called across the street chasm, "we also are

expanding. But we are going down."

"What do you mean 'expanding' and 'going down?'" Daniel removed from his lips the cigar, now burned to half its length.

"Just what I say,"Mr. Wimple answered. "Exactly what I say, no more, no less. You may depend on that. We are going down. This building will be razed to the ground. We will build below the ground. These days it is, that is to say, it is more prudent." I indicated with a tilt of his head the air above where conceivably one day hostile bombers might fly. "THE BOMB," he said, his lips carefully forming the words. And he added, "Or for when the boom is ended."

"And there below," he continued to Daniel, "there below we will expand. We will require space."

Those were the words, the crucial words, the apt ones, "We will require space." Daniel would suffer their imputations. The Wimple interests, toiling underground, expanding, requiring space . . . they would spread out, protected by the earth's crust, shrouded under its darkness, undermining the very foundations of the Wurpington Building. And across from that building there would remain, what? A heap of rubble.

The suggestion in itself was the achievement. Yet Mr. Wimple saw it all before him, as though it were a plan already concluded. He saw the rocks, the twisted girders. He saw their great shadows. The shadows were cast by moonlight and among them, casting a shadow of his own, he saw himself moving here and there, solitary, studying, while others slept, the problems to be studied. And Winnifred . . . would she be there with him? Would he confront her across some hole in the ground, or approach her over heaps of earth, under girders, climbing over old walls and relinquished office furniture? He did not know, and only pulled himself away from his musing when he saw his own figure, the figure of Alfred Wimple, adopting in this fateful progress an attitude somewhat stooped, an attitude briefly stated as tending to that of a quadruped.

In time the rubble would be cleared away, having destroyed the rental value of the Wurpington Building, and in its stead would be a place of flowers, perhaps blue geraniums, shielding the entrance to the new Wimple Building, to gain whose top-most floor one would descend thirty-five storeys into the ground.

He paced by his window. When he again looked out time had passed. Daniel's window was in shadow. It was closed, shuttered. Daniel had without doubt gone to the country a second time, "to think things over." His potted blue geraniums had once more been taken indoors. A light glimmered on one of the building's lower floors. The street below was deserted. In silence the crowds once gathered there had dispersed. Mr. Wimple was alone. Still he waited.

At last the one light in the Wurpington Building was extinguished. The door at the foot of the building opened. Winnifred stepped from it, also alone and carrying her notebook. She glanced up at Mr. Wimple, waved a paper in her hand. It was Daniel Wurpington's permit to build.

As she crossed the street, as her hand touched the door of the Wimple Building, as she ascended in the elevator, Mr. Wimple trembled, his veins warmed, his knees became unsteady. He sat down behind his desk, joying in the surge of his body, feeling himself seized by an urgent . . . what else, indeed, what else could it be, this tingling of the flesh, this puckering of the scalp, if not an urgent desire, a touch of the universal, that which made the whole world kin? He felt himself one with the great beasts of land and sea, with the amphibious hippopotamus in his swamp, whose slow blood rising in heat steams the water around him. He thought of the elephant with trunk upraised, roaring from the jungle grass, and of whales who disport themselves and come together to make tumult in the ocean.

When Winnifred had reached the twentieth floor he had thought of smaller things as well . . . of moles underground, of the mountain gopher and rabbits in the spring snow. And the porcupine . . . he wondered about the porcupine, a quilled animal, and shook his head.

As Winnifred left the elevator and entered the outer office, Mr. Wimple discovered himself on the plains where he mingled with, was a part of, was, so to speak, the outstanding characteristic of a sweating buffalo rut. He was there under a canopy of dust, among the groans, in the strife, in the lustful effort. He was one of them. Only his face, his clothes, his business engagements distinguished him from the herd.

When Winnifred knocked timidly on his door, he called her in. He told her to file away his rival's permit to build. "For the future," he said. "And as for my new plans, they will wait. We will consider them . . . they are to be brought, that is to say . . . to fruition . . . pounded into shape . . ." His words trailed off.

Abruptly bending over, like a man seized with cramp, he commanded, "Tell the office boy to go home. And the elevator man. Both of them. They are to go at once. I mean to say now — that is — at once, immediately."

While his secretary, who made no protest, and whose step seemed even quicker and lighter than usual, was absent on her mission, Mr. Wimple thought of the two of them, of himself and her, Alfred Wimple and Winnifred, with the building to themselves . . . its corridors, its elevator shafts, its offices, its long corridors. Standing, he regarded his feet. Surely they were the narrow, eager feet of a runner, say a middle-distance runner, one who could take an office in his stride and the longest corridor in several — providing, of course, that the door to the elevator shaft was closed.

Hearing Winnifred return, he drew himself up, buttoned his jacket, tightened the knot of his tie, apprehending that in love there was at times a sudden spasm. For that also — with his rival, the verse writer, Daniel Wurpington, self-banished to the country, smarting with a fast defeat and with the Wimple interests and their building newly and soundly based upon the implications of their own destruction — for that spasm, for that crisis, sudden though it might be, Mr. Wimple felt himself prepared, in a manner expectant and approaching hope.

The Woman Who Got on at Jasper Station

The daycoach, smelling of cheese sandwiches, waxpaper and opened pop bottles, at the noon hour was crowded with excursionists — a conducted party of young people passing westward through the Rockies — and when the conductor came by for the tickets, the woman in the sheared lamb wool coat who, like most of those around her, had got on at Jasper Station a few miles back, asked him if there might be another seat, one which she could have to herself, "Maybe up ahead," she said, "in the next coach."

The conductor — he was "new" on the run and she had not seen him before — punched her ticket before replying. He was a stout man with a drooping brown moustache. His lower eyelids sagged, revealing their inner redness. They gave him a semblance of rage, of bafflement, and the woman regretted that she had spoken.

"Lady," he said, leaning closer to her, "there are no seats up ahead, I've just come through. And this boy" — he glanced at the sailor by the window who shared her seat — "is ready, if the time comes, to give his life for you, for all of us. You oughtn't to mind sitting beside him."

The conductor — the old fool, she thought — went his way, panting, mumbling. The woman turned quickly to the sailor. "I did not mean to be rude," she said. "I just felt it would be more comfortable — for you."

"Don't pay him attention, ma'am. He's been reading advertisements. Besides, there's lots of room." The sailor inched away from her towards the wall of the coach. The woman supposed she had sat beside him — there were two or three other seats she might have shared — because, like herself, he was separate and aloof from the prevailing hubbub of the members of the excursion, staring wide-eyed out the windows and exclaiming at the mountains.

Now, murmuring a reply to the sailor's remark, the woman wished that he had not called her "ma'am." It set a mark upon her, put her apart, stamped her age upon her brow. Her figure was firm and trim, her carriage erect, her ankles neat. It was seldom that she was taken to be more than twenty-five.

She shuffled her shoulders, settled into her seat, surrendered herself to the immobility of travel, cheeks flat and pale, framing the red wound of her mouth, lips slightly parted as if she were about to cry aloud with its hurt. She lifted her hand, smoothed the hair upcombed from the back of her neck. Her tasselled Chinese-style hat, nodded with the motion of the coach, as though in assent to her journey. Other heads nodded too, bodies swayed, voices muttered, forests of spruce and fir and pine flowed smoothly by the window.

"I know . . ." the sailor said.

"What's that?" The woman was startled. She had forgotten the sailor.

"I know," he said. "You're not used to riding in day coaches. I saw your suitcase when you came in. It's got labels on it. You've 'been places.'"

The woman smiled. "It's an old weekend bag," she said. She was about to add that the labels also were old. Old times, old labels — not that, these days, labels meant anything at all.

"And anyway, I've travelled in many day coaches," she continued to the sailor. "This isn't the first time. Besides . . ."

The sailor interrupted. "I know. You were going to say, 'Besides, it's only a short trip I'm making,' If it were a longer trip, someone like you would have more baggage than that little bag up there in the rack above us. Of course, you may have a trunk checked up ahead . . ."

"No, I haven't," the woman interjected — and suddenly wondered why she should explain herself to the man beside her. In less than an hour she would be back "home." What would the sailor think if she told him that her "home" was a three-roomed log cabin in a railroad town of three hundred by a green mountain lake? And why should she care at all what he might think? She gnawed her lip and felt a flush of blood behind her ears. The sailor, at whom for the first time she looked fully, did not smile. A young dark-haired man with pink ears — hardly more than a boy — he seemed to await her approval before he smiled. Her eyes fell away from his. She reached into her flat, black handbag for a cigarette, searching for a match. The sailor held his lighter out to her, as if so to atone for what he had said. Over the flame his blue eyes were warm, moist, fringed with long straight lashes. Something in them — friendly, beseeching, lonely? She could not be sure.

The woman and the sailor sat for minutes in silence. She noticed, close by her own, the sailor's thigh, its curve of hard muscle showing under the dark blue trouser leg. Involuntarily, she drew back. His hand rested there upon it, heavy, competent. The back of the hand was hairy. All of him, she surmised, would be furred like that — his chest, his shoulder blades, the thigh beneath its cloth. The vagrant thought sent a tremor through her body, touched her with a gentle ecstasy. She stamped out her cigarette, rose and removed her coat, folded it on the top of her weekend bag in the rack overhead. Seating herself, she smoothed her dress, observing the dimples at the base of her fingers, the tight gold band of her wedding ring. The dress was linen and of a robin's egg blue. Up its front was a line of small white buttons, joined by narrow white embroidery. She pondered again why she had worn it. Still, it was suitable for the season, a dress for early summer. Looking down at its embroidery, she felt uneasy, as if this marked the trail of a mouse which had jumped on her straight from the tin flour bin under the kitchen table, run between her breasts and over her right shoulder.

"What were you saying?" she asked the sailor suddenly.

"Me? I wasn't talking." The sailor was surprised. He

smiled weakly, in indecision, in discomfiture.

"Don't you think the coach is very hot?" The woman spoke sharply, as in rebuke.

"Well . . . I don't rightly know. It seems good to me. It's cold up where I've been."

"And where is that?"

"Churchill — that's on Hudson Bay."

The woman said, "Oh, up there!"

The sailor told her that he was on his way to Esquimalt on Vancouver Island "to report."

"And then?" the woman asked, and at once regretted her question.

"They don't tell us," the sailor said. "Maybe — well, anywhere. We don't really know much before we sail."

He turned to look out the window and a shadow, pooled in his lean cheek, was shed with his turning.

The woman regarded the length of the coach before her, the bobbing heads, the swarthy heads, the fair heads of the young people. No more than ten years their senior, she envied them their youth, the pageant of their youth, from which she felt herself excluded, but one of whose course she partook for the brief period of her journey. A warmth and compassion suffused her for all those within the coach and, especially, for the man beside her. His sailor's uniform, contrasting with the gay shirts, sweaters and shawls about him, was like the shroud of all his young years.

"I am sorry," she said and was embarrassed to have spoken this comment on her thoughts aloud. The woman, who was childless, guessed it was war — the constant talk of war and what war's effect would be on the sailor and upon all the young people, so secure in courage, so vulnerable in flesh — what war's effect would be upon all the earth's people.

"Sorry?" the sailor repeated the word. His voice was slow and husky and, vibrating through the seat back, caressed her spine.

"I mean . . ." the woman spread her hands.

The sailor did not understand. He blinked, turned away.

After a while he asked her where she was getting off. She told him it would be at the next stop. "It's a little town by a lake. It's called Lucerne."

"Like in Switzerland," the sailor said.

"The name's the same," the woman answered. "Only in Switzerland, it's a lake. Where I am, the lake's called Yellow-head."

She had not been to Switzerland. However, she had seen pictures, read accounts of its lakes, its neat villages, its eidelweiss, its cattle grazing on the alplands and of its people given to song and dance and to blowing great curved horns. Apparently in Switzerland, unlike the Canadian Rockies there were no roundhouses belching steam and smoke, no rundown cabins and one storied frame houses with laundry strung up behind, no pool hall with lounging men outside its door, no tilted outhouses, no railroaders in oil stained overalls, no bearded trappers down from the hills sitting jack-knifed on the rail of the station platform spewing tobacco juice. She wished that she could have said to the sailor that she was going on to Vancouver, to Seattle, to San Francisco, to some place far, far away, where there were no mountains, no railroaders, no locomotives so close that, as the engineer waited for his "orders," they seemed to be panting in her own backyard — a backyard whose only fence was the jack pine forest.

"You live there . . . I mean, you live there, in this Lucerne?"

The woman spread her hands. "Of corrse, what else? My husband is the town dcotor, I left him just now in Jasper. I went with him to visit while he's on a case."

"What sort of a doctor?"

"Oh, a doctor," the woman said, "Not a specialist. A doctor for people when they are ill." She did not, at this moment, care to think of her husband, of his work, or of Lucerne. For this short hour on the train, she would partake of another life, of youth, which was slipping by her, of a promise waiting somewhere, surely, below the horizon.

She turned her eyes on the sailor, held them there. Her eyes were brown, sullen, half-lidded. She recalled in the instant what a Boer from South Africa had said to her long ago at a dinner party. It had been long ago, four years ago, in an eastern city, before she was married and came to live in a small town by the railroad tracks in the mountains. "You know," the Boer had said quietly, the tip of his tongue lightly flicking his clipped moustache, "I have been watching your eyes. They are always half-lidded, drowsy. They make

315

one think of . . ." He said no more, but hunched his heavy shoulders, pursed his lips.

Now the sailor on the train looked away, looked back at her again.

She wondered what she wanted from the sailor, this boy regarding her through a man's face. She did not know.

"It shouldn't make any difference where I get off," she said, reverting to his former question.

The sailor said, "I was only thinking . . . I guess I forgot and thought maybe we might be getting off at the same place. I mean, that you might be going through to the Coast, though I knew you weren't."

Since leaving Jasper, in the valley of the Arctic-flowing Athabaska, the train had climbed the grade along the Miette river to Yellowhead Pass and the headwaters of the Fraser which emptied into the Pacific. Now on the summit of the pass, as though upthrust by the very backbone of a continent, the coach for a moment lurched over a rough piece of track. The woman was bounced on her seat and, subsiding, her knee touched the sailor's, her thigh was next to his. This time she did not draw back.

She felt his warmth against her own, sensed the hardness of his eager body and, for the first time, caught the slight, seminal smell of beer on his breath. The train rolled on, past a waterfall and by a beaver pond reflecting the chaste, white trunk of a birch tree in its placid waters. A group of section men flashed by the window, leaning on their shovels, faces upheld to the monster of speed whose roadbed they faithfully tended. Up ahead the locomotive howled, like a thing pursued. Through the trees glimmered the green surface of Yellowhead Lake.

The sailor's shoulder touched the woman's. Against her thigh he pressed more strongly. She thought she felt its pulse, the blood urgent beneath the cloth. Lulled by the train's motion, they did not speak, they did not move, involved in a slow conspiracy of flesh. Had she tried to speak, she would have lacked the words to utter. Her mouth was dry. Chills coursed her body. Her eyes misted. The coach and its people swayed as if behind a flimsy curtain and ecstasy enfolded her like a garment.

The sailor's hand touched her knee through the skirt of

robin's egg blue. She started, as if awakened from sleep. "Look," he said softly, "I could get off when you do. A day or two doesn't matter to me, I've got leave coming, and there must be a hotel in this town of yours."

He was going to get off with her! Where could she take him? To the house, guarded by neighbour's windows? Should she ask him to come by later, to dinner, when her husband, returning on a later train, would be at home? One was at times expected to ask servicemen to dinner. No, the answer was not there. Of course, they could get off separately and arrange to meet, as it were, by chance. "Maybe we could go somewhere," the sailor's voice beside her insisted.

His words brought to her mind the station, now fast approaching where she would get down from the train. A red frame station with a cinder platform and beyond it, down a slope, the town. It was not so much a town as a boulder strewn street laid out in the wilderness stretching the quarter mile from the railroad tracks to Yellowhead Lake. Along its single street were two grocery stores, a pool hall, a combined church and school. The church-school on a little rise was across the street from the cabin where she lived and where her husband had his office. The town had no hotel, though it boasted one boardinghouse for bachelor railroaders and a homeless trapper or two.

Beyond her cabin were a few more dwellings staring stolidly at one another from across the street. Past them, by the lakeshore, the descending street became a dirt road, curving westward through a stand of jack pine to the wooden bridge which spanned the narrows. Across the bridge, on the lake's north shore and under the looming Seven Sisters, was a trapper's old cabin. From it a trail led west down the lake towards its outlet into the Fraser. Along the trail, on an idle afternoon, she had occasionally strolled. One afternoon in the recent spring, she remembered, had been grey and misty with a cool east wind from up the lake. She had sat with her back against a log and watched the waves of the lake roll in. The little waves, like the sky, were grey and she listened to each one as it dissolved with a whisper into the grey sand at her feet. Above the waves, a migrating flock of small, black birds, wheeled and dipped and twittered, like a handful of music notes thrown up against the lowering sky.

It was a deserted spot, less than a mile from town. Behind the log, against which she leaned, freshly-leafed willows surrounded a verdant patch of grass. The willows, shoulder-high, would enfold one, shield one, hide one — hide her and the sailor — from all but the clouds above.

The woman did not face the sailor when she said, "But my husband . . ."

When she spoke, she knew that he knew that she lied. Her husband could not be home, until the earliest, on the evening train. She would get down from the train, carrying her bag, and walk alone to the cabin, nodding here and there to the townspeople she passed on the way.

The sailor said, "Oh, I thought you told me . . . I mean about your husband . . ." He looked away out the window to the squalid outskirts of the town — two half-dressed children playing on the steps of a tarpaper shack. A muscle quivered on his jaw.

The woman shrank back from the scene beyond the window as though the children had been her own. To the sailor, she said, "Besides, there's no hotel in the town. Only a boardinghouse — for railroaders."

In a moment, she rose, reached up for her sheared lamb wool coat, put it on. She took down her weekend bag with its faded labels. She paused, as if about to speak again, changed her mind and walked forward down the aisle as the train came to a stop.